Last Light Falling

Legion

Book IV

By

J. E. PLEMONS

Published by Blarney Stone Publishing
304 Stubblefield Lane
Suite 1402
Liberty Hill, TX 78642

BLARNEYSTONE
PUBLISHING

ISBN: 978-1-7356623-0-5

This book is printed on acid-free paper.

Printed in the United States of America

Library of Congress Cataloging-in-Publications Data Plemons, J.E.
Legion / J.E. Plemons. — 1st ed.
p. cm. — (Last Light Falling series; bk 4)

Summary: In the fourth and final installment of the Last Light Falling saga, war between Israel and a seven nation army is reaching its pinnacle. While powers have merged among the last ten nations, many are feeling the strife that comes with a global war against Israel. Clashes among the ten have brought more turmoil to the world than expected, leaving some languishing from its pact with Russia's New World Order. But this political discord only strengthens Russia's plan to destroy Israel from a continuous and rebellious refusal to concede to the accord that rests with the rest of the world. The crippled Jewish nation is nearing a catastrophic genocide, but with the relentless resistance from Arena, she composes a convincing effort to persuade an outnumbered military in a fight that leads to a last stand for survival and freedom.

I. Title.
[Fic] — dc22
First edition, January 2020

Dedication

This book is dedicated to Mela Hudson (Nicole Marinucci) for her passion and love for humanity. Though you've left this world, we still have yet to finish our story in another. Thanks for your inspiration, dedication, and support. In loving memory, my dearest friend, you will never be forgotten.

"Hell is empty and all the devils are here."

—William Shakespeare, The Tempest

Part I

On a Crow's Watch

CHAPTER 1

A heaviness settles upon the landscape, giving way to bursts of light through gray clouds, and all is still. There's no one in sight for miles. Buildings are abandoned, and debris litters the streets. A car sits at an intersection, the doors wide open with no trace of its occupants. A rumble in the distance, the thunder signaling an oncoming storm.

Far away from the highway stands the Shaare Zedek Medical Center, a six-story building in east Jerusalem, looming like a fortress amongst a concrete jungle of apartments. High metal fencing surrounds the property except for the emergency entrance where an abandoned truck had plowed through.

Closing footsteps track behind me. Whoever they are, their pace quickens. I slip through the breeched fence and escape inside the hospital. Torches reflect behind the front window and voices clatter. My heart races. I leave the dark lobby and climb the stairs until I'm breathless.

On the fourth floor, lights flicker in the dim hallway. A door slams and shadows dance across the walls. Then I see it, just two doors down, the familiar red Rx symbol.

I pry the door open, step into the room, and lock the door behind me. *Be patient, Arena.* My eyes adjust to the dark for a few minutes. Just then, a security light twinkles in the corner, distributing a faint glow of light to half the room.

The pharmacy is ransacked. Against the back wall is a small meshed cage. A few basic medical supplies hide behind it, but nothing I need. Cabinets are bare and drawers are empty. The only thing left to scour is locked away in a couple of Pyxis Medstation carts. And of course the good drugs would be housed securely in one of these. A cracked monitor and a fingerprint identification scanner sit atop the cart. Even if this was in working order, it does me no good without security access. I tug on the metal drawers, but they remain locked. *Dammit.* The dispenser levers don't budge.

I feel along the edges for an opening to pry, but the cart is securely built for a reason. Just beneath the lid, a small lock protrudes in the front—a security override, perhaps, but where's the key? I debate whether or not to tip the damn cart on its side. Foolish thinking of course, but I'm desperate to get my hands on some antibiotics. When I fish through one of the bottom cabinets, I find two concealed hypodermic needles and a pair of slender-nosed scissors.

Suddenly, voices pass just outside the door and I crouch behind the cart. A wandering troop of rebels have followed me here. Mostly Arabic speaking, but to what tribe or country they bleed for is uncertain. Only a few are carrying guns. The majority are armed with pipes, knives, and crude metal sword-like weapons.

Russia's global grip is far from slipping. It still gains sovereign over most of the world, but smaller nations are beginning to disband from the regime's stronghold. Maybe these are some of the defected insurgents. Regardless, Jerusalem has been under attack by the world, and the only hostility afforded to breach its walls are enemies of the state. This band of unfriendly misfits is no different, plus they want to kill me, so there's that.

A flutter of footsteps swish past as voices vanish down the hall. I hastily unwrap the two needles and jiggle one of them into the Medstation override lock. The pins struggle to line, but I manage to hold them and the lid cracks open. When I open the drawers, my eyes widen. Drugs of all kind hide behind plastic dispensers, from strong pain meds like tramadol, morphine, and Norco, to milder non-narcs like ibuprofen and Benadryl. But what I really need lies elsewhere.

In the bottom drawer, each compartment houses a different drug, many of which I struggle to pronounce: *Cefazolin, gentamycin . . .*

A sudden outburst of voices argue in the next room and a door slams shut.

"Shit."

I pluck every antibiotic as fast as I can and toss them into my pack. A man's voice angrily barks as the door handle rattles back and forth.

"*Arklha!*" another voice yells.

I hide in the dark corner of the room and draw my gun. Then two shots discharge in the hall and the door swings open. Two armed men enter, one holding a lead pipe and the other equipped with a Glock. They whisper to each other in a foreign tongue while they search the dimly lit side of the room. Sweat rolls down my cheek as I realize half my boot is exposed. Quietly and carefully, I move it back into the shadow.

After a minute or so, the Glock-toting man readily gives up. Without searching the rest of the room, he withdraws his gun and mumbles to the other man, "*'Abaq huna.*" He leaves the room; it grows quiet as his footsteps disappear down the hall.

The security light in the corner flickers while the pipe-wielding rebel stands there, confused. He snoops around for a moment before advancing in my direction. The beat of my heart quickens. His eyes wander curiously toward me and he steps closer, then stops. He raises the lead pipe, cocked above his shoulder. He looks shaken, scared, perhaps paranoid. All I can hear are the slow breaths from my mouth.

I withdraw my gun and unsheathe my knife. He moves closer, just grazing the edge of the darkened portion of the room. I clench my knuckles around the knife and wait.

Another step, then another, and I can smell him, a scent of cinnamon and alcohol. Then his face pierces the shadow and our eyes meet, his glowing. He lets out a gasp, and I thrust the knife into his throat and pull him to the ground. His body shudders and his eyes glaze over. I push his dead body over and shine my torch on him. An egg-shaped grenade hangs off his belt. I quickly grab it and peek outside the room. A gunshot echoes down the hall and voices erupt in the distance.

Both ends of the hall are empty, but chattering voices grow louder. I take off and turn down the next hall through a set of double doors into a wide-open room. I freeze. All eyes are on me. Ten angry men, armed with jagged metal pieces, stand there posed for vengeance. There's nothing in the room save a metal folding chair. I hear her before she appears—the sad whimpers, the crying. A lone man steps forward, dragging a trembling woman next to him. Her face is bloodied, her clothes are ragged, and that all too familiar look of fear in her eyes does something to me. I reach for my chest holster and quickly draw both of my guns. He presses a knife on the side of her ribs and barks at me: "*Tama tajawuz eadad marrat tjawzk.*"

I have no idea what he's saying, but it's quite obvious he's going to kill this poor woman, and then probably me. I'm in no mood to negotiate. I pull the trigger and mangle his skull. He drops like a sack of potatoes, and the woman screams.

A sudden burst of anger drifts from the rest of the men. They charge me like a herd of wildebeest as I unload a fury of bullets. Entangled bodies drop to the floor one by one. When the room is quiet, I look for the woman, but she has fled.

The doors behind me rattle and the hall fills with smoke. I cover my mouth and sprint to the end of the hall. Gunshots fire, grazing the walls next to me. I barrel around the corner and down the steps to the lobby. A man jumps out of nowhere and swings his bat, just clipping my shoulder. I slide to the floor and stab him in the knee. He tumbles backward, screaming in agony. Panting, I look around and race toward the entrance, but the front doors slide open and six rebels surge in, charging in a rage. I reserve the few bullets I have left and draw my knife.

I sling the dagger at the leading rebel, and its tip anchors deep into his skull. He falls, slowing the pace of their charge. I cement my stance, raise my twin *katanas,* and wait with an anxious wrath.

Metal clashes and blood showers as I swing with fury until the last man falls dead. I catch my breath. My right shoulder is sore, and my cheek is swelling from an unexpected punch to the face. I wonder how much longer this body can handle such extremes. I step outside and sigh, "You've got to be kidding me."

Twenty or so more rebels, each donning a keffiyeh headdress, are standing there armed with no more than simple knives and metal batons, except for one cheeky fellow waving a gun and grinning from ear to ear.

"*Kuntla taleablatifatjiddaan,*" he barks with a mischievous smile.

"Blah, blah, blah, spare me your gibberish, you gobshite," I mock, not knowing what the hell he's saying.

"Ah, Irish lass, I would have pegged you for an arrogant American with that sassy response," he provokes.

"Irish, yes, but I'm from America. Sadly I can't place your origin. I'm guessing . . . *Assholian.*"

He scowls for a brief moment before shrugging it off with a half-hearted chuckle. "I'm a fair man, but you killed my men and I just can't have that. So if you stand down now, I'll go easy on you."

"Sorry, but I'm a little rusty on my 'historical culture,' but do all assholes from *Assholian* sound like you?"

"Best bite your tongue, *sharmuta.*"

"Just remember, your men tried to kill me first . . . and lost badly I might add."

His threatening grin quickly vanishes. "You're in no position to insult me."

"I beg to differ." I slide my hand over the grenade.

"You're just another stupid American woman."

This banter has gone on far too long. I grab the grenade and pull the pin. "No, I'm just another crazy bitch with a grenade."

I toss the grenade into the crowd of men and crouch down behind the door. A loud boom rattles the ground, vibrating up into my body and making my ears ring. Smoke scatters, leaving a plume of dust. I push forward through the dusty curtain of smoke with swords drawn and cut down the remaining band of rebels. In the back and resting on his knees, the cheeky asshole clutches the air. His eyes glaze and his head slumps from the force of the blast. He clumsily reaches for his gun, but I pluck it from his bloody hands.

"You're not going to get out of this war alive, you bitch. More will come," he threatens.

"Yes, and more will die," I warn.

"You won't have the numbers when it counts. Israel is all but lost, and you will burn with her."

"I'd rather burn then give in to men like you."

"Admit it, you know there's no chance of survival here. Everyone you love will perish to the likes of men like me." He smiles, revealing a gap in the front where his teeth got knocked out.

Without another word, I slide the *katanas* across his neck and dismember his head. The body falls with a thud and mingles deathly with the earth. This is a but a small taste of what Jerusalem has faced over the last six months. While he may have been too arrogant for his own good, he was right. More will most certainly come, and I'm afraid it will only grow more dangerous.

Assaults by rebels like this are infrequent, mostly small bands of radicals, but it's still too dangerous to be out here alone. West Jerusalem has seen the brunt of aggressive outbreaks from Iraqi and Syrian militants—an expendable front line of attack that Russian operatives would rather see used.

A small breeze blows past, bringing with it the stench of curdled blood. No matter how many men I've killed, I'll never get used to that smell, and if that doesn't get your stomach churning, the waste excreting from a human after death will.

A painful grunt emerges from one of the wounded men lying near the hospital entrance. He reaches forward, gasping, and slides his body across the concrete, leaving a red trail of forthcoming death. Some days I've grown past the ability to live as a merciless monster . . . *some* being the operative word. Today's his lucky day.

I push the tip of my dagger into the back of his neck. His knuckles retract like a lion's claw before he emits his last fading breath. I shuffle over to the side of the building and slide down the wall. I'm exhausted. If pain is a state of mind, then my thoughts are numb because I can't remember what it was like when pain was uncommon. My hands are weathered and cracked, crippled by relentless war, and from this small feat, I can labor no further. I'm only eighteen and a half and my body already feels the aches of a fifty-year-old. I just want to see my son and sleep for days.

Joshua . . . an unexpected gift, rests back in his bed. Fourteen months old and not a care in the world but to eat and sleep. Having a child in this wicked world is of my own doing. As foolish as it must seem, the past cannot replace my poor decisions, but it can chisel away the crap I wasn't meant to carry, and for that, I still believe in hope. I still believe there's a future for my son. I will not cease or lie down for his sake. I'll fight until the bitter end with every ounce of strength I have left, even if it kills me, and I expect my husband, Jacob, to do the same.

I reach into my pack and grab my dusty, old journal—one that I've kept in secret since the days before the world went mad. The pages are soft and yellowed, and worn from constant turning. Ink, pencil, charcoal, even blood marks the pages of my experiences. Some pages are scattered memories, others with just a few words, and some remain blank except for the date—a reminder of dark times not worth mentioning. The journal has become more than just reflective thoughts or tragic events. It's become a living story for my son now. I don't want him to only remember me by what I have written. I want him to understand the sacrifice and leadership I chose to endure for him that he will one day possess. Because one day, it will be Joshua who will be asked to lead a new people in a new world.

March 7, 2057

I'm not sure what day it really is, life has been a bit chaotic raising you. We'll just call it the seventh. It's been quite a while since I last entered a journal entry, about a month I guess. Today has been a nightmare. I had an argument with Roland, our doctor, been chased by radicals who were trying to kill me, and haven't eaten anything in twenty-four hours. I've been stir crazy of late, being cooped up in the mountain. Today I escaped, but for a good cause. Nadia, your godmother, was seriously injured a few days ago from a gunshot wound and the infection has spread. We've ran out of antibiotics, so I've taken it upon myself to search for some. Your father and uncle along with most of the men have departed for Damascus on a reconnaissance mission. It's been two weeks since they left, leaving me, Nadia, and Niki to care for you. They refused to let me go with them,

> *and I promised I wouldn't leave the mountain, but sometimes you'll have to make sacrifices for the greater good of the group. This is one of them. Without these antibiotics, Nadia may not survive, and regardless of what the others may say about my departure, I will never regret my choices. Trust may win you over with your friends, but it's sacrifice that will save them. One day, you'll understand.*

I close the journal, lean back against the wall, and gaze over a city in ruin. I should be heading back, but I'm too exhausted to move. I haven't seen the backs of my eyelids for two days now. I've been too consumed with the absence of Jacob and my twin brother, Gabe. What possible dangers have they come across? Will my husband return to me dead or alive? I'm tired of my thoughts turning against me, so I let my eyes lay heavy and turn against them.

CHAPTER 2

The cavernous fortress lying in the belly of Mount of Olives has been our home for the last year. Every night, the hundreds who chose to dwell in this underground refuge rest among the dead, below some seventy thousand tombs that reside on the slopes of the mountain. We sleep, eat, and plan our next day of survival alongside those who are buried in the Jewish cemetery. Perhaps I'll be among them soon.

Though Russia has caused much fear in the world, her allies' devastating attacks on Jerusalem have created an unsafe environment. The streets that lead to the old city remain abandoned, though sometimes an Israeli civilian may pass through, scouring for food. Many people lie low in their houses, waiting out this relentless war, while others hide in deserted commercial buildings that are surrounded by ash.

Those who have refused to join us inside the mountain remain a mystery. They steadfastly choose to live in the outer part of the city, but I assume it's out of fear. Some rumors claim they are being compensated by the Russian government in exchange for their loyalty to help persuade the rest of us to surrender. Some even come by the basin of the mountain as messengers of information in return for food and water. I'm not sure if they are spies working for us or for the Russians, but we never deny them food or water.

It's been almost two years now since we left America for a safer place, but that decision is becoming bleaker by the day. Russia has completely taken America in its stronghold. If we had stayed, we would be dead by now. Israel was our only hope for freedom. Aside from its ruin, Jerusalem still stands apart from the other nations claimed by Russian title. There is nowhere else to go except for the treacherous deserts waiting to take your life. Death surrounds us.

I crack open my eyes and feel the tiny hairs on my arm move about. An Israeli cockroach the size of a silver dollar crawls across my skin. I brush it from my arm and stomp its waxy, amber body into the concrete. No telling what creatures have crossed my path while I dozed off.

I look around and find myself still alone, but vulnerable nonetheless. It's quiet with the exception of a few flies buzzing over one of the mangled bodies, which is beginning to smell beyond the likes I can tolerate. War is unforgiving and it seems endless now. It's kill or be killed. I won this round.

Twilight approaches and I'm parched and weary. I gather my things and leave the flies to feast. The journey back to the mountain is no cakewalk. I'm not sure how long I've been gone, but I need to move quickly before a search party is sent for me.

The desert sand, once a blazing sheet of devil's heat, is cold beneath my boots. Black clouds blanket the sky, hiding the scorching sun, for it has been nine months since even a whiff of light has peeked over the horizon. Very little light distinguishes the night from day now, so trekking across the city can be quite difficult if you don't know your way around.

The outline of the mountain is in sight, but I'm only just halfway there. I can only hope no one knows I've been gone. I admit it wasn't smart going out on my own, but no one else would have taken the risk to leave, and Nadia, my closest friend, is in dire need of antibiotics. She's tough, but I'm afraid she'll lose her leg or her life without antibiotics. I trust Nadia with my life, and if anything were to happen to me, I wouldn't want anyone else to raise my son.

I've only been outside the mountain a couple of times by myself, but not inside the walls surrounding the city. I'mnot one to be afraid, but being out here is giving me the creeps. The smoky sky drapes eerily behind the crumbling buildings from war, its silhouette a haunting reminder of how cruel humanity has become. Hate has consumed us all, but I'd like to think there is still enough love within us to hold on.

A shadow flutters as the cool breeze brushes against my skin. I stop and crouch behind a broken stone wall. The breeze slows and a dead calm sets in. A flapping of feathers under a bellowing squawk brushes across me. It's him—the crow that has been following me since the beginning of my journey. He perches on a nearby stone. I think I'm cursed. This black bird and I tend to meet under strange circumstances. He's warned me on many occasions when I was in danger. Even when I neglected his presence or mocked his chattering nonsense, he's persistently come back to help me. He's even saved us, along with his murderous flock, from Egyptian soldiers at the Cairo prison where my brother was being held. When this crow arrives, I do not shutter anymore. Instead, I respect his presence, even taken a liking to him. The Israeli soldiers call them *soul eaters,* and after witnessing the murder of crows and their carnage in Cairo, I can see why. But this one in particular seems personable. He sometimes whispers to me words of advice—his voice deep and distant—and I whisper back. If crazy is the new normal, then I'm insane.

His coal-black eyes explore mine, yet his beak is still. I draw my gun and wait. The crow leaves its perch and hovers near a jarred door with broken chains. I do not dither and quickly follow after. The door opens to a deserted, old restaurant. The darkened room dims softly under a sliver of light shining from the back. Tables are stretched end to end, some covered in shrouds of blankets that are draped in dust. One of them is still warm from a body that may have lay here. I imagine the tables make for better beds than the sticky floors that smell of dried urine. A short wall to my left divides the room where a small kitchen is tucked into the corner. While this place may have served as a refuge, the only inhabitance now is silence, accompanied by the stench of stale, musty air.

The crow swoops down and flaps across the tables toward the back. He jeers a belching caw before landing beside a broken window. I approach the dusty glass and peek through the jagged edges. Small, wandering lights shine in the distance followed by mumbling voices.

"Thank you again, friend. Not sure what I would do without you," I whisper to my feathered stalker. The crow's beak, eerily agape, rattles off a chattering caw. "You do realize if we keep meeting like this, I'm forced to give you a name," I say. He erects his neck and his black eyes roll back before flying away.

The muddled voices outside move closer and become clearer . . . Russian soldiers. *Damn.* Enemy soldiers haven't moved in this close to the city for months. The pact among the Ten is loosely falling apart. This treaty, signed by the last ten sustainable nations in hopes of securing a global economy, rests solely in the hands of the sinister tyrant who created it—Gorshkov, Russia's malevolent president. Though I have seen just a sliver of his face, it is tattooed in my mind. Until I know he is dead, nothing will change.

With Israel's refusal to join and lose its precious freedoms, we wander the streets of Jerusalem in fear. While the Ten lingers in turmoil, the fate of Israel is uncertain. Few countries have remained loyal, like China, Iran, and Turkey, while most of Russia's allies fight among themselves. Tribal blood-feuds have all but vanished in the Middle East, giving up their lands in exchange to prosper under the Ten accord. Torn between the allegiance of their own people and a commitment to a lavish new empire brings uncertainty for a one-world government that may have residual risk in its political fate. While these remaining nations wither, Russia grows stronger for complete control.

I hunker by the window and keep still as the band of soldiers crosses the street. They wander near a brick façade that's left of a burned structure. Two soldiers stand guard on each side of a scorched truck while another posts on the top corner of the demolished building. Perhaps exhausted from their journey, the rest lie down against the brick wall, nestled by their guns. It's not worth the risk of an ambush; these men are heavily armed.

Their torches turn black, plunging the world into darkness. The only trace of their position are a few orange-glowing embers from their cigarettes. There's no time to wait them out. I must make haste and warn the others back in the mountain.

I grip the sides of the tables and feel my way through the dark to the front door. An unexpected voice whispers from the corner and I stop immediately and stoop to the floor. My heart jitters in my chest. Dare not to exhale, my breath holds still in the quiet. The faint voice whispers again, but shudders this time, almost as if crying.

Shoes scuffle against the floor and the clang of a metal bowl drops. I draw my gun and peek around the short wall, but it's too dark to see. A whimper draws from the darkened corner. With my gun pointed, I shine my torch below it. Hiding beneath an open sink, a woman clings to a tremoring man in a fetal position.

"*Bitte, bitte tut uns nicht weh,*" the woman cries.

"I don't unders—"

"Don't hurt us," she whispers.

"You speak English?" I ask.

"Yes." She is shaking.

"It's okay, I'm not going to hurt you." I withdraw my gun to confirm. "Let me help you."

"Bad, bad, bad," the man moans, clenching his fists.

"It's okay, it's okay . . . shhh." The woman gently rubs the man on the back.

I move closer and lower my torch away from the man's face. "I'm not going to hurt you, I promise, okay?" I slowly stretch out my arm to him. He rocks his body back and forth and shakes his head. The woman gently grabs his hand and places it near mine until we touch. He twitches a nervous tic then clenches his fist.

"Catch me now, catch me later, see me on the elevator," he whimsically sings.

For a brief moment, the man's odd behavior calms me. I watch his eyes dance strangely into his clamping fists. The woman continues to sooth him, rubbing his back ever so gently. She looks up at me with an aging face under weary exhaustion. Her matted hair blends blonde and silver, and her eyes gloss over a pale blue.

"He recalls bits and pieces from television shows and children's stories—an eidetic memory," she explains. "Rhyming is a coping mechanism. It may seem strange to you, but it helps . . . for both of us."

I sympathize with this woman's burden to care for this man, especially in times like these. I offer her a small condolence with a simple nod before extending a formal handshake. "My name is Arena."

"I'm Mia, and this wonderful boy is Godfrey." She smiles.

His peculiar nature is quite fickle as I imagine this "boy" is trapped inside a man's body. His face is grown but not worn, dressed with a bit of blond stubble. I'd guess he's in his late twenties or early thirties. Though curled up like a frightened child, I imagine he stands a little over six feet with his broad shoulders and long legs.

"A flock, a feather, mincing words, crazy lady talks to birds," Godfrey chatters.

"Uh, I can explain—"

"It's fine, it's none of our business." Mia grins as she crawls out from under the sink, clothes crumpled and stained with dirt. Godfrey moans and clutches her side.

"Shhh, it's okay. I just want to talk with Arena for a moment." Mia grabs a small rubber frog from her pocket. Godfrey lays his cheek against her hand before nabbing the toy.

"Froggy in the water, froggy take a soak, froggy swallowed bubbles, now froggy cannot croak," Godfrey sings as he squeezes the frog.

"The squeaker is broken," Mia explains. "He has a child's mind, but he can understand you. Just takes some patience."

"It's fine, I completely understand," I sympathize. I lead Mia out of earshot from Godfrey and begin to pry. "How long have you been living here?"

"About a week. There were others, but they left a few days ago and haven't returned. We left Germany a year ago before war began in our country. Some stayed, and many died trying to flee. Godfrey lost his parents, Edmund and Carolyn, during Germany's shift in power. Edmund held a strong position in the Bundestag, an expendable assembly to the Russians. When the Ten was established, all members were told to relinquish their positions and confide to the loyalty of the Ten's regulations. Though this was a forcible suggestion, Edmund had no intentions of abolishing history, so he and many other legislators fought back with a clear and relentless vision to preserve Germany's governing body. And because they refused to disband their positions, each legislator and their family members were executed."

My heart sinks. "How did Godfrey survive?"

"Upon hearing the news of Russia's coup, Carolyn took preventative caution as she was instructed and moved Godfrey to Frankfurt with me. I've known Edmund and Carolyn for the better part of twenty years and was employed to be Godfrey's caretaker for the past ten. I guess they knew no one else they could trust.

"After parliament was abolished, China seized Germany's southern region and took reign while Russian leadership gained full political control. And that's when the devil showed his face. Citizens were given unviable options to either withdraw their allegiance and adapt to a new political slavery or seek fruitful endeavors of conformity through prison labor. With someone like Godfrey," she cries, "I just couldn't see any other way out of this tortuous inevitability . . . so we fled."

"I'm so sorry," I say. I look back at Godfrey—he's playing with a button on his shirt in a childlike manner. "Does he know?"

"No, nor should he," she affirms, eyes fixed. "His parents' death shall remain in secret."

"You have my word," I whisper. I can only imagine what these two have been through, fighting through hell to find what little peace may lie before them. Godfrey's innocence in this broken world echoes why I will never stop fighting for hope. Godfrey is not dumb nor oblivious to pain. He hungers for joy just like anyone else. Why should he be any different? A child's mind should never be consumed with tragedy.

"Are you alone?" Mia asks.

"No, and you and Godfrey don't have to be either. I have trusting friends and a place of refuge that you can be a part of too. When is the last time you've eaten?"

"Not sure, two days maybe," she says.

"If you come with me, I can find you a place that's safe with plenty of food and water."

"Candy please, candy please," Godfrey chatters.

Mia digs into her pocket and pulls out a candy wrapper. "I'm sorry, sweetie, I don't have any more."

"Wait, I may have something." I rustle through the bottom of my pack and pull out a stick of gum. "Can he have this?" I ask Mia.

"Gum!" Godfrey shouts.

"Shhh," I gesture tamely. I grab my gun and fix my eyes toward the back window, waiting for torches to brighten.

"Everything okay?" asks Mia.

"We're not alone."

Mia calms Godfrey before handing him the gum. A smile stretches across his face as he jingles, "Gum is fun, come and follow, only chew and never swallow."

Mia's worried face draws closer to me. "Are we in danger?" she whispers.

I hold my tongue. The expressions on Godfrey and Mia's faces couldn't be any more different. But Mia must know the truth. "There's a small Russian squad camped just across the street, and I don't see any signs of them moving anytime soon. If we want to make it out of here, we need to be very quiet."

"What do you suggest?"

"We could risk holding out here and hope they don't search this place, or we can quietly walk out the front door and double back to the south."

Mia's face pales. She looks back at Godfrey, who is happily chewing his gum. "What are our chances staying here . . . and don't lie to me."

"It'd be foolish of me to tell you we'd be okay here, but I know how these soldiers' minds work. They don't leave any place untouched. We must go."

"What about Godfrey? We can't count on him staying quiet."

Godfrey is staring into space and quietly humming a tune. *What have I gotten myself into?* He stops humming and calmly turns to me, his face as still as a mannequin.

"Are you okay, sweetie?" Mia asks.

He doesn't respond, provoking Mia to worry. "Godfrey, honey. What's wrong?" she asks. Still he says nothing. This unusual behavior grows beyond his already odd nature.

Suddenly, his eyes roll back white and his mouth stretches open like someone possessed. Mia and I jump back, frightened. He crawls out from under the sink and stands motionless like a robot—no tics, no fist clenching, nothing. Mia scuttles behind me, terrified. Godfrey points toward the window and whispers in an deep eerie voice, "Bad men coming."

A gunshot fires from outside. I race to the window and glance across the street. Two shadows move past and a few torches light up. "Shit, we got to go, now," I urge.

Godfrey is now sitting on the ground, rocking back and forth in a nervous manner. The white in his eyes have vanished and the normal mannerisms he possesses have resumed. Mia urges him to move, but he moans loudly to himself, refusing to budge.

"He's going to get us killed," I warn.

"Shh, shh, Godfrey, it's okay," she comforts.

"Candy, candy, good for you, no more candy, makes me blue!"

Mia frantically digs in her pocket but comes up empty. "What are we going to do?" she frets.

I stoop down next to Godfrey so we're at eye level and gently touch his hand. "Godfrey, do you like games?"

"I play games," he says excitedly.

"Okay, but this game is special, because if you win, you get all the candy you can eat." His eyes light up. "It's an easy game. All you have to do is be quiet until I say stop. That means no talking and no humming."

"I can clap? " he asks, slamming his brawny hands together.

"No, no, no, not even one clap or you lose the game and lose all the candy."

"Candy!"

"Shh," Mia urges. She turns to me. "This isn't going to work."

I glance toward the window. Torches begin to move. "All right, Godfrey, there's one thing I left out about this game. If you make even one sound, not only will you lose all the candy, but the bad people will come for you."

A sudden fear blankets his face. "That's right, Godfrey. They will come for you, for Mia, and for me, and they won't be nice. They will rip our arms and legs from our sockets like monsters." He draws his fists and rocks back and forth. "We don't want the monsters to win, do we?"

"I don't like this game," he stutters.

"I don't either, but we have no choice, Godfrey. We must play . . . and we will win."

Another gunshot echoes outside.

"Don't leave me," he whimpers.

"I won't. Stay close to me and I will protect you from the monsters."

The door suddenly creeps open. I grab my dagger and sidle against the wall. A Russian soldier enters, an assault rifle dangling against his hip. Godfrey and Mia are hunched over in the shadow.

A Russian voice crackles on the man's radio, "What's your status?" The soldier shines his torch in the corner just above Godfrey's back. I hold my breath, my dagger raised. Our eyes meet. He drops the radio and reaches for his gun, but I plunge forward and jab the blade through his neck. Clutching the air, he staggers toward Godfrey before falling lifeless to the floor. I retrieve the radio and respond back in a deep Russian voice, "Clear."

Mia stares blankly at me, and Godfrey stops clenching his fists. "Shhh," I gesture quietly. "The game begins."

CHAPTER 3

The small glow of amber dips below the horizon, providing the lasting rays of daylight before plunging into darkness. The air smells of fire as another string of short-burst gunfire erupts. Mia's bold escape from Germany has earned my respect for her, but shit's about to get real.

The empty sidewalks look promising, but the open space in either direction makes it too risky to escape. Across the street, rows of apartments crowd tightly around clusters of commercial buildings. The gaps in-between follow darkened backstreets, which is where we should be. Mia and Godfrey huddle close behind. "Stay close to me, and remember, Godfrey, lots of candy." I quickly grab his hand.

We scamper across the street and lay low behind a large dumpster. Moments later, two soldiers carrying assault rifles walk up and down the street, pointing their guns aimlessly in the dark. They roam closer, then stop on the other side of the dumpster. Godfrey curls next to me with his head hiding between his knees. A torch shines just near Mia's shoe. Her eyes grow wide, but I motion for her to stay put.

A static voice calls out over one of the soldier's radio in Russian, "Forty-six Wolf."

"Go ahead," the soldier responds.

"Sweep the east block and hold."

"Roger."

"Stay here and wait for my signal," one soldier says to the other. Apparently, the protocol of two is loosely followed.

I peek underneath the dumpster and see a single pair of boots. I grit my teeth in frustration. Mia looks frightened as she hangs tightly against Godfrey. We wait patiently, under controlled breaths, for the soldier to vacate. Not a moment too soon, the ground scuffs repeatedly as the soldier stomps out a cigarette with the tip of his boot. He tussles with his gear and slowly walks off.

I sigh with relief. When I motion to Mia and Godfrey that we're in the clear, I pause. Mia looks distressed; her hand is clamped firmly over her mouth and she's pinching her nose with two fingers. Her eyes are watering. I'm confused. Then she lowers her hand and exhales with relief, but it's too late. She can't stop herself and she lets out a loud sneeze.

I hold still and listen—the air is quiet, and the sound of boots have vanished into the night. Not convinced, I glance around the edge of the dumpster. A sliver of light shine's from a torch and a shadow approaches. I grab my knife and slink against the metal corner. Godfrey quivers like a leaf in the wind as a silhouette of a soldier creeps closer. His rifle barrel is just inches beyond the edge, and I'm ready to grab it with all my might and jab my dagger when shouting erupts across the street, "*Soldat vinz, soldat vinz!*" His rifle barrel advances no further. They've discovered the dead soldier.

I clench my teeth in frustration. Mia clings to Godfrey and buries her head into his shoulder.

"*Boevik na khodu!*" a voice shouts over the soldier's radio. Russian tongues argue back and forth. There's no hiding—they know we're here now—but I will not let Mia and Godfrey's hope for survival end here. I signal for them to stay put. Then I take a deep breath and swing around the corner with my knife at the ready.

The soldier grabs my arm and shoves me hard against the dumpster. Black dots dance in my vision, but I blink rapidly to clear my head. His hand presses against my throat, his face is inches from mine. The pores on his nose are large and his eyes are glinting in the lowlight, and suddenly I'm starting to lose my vision. Just then, gunshots ricochet against the concrete and echo in the alleyway, snapping me out of this trance. Pain tears into my throat—I'm afraid he's crushing my windpipe. In the distance, I make eye contact with Godfrey, who's crouched in the shadows with Mia, too frightened to move. More gunshots, and my attacker flinches, just the opening I need. Somehow, my knee slams into his groin and he stumbles back. I gasp, the air flooding my lungs in painful heaves. The ground is swirling, and I'm afraid I'm going to pass out. My eyes try to focus as I regain consciousness, and it takes a moment for my brain to comprehend what I'm seeing. Godfrey has the soldier in a chokehold while Mia tries to wrangle the soldier's flailing arms.

I shake my head, grab my knife from the pavement, and plunge at him.

"Keep holding him tight," I say to Godfrey. "And close your eyes." Godfrey complies, and I thrust the blade into the soldier's heart. He gasps a small breath before his body goes limp in Godfrey's arms. "Thank you," I say. "You saved my life."

"Playing a game, it's all the same," he sings. I wonder if he knows the full extent of what has happened.

"I'm sorry," I say to Mia, "but we're not out of the woods just yet." A small glimpse of relief is painted on her face, but I can tell she's in shock.

Suddenly, an outcry of shouting explodes from the restaurant and soldiers bustle down the street. A gunshot zings past and tags the side of the dumpster. Damn, they've spotted us.

"*Ya vizhu ikh, tam, tam!*" yells one of the soldiers.

I grab Godfrey's hand and say, "Run!"

A blazing burst of gunfire showers the sky, chasing us through a gate and down a small flight of steps. Bullets scatter, zipping past like angry wasps.

"This way!" I shout.

We sprint down a row of apartments and exit into a maze of cluttered dwellings stacked on top of one another. We dart around in search of an escape, but it's hopeless. Every direction appears the same. Buildings mirror each other, and we're cramped tightly in the dark among the unknown. I've lost my bearings. Though it's well hidden, we've failed to distance ourselves from the soldiers. Gunshots follow us.

We press forward, down the backside of the neglected dwellings and into an enclave of deserted retail shops—a nestled district in derelict. After turning down one alley and into another, we find ourselves misplaced in an urban sea.

Mia gasps for air, bent over with exhaustion. Godfrey mimics, fatigued and weary. I'm also spent, but we can't we can't stop now, we must find a place to hide. I take Mia's hand and urge her to move. She wheezes a few breaths and slowly stands upright. Godfrey grabs her waist and assists her around the corner where the street narrows. Rows of shops line both sides of the cracked sidewalks.

The doors on each storefront are locked, except for one—an old clothing store with barred windows. I push on the front door, but it only opens up a few inches. Something has jammed it from the other side. Mia struggles to walk and clutches my arm.

"I'm so sorry, but I need to rest a bit," she pants as she leans against the wall.

Suddenly, voices mingle around the corner. I lunge at the door, but it still won't open. I'm not strong enough.

"Godfrey, I need you to push on this door as hard as you can, okay?"

Clamoring voices grow louder. Someone says, "Check all the doors. They're in here somewhere."

With one big heave, Godfrey is able to push the door open, and the three of us rush inside. A chair blocking it slides across the floor. The door knocks loosely against the frame. I turn the lock, but it's broken. At the bottom is a shredded baseplate and a metal wedge.

"Godfrey, help!" I say, and together we prop the chair against the door, but I don't know how long it will hold.

"Move on!" shouts a Russian voice. They're squabbling just around the storefront.

"Go," I whisper.

Mia and Godfrey dart across the room in the dark and bump into a metal clothes rack. They quickly crouch below it while I wait nervously across from them. Boots scuffle toward the front entrance and the door rattles. I hold still, nearly breathless with my gun drawn.

Godfrey rocks back and forth and quietly clasps his hands. I'm surprised he's stayed quiet this long without humming one of his rhyming afflictions. Tears run from Mia's eyes, a face fighting a hopeless end. The door shudders once more, almost jarring loose, but it holds secure.

"It's clear," a muffled voice confirms.

I can't believe it. Mia happily exhales as we reach a rare break in our favor, but the moment doesn't last. A shadow dances from the back of the room and flutters swiftly across the floor. An empty clothes rack falls forward and clangs to the floor.

The front entrance shakes with a violent thud. Then the chair scratches across the floor as the door slowly creaks open. Two soldiers stand in the doorway. I draw my guns, ready to kill, when the unexpected happens. A ragged, old cat saunters from the dark and circles around before fixing itself in front of the entrance. The soldiers stay planted in an odd stalemate with this neglected feline.

"Never mind, it's just a damn cat," the soldier says.

The cat arches its back and leans forward on its front paws. Not sure what pissed in this cat's Cheerios, but it's not happy. It rears its ears back into its matted black fur and caterwauls with contempt. Either this cat is blind or I'm not interesting enough for it to notice me. I avoid eye contact nonetheless.

"Stupid cat, want to eat a bullet?" the soldier mocks. The cat purrs. "Pounce on me and I'll rip that scrawny head off." The cat retracts and sits upright.

"Come on, let's go. Leave the damn cat alone," a voice orders outside.

"Fine," the soldier snaps.

Without warning, the cat's eyes lock on me, and it jumps back. It stretches back its mouth, exposing sharp teeth, and hisses at me like a startled snake.

"Wait," a voice murmurs at the door.

You damn cat.

The soldier advances forward and his torch shines near me. I grip tight, turn, and unload, the sound of the gunfire deafening in such a small space. Both men fall dead. The cat has scampered outside in fear.

"Go out the back door, now!" I shout.

Godfrey grabs Mia's hand and vanishes into the dark, and I sprint after them. Russian voices spew from outside as several men rush the front entrance and fire their guns. . Bullets graze past, clipping the air. I dodge them blindly in the dark, and then pain rips through my shoulder—a bullet has caught me. I scream in pain and hold my arm, but every movement is agony. I stumble toward the back door, my legs burning. I push it open and slam it shut, then collapse to the ground.

"Shit," I fume. My sleeve is covered in blood. The wound in my shoulder is burning.

I rush down the left side of the alley and escape south into the next backstreet. It's eerily quiet and empty except for a couple of dumpsters and the rats scurrying from them. My heart sinks over Mia and Godfrey. I've lost them. How long will they survive out here, or are they already dead? I draw one of my swords and creep cautiously down the street.

A backdoor creaks open. Mia, hands raised, slowly steps out followed by a gun resting behind her head. A Russian soldier emerges behind her, his face bloodied and angry.

"Drop the sword or the bitch dies," he scoffs.

Mia's lips tremble as tears slip down her terrified face.

"Now!" he orders.

I can't risk Mia's life even though I know I can kill this man. I'm out of options. I lower my sword and toss it to the ground. I rest my hand beside my dagger and take a step forward.

"Stop!" He backs next to the dumpster. "Don't you take one more step."

"Okay, just let her go," I calmly assert.

"Where are the rest of you?"

"Let her go first and I'll tell you."

"Don't trifle with me, woman."

He pauses for a moment, grits his teeth, and shoves Mia to the ground. She releases a painful yelp and holds her limp wrist.

"You bastard!" I fume.

She crawls weakly toward me and lies face down like a frightened opossum. The soldier points his gun at me and wrinkles his brow. He has no intentions of letting us go. I bend down to Mia and covertly grab the handle of my dagger.

"You can make this easy on yourself and her. Tell me now and I'll be merciful," he offers.

I stand to my feet. "You might as well point that gun to your head and pull the trigger, because when I'm through with you, you're going to wish you had," I retort.

The soldier aims his gun and sneers, "I don't think so."

Before I can even pull out my dagger, a large shadow rises from behind the dumpster and bludgeons the soldier over the head. The gun slips from his grasp and he tumbles to the ground.

Godfrey is standing behind the unconscious soldier holding a bloody two-by-four. He drops the wood and points at the soldier. "Bad man."

Hardly appropriate because we almost died, but I can't help but chuckle. "Yes, very bad," I say.

I help Mia from the ground as she wobbles to her feet. She holds her wrist against her chest and rushes over to Godfrey. Though his gentle face blossoms with innocence, it's but a mask hiding his unexpected bravery.

"Friends protect friends," he clearly expresses.

I look upon him and see a man before me. "You've just earned yourself a life supply of candy," I say. Nearly emotionless, he struggles to grin. I can only imagine the fear that's swimming in his head. Godfrey has seen enough bloodshed, so I tie the soldier's hands to his feet with a piece of twine and leave him to agonize instead. I snatch his rifle and wince. It's like a sharp sting from a scorpion's tail. My shoulder bleeds freely. I press on the wound to try to hide my grimace, but it's useless. I lose my balance and tumble to the ground.

"Arena, you okay?" Mia worries.

"Yeah, I'm fine, just a bit fatigued," I lie.

I pull myself up and press forward as if nothing happened. They've put their trust in me to get them to safety. We exit the alley and trudge cross the battered street, silence broken only by our footsteps. The farther we walk, the quieter it becomes and the more painful my shoulder throbs. I can only hope that the worst has past, but I'm not convinced. My legs slow to the pace of a tortoise and my eyelids twitch with exhaustion. While the darkness may conceal my wound, it cannot hide my blood-stained hand.

"My God, honey, you're bleeding!" Mia rouses.

"It looks worse than it is. I'll be fine," I quickly diffuse.

"You need a doctor."

"I'll make it."

"How much further?"

"Shh, wait," I interrupt.

A tin can clatters to the ground and rolls past in the distance. I retreat back into the alley, keeping Mia and Godfrey securely behind me. A shadow rustles across the street. A few moments later, we're being assaulted with gunfire.

We double-back down the alley and exit two streets over. Mia and Godfrey lay low a few steps behind against the wall. I crouch near the corner of the building and spy the back of a lone soldier planted atop an old bus. I steady my aim with the rifle, ignoring the searing pain in my shoulder, and snipe him from his perch. The shot echoes before turning eerily silent. I rush to my feet, but fall dizzy back to the ground. The weight of the rifle slips from my weak grasp. Mia rushes to my side and lays her hand on my cold, sweaty forehead. Everything is spinning.

With the help of Godfrey, I'm able to rise to my feet and retreat wearily down the street. I do everything to keep myself together, but I'm waning. All I can think about is holding my son close to my skin.

Just then, a soldier limps around the corner, his clothes torn and bloodied, and we all stop. I grab for my gun, but I haven't the strength to unholster it.

The battered soldier points his rifle and grins behind a churlish glare. Surely this isn't how I die. Not here, not like this. I search deep into the stony eyes of this evil man, trying to find some humanity, some warmth, but there's nothing.

Bang!

Blood exits the side of the soldier's ear and he crashes to the ground. A man in civilian clothes, emerges from the dark carrying an assault rifle. My vision blurs as my surrounding escapes me. I reach out to him, but my legs buckle and I fall to the ground. His voice mumbles into an empty shell and his face vanishes. A bright light shines before everything fades to black.

CHAPTER 4

"Arena, Arena?" a faint voice calls.

I open my eyes, but it's all too fuzzy. A dim light blankets my face and a blurry figure passes by. I'm not alone. I lift my head from a pillow and realize I'm lying in a bed. How did I get here, and more importantly, am I dead or alive?

"Arena?" the voice whispers again.

I focus my eyes and awake to a familiar face. Niki, my stepsister, is sitting next to my bedside and holding my hand. Her stringy blond hair dangles over her eye and hides part of her pale face. I've made it back to the mountainside, but how did I get here?

"Shh, just sit back and rest, sis," she comforts. Her warm smile and kind heart is all that's left of my foster family. Her parents, Mya and Daniel have been long dead, but I'm afraid their fatal suffering inside that Russian prison will never leave us. Gone are the days of that world except for the memories she brings with it. To see her now is soothing, but I fear the day that may come when we part.

She lifts the bandage from my shoulder and cleans the skin around my wound. "Does it hurt?" she asks.

"No," I grimace.

"Look, you don't have to act tough around me. We're family."

"Yes, it hurts like hell." In fact, it feels like someone is pounding my shoulder with a ball-ping hammer."

"Lucky for you, you ran across a paramedic," Roland chimes in. Roland is the only trained medical doctor in the group. He was one of a few remaining survivors who escaped from Cairo. After rescuing Gabe from the prison there, our fellowship drastically changed. We are fortunate to have him with us. Egypt seems like a long time ago now.

We shipped from America with thousands of survivors only to land in a world with more turmoil than what we had left behind. Our numbers diminished on the rough seas, thwarted by a Russian sub and claiming a few of our ships. Thousands of frightened men, women, and children turned into hundreds and hundreds reduced to the few who endured the tumultuous journey. While those who died at sea, some stayed back in Alexandria, but many risked everything to depart the fellowship with a mysterious man who claimed to be their liberator. Unfortunately, their decision to leave cost them a chance of freedom to a devil in sheep's clothing. I'm not sure what we have found in Jerusalem is much better as we live in fear now, hoping to survive another day.

"He did a good job dressing your wound," Roland continues.

"Who?" I ask.

A medium-build man with dark tousled hair and caramel skin walks over to the side of the bed. Dirt covers his face and neck. I don't recognize him. "I guess we haven't formally met. I'm Attimus," he says. His unusual accent mingles together Italian and British, but neither suggest where he's from.

"Thank you," I reply softly.

"No, thank you. I wouldn't have made it here if you hadn't cleared out an entire Russian platoon. I was lucky enough to be at the right place at the right time or we wouldn't be having this conversation right now. "

"Wait!" I sit upright and wince. "Where's Godfrey and Mia? Did they make it here?"

"Yes, Mia's resting, and I think Godfrey is in his room counting candy wrappers. Not sure what that's about," Attimus says.

"Sit back," Roland says as he jabs a needle into my arm. "Just a little medicine to numb the pain. I know I shouldn't be telling you what you already know, but I'm going to say it anyway. What the hell were you thinking going out there alone like that?"

"If you check my pack, you'll see," I assert.

Roland rummages through the contents and pulls out the antibiotics. He sighs. "As your friend, I strongly advise against you ever attempting something like this again without help, but as your regular care physician, I redact my former remarks and apologize."

Roland is about as fatherly as a lion is to a fawn, but I can't discard his concerns. He's right—I shouldn't have gone out alone—but I'm too stubborn to admit it, so I just smile.

"I believe you are in good hands here," Roland says with a wink. "I shall go tend to Miss Nadia now. I know she'll be happy to see you."

"We should leave you to rest, Arena," Niki says.

The medicine Roland injected me with has numbed the pain in my shoulder, but it's also caused my eyelids to weigh heavy. With every second that passes, they shudder until I fall back asleep.

* * *

I peel open my eyes. I'm groggy but feel well rested. Nadia enters the room with Joshua nestled in her arms. She hovers over me with a gentle smile. Aside from Jacob and Gabe, no person in the world means more to me than Nadia. In the small time we have known each other, she's been my side through thick and thin, saving my life on more than one occasion. She's my friend for life—my sword, my shield, and the mother of my child if I should pass.

"Feeling better?" she asks.

"Yeah, sore, but I'll live," I answer plainly. "How's your leg?"

"Sore, but I'll live," she copies, jestingly. Nadia's leg was shot just below and behind the knee during a food run a week ago. She was caught in a crossfire from a band of lawless radicals.

Joshua squirms in her arms and coos. There's no pain in the world that can't be cured by the sweet, innocent sounds from an infant. She carefully hands him over and the very second he touches my skin, tears fall from my eyes. My heart warms over while he gurgles in his sleep, sucking his tiny thumb. His puckering lips mirror mine, but he has the softest azure eyes like his father.

Nadia carefully lifts my arm and redresses the wound. "You sure do like to attract bullets," she teases.

"At least it'll match the other shoulder now."

I have no illusions of my blemished body anymore. From scratches, knife cuts, bruises, and gunshots, it's a safe bet I won't be modeling a two-piece bikini.

Nadia probes at the gauze. "I appreciate all the things you've sacrificed for us, I really do. It's just . . ."

"I did what I had to do," I say.

"It scares me when you go into things alone."

"I had no choice."

"You could have at least asked him."

"He wouldn't have approved, and you know that. Hell, he's more protective than my father was."

"Father Joseph isn't your enemy."

"He's not my father either."

"Maybe so, but you can't just leave us in the dark like that."

"I admit it was risky—"

"Risky? It was stupid. You could have been killed!"

"I did it for you."

"I appreciate that, but I'd much rather see you with your son than worrying about my problems. He needs you more than he needs me." Her words cut deep, pressing into me a fraught of guilt.

"I know it may seem pessimistic of me, but we can't know what tomorrow is going to bring. Believe me, I don't take joy in thinking about these things, but we must be prepared. If Jacob and I aren't around, you are my only choice for Joshua to have a life with."

Nadia lets out a large sigh. "And what about Niki?"

"He needs more than love. I adore my sister, but Joshua needs a mother who can protect him. I'm trying to make this world a better place for him, you must understand that."

"Then you must understand I'm here to protect you," she retorts.

"Fair enough," I agree.

"So we're good here?"

"As long as you don't mention me leaving the mountain to Jacob, we got a deal."

"Good luck hiding that from him." Nadia turns away, smiling. She finishes the bandage and pulls the bed cover around Joshua.

"I guess you met Godfrey, Mia, and—"

"Attimus, yes. I met him . . . I mean them." She grins. "Attimus is a good man. We're lucky to have him."

"Do I detect a hint of adoration?"

She stares into space for a moment, dodging to answer. Finally, she says, "Absolutely not."

"I do believe you're smitten with him."

"He's nice to look at I suppose," she says with a chuckle. "All right, that's enough. Get some rest. I'll check in later." She blushes as she leaves the room.

I snuggle my son against my chest and watch him lie still as he dreams, his nose twitching and lips smacking. I can't help but muse over Nadia's words. It's terrible to imagine what Joshua's life would be without me. I'm not ready to die. He needs me just as much as I need him.

The door creeks open and in walks Father Joseph. He's dressed in a dark coat, faded and frayed at the ends. His shirt, untucked and worn, matches his salt and pepper tousled hair. I'm not in the mood for one of his parental speeches. I love him like a father, but right now I just want to be alone with my son. He stands next to me, silent, and offers a courteous smile—an unusual approach considering I left the mountain without telling him. But I know him well enough to know that he's not going to let this go, so I preemptively strike the inevitable conversation. "You can save the lecture."

"I'm not here to tell you what you already know," he says behind a stoic face.

"I left without your permission because I know you weren't going to allow me to go and search for medical supplies we so desperately need."

"Like I said, you've already accepted your immature decision that put your life at risk and everyone else's in danger."

"And there it is."

"Is it?"

"You just couldn't wait to throw that in my face."

"I believe you did a tremendous job all on your own."

I lift my head from the pillow and writhe from my shoulder. "Damn."

"If you stayed where you were supposed to, you wouldn't be in such pain," Father Joseph chides.

"I'm a grown-ass woman. I can make my own decisions."

"You're barely an adult."

"I'm eighteen and a half."

"Oh, well in that case," he concedes with a sarcastic smirk.

And so these conversations go. Father Joseph always makes me feel so big and small all at once. "Do you enjoy giving me a hard time?" I ask.

Father Joseph sits down in a nearby chair and rubs his temples. The dark circles under his eyes indicate he hasn't slept much. "Don't be daft, Arena. If it seems like I give you a hard time, it's only because I care about you. I'm not here to battle every decision you make. I'm here to stand by those decisions and support you, even if they are unpopular. I don't fight with you, I fight beside you because you matter most to me. Trust grows beyond what you can see. I'm here to protect that."

"Even my bad decisions?"

"It's my fault that you have to make any decision at all. I'm the one who brought you and Gabe into all of this. If there's anyone to blame, it's solely on me."

"We made the choice to follow."

"And I'm glad you did. You've made me a better person for it."

Father Joseph places his hand on my arm and I feel an urge to cry. We've been through so much together these last three years, escaping one tragedy from the next. I was much ornerier toward him when we first met, but something inside me changed when he confessed his connection to my mother. I knew there was something special about him, though I had refused to show it. While I've made plenty of questionable decisions on this journey, he never abandoned us. He's seen me at my most vulnerable and I have witnessed his. Even when I was at my weakest and ready to end my life, still he believed in me. If we were not born to be bound to one another, then I may never know what any of this means. I remind myself every day that if he hadn't protected over us, Gabe and I would have most likely not survived, from the moment of our first breath to this seemingly endless war.

"I'll leave you two alone. You're going to need all the rest you can get before Jacob and the others return," he says.

Sadiq, special operations commander of the Israel Defense Force and my respected friend, has led Jacob, my brother, and a dozen other men tasked to survey potential troop movement across the southern Syrian border. The one region of Israel that's vulnerable to breach lies north of Tel Aviv. If enemy soldiers reach that far west, it could spell doom for our southern camps. Any help from our Independent Syrian allies could ease those concerns.

"You're not going to tell Jacob about any of this, are you?" I plead.

"Oh, I'm staying out of that conversation. This is between you and him if you decide to mention it. You are of course a—how did you put it, a *grown-ass woman*?"

"Now you're getting it."

"Oh, and for the record, if you would have asked me to leave to go get medical supplies, I would have gladly gone with you." Father Joseph smiles and walks out the door.

CHAPTER 5

It's been a week since Jacob and the others left for Damascus. Sadiq's well-trained squad should give me comfort, yet a simple recon mission gone awry lies heavy on my thoughts. I should be with them, but instead I'm left here to worry, and with my arm now in a sling. Joshua burrows against my chest and curls his monkey-like toes.

Whenever we're alone, I often sing Irish lullabies or retell stories of my childhood to him. And while my voice vibrates against his skin, I'm often interrupted by his reciprocal babbling. Whenever I worry, I just hold my son and escape into his simple life. It keeps me in a place of calm in a world that isn't. If I had the likes of his mind, I'd go there and never return. Sadly, I'm bound to my reality. Should he ever know the cruelty humanity has brought onto this punishable world, it will come by our failure to secure a better one. I will not let that happen.

The door opens to my quarters and Allison walks in looking bright-eyed. She's holding a small basket of food in one hand, and a copper vase filled with water in the other. She's only twelve and has seen too much horror. After her mother died, she was left in my keep, and despite following me through tragedy and misfortunes, she still looks up to me as a mother.

"Hi, love." I smile upon her cheery face.

"I brought you some goodies from the cupboard," she beams, eagerly lifting the cloth from the basket. Among the treats is a small jar of blueberry preserves, and I pluck it from the basket. I'm reminded of Luke and tears brim my eyes. A year ago, we all left America on the cargo ship, fleeing for our lives from a Russian invasion. Allison and Luke had eaten so many jars of blueberry preserves; I'd found them in a hideaway with blue lips and belly aches. Luke has since been taken from us in an unfortunate car crash near ten months ago. Not a day goes go by without being haunted by his limp body.

Allison pries the jar from my hand and sets it on the table. "I'm sorry," she laments. Luke was like a little brother to her.

"You have nothing to apologize for, my love. Life can be cruel sometimes, but we keep going until we can't."

"Then I don't want to keep going."

"Don't ever say that. Don't even think it."

"What's the point? We lose everyone we love in the end anyway. Why should we have to suffer through it?" The smile leaves her face as she rubs her glassy eyes.

"I don't know." I understand her anger, and I wish I could take it away, but I have no words that can change how she feels.

I walk over to the crib and place Joshua in his bed. I gaze upon his innocence with uncertainty and lost myself. What is to come of our fellowship? Have I doomed us all? I look over at Allison; she looks like she's about to break.

"I'm so sorry," she mutters behind trembling lips.

I open my arms and engulf her with an endless hug. She squeezes tightly, holding on to every moment. I can't replace her mother, but I know I don't need to. She means the world to me.

"I can't bring him back, God knows I would. We press on because it's what we do." I calmly stroke her hair.

She unburies her head, eyes sloped, and reaches into her pocket. She opens her palm and shows me a pair of dice. "Don't know why, but Luke always carried these with him." She hands me one die and returns the other to her pocket. "But now we can both carry a part of Luke with us."

I'm afraid the pain she carries may consume her, but sometimes it's that pain that will eventually heal us. She opens the jar of preserves and tears off a piece of naan from the basket. I grab a spoon from the table and admire the small smile lifting from her face.

"To Luke," she praises as she spreads the jam over the bread.

"To Luke," I concur with delight. Though I take part in this honor of Luke, I'm afraid the sweet fruity nectar will forever leave me with a bitter memory. For the many hardships Allison has had to endure, it's hard to believe she's survived this long. She is living truth that hope remains alive, and despite dwelling in a dangerously dark place, she leaves the room in a better one that I hope she takes with her until the end.

* * *

The day's end has approached and everyone's asleep in their quarters while I tussle restlessly in mine. The bed is empty on one side as Jacob has yet to return to it. His necklace dangles lonely on a hook, waiting for him to wear it. He left it to remind me of him while he's gone, but I don't need to see it to remember his face. The metal cross, hanging from it is as weathered as the journey we've led since we first met. We've been through hell and back and I'll let nothing tear us apart. When will he return, I don't know, and my anxiety is not my friend right now. Some distraction is in order. Maybe I'll clean my blades.

I move quietly across the floor and fetch my swords, a piece of leather, machine oil, and a polishing cloth. The sigh from my sleeping baby warms my heart as Joshua exhales tiny breaths. He secures his small blanket in his tiny fists and dreams quietly in his crib.

I lie the swords next to each other on my bed. Both have seen better days—long before they've touched my hands. I slide one of the blades against the leather and remove any unwanted barbs still clinging. These twin beauties have become a part of me, more than they probably should, but I trust them. They don't talk back, question my integrity, give me unsolicited advice, or judge me. I have an unhealthy relationship with these swords, but they get the job done.

I've even given them names. Valdis is *spirited in war* and resembles death. Her edge is as sharp as a liar's tongue and swings like a dancing feather in the wind. She has balance like no other sword and will ruin a man in a split second. Her twin, Agrona, meaning *to slaughter*, is equally matched, but has seen more battle than her sister. Her blade, covered in scars, dulls under the light, but it's the small chip just above the handle guard that differentiates the two. Agrona has wreaked havoc on many and is second to none, but even she knows there's a threshold to violence. Sometimes I might feel one becomes jealous of the other, so I switch them from their sheaths every so often. Yes, I'm nuts, but whatever keeps me going, so be it.

The dull luster of the blades shines despite their imperfections, but for how long? After a finishing rub, I return them to their sheathes and keep them quiet until they're stained red again. They were forged for no other reason than to kill, but I often wonder who truly is in charge, the sword or the person who wields it?

The chance to sleep passes me by. I've grown somewhat bored and a bit stir-crazy in this mountain. Fresh air is calling my name. leave Joshua to his dreams and take advantage of this rare opportunity to go outside. I tiptoe across the cold concrete floors down the long corridor and ascend a flight of stony stairs. Two soldiers stand twenty feet from the edge, guarding an iron gate. Behind that lies a highly secured entrance to the outside world, a formidable escape for anyone trying to leave without permission, though I've done it twice. Two hallways lead into the dark on either side of the gate. One joins the medical wing, the other to the mess hall.

The two army greenhorns look so young, I'm not sure they've ever shaven. Their eyes follow me as I scoot closer to the gate. The young man on the right eagerly rises from a stoop and secures his rifle. "Amdur" is stitched on a small rectangular patch attached to his uniform. The other follows me with a nervous twitch in his fingers. I stop just shy of the men and wait for them to open the gate, but neither budge.

"So, am I going to have to ask or are we pretending to be sloths?" I mock.

"No one leaves the caves unless we've been notified first," Amdur barks.

"On who's authority?"

"General Eizenkot, ma'am."

General Alexander Eizenkot, the Chief of the General Staff holds the highest administration privilege to the entire Israeli unit. He's a man of determination and grit and can often be a mean old buzzard. I find his more softer side appealing when we converse. I believe it's our mutual respect for each other that may tame his stern and persuasive persona, although it was that same manner that convinced me to help lead this war. However, if there's any communication between us, it's normally conveyed to me through Father Joseph. Perhaps our conflicting ideals keep us from talking face to face.

"Look, I can see you two are loyal, but how about you show a lady some respect," I wink.

"I have my orders," he says firmly.

I pull the knife from behind my back and casually clean my fingernails with it. The soldier on the left slowly backs away from the gate while the other stands firm.

"Funny, that's exactly what Private Rudma said. Now he has to sit down to take a piss," I say casually. The soldier's eyes grow wide.

"Ah, Private Rudma . . . yes, such a shame what happened to him," a voice enters from the hall on the right.

"Father?" My stomach tenses.

The soldier steps back, edging his body against the gate.

"Is there a problem here?" Father Joseph grins.

"I was just going to get some fresh air," I say.

"Well, are you gonna let the lady pass or does she need to make another illustration?" he advises the soldier.

The nervous guard fiddles with the key before he pushes open the iron bars. Behind the gate stands a grand door made of blackened steel with concreate pillars erected on each side. He swipes his badge across the security lock but is denied access. Slightly confused, he swipes again but is still denied.

"Not sure what's going on." He shrugs, puzzled.

Father Joseph swipes his security badge and the door unlocks. "Probably just a system glitch."

The doors open out to a stony interior large enough to fit six armored tanks. I turn around and mock with a curtsey before the doors close shut with a bellowing thud. Father Joseph stands composed with his hands tucked into his pockets and avoids eye contact.

"Foolhardy for you to leave the mountain after what happened last time," he says disappointed.

"System glitch my ass," I retort crossly.

He looks into my eyes and says in a gentler tone, "It was a change in protocol, a mere suggestion—"

"By whom, you?"

"No, by others who care about you, Arena. Look, I understand sometimes why you do the things that you do, often reckless, but I get it. You have to realize that not everything you decide should solely be on you. Risks taken, I know, but we do them together."

"I'm alive, aren't I?"

"Being a bit cavalier are we? Alive, yes, but for how long?"

His eyes draw upon me like a loving father, worry and stress trapped behind those pupils. I wish I knew my future, but I must live for now and honor his words. He's right. We are all going to die in the end, but we shouldn't have to die in vain. If I give him an inch, he'll take a mile, so I change the subject.

"The interior security of this cavernous fortress lacks attention to detail. Might want to mention that to the General Eizenkot at the next meeting. Not sure putting greenhorns at the gate is a terrifically good idea."

"I'll be sure to make note of that," he chuckles. "I'm sure he'll want to know why a wounded woman charmed her way past the gate with an outlandishly threatening story. Rudma, seriously? Where in the hell did you come upwith that?"

"It was stitched on the guard's uniform . . . 'Amdur' spelled backwards." He looks at me with a ridiculous smirk. "Didn't say it was profound story," I continue.

"You're something else."

"I try."

We pass through the open lobby with its vast vaulted ceiling hanging majestically above us, and cross the cold, rocky slate. It's simply amazing how much time and effort was poured out over the past one-hundred years into this grandiose solitude, but the scale of what lies below us is even more incredible.

We walk down a long, dimly lit corridor and approach a small door. Father Joseph swipes his badge and the door creeks opens. Just on the other side a jagged stony crevice opens to a small set of pale limestone steps to the stale air outside. The Mount of Olives peaks just over twenty-seven-hundred feet. Below the mountain entrance, about a thousand feet, several soldiers on alert pace back and forth on the outer edge. Several more are standing atop camouflaged stands that are embedded into the mountainside and blend into the terrain.

The rocky steps descend to the base, but I detour to the left on a slightly altered path instead. Father Joseph follows me as I round the corner and up to a small vegetated cove where I sit back and examine the dark city. Though it seems so peaceful up here, it's quite a different story down there. I shiver as the tiny hairs on my arms dance about.

"Here, I figure you might need this." Father Joseph offers me his jacket to fight off the brisk cool evening.

"Thank you."

"You know I have to ask, though I don't expect you to tell me, but how the hell did you escape from here?"

"Do you really want to know?"

He looks at me and grins. "I suspect you wouldn't tell me the truth."

"I have no reason to lie to you."

"Well, that's good to know, but I don't expect you need to tell me everything."

I lean my weary head against his shoulder and feel his bristly facial hairs when he dips his head to me. I wish my dad were here with me, but this is the second-best thing I can hang onto. I search my memories and wonder what kind of relationship Father Joseph and my dad had, or if Father Joseph was ever as kind and patient with my mother as he is with me. Everything about him is a mystery, but I feel as close to him as I ever had.

Some days I find it difficult to remember the littledetails of my parents and then there are times like now I'm able to relive small tender moments; like the stubble from my dad's chin rubbing against my cheek or my mother's wise and comforting words. I have many memories of them both, but only one still haunts me—the day they were killed in a car crash when I was nine. I'm afraid nothing can tear me away from that.

The sky moans with a rumble of thunder for the first time in nearly a month. Discordant voices chatter in the distance, as if chanting out of rhythm. "What is that?" I ask, puzzled.

I climb up the ledge a few steps and peek over one of the stoned walls where rows of tombs blanket the side of the mountain. The voices continue, but I cannot see from where they are coming from. A sea of limestone blocks outlines the Jewish cemetery. Trees pepper the mountainside, climbing to the top where an array of abandoned buildings lie in ash. The prattling voices continue to lament in the dark. It's quite creepy.

Father Joseph climbs up next to me. "Some of the elders still come up here to pray. When not at the West Wall, many of the orthodox Jews would come here and plead to God for forgiveness," he explains.

"Among the tombs?"

"No, you can't see it from here, but there's a mysterious olive tree that grows from the rocks. Some say it's been there since the beginning. They kneel before the tree and pray for hours on end once a month."

"There're many trees on the mountainside. Why this one?"

"It's not like the others. One side, green and luscious, flourishes to the west, while the other is vacant, withered, and dead. Some believe the tree represents a balance of life and death, two worlds separated by the breath of God. The elders do not worship or pray to the tree itself, but use it only as a conduit to talking to God. While the luscious green represents the side of the Holy Land, the dead represents the world against it. They pray that one day the entire tree will spring leaves of life, bridging a final moment of peace."

"That's a bit optimistic."

"Strangely, leaves have begun to fall during the past month."

Its curious mystery is too intriguing not to see. I swing my leg up over the stony barrier, but Father Joseph grabs my ankle, keeping me from climbing over.

"What do think you're doing?" He expresses under that fatherly tone.

"You've piqued my interest. I'm going to go have a look for myself."

"This isn't to be taken lightly. The tree is as sacred as the prayers it listens to, and it isn't to be touched."

"What do you mean?"

"For as long as the tree has been here, it's forbidden to be touched. The Jews believe the power of balance should never be disturbed by man."

"I'm not going to touch it. I just want to have a look." Father Joseph's eyes squint with an uncertain detainment. "Trust me," I reaffirm.

Unsure of himself, he slowly releases my ankle and grumbles beneath his breath. "You promise to stay within the walls this time?"

"Have we not already discussed this?"

"Perhaps, but can you give me your word anyway?"

"Look, I just need some time to myself and to clear my mind. This is a perfect opportunity." He scrutinizes me and I squirm under his gaze. "Fine, I give you my word. Besides, what could possibly happen up here anyway?"

"With you, plenty." He smiles and walks away, but I know hiding behind that grin is a nervous man just trying to look out for my well-being.

I search over the rows of tombs and quietly walk among the dead. The ceremonial chanting grows louder with every step. Dark clouds bury the mountainside into shadow. Only the small light from a lantern glows in the distance where a melody of prayers linger into the humid night. It's quite haunting.

Like a prowling cat, I prance lightly behind the headstones. The chanting suddenly stops and the lantern moves about. I creep closer to the rocky edge where several men wander around the mountain. Two men stay behind and kneel before the mysterious tree.

They recite in unison under their Hebrew tongues, *"Barukh ata Adonai Eloheinu, melekh ha`olam, Barukh ata Adonai Eloheinu, melekh ha`olam."*

A cool breeze blows past with a shiver and the leaves on the tree flutter. The two men rise to their feet and vanish into the darkness around the mountain. I pause before moving closer, observing my surroundings. It's quiet and still. I'm all alone, or am I? The tree, erected on the edge of a cliff, stands solid, stately, and very much alive. Strangely, I feel it searching me as I stand near it. Its roots cling to the rocky soil, spiraling into a woven knot of old age.

It's very much as Father Joseph described. Half of the limbs are blanketed with leaves of green, while the others have been banished with a cold emptiness, left to wither and die. The peculiar branches are mesmerizing. I'm hypnotically drawn to it and can't turn away. My legs begin to weaken as I approach the tangled roots, but I dare not touch it as Father Joseph instructed.

My eyes blur into its grainy trunk. Closer and closer, I scoot almost uncontrollably. A low hum rumbles from the ground and the tree sways. A decay of grating voices warble a deathly melody over me. I'm struck by their cacophonous chords weaving inside of my head. I'm stranded before this mysterious tree, hypnotized with weary eyes lost in its branches. Without any resistance, I stay transfixed, my body moving closer. My hand stretches toward the tree. I try to retreat, but something inside me pulls me in. My skin tingles. My body and mind leave me. Closer and closer like a magnet, I reach forward to the spellbinding tree. My hand glows white as I grab the trunk. Suddenly, a knot in the tree splits like an open wound, and a shrill of tormented voices spew with pain. Distorted faces emerge from the bark while shadowy figures erupt from their mouths and into the dark sky. The entire tree suddenly glows white, and my hand begins to burn.

Boom! The sky breaks in a thunderous roar as a wave of energy ripples across Jerusalem. My feet lift from the ground as my body flings from the tree. Like a broken spell, my mind releases and my eyes come back into focus. What the hell just happened?

A sharp sting crawls up my arm as I slowly rise to my feet. I carefully remove the sling from my throbbing shoulder, exposing a blood-soaked bandage. The stiches have torn open. I rotate my arm and press against the wound, but the small prickle now burns. I must have bumped my head against a rock, because my eyes begin to deceive me. The skin on my arm glows a pale blue, and my veins flicker like tiny lightning in a storm. Mesmerized by this hallucination, I nearly forget what sent me tumbling in the first place, but only for a moment do I lose sight. Because if what just happened wasn't strange enough, the peculiar event continues.

A dead silence drapes over me, like in my nightmares, but this is no dream. I turn to the olive tree, frightened and shaken by what might haunt me next. Every leaf is still as if it has been painted. No wind, not even the slightest breeze blows. The nightly sounds of birds and crickets have vanished. Everything around me appears to have stopped, even time. Not much surprises me anymore until I notice something unhinged from the laws of physics — tiny dried leaves suspend in the air. I pluck one of them from their altered state just to make sure I'm not losing my senses. It crunches in the palm of my hand. Has time truly stopped? I feel like a painter's brush dragging across an empty canvas?

A shadow passes over me and into the tree. My feathered friend is perched on one of the dead limbs. How poetic that this crow sits atop something in a deathly state. He glowers at me, and then something most unusual happens.

The crow stretches its wings, wide as the limb, and squawks. His glassy cobalt eyes vanish behind their sockets, and his gaping beak folds back. Feathers droop like glue and descend closer to the trunk. The fowl leans forward, expanding its contorted body into a frightful shadow as it touches the stony ground. His chest splits open and the waxy feathers disappear. I step back, breathless at the chilling deformity. It moves closer to me. My spine tingles beneath my cold skin. The distorting shape of a crow shifts into a frightening new discovery: a human-like figure, as black as night, standing before me.

The figure hides behind a dark cloak with a draping cover. I shiver when it lifts back the hood. A faceless figure as black as coal moves like rippling water. I can almost see my reflection in-between the flowing waves. I feel eyes staring through me. I want to run, but I cannot move. My feet are planted heavy to the ground.

The faceless creature reaches its hand out to me. Perhaps a conceding gesture, but I'm scared to death nonetheless. I carefully stretch my hand forward, but the creature does not acknowledge it. Instead, he grabs my wounded shoulder and presses on it. I stand fearfully still, for I have no power over this being. A warm sensation suddenly grows from my wound and tiny spikes of lightning flashes blue in my veins. The warm sensation burns hot now. Am I being punished for touching the sacred tree? My undoing cannot overcome this. The harder this creature-like human presses, the greater the sting. My eyes water as the fiery pain engulfs my entire body. The scorching agony suddenly stops and the creature releases my shoulder. Just as quick as the heat boiled, it leaves my skin cool and unscathed.

I search my arm for the torn stiches, but the wound has disappeared. Not a hint of a scar lingers. What unearthly power stands before me? A demon that heals? Suddenly, a pair of crow's wings emerge from the creature's back, and black feathers stretch wide. The creature echoes a shrilling caw, and like a yawn from a cat, the wings extend outward before resting down near its sides. This is no demon. It's the angel of death, and it's come for me.

Shrieking whispers emit from the faceless angel, but I can't understand it. The hissing chatter evolves through a course of different languages, many of which are Semitic, until one catches my attention.

"*Nim vasáiof.*"

Strangely, I understand it completely. Though it sounds like gibberish, it's plainly translated to my ear as, "Do not be afraid."

"No, of course not. Why would anyone be afraid of a faceless, shape-shifting crow that can heal wounds?" I joke in a nervous manner.

Silence from the creature marks an eerie response. Either it's pissed or it fails to get sarcasm. The dark angel assertively steps forward and parks its liquid face a few inches from mine. A lump of air slides down my throat.

"I was just joking . . . as maybe too often I do," I attempt to apologize. I think I liked it better when it perched on my shoulder.

The dark, fluttering water slowly dissolves, and a human face forms underneath the distorted ripples. My jaw drops and I fall back on my ass.

"What . . . it can't be? Wh-what are you?" I gasp.

The water clears, leaving a familiar face in its place . . . Finnegan.

CHAPTER 6

The ground rumbles a gentle bass as the angel advances toward me. He extends his hand for mine, but I withdraw. I stand to my own accord and stare eagerly into the face of my dead uncle, the former special ops commander who withdrew from a politically corrupt government. The last time I looked upon Finnegan's face, he had died in my arms, risking his life to save mine. We began this deadly journey together . . . sadly, he wasn't able to finish it. Though he lies buried back in America, his death made me stronger to continue what we started. And now, here we stand looking back at each other under a familiar, but strange gaze. I recognize those soft blue eyes, the broad slope of his nose, even the three-line crease in his forehead.

"Does this not give you comfort?" the angel asks. His voice is the same, just how I remembered it. But I know it's not him. I try to remember him as the man I knew before he was killed—a strong, patient, and wise man with the ability to be forgiving, but vengeful when needed.

I try to gather my thoughts, but they come out a sarcastic mess. " I think it's fair to say that comfort is a bit overreaching considering a deceased relative is speaking to me right now."

"Shall I change back?"

"No! No offense, but I'm not sure what's more disturbing right now. At least here we can see eye to eye . . . so to speak." Maybe I wouldn't be so creeped out if Finnegan's entire body manifested, but to see just his face makes this conversation a bit unsettling..

"I'm sure you have a lot of questions you want answered."

"Nah, I was hoping to keep this creepy encounter a mystery . . . for dramatic effect."

His stoic expression deflects my attempt at sarcasm "I understand your frustration through all of this—"

"Do you?" I explode with contempt.

The angel pulls a sword from underneath his long draping cloak and slams it into the ground. Flames ignite like forged steel quenched in water. I retreat back, my eyes widen. The fiery blade immediately calms, leaving a glowing ember along the sharp, tempered edges.

"I feel the anger coursing through your veins every day, Arena. I know the sting that sticks in your crawl. That moment when you realize everything around you crumbles but leaves you there wondering why you didn't fall with it. Yes, I know the pain that haunts you, wondering why it's you who are here instead of someone else."

Tears burn my eyes. "I didn't ask for this."

"No one does, but you've been chosen, and how you choose to deal with it determines everything for everyone. Those demons inside of you can't live forever. You think you've been dealt a bad hand, but here you are wanting more than just answers."

"I deserve the truth!" I shout.

A subtle smirk crosses Finnegan's face. "You don't want the truth because deep down you already know," he counters.

My blood boils, but I will not give in to his smug grilling. "You know nothing of what I want—"

"It's quite obvious." He steps forward.

"Leave me!"

"It's written all over your face."

"Stop it!"

"Don't fight it."

"Go away!" I step back again, feeling trapped.

"Say it!"

"Revenge!" I expel. Tears trickle down my cheeks.

His squabbling tongue ceases, leaving us in silence. Adrenaline flowing and heart pumping a thunderous beat, my fists clench with rancor.

"Where has this Arena been hiding?" he asks.

"I'm not what you think I am." My fists relax and my trembling body calms.

"The revenge you seek is not shameful, but it can be dangerous. Anger leads to hate, and that is what harbors mistakes."

"I'm not that Arena anymore. I have a son now—"

"And if you want your son to live beyond this, then you're going to have to accept what you've become."

"I didn't ask to be a killer," I say in a small voice.

"But you were born to be a leader. Killing is an inevitable just. It's what you and I were created to do. I sympathize with your plight, but before you and I can move forward, you're going to have to put aside those feelings and trust me."

I gaze beyond the face of my uncle and find curiosity looming. Why does this creature encourage such dark things? "Who are you?"

"The one who gives purpose and direction, leader of righteousness and justice, protector of providence. A warrior who wields his sword against all evil. I'm the lord of my kind in the presence of my seven brothers. General over the many and the deliverer to the few. I am the Archangel Michael, and I've come to help see your way through."

"Through what?" I dare ask.

"The war of all wars."

My loved ones flash through my mind. "My son . . . is he in danger?"

"All are in danger, that is all I can say. I'm only here to help. I cannot see your future, but I do know your past. I've watched you grow, suffer, and toil. I've witnessed the sacrifices you've made, but I cannot in good judgment tell you how this will all end. I only know my part in this is to protect you and your brother. Outside of that is beyond my scope."

I'm taken aback at the mention of Gabe. Uncle Finnegan was right all this time, that Gabe and I have not only been chosen, but that we are being watched and protected. I think of the many horrible things that have happened since our journey began, all those times when I cried out to my heavenly Father for help and felt so alone, not understanding how tragedy could befall such good people. And all those times I have felt alone, felt like I was being called to the darkness.

"If you truly are here to protect us . . . then what's coming for us?" I say.

"For many years armies from the north, east, and west have been preparing for complete annihilation of Israel, but now it's becoming a reality. The accord of the Ten nations have diminished, countries scrapping among each other and leaving their spoils for a hungrier nation. Chaos has ravaged the weak, but it has secured a military stronghold for others. The kingdom to the north is coming, and with it a multitude of mindless men ready to destroy. Seven armies have come together and will soon strike. Jerusalem will fall into ash."

My eyes widen. "How many soldiers, and don't sugar-coat it. Tell me the truth."

"Israel is outnumbered ten to one. Ten days from now, those armies will advance from Turkey to Iran, and nothing—not even the best negotiating skills or political submission—will stop them. When the moon glows red against the sky, you will know it is time. What has been set cannot be undone."

My heart sinks. I've led my friends and loved ones here to perish. What have I done?

"Israel is strong. She can withstand much," he continues.

"For a while, maybe, but even these odds are too great. I will not leave my son to die here. We must leave now!" I quickly turn away.

"Wait!" he shouts.

My feet stop, planted on the rocky ground. I reach forward, but an invisible wall prevents me from going any further. "Let me go," I demand.

"You leave Jerusalem now and all will be destroyed."

"And how will it be any different if I don't?"

"Your fate brought you here, do you not believe that?"

"Brought me here to die?" I counter.

"You cannot just wield life like a sword—"

"I can certainly try." The angel scoops up a handful of sand and holds it before me. The tiny grains sift through his parted fingers, leaving his palm empty. "The choices we make can either free us or bury us. Either way, you cannot conquer death, but you can choose to embrace it for a new life . . . a better one."

"Why would my fate lead me here to die?"

"You so sure of that, are you?"

"Jerusalem will fall, you said it yourself," I say.

"Your journey led you here because you are a sign of hope. God is with you, Arena. He always has been. From the moment of your birth, to the death of your parents, to bearing a child. The people here look upon you and believe there may still be peace. You must believe that you can make a difference in this war. Soldiers respect you, the general respects you, but you must convince them, despite the odds, that they must fight until the end. Israel may fall, but she will rise again. You must stay and fight, Arena."

"And what becomes of my son? He may die in all of this?"

"If you seek a peaceful world for your son to live in, then you must fight to ensure that. It's up to you. I cannot force you to choose your own path. If you leave, you and your son may live a few days, but death will soon come crashing down on you. Stay and fight. Provide hope to those who will stand and fight with you. Because in the end, it's not who you are fighting for, but what you're fighting for."

"And what is that, a world free of bitter men?"

"No, a world free of chains."

Finnegan's face vanishes back into the angel's head made of moving water. Michael pulls his glowing sword from the ground and tucks it inside his cloak. His wings stretch upward before shrinking and folding back behind his head. His body eerily contorts, and the shadow of a man quickly transforms back into a crow and flies away into the dark sky.

The suspended leaves float down to the earth and a cool breeze pushes past me. The moon shimmers a dusty red as a nightly chorus of insects return. I leave the mountainside at peace, but I'm conflicted. My path grows more uncertain. My mind, riddled with a thousand questions, rests with only one: How am I to lead an army into a war we cannot win?

I haven't been this frightened in a long time, and to suggest any different would be foolish. But everything makes sense now. Israel is falling right into a pit of lies. Rumors have surfaced of a possible peace pact with Russia, but I can't see Israel converting like other unfortunate nations that signed a treaty of deceit. Now those countries suffer under a regime that was never willing to offer a chance of civil peace. Slave countries they have become, bound to an evil that's not worth living.

I realize how much my focus has shifted ever since I became a mother, but I recognize how my path is one and the same: Joshua is my hope. I'm no savior to the world, but I can help free us from being bound to it. No, I will not give in, nor will I let this nation fall to its demise. We must stand and fight to preserve the decency of man. If the rumors are still true, then I must do what I can to dilute them. We cannot negotiate no matter the odds that fall against us.

No longer are the thoughts to run and hide with my son. No longer will I consider stepping away from being a warrior for the comforts of motherhood. I will not abandon the people. I must leave behind a part of me that surely cannot return. If I truly was born for this, then I will embrace it for the greater good of all. This is who I am, who I was, and who I will forever be. I'm more than just a mother to an innocent child. I'm a shield for the broken and a call to death all the same.

CHAPTER 7

I often wonder what the world would have been like if Gabe and I had never met Father Joseph. Would our journey have met less tragedy? I don't know, but the simple truth of it all is that our fate would not have changed. I believe the thought of a revolution was planted far before my hands ever touched my swords, perhaps even before my first breath.

America has long fallen and its freedoms have withered away. With or without my rebellious push to kill its corrupt president three years ago, it would still remain in the tight clutches of Gorshkov's malevolent rule. And here we are, hiding deep inside a mountain and fearing the same sinister regime that chased us here, all because I set in motion this rebellion that started it all. We can never go back now. I must face the consequences. President Gorshkov must die. He's the only one who stands between preserving freedom and falling to slavery.

Standing just outside the exterior gates of the mountain, Father Joseph waits eagerly next to a couple of IDF guards. Though not fully responsible, I anticipate a bombardment of questions about my rebellious disregard for the sacred tree, but to my surprise I get anything but.

"Why are you back so early? Thought you wanted some alone time."

"I...I, uh?" I sputter.

"You okay, you look like you've seen a ghost?"

"Didn't you hear the . . ."

"Hear what?" he asks. I'm not sure what to think or if I should say anything at all. The guards look at me as if I'm

"He's getting big, and so handsome too," Gabe bubbles.

"He's a handful."

"Whoa! He's ripe. I believe we got a fully loaded one here." Gabe holds Joshua up and grimaces. "You can have him back now."

"Oh no, you can change at least one diaper. I've changed plenty. Besides, it'll make a better man out of you."

"That's debatable." Gabe carefully places Joshua on the bed as if he's an unstable piece of explosive.

"He's not made of glass, goofy."

"I really don't know what to do here."

"It's not rocket science. Clean everything that has shit on it."

"First day back and I'm dealing with this? You did this on purpose, didn't you?"

I chuckle. It's funny to see my twin brother trying to wrangle a squirming baby. "You're lucky he hasn't pissed in your eye." I hand him a fresh diaper. The puzzled look on his face is priceless. He's got all the book smarts, but common sense has left the building. The diaper is on backward, and nearly all of Joshua's butt is hanging out. He might as well be naked.

"How's that?" Gabe asks hesitantly.

"Are ya mad, now? His butt crack is smiling at me. Turn the diaper around, Einstein."

"Well, aren't you a bag of weasels. How the hell am I supposed to bloody know?"

"I worry common sense has departed from ya."

Gabe flips the baby around and I stop myself from intervening. After some huffing and puffing, it seems everything has righted itself. "There, is that better?" he asks.

"Perfect, now you're a real man."

Gabe rolls his eyes, picks up Joshua, and whispers in his ear, "Your mother is a real hard ass, isn't she?"

The door creeks open. "Sorry, am I interrupting something?" Nadia asks politely.

"No, I'm just giving my brother some paternity lessons. Come in."

"Nothing like seeing a handsome man with a baby," she says, and her cheeks blush. She turns to me. "I just thought I'd check in on you, Arena. How's your wound?"

"Wound?" Gabe curiously interrupts. Nadia looks down and seems embarrassed. My secret is out of the bag.

"It's much better, thank you," I say to Nadia. "Well, I guess it's time to feed the child," I quickly deviate from the conversation.

"I'll take him off your hands, "Nadia offers. "I'm sure you two have plenty to catch up on." She grabs Joshua and leans close. "I'm sorry," she whispers. She closes the door behind her..

"Spill it," Gabe snaps.

"It's nothing, just a scratch. In fact, it's not even there anymore so it doesn't matter."

"We don't keep secrets from one another, you know the rules."

"It's a long story."

"I have all the time in the world." He smugly crosses his arms and lies comfortably on my bed.

Normally I would smack him on the back of the head, but my brother has been through a lot. It's been just over a year since Juliana died. Ever since, Gabe has become reclusive in his own mind, unable to process what was once a reliable intuition. Sadly, my brother's conscience had followed down a dark path rendering him incapable of tapping into a special kind of clairvoyance he once possessed. Juliana's death affected us all, but none more than Gabe. It happened during the first enemy raid in central Jerusalem, which is what initially forced us to escape inside the mountain. We fled across the old city, but found misfortune during our retreat. Juliana caught a chasing bullet to the heart before we could reach safety. We've long set for a different life since leaving her grave. That moment is a permanent stain on my brother's heart. The first and only love of his young life now casts dark shadows within him. Life can be cruel, but what we make of the consequences will either lift us in light or blind us in darkness. Sadly, Gabe may be walking an unstable line between both. As twins, we are in this together through the good and bad. He deserves more than a curtailing of my experiences. Our relationship merits the truth, all of it.

"Okay, but I warn you. You'll think I'm insane," I say.

"I think you've already established that long ago, but go ahead, nothing surprises me anymore."

I detail the past events that have led up to my mysterious encounter with Michael at the sacred tree. It's almost like Gabe already knew. Nothing seems to shake him anymore, not since he lost Juliana. I believe deep down Gabe's clairvoyant power is crippling his mind. Sometimes I think he may have foreseen Juliana's death. Blessed with a gift has malformed into a curse, and because of that my brother may be trapped in between. Suppressing prophetic thoughts could either hurt him or hinder us all, but it's his decision and no one else's. There are just some things I can't explain. Our special connection is one of them. From birth to death, we cannot be apart. I believe we have a kindred spirit like no other. If one feels pain, so does the other, but I'm afraid that if one of us dies, so does the other.

Gabe's unbreakable silence is a response no words can share, but I know he knows our future here is bleak if we do not act now.

"We started this war . . . it's time to finish it," I say.

Somewhere drawn on his face lies a hidden purpose, but I can't extract it. He's become less readable. He gets up and strolls across the room to the door. "You sure about this?"

"We fight, no matter what," I reaffirm.

"Then I hope you have a bloody good plan." He smiles before leaving the room.

A war without a plan is a body without a soul. We must not give our enemies an illusion of fear or we are already defeated. The odds are against us in every way, and I have nothing to offer but to fight.

I leave my room and wander the halls, anxiously waiting for Jacob to return with the others. My mind is racing. Jerusalem is in grave danger, but this hasn't been the first time. This city has witnessed tragedy throughout its storied history and it's about to get worse. So much in this world has changed, especially the political climate. Nations that have been sworn enemies with other nations are now allies. Friends of others have become enemies. Israel stands alone with the exception of a few underground ties with the Ukraine, Saudi Arabia, and Egypt. Even parts of Syria have demonstrated an unusual relationship with Israel. Though the tie may be influenced by economics, Syria is an ally worth having now. Since the great Syrian War with Russia and Iraq, the once prominent piece of land has fallen into an economical disaster—a poverty-stricken country now in complete turmoil. Its religious melting pot is no more as people fled, risking their lives from being secluded under harsh rule. After a ten-year occupation by the Russian regime, the country's petroleum beds ran dry, leaving Iraq to govern the territory. Then a civil war broke the chains from Iraq's rule and the nation's southern territory was forced to split by an insurgence of Syrian rebels that is now known as the "free zone" or the Lower Syrian Parallel.

This is what Israel has come to now, seeking feisty rebels to fight with them to undo a decade of Russian oppression and weed out a world that is dangerously under fire. Political egos, power, and greed have nearly eradicated human decency. The New World Order is not a solution; it's a death sentencing.

As I walk throughout the underbelly of this complex, I question how much longer we will be trapped in here before we are eradicated. Everything suddenly looks bleaker now.

I pass by a messy room where Mia is lying on her bed. Godfrey sits against the wall holding a square tin in his lap. He deserves better than this.

"Hi, Godfrey," I address softly.

"Arena, you come see me?" He grins.

"Of course, may I come in?"

He pats his hand on the floor, ushering me to sit next to him. The kindness in his heart is not overstated. "Crazy girl talks to birds," he says.

I smile. "I suppose. Does it frighten you?"

"No, it's funny."

"What's in the tin?"

His grip tightens around it. "Sweet, sweet candy almost gone."

"Well, that's no good. How about you come with me so we can refill it."

A grin lifts from his face as he quickly stands up. "Fill it, fill it to the top, in my tummy till I pop."

"That's the spirit," I encourage. Godfrey stops near the door and gently grabs my arm. His eyes drift away momentarily before looking back at Mia. "She'll be okay," I reassure him.

"Mia sleepy too much."

"She needs her rest so she can be strong again." Godfrey gazes at her somewhat sadly. "Are you ready to get that candy now?" I say as a distraction.

He returns his eyes to the tin, then smiles. "Aye, aye, Captain," he salutes. If I ever need to smile, I'll just go to Godfrey now.

We pass the dining hall near the second corridor of sleeping quarters and enter the main kitchen area.

Around the corner Veronica comes racing and bumps into me. She tucks a lock of brown hair behind her ear. "Oh, excuse me," she says.

"We were just headed to the pantry for some more candy," I explain.

"And how is Mr. Godfrey today?" she asks.

"Fine I suppose." He hands Veronica the square tin. Since we've returned from the city, Veronica has cared for Godfrey as her own. They seem to connect well with each other. Veronica is one of the many who has left the western part of the city to seek refuge here with us. She can speak five languages and was a schoolteacher before her school was left in ruin. Originally from Syria, before the Great Divide during the Russian wars, Veronica fled to Jerusalem to find peace. I'm afraid that conflict has followed her here.

"I'm sure we can find you some candy for you," Veronica smiles.

Familiar voices linger from the floor above. My eyes grow wide. "They're back," I beam with excitement.

Ari, Sadiq, Henry, and Jacob descend the long stairs to the main hall. Their faces are bleak, a sight I wasn't expecting. Surely they'll have better news to squash any negotiating rumors from manifesting. Ari, a brave man who's been with us since the Cairo prison where Gabe was locked in, leadsin front down the steps. His gritty face, wrinkled like leather stares blankly with fatigue. Sadiq, the most experienced soldier, slinks behind, but manages to keep his chiseled jaw upright and lips pursed—the staid look of a commander who refuses to reveal his emotions. His six-foot frame is cut into a soldier's mold, muscular and stout. His demeanor rarely wavers from the leadership he was appointed. Even under the arduous travels and grueling conditions, he still manages to keep his dark hair trimmed closely to his skin and slightly above his ears. He may seem rigid, but I've witnessed his softer side, and though we've had our differences in the past, we've become close friends on the battlefield.

Henry follows, dragging his heavy boots down the steps. Of all the men who I expected to keep a stoic and confident expression, he surprisingly dips his weary head and slumbers. Dark stubble covers his shaven head. Henry has been my godsend throughout the years. Aside from his martial arts training, his shared wisdom has secured me during my journey and has kept me from straying the course. His words are always comforting and earnest, but I'm afraid his grim face may tell me something I don't want to hear.

Just a few steps behind him, descends the man my eyes have been anxiously waiting for. Jacob wearily looks down without a hint of noticing me at the bottom of the stairs. Two weeks apart from my husband and still I cannot look upon his face. His shaggy blond hair shades the gloom I suspect suppresses it. His olive-green uniform is crumpled and shredded above the knee. My heart aches and yet flutters with every step closer he takes.

Ari, Sadiq, and Henry pass by me with a meager pat on the shoulder, but my face strains the attention of my husband whose face has yet to find me.

"Jacob," I beam. Finally, our eyes meet, but he only offers a weak smile. I jump into his arms and kiss his chapped lips. "Are you not glad to see me?" I ask.

"On the contrary, my love. I've missed you so much."

"Why so gloomy then?"

He pauses when he sees Godfrey and reaches out his hand to him. "Hi there, I'm Jacob."

"Chicken little, chicken quick, farmer beat him with a stick," Godfrey sings.

"Uh, excuse me?" Jacob's face draws blank.

"This is Godfrey. He's my friend," I say.

"Arena talks to birds," Godfrey adds.

"Does she?" Sadiq smirks.

"She kill bad men and—"

"Hey, Veronica, why don't you fill Godfrey's tin with candy," I quickly say.

"Come on, Godfrey, let's go fill this up,"Veronica insists. She glances at me uncomfortably before leading Godfrey through the kitchen and out of sight.

"What did he mean by that?" Jacob prods.

"Nothing. He says a lot of things that don't make sense, but he has a very kind soul. He and his caretaker, Mia, were wandering the streets, so we took them in. Why don't you all come sit down in the dining hall and we'll get some real food to eat. It's been a long journey."

The dining hall stretches nearly fifty yards, and it seems massive now that it's empty. . The five of us sit near the front where two double doors lead to the front of the kitchen. Ari, Henry, and Sadiq sit on one side of the table while Jacob and I sit on the other. Sadiq removes his hat and tosses it on the table. His face, worn from the journey, matches that of the others. I'm not sure I want to know what news they bring, but before I can ask, Veronica pushes through the kitchen doors with Godfrey.

"Excuse me, gentlemen, but I'm just letting you know we'll have some food prepared for you shortly."

"Thank you so much, Veronica," Sadiq politely addresses. Godfrey holds his tin as he stares at Sadiq. "In the garbage throw out junk, something smells like stinky skunk." Sadiq's face reddens with embarrassment.

"Come on, Godfrey, it's time to go back," Veronica quickly shuffles off, chuckling.

Sadiq grins as he sniffs his armpit. "Hey, it's been a long journey. We can't all have the privilege of hot showers every day."

"I expect nothing less," I chide.

The jovial moment fades as a surprise visit from General Eizenkot enters the room. He is dressed in a dark green single breasted, three button suit with a red beret slightly tilted on his head. His wide shoulders fill the tips of his jacket, and his stomach stretches the front flap beyond the buttons' clasp. He stands a bit over six feet, but walks in like he's ten. "I thought I'd find you all here," he addresses with a raspy grumble. His face, aged and tired is lined with wrinkles with a scar nested above his left brow.

"General," Sadiq says as he quickly stands up.

"Please sit down. I know you all have had a long journey. I expect you to be well fed before we discuss matters. Colonel Dahan and his men have the prisoner in custody—"

"Prisoner?" I stand to my feet.

"Arena, wait," Jacob calmly gestures.

"I know you must have questions, Arena, but please let the colonel do his job before you think about doing anything rash," Eizenkot advises. His pointy chin stiffens, and his eyes stay firmly on mine. Now's not the time for conflict, though I have a few choice words. I sit back down to appease the general's request.

Eizenkot looks at the men and says, "Let's meet at oh eight hundred in the council room. We have much to discuss and plan. In the meantime, get some rest, and be with your loved ones. And Jacob, let's keep this debriefing among the scout team. Distractions only further complicate things." His eyes avoid mine before he escorts himself out as hastily as he walked in. The general is a man of few words, which is why he's in charge. In the military, it's best to know something about a little than nothing about a lot. However, I'm confused by his cryptic order to Jacob.

"What the hell was that supposed to mean?" I ask Jacob.

"Nothing," Jacob dismisses.

There's silence for a few minutes as we sit under the dim lights. Not even the smells from the kitchen can stir a conversation under their fatigue. Two weeks of scouting and I have yet to hear a word about any of it.

"Look, I know you guys are tired, and some of you are greatly in need of a shower, but can you just level with me? What the hell happened in Damascus because I'd really hate to find out later in the meeting," I say.

Jacob's eyes disengage from the conversation. Henry and Ari look down at the table. They're acting so weird.

"What's going on?" I snap, and then it hits me. "Oh, I get it. Eizenkot was referring to me, wasn't he? I'm not invited to the meeting. Is that what this awkward silence is about? I find it a bit childish . . . even for you, Henry."

Jacob grabs my hand with a gentle touch, "Look, Arena, we think—"

"We?" Henry chimes in.

Jacob looks up at me. "Okay . . . *I* think it might be best if you skip the meeting."

"Skip it? You don't trust me now?" My blood is boiling.

"I trust you plenty, but with you roaming off in the city and nearly getting yourself killed, I'm not sure the Defense Council is ready to take suggestions. You stirred up a hornets' nest out there." His words ring with disappointment.

My stomach knots up. This is not how this was supposed to go. "Who told you?"

"Arena, it's hard to keep secrets in a highly guarded facility. Would you have lied to me?"

Ouch, and the hits just keep on coming. I'm not sure I could have kept it from him, but I can't say for sure I would have said anything at all. Ari, Henry, and Sadiq all look uncomfortable as they witness this conversation between me and Jacob.

"I do for the greater good of the people here, nothing less," I say.

"That's why I trust you here . . . with Joshua."

"So you side with the general?"

"No, I side with my family, one I want to keep alive," Jacob says with fire in his eyes. "Let the Defense Council grumble over the decisions. We did our job, and sometimes that's all we need to do."

I lock my jaw to keep from crying. Jacob's words run deep, but only because they are true. We rarely argue, especially not in front of people. It usually takes a few days for me to process my emotions, while Jacob can be fine in a few hours. The kitchen doors open as two men with three large trays of food saunter in. Even if I were hungry, I don't think I could eat a morsel. I quickly wipe a tear hanging from my eye and leave the table.

"I've bothered you all enough. I'll let you eat in peace. I need to go tend to Joshua anyway."

"Arena, wait," Jacob insists.

I exit the dining area, fuming and nearly run over my brother in the hall. He stumbles back. "Where are you going off in such a hurry?"

"Nowhere, I'm just . . . it's not your worry, okay!" I snap. I'm so angry I can feel the heat radiating from my face and yet I want to cry.

"Geez, what's up your ass?"

I dip my head and sigh. "I'm sorry, I didn't mean to bark at you. I just have a lot on my mind."

"It's fine, I understand. I'm assuming they must have told you about the prisoner then?"

"As a matter of fact, no."

"Well, I wouldn't worry about it too much, besides, you've got enough going on."

I grab his arm. "Tell me . . . please?"

Gabe's eyes drift wearily into mine as he explains a skirmish across the Syrian border. A small band of northern radicals descended into Damascus and found themselves outmatched by Syrian rebels. The raid left most of them dead, but the few left alive were forced to retreat back in the hills, except one.

"Why only him?" I ask.

"Don't know. Seemed strange at the time, especially from a northern insurgence. They aren't the kind to easily surrender without some sort of resistance, but this one did."

"Iranian?"

"Not sure, but a Russian sympathizer nonetheless. Our Syrian allies said they've been surging in small groups across Damascus more often than normal."

"Hey, I appreciate you telling me."

"Of course, but like I said, I wouldn't worry too much over it."

I walk away feeling even more disappointed with Jacob's exchange. My heart sinks as his words echo in my head. Why am I being so sensitive? Maybe because I've waited so long to be whisked away in the arms of my husband, but instead I receive his rebuke. My eyes swell until they drip. How am I supposed to suck it up and follow protocol when I'm expected to somehow lead this group? I'm suddenly angry at Jacob for making me feel so small. I don't care how rebellious it may seem, I must go to that meeting.

Nadia emerges from the medical bay with Joshua nestled against her chest. Attimus, hair tussled, follows closely behind. I quickly wipe the tears from my cheek.

"There you are," Nadia smiles.

"Sorry, I was meeting with Jacob and the others back from Damascus."

She wrinkles her brow. "You have weary eyes. Everything okay?"

"You have a minute to speak?" I ask.

"Sure, of course." She turns to Attimus. "Excuse us, Attimus."

"I'll go check in on Mia," he says, leaving the hall.

"Did I interrupt something?" I prod.

"No, we were just going over medical supplies."

"Sure you were."

Nadia stiffens. "I'm positive."

"Come on, it's me. What's the deal? You're beautiful, he's cute—"

"Well, he . . . he's gay," she whispers.

I never would have guessed that about Attimus. "That's a bloody shame. You two look cute together."

"Yeah, and it's always the cute ones," Nadia attests. She hands Joshua over to me. His eyes open then shut. He emits a small sigh before falling back to sleep.

We pause for a moment in the empty hallway. "I want to ask you something, and I want you to be brutally honest," I say.

Nadia nods. "Yes, of course."

"Do you trust me? If your life or anyone else's was on the line, knowing that a decision I might have to make could be a tragic one but would ultimately serve the greater good for us all?"

Nadia places her hand on my shoulder. "I would follow you to my death if it meant it would save lives. No one believes in you more than me. You were born with a power unlike any of us have seen, a power beyond strength or sacrifice. Your authority comes from something greater. You have the power to believe, a place of faith that rises against the odds. Warriors may be fierce, but you are not the warrior who draws the fire because you *are* the fire. And as long as you lead, that fire burns with us."

"Thank you," I manage as I hug Nadia. I would have no future without this great woman. In Alexandria, Nadia saved me from taking my own life. At that time, after losing Uncle Finnegan, Juliana, Luke, and countless others, I really did feel like nothing I did mattered. But now I know deep in my being that this world needs me. If my days pass, I could ask of no other to raise my son except for this woman.

Joshua yawns and stirs, and I kiss his forehead. With a heavy breath, I say, "Something evil is brewing beyond what you can imagine."

Nadia is startled. "Are we in danger here?"

"Something tells me grave news has been brought back from Damascus. It's no surprise the Israeli defense is outnumbered, but no matter the odds, we cannot give in."

"Do we have a choice?"

"The choices we make will either free us or bury us. I'd rather fight for what's right than die in vain. Listen to me: No matter how difficult it seems, no matter what we are up against, we must fight. Any other alternative will bring us to death eventually. You can't negotiate against a tyrant, and you and I need to convince the others of that."

"How?" she asks hesitantly.

"If you truly believe in me, then I want you by my side tomorrow morning because you're coming with me to the Defense Council debriefing."

"I trust you'll figure out a way to get in," she says witha smirk, "but once we're there, what are we going to do?"

"This nation needs some motivation. I'm gonna pick a fight."

I leave Nadia standing there with a nervous twitch in her eye, but she's a strong woman and I know I can trust her to support my decisions no matter what.

I take Joshua back to our quarters and anxiously wait for Jacob. Though my son fills the room with warmth, my bed still lies cold without Jacob in it. My muscles tense and my mind spins. I have to figure out how to approach Jacob about my stance on the meeting. After what he pulled in the dining room, I almost don't want to tell him anything. I push the thought away . . . I don't like being at odds with the man I love.

Jacob finally enters the room, his eyes distressed. The journey has taken a toll on him just by the sheer weariness as he walks past. Not a word is spoken. I've done nothing to be alienated like this, but I give him the benefit of the doubt nonetheless. He sits on the bed just ten feet away in silence. Is he too stubborn to address me, or am I too proud to respond? This isn't who we are, and if I don't say anything soon, it could be who we become. Anything would be better than this awkward exchange.

"I'm a good mother, you know," I break the stillness. I waver to face him even in my own stubbornness.

Jacob lets out a heavy sigh. "I've never questioned that, Arena. Not a single thought has crossed my mind that would ever entertain the idea." The small hairs on the back of my arm rise up. Jacob wraps his arms from behind and kisses my neck. "I don't think you're good mother, I believe you're a great one," he says as he nibbles sweet kisses below my ear.

I turn around and plant my lips on his. My heart warms for a moment, but I realize I'm much more than just a mother to my son. I pull away. "It takes more than kisses to convince me you fully trust me," I say. I wonder if Jacob and I are on the same page.

"I have always trusted you."

"Then why do you keep me in the dark? I'm just as much a part of this fight as anyone else here."

"Call me selfish, but I don't want to lose you. I thought you would feel the same."

"Keeping me underground won't help, Jacob. You want what's best for our son, yes?"

"What's best for our son is a future where he can wake up to one of his parents."

I grit my teeth. "I'm doing this for his future. He won't have one if I don't help lead this fight."

"Yeah, but at what cost? I thought the old Arena died when you became a mother."

His words pierce sharp into my heart. It's a formidable pill to swallow and I can't really fault him for saying them, but it still hurts. Maybe deep down I haven't changed, or maybe the old and new me are one in the same. I admit, the old me was reckless and merciless and often made rash decisions. Motherhood has softened those rough edges, but it hasn't made me lose sight of reality. I love my son, but I refuse to rest idle and allow an oppressive nation take his future away.

A rush of anger courses through me and I stifle it. In a steady tone, I say, "You and I both know that we can't escape what's coming. Negotiating a peace pact with Russia is fruitless. Where are we going to go other than in the hands of a tyrant to subjugate us? I will not stand by and wait to be a bargaining chip for slavery or slaughtered in the masses. Our son deserves better that that, and deep down you know it's the right thing to do."

"Leading us into war is not what bothers me; it's fighting in one I'm not sure we can win."

Michael's words echo in my head. How can I explain this to Jacob without sounding like I've lost my mind? "Every breath we take is a gift," I say. "War is just a deterrent for those gifts we take for granite, and this is a war we have no choice but to win."

"Why you so certain?"

I pause for a moment. I can hear Uncle Finnegan's laugh—his real laugh—in my mind, and I'm filled with sadness and hope all wrapped into one. "There are many things in this world unexplained. Attempting to understand them can drive us mad. Many would rather avoid the unknown just to preserve their beliefs . . . or lack of. But even in the worst moments of despair, I would never surrender my convictions. I will stand by them until my last dying breath. I would never put our son in danger, but sitting back and doing nothing certainly will. If there is any better time to trust me, it's now."

He gently touches my cheek with a callused hand and holds my waist with the other. "Even when things didn't go as planned, I trusted you then. I never stopped trusting you, Arena. I get it, I understand. I'm not here to stop you from doing what you think is right. I believe in you. I just want you to know for sure, that's all."

"I've never been more sure, but I'll need your full support on this when I go to the meeting tomorrow morning."

Jacob breaks the tense moment with a smile. "I had no chance of stopping you from going anyway, did I?"

"Nope," I assert with a grin. I lay my head on his chest and realize the true person I've become. "I was wrong, ya know."

"What do you mean?" he asks.

"The old Arena was never dead. She just needed some time to sort things out. Whatever part of me left is very much alive."

"I'm just glad to have any part of you."

"So we're good?" I peer into his fixed blue eyes.

"Yeah, we're good. But I really just wanted to see my wife after a long journey. Is she here, because I really—"

"Shut up and kiss me."

Finally, alone with my husband after weeks of worrying whether or not he would make it back, I find a rare moment of peaceful sleep. Tonight, I embrace the calm without concern, but tomorrow a new beginning will give rise that may bring risk to us all.

CHAPTER 8

The bed is empty, but the sheet is still warm from Jacob's body. I adjust my blurry eyes over Joshua's crib and find him missing. The door knocks before cracking open.

"You sleep okay?" Nadia stands at the door.

"Yeah, maybe too good. What time is it, where's Joshua?" I ask with a bit of confusion.

"Niki took Joshua so you could sleep. I waited for you outside the meeting chamber, but you never showed up."

"Shit! What time is it?"

"Eight-fifteen."

"Damn, we can't miss this."

I throw on some clothes and dash out the door with Nadia. The meeting quarters sit tucked in a corner two floors down near the other end of the compound. We sprint down the halls, nearly bumping into others as faces blur past. Blood pumps swiftly though my veins as I fear I may have missed something important.

The bottom level smells musty and the walls leave a mosaic impression of cracked paint. Unlike the upper levels, quietness lives down here, unfortunately along with a breeding ground of unwanted tiny insects.

We pass through a set of double doors that lead into a long corridor of steel-reinforced concrete stretching nearly fifty yards. A voice echoes around the corner toward the end of the northern wing of the compound. We meet nearly head-on with Gabe who is standing just outside the council chamber.

"Where the hell have you been? Jacob has been asking about you," Gabe huffs.

"Overslept. I wasn't expecting Jacob to leave without me."

"So much for a quick briefing. You better get there, and don't expect a warm greeting. You weren't invited, remember?"

"I wouldn't have it any other way."

Behind these closed doors marks a new chapter in history that could change us forever. I just hope I know what I'm getting us into. I take a deep breath, clear my mind, and walk in. Heads swivel in my direction. Whatever chatter among this lively bunch of ranking officers ceases. The room smells of sweat and swelling egos. Its ceiling hovers low, but the vast space inside could fit a hundred soldiers. In the center is a large rectangular table where twenty men in uniform sit. A major and a lieutenant-colonel are among some of these distinguished gentlemen.

General Eizenkot glowers at me in confusion. Father Joseph, standing just beside him, gestures me over. I quietly make my way around the large table, glares notwithstanding. Jacob sits to my right, along with Ari, Henry, and Sadiq.

"Quite an entrance you made . . . was beginning to worry about you," Jacob whispers.

Multiple field officers fill the rest of the seats in this the private council, with the exception of Sir Maarku, a retired political dignitary from the Parliament of Egypt. Colonel Dahan, second in command of the Israeli Defense Force, stands at the helm with a sour look on his face. He's a thin man with slightly sunken cheeks and the skin tone of a camel's hide. His brows, dark as charcoal, nearly run together as one. They are so pronounced that even the slightest lift from them gives him a permeant grimace. The colonel and I haven't been exactly the best of friends the few times we've met. Our arguments often escalate into dueling insults and nonsensical banter. Though my ideals and military philosophy differ greatly from his, I must respect the position he was appointed.

"This is a private affair. Can we help you?" the colonel addresses firmly.

"No, but I believe I can help you," I say. The flustered look on Colonel Dahan's face turns into a scowl. Ego certainly has a knack for getting in the way of important conversation.

He balls his fist next to his side and the vein on his neck bulges. "With all due respect—"

"Respect? I'm sure anything but is about to follow that statement," I reply sharply.

"I get more decorum from a dog than your—"

"Okay, let's just calm down," Eizenkot chimes in. "Arena, I'm at a loss of words why you are here, but I assume you have a good explanation."

"My apologies for the interruption, gentlemen, but I feel I deserve to be just as much a part of this as any of you here. I represent the citizens of this compound, and anything reported in here that may affect them should be in their best interest. I'm not a soldier, but I am a survivor, and I will do everything I can for these people to obtain a future without repression, especially my son."

"I sympathize with your cause, but let us do our job before you belittle the integrity of this council," Colonel Dahan scoffs.

"Excuse me?"

"Easy, Arena," Father Joseph braces me.

"I'm here to listen, not exploit your incompetence, so by all means, continue, Colonel," I snap. Okay, so I'm not making the best impression. Insults aside, adrenaline has me flustered beyond my control, not to mention a colonel with pride bigger than my own. I pull up a chair and sit beside Jacob to cool down. The smirk on Colonel Dahan's face isn't helping.

"Since you missed Sadiq's debriefing, I think a quick refresh wouldn't hurt, do you agree, Colonel?" Eizenkot asks.

"Of course," the colonel says through gritted teeth. He flutters about before opening a folder and bringing me up to date. "131st division was pushed back from the western line and they'd set a resistance line of defense further north in an effort to gain sympathizers and possible political allies, those of which include the lower Syrian parallel.

"With the recent surge of hostile adversaries to the east, more support is needed to thwart infiltration along the Jordanian border. Sadiq and a small reconnaissance team set off for Damascus in an attempt to sign a treaty of resistance with the like-minded Syrian rebels, but despite efforts to gain forces, our intelligence operations have indicated a much stronger resistance along the western regions of Turkey. And they will head straight through Damascus. A potential breach through the northern zone of Tel Aviv could be our downfall." None of this sounds good and makes it even more difficult to convince these people we must fight.

Sadiq turns to me. "Very few soldiers remain, though a strategic positioning of defense could be useful . . . of course, under the protection from the lower parallel government, but . . ." he hesitates.

"But what?" I prod.

"Even if we were able to establish a base in Damascus, it would still be ineffective," Sadiq says.

"We are very alone in this war, Arena, and every damn country still pushing forward isn't in the job of supporting a lost cause, a defector of the world," Colonel Dahan explains. "Israel is evil in the eyes of those who refuse to surrender to Russian politics. Helping us would only hurt them."

"Yes, but the Ten is broken. Its armor has become fragile. You and I both know everything has a weakness, and Russia is no different. Don't underestimate the vulnerability in one's ego. Eventually, nations will suffer and rebel," I counter.

"While that may be true, the treaty is still much alive," Sadiq cautions. "The Ten has come under severe scrutiny from the European Republic. For months, political squabbling has torn apart a once-prominent relation with Russia and China, but even this has been tested under the New Order rule. And because of that, nations have gone to war with each other, eliminating the weak and building the strong. Now, three of those rebelling nations are no longer a problem child to deal with; they have been conquered, reorganized, and absorbed."

"Surely you can't compare the stronghold of this nation to those who have fallen?" I argue.

"No, but everything has its limits, and what remains is far more dangerous now. The seven nations left have given no opposition to the pact. And that is what is concerning," the colonel retorts.

"We have seen abroad what the accord can do. The world has changed, Arena," Eizenkot chimes in.

"Your experimental EMP catastrophe caused that," I remind him.

"Regretfully, it has limited our own lack of technological weaponry, but tough decisions require tough sacrifices. Sometimes we have to go backwards in order to move forward. It had to be done."

Nearly two years ago, Israel launched Project X9, a devastating geomagnetic storm of fifty kiloton E6 missiles that rendered most of the world in darkness. The nuclear explosion above the earth's atmosphere disrupted power grids and disabled all electronics abroad. It inevitably killed ammunition factories, immobilized heavy military arsenals, ceased production of ballistic arms, and have caused total extinction of air to air combat.

"Your tough decisions may have just given us a break. Finally, a breath of fresh air. I commend you, General."

"Why's that?"

"Because it gives us an even playing field now."

"Even?" Colonel Dahan dismisses.

"Without disastrous weapons placed in the wrong hands, we can survive," I explain.

"Perhaps, but it hasn't stopped a rise in Russia's military forces. Nations have given up trying to find a solution to distant themselves from the accord. Their only hope to sustain now is meeting the needs of the New Order."

"I don't give a damn about what appeals to the New Order. I care about our freedom. We must fight."

"I understand your passion, really I do, Arena, but there's more to this than you may realize," Sadiq explains. "Our intel with Syrian operatives uncovered some grave news from the north. The accord goes beyond a global network of nations feeding into an ideology. It's created a monster. A real devil in the flesh. Those nations we hear so much about with their economical endeavors are just a fraction of what President Gorshkov was creating. His army hasn't just risen; it has metastasized beyond anyone's control. I'm afraid we won't survive this war, even with our numbers."

"So, you all have already decided to give up and allow that Russian prick to have all the power? As long as Gorshkov is alive, our sovereignty is no more than a delusion." I'm angry. I didn't just risk my life all these years for nothing.

"No one has decided anything yet, but a negotiation tactic is certainly an option," Eizenkot clarifies.

"He's selling you the illusion of freedom!" I shout.

"No one in this room is proud of what may become, I assure you of that. For now, it's just a setback," Colonel Dahan adds.

"Setback!" I bark. I look around the room at their defeated faces. Sadly, they seem willing to salvage an imaginary hope from Gorshkov. This is anything but a setback. Am I delusional, or is this where the end truly begins?

"Arena, I wish we would have found better news in Damascus. I'd fight alongside you until the end, but at what cost?" Sadiq says softly. "We could fend off a surge from the northern territories, but it could deplete our numbers quickly. With supplies limited, we'd find ourselves scraping with one army, only to be crushed by another advancing from the western nations."

The colonel clears his throat and looks remorseful. "You see, even the best know where their limits are drawn. There's no shame in knowing you've been beaten. I'm sorry if you really thought you could actually do something. The team's deeply disturbing news has given us no other choice but to alter our course of action."

"Disturbing enough to give in and allow the rest of us, who are hiding in this underground tomb, to wake up one day slave-bound to the Russians? Is that what you really want?"

"Slavery is not our intention, and it will not be a part of any negotiations!"

"But you can't guarantee that, and you know it. Wehave to fight this war. It's our only choice for freedom. We can't just sit back wondering what-if. It's time to take a stand."

"Military tactics isn't something you play on a board game. There are many pieces at play surrounding the future of Israel you simply can't understand."

"Don't coddle me with your bullshit, Colonel. I'm perfectly capable of interpreting what a deserter looks like." Colonel Dahan's face glows red with anger as he approaches me. "Politics runs games. A misguided war eliminates players. We simply don't have the manpower to overcome this war."

I stand up and plant my feet firmly in front of the colonel. "That's why you need a woman to lead, you coward."

The colonel pushes forward, unhinged, and balls his fists. His raging fit of anger is stopped by Sadiq and Ari. Jacob stands between me and the brutish colonel.

"Stop this at once!" shouts Eizenkot. "Are we not on the same side here?"

Colonel Dahan backs away and straightens his ruffled jacket. The other officers quietly sit back in their chairs as the unraveling argument ceases. Nadia and Gabe stand by the open door where Ananiah looks on. How long he's been standing there watching is uncertain, but long enough to understand my frustration.

"Looks like we may have met an impasse," Ananiah states with a slight grin. His words always seem appropriate at inappropriate moments. It's probably the reason we get along so well. Longtime friend of Uncle Finnegan, retired general of the IDF, and avid supporter of my well-being, Ananiah resigns steadfastly as the supreme lender of truth and honesty. You can't bullshit a bullshit artist, and he's no exception.

"Ananiah, good to see you, old friend" Father Joseph greets. General Eizenkot respectfully shakes Ananiah's hand. The two clearly have a history with mutual understanding.

Ananiah's last visit was nearly three months ago before citizens began abandoning the city and headed south toward the Israeli border. Some turned to Cairo for refuge, which is dangerous, but unlike what Jerusalem has suffered.

Ananiah led many into Egypt where he and his brother-in-law, Mubarak, continue to maintain strong political and militant ties with Egyptian allies. These successful and secret negotiations have given the Israeli defense some protection along the southern border. Ananiah continues to ride these fruitful discussions, which probably explains why Sir Maarku is here with us today.

"I don't mean to interrupt this enlightening conversation, but if I may offer a sense of . . . delusion here?" Ananiah looks at me and grins.

"By all means," Eizenkot consents.

"Aside from a potential catastrophic fallout the colonel here suggests, I'm not so sure what Arena proposes is so crazy."

I breathe a sigh of relief. There's nothing better than a little validation.

"I second that!" Nadia excitedly agrees.

"Just hold on before we declare World War III," Colonel Dahan reasons. "Though I respect your credulous opinion in the matter, Ananiah, it's imperative we look at our options from a factual viewpoint of what we know not what we want to see."

Ananiah walks over and takes a seat at the far end of the table. "If humans decided everything based solely on facts and logic, we'd all be dead."

The Colonel sits down as well. "I've been fighting in battles for the better part of ten years and nothing I've experienced has changed for the better."

"Arena has changed more in three years than the world has seen in fifty. You might want to at least hear what she has to offer."

Colonel Dahan glares at me. "Sometimes our overzealous minds get in the way of what is best. Convincing the people here to rebel is detrimental to their well-being and to a larger degree, this nation. Not everything we think is good is for the greater good."

"Whose interest are you serving then?" I coax.

The colonel softens a bit. "Our intent is to serve the interest of everyone here. The people just need to know they will be safe. It's not their job to worry, it's ours to maintain."

"I'm sure if their lives are at stake, they would want to know the whole truth," I say.

"Sometimes the details must maintain a sense of secrecy," the colonel huffs.

"The devil is always in the details." I smile.

"Tell me, what are you hoping to gain here except for the uncertainty of these people's safety?"

"Making sure we don't make the same mistake that put

us in this situation."

"Mistakes are made every day. Negotiating a peace treaty isn't one of them."

"I can assure you every option has been explored," Eizenkot points out, "but we must not delineate our plans because of our emotions. Understand we're just trying to unravel the best proposal."

Disappointment is such a powerful emotion, and that's what I feel as I stare into Eizenkot's eyes. I've never witnessed so much stubbornness among a bunch of bickering men. "Is that your diplomatic political speak? Tell me, what happened to the general who believed in me? The one who convinced me to never to back down from a fight and push forward no matter the cost? A year ago, I stood before a man who despised the word 'negotiate.' And now all he wants to do is surrender a plea. This isn't who you are. Brave men do not cuddle with the enemy."

"Enough!" Eizenkot slams his fist into the table. "Mend your words. I didn't become a general sitting at a desk. I can see it in your eyes that you want nothing to do with surrender. It's boiling inside of you, not because I've made you angry . . . hell, that's not difficult at all. It's because that's who you are and why you have survived so long. But this is the option we've brought to the table to discuss."

Heat burns my cheeks and I steady my breath. The thought of surrendering to the Russians is enough to make my head spin.

"I have to agree with Arena on this. Maybe we are a bit premature with our approach," Father Joseph suggests.

"Just like that, you're all going to let this girl change your minds because she has a knack for picking fights?" Colonel Dahan, argues.

"Albeit it's unorthodox, but she has yet to steer us wrong, and confidence has been quite absent these days. Maybe it's what we've been needing," Ananiah acknowledges.

"I'm at a loss here, but I'll bite," Eizenkot accepts. He faces me with a bitter curiosity. "What is it you think we are capable of doing to change the course of our fate?"

The vein on Colonel Dahan's forehead bulges as he shouts, "I'm sorry, but I need to step in. The council isn't interested in the advice from a reckless endangerment."

"I'm reckless?" I seethe.

"Let's keep this civil," Eizenkot says, exacerbated.

"Your discipline of basic house rules is a danger to us all. How many lives is worth putting in danger because you can't obey the simplest of rules. I would have kept you chained to your chamber if I knew I had to risk any of my men to fetch you from the dangerous streets. You have been a liability to us all and it's going to get you killed," the colonel scolds.

"If I wanted kill myself, I'd climb your ego and jump to your IQ."

The meeting erupts into a cacophonous clatter of arguing. Father Joseph pulls me aside and whispers, "There's a better way to win your peers over. I'm with you one hundred percent, but you have to give them a reason to fight, so quit the squabbling and convince them."

"Stop!" Eizenkot shouts above the ruckus. "When did this become a daycare? Do I need to remind you all the importance of why we are here? Now put away this childish banter and let's return to some civil discourse."

The room settles and I sit back down. *Stay calm,* I remind myself.

"Arena, if you have any advice to offer that we haven't already heard, I implore you to lead us there soon," Eizenkot says.

Convincing these men to give up everything and fight against the odds we cannot possibly overcome is futile. How can I change their minds? I look upon Nadia and Gabe who proudly behold with confidence while the others rest their eyes bleakly toward me. This is my only chance to change everything. God help me.

"My apologies, General. I didn't come here to divide us. I just want what's best for everyone, but I can't make you see through your own blindness. You have to believe that there's always a way around a perceived hopelessness, otherwise what's the point of existing? I look around at some of the faces and I see fear. And that's okay. I don't shame you for wanting to live, but for how long?

"These delusions of peace you conjure have blinded you. There is no peace treaty with Russian loyalty. The rest of the world knows this. Why can't you? If you accept a negotiating deal, you might as well dig your own grave on the mountainside now. This nation has resisted since its birth and has held itself independently from all walks of tyranny. So don't think for one second that your enemy will suddenly have a change of heart. You won't be lucky enough to be held captive like the rest, I assure you.

"Fight and you have a chance to preserve freedom for generations to come. Surrender and you lead a people into damnation. I will not let my son live in bondage. I'd much rather die fighting than live one day in slavery. I beg of you all. Don't take us to a place of misery. Lead us to a new world of freedom. Because in the end you can't erase regrets, but you can forge hope. That is where our future lies."

Eizenkot lifts his face from his palms. "Assuming you are correct and there is somehow a glimmer of hope left, how are we expected to fight against an army that outnumbers us three to one?"

"Because you aren't. You're going to be expected to fight against an army that outnumbers you ten to one."

The room erupts into chaos. Jacob wrinkles his brow in confusion.

"Excuse me?" one officers asks.

"Gentlemen, please listen," I say. "Nearly three million men, many forced to fight, are gathering just across the border of Iran as we speak. That army is going to divide. The eastern regiments will hold in central Jordan while a western front from Syria will advance an assault on the northern and western Israeli border. In ten days, Hell's gates are going to open and nothing is going to slow its motion, not even a peace treaty. Gorchakov and his Russian forces are preparing to conquer, and they have no illusions of stopping."

The room erupts again, the men murmuring among themselves. Eizenkot has to quiet the group once more.

"Don't play games with me," Colonel Dahan shouts.

"Why would I make this up?"

"Because you'll say anything to change our minds," he responds.

"Are you willing to take that risk?"

"I'm in no mood to be toyed with," Eizenkot fumes. "Can you give me a good explanation of how you came by all this information?"

I know I can't disclose my conversation with Michael to these men. They will never respect me. I can live with that I suppose, but I don't like the way Jacob is looking at me, asif he's staring through me. I understand he trusts me, but this I cannot share but with my brother, for now. I know I'll have to tell him at some point.

"Let's just say a little birdy told me," I say cheekily.

"You think this is funny?" the colonel scoffs.

"Just wait a minute, Colonel," Ananiah asserts. "What do you mean, Arena?"

What have I gotten myself into now? All I had to do was convince them to fight, and now I'm supposed to convince them I have an angel looking after me? In all honesty, I just don't care anymore. We're running out of time. Let them think what they want.

"You think it was a coincidence I made it here in Jerusalem? Do you have any clue what the hell I've been through to reach this point? I should have been killed, multiple times, but I somehow made it out alive. Not because I'm superhuman or lucky. I believe my brother and I have been chosen to be here . . . for reasons I can never explain. I don't have proof for you to see, but I have enough experience to conclude that someone has been watching over me and my brother throughout this journey. Maybe now I'm supposed to be watching over you. How I got here is simply a miracle. I left a nation in turmoil with every damn soldier wanting me dead."

"I can vouch for that," Father Joseph chimes in.

"I crossed a violent ocean that should have swallowed me up and escaped a Russian submarine attack that should have fed me to the sea. I somehow survived Alexandria when I shouldn't have. For Christ's sake, I tried to take my own life. But here I am, full of scars, bullet wounds, a bruised ego, and a lot of regrets I can't erase."

"I'm sorry for what you had to go through," Eizenkot offers.

"Humility is a funny thing. No one desires it, but at the same time, you can't move forward without it. As stubborn as I may be, I know now I cannot change my fate. So I beg you, all of you, to reconsider what you think is right."

Colonel Dahan leans his hands on the table and smirks. "You're throwing out numbers and specifics that haven't been confirmed. And what if you are wrong?"

"I'd rather die fighting for what's right than live one day in slavery. We can play what-ifs all day long, but unless you take a stand and do something about it, that's all they will ever be. Some times you have to reach beyond the lies we tell ourselves even if it makes us uncomfortable. Just know that I've warned you all. You don't have to believe me, but I assure you, on my mother's grave, you soon will have no choice but to believe me. "

An eerie silence casts over the room. No one will make eye contact. Suddenly, an officer bursts through the door clutching a piece of paper in his right hand. "Sorry to interrupt, General Eizenkot, but you need to see this."

Eizenkot grabs the paper and carefully scans the document. The reddened glow dispels from his aging face and leaves a pallid gloom.

"General?" the colonel asks, concerned.

The general hands the piece of paper to Colonel Dahan and turns to me with his rigid jaw and sullen eyes. "Perhaps we owe Arena an apology."

The colonel's face drops. His voice breaks with surprise. "You knew about this?" he quizzes me under an agitated tone.

"I haven't the slightest clue what you are talking about," I say.

The colonel drops the paper on the floor. "Beriah is dead."

"Excuse me, not to be insensitive here, but who is Beriah?" Henry asks.

"Beriah Covitz," Eizenkot answers. "Head of International Affairs council. He, among a few other Egyptian dignitaries advised by Maarku, formed an underground peace agreement with our neighboring countries. Somewhat turbulent at times, depending on how generous a deal they made with the Ten accord. A dangerously rocky operation, but necessary all the same.

"Up until a few weeks ago, we had established what we thought were hopeful talks with an unexpected surprise from British intelligence and a Saudi insurgence. The private conference seemed like a success for support, but days later it came to a decisive end. Not only did Britain and Saudi officials back away from the deal, but so did our long-time Ukrainian ally whom we have depended on the past two years. We surmise a hefty exchange with Russian intimidation and back-door deals. That's when we knew for sure that we were on our own.

"Under a stronghold across our borders and the potential for a catastrophic fallout with the rest of the world, we decided to send Beriah to an Iranian summit arranged by Russian leaders to make a plea bargain under a worst-case scenario . . . an insurance policy, if you will. That was four days ago. We had no reason to believe Beriah would return with bad news, but after this transmission from special intelligence in Iran, everything changes. The Iranians are no more than a puppet under their Russian master. It was a fool's errand to trust them and now they've killed our acting chancellor of negotiations. Beriah was our last hope for peace."

"Peace? I'm pretty sure we're past that, aren't we?" I say.

"Suppose we do go to war," Dahan says. "How are we to overcome these odds? It will be a massacre."

"I'm not one for cowering, but the colonel is right. In order to deal with these numbers, we must fight smart," I admit.

"From what we gathered with Syrian intelligence, southern Turkey will most likely be the heaviest troop deployment. East of Damascus is in shambles from relentless wars. The desert has swallowed most of the territory as far west as Al-Midan. That scarred terrain isn't traversable and wouldn't be ideal for transporting ground divisions or supplies. Our best bet is to hold their troops along the Rachalya pass in Lebanon," Sadiq suggests.

"And if they get through, they'll have easy access to the roads right through Tel Aviv and straight down to Jerusalem. To avoid such a calamity, we'll have to plant our largest line of defense along the West Bank and hope we can divert them back to our east. It may give us enough time to mount a counter-surge from Amman in northern Jordan and hit them from both sides," Colonel Dahan says.

"Still, with these numbers that have been projected, it would deplete our supplies and put a heavy dent in our forces. We still have to protect eastern Jerusalem and this complex from falling," Eizenkot chimes in.

Listening to these men plan for a war that is almost impossible to overcome no matter how they strategize gives me a migraine. Voices inside my head mingle in chorus with one another. If I had a better idea to suggest, I would. I did my job. I've convinced them to fight, but I'm not prepared to debate some of the tough questions surrounding their strategic approach.

I search Gabe's blank face as he stares at me. An impression of our scattered thoughts mingle with one another, a gift only he and I can understand. I trudge through lost ideas,hoping there's something hiding that's worth finding. There has to be a way around all of this. Why would Michael put me in this situation if there wasn't a way out?

My mind takes me through a series of strategic campaigns from historical wars. Military tactics that were brilliant under much different circumstances and others that were formidable. All seem hopeless with our numbers. Not even the unimaginable quest of the three hundred Spartans could prevail in this war. None of my ideas would work. And then it hits me, the Trojan Horse. After a fruitless ten-year siege during the Trojan War, the Greeks constructed a wooden horse as a ruse. They pretended to retreat to Greece, leaving the wooden structure behind and hoping the Trojans would take it into their city as a victory trophy. The Greeks had hid an elite force of soldiers inside the horse, and when the time came, the soldiers snuck out, opened the formidable gates to the city, and destroyed the city of Troy.

"You said the heaviest troop deployment would most likely march from Turkey's southern border and western Syria, correct?" I ask Sadiq.

"If they're smart, yes. According to Syrian intelligence, Turkish and Russian troops have been prepping along the border as we speak. It would be the easiest way in," he answers.

"And they know our defense will be ready for them?"

"I'm sure they've anticipated that as well."

"What are you getting at?" Eizenkot probes.

"I may have a plan to keep most of our troops cemented on the eastern border while defeating the northern troops without any casualties."

"I really have nothing left to lose at this point. Please indulge us with such a tactic."

I take a deep breath. "I'm sure you all have heard the tale of the Trojan Horse?"

Mumbles erupts in the room. Even Sadiq looks like he's trying to hide his smile.

"You expect us to build a wooden horse in ten days?" one of the officers mocks.

"No, we already have the horse. We just need to hide the soldiers."

"Count me in as being sorely confused," Ari says.

"Jerusalem is our horse. We're going to lure Troy to the Greek Army."

Colonel Dahan shakes his head in frustration. "I haven't a fucking clue what you're getting at."

"You would be pressed to obtain settlement at the Almon military base, though it would be ideal later down the line. Just too far away from the city. Any military advancement on enemy soil should always be taken to the heart of the city where government officials reside. This is the common stance for any military establishment by force, It's the perfect place for occupation to control a city under siege. That would be Kiryat HaMemshala, the precinct of the State of Israel, home of the prime minister.

"And if you're Russia, you want to conquer territory,not citizens," I say. "You want to keep people under rule, not below ground. You would push troops further back from their own borders until they are depleted of supplies. They would soon surrender if not killed already. Then you would only have one thing left to do."

"What is that?"

"Plant your flag and solidify a victory."

"Is it even possible to divert them into the city . . . the Kiryat HaMemshala?" Father Joseph ponders.

"Arena, I'm not sure where you are going with this, but are you suggesting we purposefully lead them here?" Sadiq asks.

"Exactly."

"Have you gone completely mad?" the colonel snaps.

"Perhaps, but it's the perfect setup. We lure their largest deployment into the city right to Kiryat HaMemshala. We hit them with little resistance to slow their pace but give them a taste of victory. I want us to retreat, and we need to let them see us do so. Give them a day to gather all their troops inside and revel in the successful battle. That should give them enough time to set up communications with Gorshkov. I want him to think that Israel is easy prey. It will give him good reason to send back any other incoming troops."

"Then what?"

"Then we do as the Greeks did, release the Trojan Horse."

"I'm liking this. So, when do I get started with the explosives?" Gabe says with a chuckle.

"Explosives?" Eizenkot puzzles.

"Kiryat HaMemshala is our Trojan Horse, and Gabe's homemade explosives are our Greek elite force. We can take out most of their troops without risking our own. It gives us some breathing room, confidence, and most importantly a chance to make Gorshkov shit his pants. If we can't lure him in with his troops, we can at least give him reason to doubt his overconfidence. You want to dismantle a regime quickly? Destroy its ego."

"I know I don't speak for everyone, but this is a pretty sound plan," Sadiq admits, "but I'm not sure where we are going to get a hold of properly stable explosives. The ammo yards are limited with supplies. Some still may have what you need, but most of it is non-working tech with aging rockets, unstable mines, and non-active warheads."

"I've seen the inventory. You have more than enough to light up more than this city. Trust me, I'll make it work. We may have to go analog, but I guarantee a bonfire for the ages," Gabe explains.

"Colonel, what do you think?" Ananiah asks.

Colonel Dahan doesn't answer right away. He's looking at his lap, twirling his fingers. Then he looks up at me and says, "I think I'm still in command of logistics, but I'll yield to the General."

"I believe Arena has a conceivable plan, and I believe she's just earned herself a promotion," Eizenkot affirms.

"I'll second that," Father Joseph agrees.

The men continue to debate a plan of action and agree to send twenty five thousand troops to Damascus in hopes of curtailing the Turkish troops and force them to deflect toward the east and into to central Jerusalem. For my efforts, I've been tasked to help lead the parting battalion, but I believe my advancement has further insulted the colonel's ego. Jacob lifts a playful grin at me from across the table. We may not agree on everything, but his trust in me strengthens in that subtle, proud moment.

Colonel Dahan looks to me with his beady eyes and his lips stiffen. "I'm still in charge of these troops whether you believe all this is possible."

"We are smarter, faster, stronger, and more determined to survive than any nation still standing. This is a well-oiled machine ready to be put on display for the world to see. And whether it carries us to victory or not, other nations will take notice and eventually follow our revolution to the halls of victory."

"I hope for your sake you're right. Overconfidence can lead to a very bad place."

"I have two hundred and fifty thousand men and women ready and willing to fight with you, Arena," Eizenkot says.

"Just remember, they are risking their lives for a cause greater than all of us. I'm in no way forcing anything upon them against their will, but if they are willing to serve, then I will gladly have them."

"They've been preparing for this their entire lives. I can assure you, they've been well trained and will follow orders."

"Good, because I need a soldier carrying a gun, not a conscience."

Ananiah smiles at me. "Just like your uncle, I see. Don't ever let that change. It's what made him believe in you . . . and in all of us now," he expresses wholeheartedly.

The colonel's eyes follow me from across the room with a scowl resting above them. A smile struggles to lift from the trembling corners of his mouth. His mulish behavior and resistance to all this begs me to further question his interrogation with our prisoner. "So, what shall I tell my men to expect of you?" he sneers before I leave.

"You tell them to expect nothing less than hell itself, and when it opens, I'll be there to shove those rusty fucking gates right back up Lucifer's ass. I'll fight until my last dying breath and I hope they do the same. It may not be the answer you're looking for, but you won't need one, because they'll know what they're fighting for. So you can tell them whatever you want. It won't change who I am, though I caution you, because it may change who they become."

"You sure you want that responsibility on your shoulders?"

"From here on out, we all carry a bit of the burden."

"There's a war of evil out there, waiting for us unlike we have ever seen. You sure you're ready to pick a fight with the devil"

"I'm not afraid of the devil, Colonel, but I'm bloody certain he's afraid of me."

CHAPTER 9

A canopy of black clouds rolls in from the north. I survey the eastern side of Mount Olive and wonder if I'll ever see these lands again. If I don't return, then I shall always remember its mysterious beauty. For a slight moment, the eastern horizon glows blue before vanishing in the cool wind. My body shivers, and not from the slight March breeze. Curious shadows dance along the border below, howling sinister whispers in my ear. Wild dogs perhaps, or just rowdy scavengers searching for food. Or maybe it's the distant tremors from Hell's gates waiting to purge. Whatever roams these lands better know they're in for a fight.

The sacred tree, its gnarled trunk once resting to the east, leans to the west now. Leaves flutter from its lively limbs while the dead, rotting leaves turn black. Tombstones poke from the earth, reminding me of the spirits resting here. The thunderous sky bellows across the city as flocks of birds retreat south. An unnerving sign of things to come for sure.

I head just south of the mountain where Jacob, Henry, and Ari explore the underground weapons compound. Not even a day passes since these brave men have returned from one journey to anxiously prep for a dangerous mission that may prove to be our end.

The underground compound has ten reinforced steel bunkers and a supply of an assortment of weapons. There are many guns, but the ammunition supplies have been purged beyond my liking. This war will be won not by a game of numbers but by the threshold of sheer will.

While they sort through an array of weapons, I leisurely explore the rest of the compound to find my brother. Gabe and a team of skillful explosive specialists reside somewhere in this maze, forging a stock of deadly bombs for our enemy.

The bunkers, with ceilings no more than seven feet tall, link to each other through a web of connecting tunnels. If you suffer from claustrophobia, this would be your personal prison. There are white numbers painted above each weapons room. A unique symbol marks the door,indicating the type of danger represented behind it.

Each bunker holds a specific type of deadly weapon, but none more dangerous than bunker five—the entryway to the nuclear explosives chamber, the best place to forge heavy explosives. . The change in air pressure gives me a headache as I descend lower underground. The damp and dingy corridor ends in front of ten-inch-thick steel doors marked with a faded radioactive symbol.

A small camera, sitting atop the entrance, rotates in my direction. I bang on the door and wait. Gusts of trapped air rumbles past and echoes a lowly bass through the tunnels. My ears pop. The settling steel entry moans and screeches before the rusty doors creak open.

Two men dressed in military apparel greet me on the other side. One awkwardly salutes to me. The massive room sprawls nearly one hundred yards in every direction. Rows of shelves, bolted to the concrete floor, stock weapon parts that nearly crest the tip of the ceiling. Long-range missiles, many of which are inactive, are stacked on one another. Huge dollies that transport them sit empty next to several rocket-launching vehicles. Large halogen lamps dangle beneath the towering ceiling that stretches equally to all four corners of the echoing chamber. This bunker, without doubt, reflects the worn symbol that's plastered outside the door: brisk, bleak, and filled with a variety of dangerous toys.

The officers escort me near the back where a mechanic skillfully guides a cutting torch around a cylindrical piece of metal. Glowing shards of ember shower like a display of fireworks.

My brother, clothed in a leather apron and wearing a pair of magnifying glasses, works methodically behind a long table, as he diligently crafts an assortment of circuitry next to a small domed warhead. Not many people in this world possess the skills he was born with. He's been in love with science and electrical engineering ever since I've known him. Finnegan had a special kind of connection with my brother's talents. He even offered the military a few of Gabe's inventions. My brother's remarkable gift is greatly understated. Though his intellect flourishes well beyond his age, it's his social skills I'm afraid that hinders him. I remember the days he would correct our teachers in class, making fools of them, or when he would geek out over some mathematical theorem in front of girls when they clearly were not interested. He's older and wiser now I guess. I do worry about my brother wielding such things, but he's a cautious man. I trust his knowledge is as keen as his attention, though I still can't help but give him some motherly advice.

"Don't blow us all up," I joke. I never said it would be profound advice.

"Says the woman who got us in to this," he chuckles.

"So what are these?"

"Detonators," he says quickly. "You gonna stand there and watch, or ya gonna help me?"

"How about a please?"

"Hold this wire right here . . . *please.*" Damn, my brother is bossy. I do as I'm told. He solders the wire with thorough precision and blows cool the circuit board until the wire stiffens.

"How many more like this?"

"That's the last one." Gabe connects a lead wire from a small battery in his hands to a jack on the board. After a red light glows from a bulb on the circuit, he disconnects it and sets it down on a table behind him with the other detonators.

"So, what are we going to detonate?"

"Some of the experts have been playing around with RDX and PETN, but they have proven to be a bit unstable, so we just decided to dismantle a few insensitive munition bombs and detonate them remotely. They're bloody big so we'll need to cloak them, most likely underground. We can plant simple Semtex charges on the interior of the buildings, but it probably won't matter since the bombs will blow everything to hell anyway."

"You sure it's going to be enough?"

"You wanted a Trojan Horse? I have enough explosive power for a harem."

"Got it . . . and I could have done without the sexual innuendo, but clever."

A familiar voice and a scraping of metal rattles just behind a stack of pallets. Sadiq and two other bomb specialists glean through a pile of dangerous warheads—parts most likely being used to create our mighty Trojan Horse. Powerful, yes, but the stability of that power has yet to be seen. I'm not so sure I want to be around when they are planting them.

With just two days to build and strategically set these menacing explosives in the government complex, I leave the men to their tedious work. If all goes to plan, not long from now, tens of thousands of enemy soldiers will be receiving an explosive surprise.

I escort myself back to the bunker entrance when Nadia surprisingly passes by.

"What are you doing down here?" Nadia casually asks.

"Funny, I was just about to ask you the same thing."

"Thought I would see if they needed any help. I feel a bit useless just waiting in my quarters."

"I'm sure they could use a woman's touch, especially my brother."

"Yeah, he's a special kind of guy," Nadia adds with a twinkle in her eye.

"Uh, sure . . . wait, what?"

"You know, just with all that he's been through the past year."

"Of course, yeah. Well, I better get back. Niki's with Joshua and probably wondering where I am."

Nadia scoots off with a blushing grin and an unusual delight in her step. I stand there with the intension of exiting the bunker, but I find myself engaged to her mysterious behavior instead.

I watch from afar as Nadia scuttles near the back and meets Gabe with a long, affectionate hug. I don't usually go snooping into other people's business, but what the bloody hell? That's my brother. What happens next leaves me in utter shock. Gabe plants a long kiss on Nadia's lips. I quickly exit the bunker without them noticing.

So that just happened? I stand on the other side of the door and wonder how long this charade has been going on, and how in the hell did I not see this. Why would they keep this from me? I mean, seriously, what the bloody hell? Has my brother completely forgotten about Juliana? I'm all for putting the past behind, but I'm shocked my brother has moved on this fast.

Juliana's death changed Gabe for the worst. My shy little brother with a kind heart had vanished. Hate and bitterness replaced the brother I knew. As months passed, he gradually left that bitter heart behind, but I really never got a sense he fully healed. Not until seeing him return from Damascus have I witnessed a stronger man. He talks to me more and that infectious smile he used to carry has come back. Maybe I'm the one who hasn't gotten over Juliana's death. I want to cry and yet part of me finds joy. If by moving forward with his life is connected by Nadia's affection, then so be it. I'm just glad there's still a smile left in him.

I walk away knowing less about my brother's true feelings and more about the insecurities of my own. Some things are just best left alone until they are ready to be opened. Not today. Right now I need to hold my son. I exit the compound and return to the cavernous belly of the mountain.

The dingy passages in the complex are quite a pleasantry compared to the narrow ones connecting the bunkers. Every step I take down these halls becomes a guilty reminder of the loved ones I will be leaving behind. Every open door I pass, a piece of me breaks inside, watching families huddle together, taking advantage of the last quiet days that may remain. News has already spread among the people about what we will be facing. They must all prepare for the worst because anything less is delusional.

I pause just outside a door where Allison clings to her pillow and curls up in a ball while Godfrey rests beside her. I desperately want to console her, but I know she will only try to talk me out of fighting. She looks up to me far too often, and that's why I must leave her with Godfrey. It sounds heartless, but sometimes the things we must do for our loved ones doesn't always resolve to precious moments. There will be a time to part with words, but not now. I must make preparations before I deploy with my unit. We have a long haul to Damascus. No matter how many enemy troops we may face there, We cannot let them through. It's up to us to staunch them. My hope rests beyond these stony walls, but it's my son who anchors that courage. We all have a purpose in this fight, but our reasons sometimes lie in what we cannot see. If we could, we would never make the impossible possible.

My heart beats just a wee bit faster as I head down the hallway. A strange anomaly surfaced the day my son was born. Our hearts were synched the very moment my son gasped for his first breath. Ever since, I've been able to recognize Joshua's presence by the simple beat of my heart pumping. Like with my brother, there's a mystical link between my son and I. It's reached a point where nothing has become out of the ordinary.

Faster and faster my heart drums as I press down the long grayish halls. Just a stone's throw from the medical bay entrance, Henry and Roland storm out. "What's the hurry?" I ask.

"Our prisoner tried to escape and injured a couple of guards," Henry explains.

"I'll kill him!" I grit my teeth.

"No, you stay here, we can handle this." Henry and Roland sprint off, leaving me irritated.

Just then, my son's lonely cry echoes down the hall, reaching my ears. I rush toward my quarters and halt in the doorway. Joshua is squirming in a basket on a crumpled quilt. Niki tenderly picks him up and coddles my hungry son with a bottle she has prepared.

How can I leave my son behind? A mother should be with her child, but here I am, watching from a distance as someone else nurtures him. *You're a good mother,* I remind myself as I fight back my tears.

Niki smiles and pats the dingy bedcover, offering me a place to sit. "How are you, sis? Sorry, that's a silly question—"

"No, no, it's fine. I'm just making my rounds before . . ." The words refuse to slip from my tongue. Leaving my loved ones behind stings deep.

"You're doing the right thing you know," she encourages.

"I wouldn't be doing this if we had another choice."

"I know . . . and so do the others. They trust you."

A sudden burden weighs on me as I notice the glowing contentment on Niki's face. Joshua has his eyes closed as he drinks his bottle, and I want him to open them, to see me, his mother. I rub his chubby leg and he grips my index finger tightly. I know my son is in good hands with Niki, but I'm afraid that even this formidable underground complex is subject to fall. If that is to happen, there is but only one place to retreat—deeper into the ancient belly of the old city where there's a subterranean space of ancient tunnels.

A parallel city, shifting throughout history, lies dormant underground, cursed. Though engineered excavations once thrived, leaving caverns, halls, and open-spaced chambers habitable, the seven-year border war ravished many of the canals. Narrow walls collapsed, burying much of the ancient dwelling, but for the few that remain intact, they have now become the most important passages if we want to survive.

The lower chambers hide deep below, locked behind a stony door the priests call the Prophets Path, also known to everyone as Elhiym's Hollow. It can only be opened from one side and is the last stable entry in safe proximity to the under city. Many believe the other side of the door is haunted, a gate to the underworld. A fool's thought perhaps, just to keep people from entering the unstable channels, but eerie all the same.

The path extends to the Ninth Gate, a vast edifice encasing King Herod's street near the great doors to the Temple Mount. This chamber is the only place left to hide if our complex becomes unprotected. But without ample food or water, survival could become grim after a week down there. It may be all we have left.

My mind races to the worst, leading me to caution, "If anything should happen—"

"Arena, we're not completely without protection here. This place is well defended and secluded," Niki quickly reassures.

"Perhaps, but I must consider that nothing can be truly safe anymore."

She smiles at Joshua. "I'll guard him with my life."

"I know you will, but even the slightest moment you feel unsure, you know where you have to go."

Niki gasps. "No one dares go down there, not even the people from here."

"Sadiq has journeyed these chambers more than once, so I would ignore all the village rumors about Elhiym's Hollow. They're no more than just kids' stories of embellishment." I haven't ventured down there either, so I understand where Niki's fear is coming from, but I want her to be prepared for anything.

Niki's wandering eyes lie deep in doubt. "But is it safe?"

"Safer than out there, I assure you."

"You realize that we cannot reenter once the chamber door is closed."

"Yeah, but it will keep you and Joshua alive."

"And what about the rest of the people here?"

"They're fully aware of what may happen and are wisely capable of making their own decisions. Just make sure you keep Allison and Godfrey close by and take them with you into the tunnel. In case something should happen and I don't expect it to, show them both where the entrance lies. Better safe than sorry."

"We've been through tougher times, right?" She rubs Joshua's head.

"We didn't come this far to give up now."

"I'll do everything to keep them safe." Her plaintive words drape her face like a veil of burden.

"I know it's a lot to ask of you, but I know I can trust you."

Niki pauses for a moment. Her face has paled. "I won't lie to you, I'm scared, Arena . . . for everyone."

"You're not alone, which is why I've asked Harold to stay back." Harold, Niki's zealous beau, has been my devoted friend since the beginning of this chaos, well before he and Niki ever met. After his persistent protesting, he finally accepted my request to stay, mainly out of his personal loyalty to me.

"What?"

"There's no reason to separate everyone. Harold has done more than enough for me, Gabe, and everyone else. At least someone deserves some good fortune."

A small tear trickles down Niki's cheek. "Thank you," she weeps, and she squeezes me. We've hugged many times upon departures and returned to each other just the same. I can only hope this one is no different.

"Look at me," I say. She raises her head from my shoulder. "You don't hesitate to leave if those gates are breached, all right?"

"I won't, but if it is our last resort, we can never return here."

"Then let's hope it doesn't come to that."

I hover over the padded blanket and watch at the delight of Joshua's tiny lips slurping up the milk. I cradle him inmy arms, feeling his warmth and movement. My son's eyes, blue as the summer sky, beam back at me, wading with innocence. A part of me breaks inside as I hold him against me. Every moment I have to remind myself that I'm not abandoning him. I'm giving him a chance at life.

CHAPTER 10

As dusk sweeps in, Gabe and nearly one hundred men begin preparations inside the government district near Wohl Rose Garden—a tedious task of strategically planting ten dangerous explosives tethered together capable of destroying forty city blocks. A section of the old city where the once-stately structures stood are crumbling from existence. The namesake of these pillars may stand with pride, but their future is forgone. We have no alternative. This piece of historical land must be sacrificed if we are to have a fighting chance in this war.

A sign of fear erupts in the dining hall as two men brawl over a petty dinner plate. They scrap on the floor while bystanders watch in shock. I push myself through the crowd and grab one of the men from the back of his jacket while Harold pulls back the other. The two men—one large and one small—sneer at each other before standing to their feet, but I trust their differences have yet to be resolved. I move between the men and draw my gun to make it plainly clear.

"Don't even think about it," I warn.

"What, are you going to shoot us?" the large man barks.

"Is that what you want, huh? While you two are acting like buffoons in front of your friends and family, have you forgotten what's going on out there? I suggest you put your focus elsewhere. The last thing anyone needs to be worrying about is breaking up a trivial fight over a fucking chicken wing."

The men stare at each other, but their eyes refuse to meet. Allison quietly emerges from the crowd with a plate of food and places it on the nearby table.

"You can have my food, sirs. I'm not very hungry," she humbly offers. Their faces redden with shameful discontent over the fruitless display.

"Thank you kindly," the small man mumbles. The large man slowly takes a step forward with a nasty scowl on his face. I draw my knife from its sheath and hold tightly to it. He clenches his fist.

"Don't do anything stupid," I advise.

Allison grabs my hand and lowers the knife to my side. "It's okay," she whispers. She cautiously buffers herself between the two men and stands quietly. The man loosens his fist and relaxes his face. Allison is no longer a broken girl withering away from grief. She's a young woman with a strong will holding the broken pieces of her life together.

"Well? You gonna shake hands or do you need some encouragement," I urge with my knife.

"I would do what she says. These things often end ugly on the side of stupid," Allison says lightheartedly. The two men smirk before grasping each other's hand. Whether or not it's a false gesture for my sake, they mend their differences. The large man picks up an empty plate and divides the food equally before handing it to the other man. The crowd disperses as both men part ways.

"You don't need me around here to protect you, Allison. I do believe you can take care of yourself." She wraps her arms around me and buries her face. Her tears soak through my shirt.

"Maybe, but who's going to protect you?" she whispers.

I have nothing to offer but the comfort of a hug because I don't have an answer. As I embrace the daughter I never had, I can only hope that we will see each other again after tomorrow.

Ananiah walks into the dining hall looking grim and worried. Just then, the lights dim and there's a thunderous rumble.

"What was that?" Allison trembles.

"Nothing, love. Gabe and the others are probably just testing some explosives." Even I doubt my own explanation, but it's all I can come up with.

"You sure?"

"Yes, nothing for you to worry about. Tell you what, how about you stay with me tonight?"

"Really?"

"Sure, why don't you go on and get your things and take them to my quarters." A smile lifts from her face as she scampers off into the hall.

"Please tell me I just didn't lie to her," I ask Ananiah.

"I must say, you're as perceptive as your brother, but I guess you already know that."

"A simple yes would have done. So what brings you here?"

"We need a favor to ask of you."

"We?"

As if on cue, Father Joseph saunters over. "Well, *we* is an inclusionary term, but I think it's best to keep this matter just between us three." He digs through his jack and hands Ananiah a set of keys.

"Just what have you two cooked up?" I ask.

"Arena, I understand you have a . . . skill—"

"Affliction," Father Joseph smirks.

"For interrogating," Ananiah continues.

My brows knit together as I glare at Father Joseph. I find his remark a bit tasteless, but true. "Interrogating who, the colonel's prisoner?"

"I'm sure you are aware that our he tried to escape this afternoon? " Ananiah says, and I nod. "Well, after apprehending the cockroach from a brief scuffle with one of the guards, we found this sewn into the neck of his shirt."

A small metal cylinder the size of a quarter sits in Ananiah's palm. I grab the object and examine it.

"What is it, some kind of tracking device?"

"No, but what's inside of it is concerning."

I rub my thumb over a small cap that's screwed into the cylinder and open it. There's a rolled-up piece of parchment inside. I unravel the paper and find a random set of letters and numbers written down.

"What is this supposed to indicate?" I ask.

"We don't know, a code perhaps. Could mean anything, but we know for certain the man carrying this around is a liability," Ananiah states.

"Have you told anyone else about this?"

"No, and we want to keep it that way . . . for now," Father Joseph adamantly insists.

"I think you ought to let the colonel—"

"No. We've been explicitly instructed not to involve ourselves with the prisoner. Colonel Dahan has made it plainly clear that he is running the interrogation process and no one is to interfere."

"Yeah, I was briefed earlier about it. So how did you retrieve this without him knowing?"

"Henry sifted it off the floor. It must have torn loose from the prisoner's shirt during the brawl with one of the guards. Henry came to me first about it, and I've kept it in my possession since," Ananiah says.

"So why the secrets?"

"At first glance I didn't really think much of it, but then I remembered seeing one of these before," Ananiah says.

"Before?"

"Sitting on the colonel's desk," he confesses.

My blood boils in a steam of rage. "That son of a bitch!"
"Now just calm your kettle, Arena," Ananiah urges. "We don't know all the details right now. It's just speculation at the moment, but a serious matter nonetheless. We need to approach this wisely. We have no reason not to trust the colonel."

"That's what scares me."

"Don't let it overcome you now. I know you two don't get along, but be mindful of your loyalty."

"My loyalty? I just don't want to be caught in the snare of a liar's tongue." I can hardly breathe. My insides are tearing any sliver of sympathy I may have had for that asshole colonel.

"Let's keep our wits about ourselves," Father Joseph says calmly. "The colonel doesn't know we have the item, so we go on about our business. No one else is privy to this information except us three. I plan on keeping it that way."

"So what is it you need from me?" I ask.

"You know I don't condone lying or keeping secrets, especially behind the Ministry of Defense's back, but sometimes we have to bend the rules to break through some answers."

"So you want me to interrogate the prisoner?"

"To be absolutely sure . . . yes," Father Joseph whispers.

I look at Ananiah. "And you're okay with this?"

"Can't make an omelet without breaking a few eggs." He shrugs.

"The prisoner is restricted from seeing anyone. How the hell am I supposed to get inside?"

Ananiah hands me the set of keys that Father Joseph gave him. I can't help but chuckle at what went through Father Joseph's mind as he swiped these.

"You sly, old bastard. You stole these, didn't you?"

"I borrowed them." His eyes squint with discontent.

"And how, exactly, am I to get past the guards?"

"We thought you could help us with that," Ananiah confesses.

"What, you want me to shoot them?" I say in a sarcastic tone.

"I don't know . . . improvise. Use you womanly tactics," Ananiah says.

I roll my eyes. "I'm not seducing the guards. Jesus, you guys suck at planning."

"We just need to distract them long enough for you to get past the gate and through the cell door," Father Joseph explains.

"And suppose we do that. What about the cameras?"

"There are no cameras in solidary confinement for reasons you can guess."

I sigh. This might be harder than I thought. "Okay, let's say the prisoner squeals like a pig and reveals everything we need to know. How are we going to prove that to the others, especially since we're unauthorized personnel who've stolen keys and snuck inside a well-secured cell?"

Father Joseph hands me a small black device with two blue buttons. "It's a recording device. If there's a confession, it'll be documented."

"And if he doesn't spill?"

"That's why we have you. Make sure that he does," Ananiah stresses.

"Do what you have to do. We will fully back you with the consequences," Father Joseph adds. "If we're going to war, then we bloody better have a trust we can anchor in this fight. I know Eizenkot well, he's a smart man. He believes in you, and I don't doubt for a second he would ever turn his back from you, regardless of an accusation against Colonel Dahan . . . if it comes to that."

I consider our options moving forward with this, but these men are right. Trust cannot be taken lightly, especially now. "Okay, so when is this going to happen?"

"The colonel and all ranking officers will be meeting at oh nine hundred tonight with the general for a last pre-plan before deployment. The lower levels will be empty for preparations with the exception of the cell block, which contains two guards and our prisoner," Ananiah explains.

"And why was I not invited to this meeting?"

"I informed the general that you needed some time alone," Father Joseph responds.

"So that gives us about thirty minutes to prepare. I think I may have a solution for detaining our two guards. Meet me in the medical bay in fifteen, and grab a bottle of wine from your stock."

"Stock?" Father Joseph says.

"Don't toy with me. I know what you have."

"Well, so much for privacy."

"Hey, don't look at me," Ananiah chuckles.

"Just bring the bottle with you, okay? I need to check in on Allison."

Father Joseph and Ananiah exit the dining hall, poised and resolute. But I have pending doubts of the outcome. Allison is in my quarters curled up next to my pillow. A fading candle flickers on a wooden stand dripping a glacier flow of wax to one side.

I lie down next to Allison and stroke her brown hair ever so gently. This is the calm I've longed for, but I know it's short-lived. I must confess, I've been torn between two worlds wrapped up inside of me: hope and despair. It hurts knowing I cannot bring my loved ones back, and yet I struggle with the confidence to protect the ones I still have. What has come of me to break my faith like this? I know this will all end one day, but when will I finally see peace?

A gentle but steady knock rattles the loosely hinged door. I open it and find a most enjoyable face greeting me.

"Hi, Godfrey, everything okay?"

"I'm scared . . . s–c–a–r–e–d, scared," he says.

"Where's Mia?"

"She not feel well."

"Well, you can stay here. Allison is resting, but I'm quite sure she would love the company."

"I come to protect Allison."

"And you're the perfect person for the job. Come in."

Without a hitch in his step, Godfrey comfortably walks in and sits in the chair next to the bed.

"Close your eyes, not a peep, happy dreams, now go to sleep."

His eyes float about, and within seconds he mumbles softly into a slumber. What keeps us from going mad? Embracing the small joys in life instead of waiting for great expectations to arrive. These two give me joy and a small hope that good will eventually prevails.

Suddenly, a ghostly image of Luke appears next to Allison. Once again, my eyes deceive me, but only for a brief moment as his image vanishes. I want to believe he's there, watching over her, but I can never truly know. I shut my eyes and remember Allison and Godfrey in this peaceful moment as their wild minds drift into a land of dreams.

CHAPTER 11

Cracks in the walls, eroded over time, scatter like veins. At the end of the hall is a rusted gate broken beyond repair. The gate opens without any effort. Through the other side, a dimly lit passage stretches in two directions: one to the medical bay and the other gradually trails off into the shadows.

Footsteps faintly scuffle across the frigid floor and a shadowy figure emerges of a man in tattered clothing, carrying a book in one hand and a balled fist in the other. He shuffles with a decisive limp closer to me. Aged and disheveled, the old man stops next to me and draws a blank stare from his wrinkled face.

"Sir, can I help you?" I ask in an attempt to draw him from his near catatonic state. He says nothing. "Sir," I call once more. Still no response. Not to be rude, but Father Joseph and Ananiah are waiting, so I turn away and leave the old man to himself.

"Have you lost your way, my dear? " the old man suddenly speaks. His words stir me to stop.

"What?"

"No one is without pain I'm afraid, but it doesn't have to define you."

I'm not one to argue with an old man, but something has put a stick in my crawl. "I haven't given up, if that's what you're implying. But sure, some days it hurts worse than others. I can feel it deep inside of me struggling to escape. Does that make me any different than anyone else?"

"Of course not, but you're not anyone else, are you?"

"I can't help it if my feelings alter my faith."

"Ah, but that's exactly where you do not want to be. Faith is not a feeling. It overcomes our feelings. When you lack conviction, the human element cannot be sustainable in a world filled with uncertainties."

"Who are you?"

"Just an old man."

The mystery behind this old codger raises great suspicion, yet I find myself drawn to him. He has not once faced me since he spoke, and I believe there's much more to him I do not understand. I search his face again and notice his eyes are cloudy. I'm no expert, but I recognize a man who struggles to see, for this poor man is blind.

"My faith is what led me here—I cannot deny that—but I can't do this on my own," I say.

"You won't have to, but are you willing to act on that faith, no matter what?"

"Of course."

"Then ask yourself, would you sacrifice the life of one you love to save the lives of thousands you do not know?"

"I . . . I can't . . ."

"Because you won't have to make that choice if you lead by faith first."

My hands tremble, and the back of my arms fill with goosebumps. This is no ordinary man. Words from wise men have changed lives, but his have plucked the living pain out of my soul. I'm nearly immovable and struck with reverence by his presence.

"Hold out your hand," he says. He opens his book, grabs a small skeleton key nested inside the pages, and gently places it my palm.

"What is this for?" I ask.

"A parting gift." He closes the book and slowly limps away.

"Wait, where are you going?"

"I must get back now. The dust in these halls don't take kindly to my lungs."

"Well, let me at least help walk you back. It's quite the maze down here if you don't know where you're going."

"Oh no, my dear child. I do not need my eyes to see anymore. I know exactly where I'm going, which is far greater than where I've been. Strength be with you on your journey, Arena."

"Wait, how did you know my name?"

The clank of doors slam shut down the hall, and I look away for just a moment, but when I turn back, the old man is gone.

I'm in too deep with my own insanity to approach anything pragmatically anymore. If I let my mind manifest anything, it surely wouldn't be old men, but this is my world now whether I accept it or not. I examine the small tarnished key. It's as real as anything else, but I haven't the time to understand its purpose. I tuck it in my pocket and dash to the medical bay.

Father Joseph and Ananiah are waiting anxiously, pacing about. When people become ill, they come here. It's one of two medical facilities in the complex, but it's the only one utilized with the best conditions. The other is deeper below, un-kept and undersupplied. Medical instruments, gurneys, and a few beds reside in the main room.

"You want to tell us why we are here and why I have this rare bottle of wine in my hand?" Father Joseph ask.

"Don't worry your panties off, Father. It's just one bottle, you have plenty more," I playfully quip.

"Note to self, keep door locked," Ananiah banters back.

"I'm assuming there's a good plan in all this?" Father Joseph sighs.

"A plan, yes, but it's debatable whether it's good. Just follow me."

I lead them to the back of the main room and unlock the secure doors that lead to a small room of medical supplies including a vast assortment of prescription drugs in pantry cages.

"How the hell did you get a key to this room? Roland is the only authorized user," Father Joseph asks..

"I—how did you say it before—*borrowed* it."

"Of course, what a stupid question."

"So what are we searching for?" Ananiah asks.

"A sedative, preferably something that won't put the two guards in a coma. It's the only diversion without being completely suspicious. I don't see any other way we can lure them from their post for a few hours."

"And just how are you going to get them to take the sedative?" A puzzling look crosses Father Joseph's face.

"I'm working on it." I scan the shelves one by one, deciphering each bottle and vial, but nothing jumps out at me that's familiar.

"I have no idea what drug I'm looking for," Ananiah says.

"Hell, I can't even pronounce most of these," I add.

"I think you'll find what you're looking for right here."

I jump back, knocking my head into the cage behind me, and Ananiah drops a bottle of pills. Roland is standing there with his arms crossed.

"How long have you been standing there?" I sputter.

"Long enough to not ask questions."

"We . . . were just—"

"Look, I don't need to know the particulars, in fact I don't want to know anything, but if there was a need for a person to *aid* another person's—let's call it *pain*—I would find it in here." Roland points to the back cage.

I search the shelf. "Next to the blue bottle," Roland adds as I grab the pills. "The other blue bottle," he corrects. I examine the entire shelf once more and find a small amber container of liquid.

"So, if said person needed some time to rest *quickly,* I would give that person, say one hundred and fifty milligrams?"

"Sweet Jesus, no, not unless you want the person to stop breathing. You want said person to take a nap?"

"Yes, as quickly as possible."

"Then twenty milligrams will do the trick. Anymore than that and you'll put them in a state of decay. And I'm no detective here, but I'm assuming that bottle of libations will be used to take the sedative?"

"You have quite the keen eye. You sure you're just a doctor?"

"I'm many things, but a psycho-crazed lunatic, I'm not."

I furrow my brows at his insult.

"Look, I think we got what we need. We'll be leaving now," Father Joseph calmly implores. "And I can explain if you—"

"No need. You were never here, out of sight, out of mind," Roland says. "I wash my hands of this . . . whatever *this* is."

"Thank you." Ananiah nods graciously as we leave. I deflect my eyes from Roland and hurry toward the exit. I've suffered enough embarrassment.

"Arena," Roland barks, and I turn around. He's holding out his hand. "You forgetting something?"

I pull the supply room key from my pocket and place it into his palm. "I was going to return it, honest," I apologize. "Next time, just ask. You might be surprised by the results." Roland hands me a syringe and smiles. He has never deterred his support for me. He's that friend who brings the shovel to help hide the body. I wish I could leave him under better circumstances.

The three of us quietly step down the deserted halls as the time for our plan quickly approaches.

"Wait," I whisper, detouring into the kitchen. I grab a couple of wineglasses. "Anyone see a corkscrew?"

Ananiah rummages through a couple of drawers and swipes a corkscrew. "Got it."

"Perfect, now let's go."

My heart beats fast as we reach the lower levels. A cold, damp crawl lingers through the dark passage to solidary confinement, a morbid poetic sentiment for such a dreadful place. We pause and I peak around the corner. A large space that stretches twenty meters across is dusty and dank. The ceiling, carved out from the jagged mountain, hovers like a vaulted cave. Two men stand in front of an iron gate that divides the room. They're dressed in full gear and have rifles strapped to their torsos. A metal door behind the gate leads to a small interrogating cell where half is encased in the stone walls. The guard's post is drab and dim with just a couple of low wattage bulbs glowing outside the cell.

"It's now or never. I'm gonna have a drink with my friends."

"And if they refuse?" Father Joseph asks.

"I don't know, I'll knock the shit out of 'em with my boot."

"That's plan *C*, right?"

"Just stay here and wait."

I quickly measure thirty milligrams of the sedative into each glass. Father Joseph and Ananiah look at me as if I have two heads. I peer around the corner at the young guards. A cold sweat runs down my neck, and my gut dances with butterflies. I'm starting to second-guess my plan. My head swarms with ideas, but only one seems promising. This isn't going to be pleasant.

"Here, hold these." I hand him the bottle of wine and glasses and bashfully remove my clothes down to my undergarments.

"What the hell are you doing?" Ananiah whispers.

"It's going to be hard enough to get two well-trained stationed men to take a drink of alcohol on duty. So maybe a half-naked woman will entice them."

I take the wine, glasses, and shuffle off down the hall. It doesn't take long for the two guards to notice a woman in her bra and panties.

"Stop! What do you think you're doing down here," one of the guards shouts as he ogles me. He has a nasty scar on his cheek. The other guard has a thick brown mustache that hangs over his top lip. It's horribly unfashionable.

"Oh, I'm so, so sorry. From a distance I thought you looked like my husband," I giggle childishly. "It's our anniversary and I thought I would surprise him. I'm so embarrassed."

"It's okay, ma'am, no harm, but why do you think he would be down here?" the first one asks.

"He said he would be working in the lower levels, but I guess I got lost. Stupid me. I'm glad I didn't decide to meet him in my birthday suit." I stick my chest out and smile. Their perverted eyes explore every inch as I stand there babbling like a clueless sorority girl.

"You're not stupid. It could happen to anyone down here in this maze. It can be confusing. Maybe we can help you. Who exactly is it you're looking for, ma'am, if you don't mind me asking?" the other inquires.

"Jacob, but I shouldn't be bothering you two. You have a very important job to tend to."

"Oh no, it's fine, and you don't have to leave on our account. I believe your husband is in a private meeting with General Eizenkot."

"Oh, rats. I guess I misunderstood. Well, that's just great. What am I supposed to do with all this wine? I really hate drinking alone. Maybe you two can have a drink with me?"

"Ma'am, were on duty. I don't think it's—"

The first guard elbows his comrade in the shoulder. "We're not supposed to drink, but I guess just one won't hurt."

"Fantastic. Would one of you strong men please help me uncork the bottle?" Both men eagerly step forward, leaving their post without a care, and one of them removes the wine cork. I fill both glasses and offer one to each of them.

"Where's your glass?" the other asks.

"Oh, an Irish woman is just fine resting with her bottle. Glasses up, lads."

> I drink to your health when I'm with you,
> I drink to your health when I'm alone,
> I drink to your health so often,
> I'm starting to worry about my own!"

I tip the bottle to my lips and watch the two guards empty their glasses. It's only a matter of time until these blokes greet the concrete floor.

"Well, I'll let you good gents return to your duties. I must be getting on my way now."

"What, so soon?"

"I don't want to get you boys in trouble, much less my own if I know what's good for me. I appreciate you having a drink with me, but I do have to go."

"Come back anytime and thanks for the drink." They grin especially big as I grab their glasses. I can feel their eyes planted on me as I exit down the dark hall and around the corner.

"Well, did they take it?" Father Joseph whispers.

"Oh, they took it, creepy bastards." I redress and rest against the wall and wait. Father Joseph and Ananiah take turns stealing sips of wine.

"I'm not going to let this expensive wine go to waste," Father Joseph assures.

Almost ten minutes pass until a sudden thud crashes down the hall. Both guards are curled on the floor just outside the gate.

"Shit, that was quick. Might want to check their pulse," I joke.

With the keys in hand, I rush to the end of the room and unlock the gate. I wait outside the cell door and wave for Father Joseph and Ananiah. They come running over.

"They're fine, still breathing," Father Joseph confirms the guard's pulse. He pulls a set of keys from the man's belt and hands them to me.

"Okay, no turning back now. Wish me luck." I exhale a calming breath before unlocking the cell door.

"Arena."

"Yes?"

"By any means necessary," Ananiah says.

I slowly open the door and lock it behind me. The cell is dark and appears empty except for an old, rickety wooden chair resting in the middle of the floor. I remove the recording device from my pocket, press record, and place it on a dust-covered table next to the crackled wall.

The small concrete room smells of an odor only a fishmonger could tolerate. A small recessed amber bulb dimly glows in the center while the corners rest in the shadows. The danger when interrogating a prisoner can vary. After this one tried to escape with complete disregard for the consequences, I expect him to be hostile.

A chain is bolted to the middle of the floor and stretches to one of the dark corners. It rattles against the cold concrete as a man draped in filthy rags emerges from the shadows. His dirty hair clings to his oily leathery face.

"Ah, a visitor, and a pretty one. How indulging. What have I done to be spoiled like this?" he spews. I can detect a slight Russian slur in his enunciation, but he cleverly hides it with a Turkish accent.

"The tongue of the devil is as sharp as the thorn in his ass," I strike back. "So tell me, how does a Syrian defector get caught on the southern border?"

"Wrong place, wrong time."

"Only a fool would say that. Am I to take you as fool then?"

He glares at me with hatred. "Who the hell are you?"

"Your best friend, or your worst nightmare, depending on how you cooperate."

"This childish grilling will get you nowhere, I'm afraid. I've been thoroughly questioned and threatened, and look where it's got me." He holds out his bound hands and feet.

"Maybe you were just dealing with the wrong people." I grab the chair and move it closer to him. "Go ahead, have a seat. We can at least be civilized."

He chuckles in jest and shuffles over to the chair. It doesn't take long to recognize the slightest mannerisms of a common drifter. From the insecure posture to the small crooked smile. Behind that devilish smirk is no killer. This traitor portrays the workings of a simple con man who made a very bad deal. But he won't get any sympathy from me.

"Are you frightened of me?" he sneers.

"Not in the slightest."

"Well, you should be."

"The only thing that scares me is suffocating from the ego that fills this tiny cell."

He laughs. "So what makes you so damn special that they would send you in here with me?"

"Trust me, if any responsible officer knew I were in here, they would be calling the entire battalion to come get me."

He cocks his head, seemingly interested. "Well, as you can plainly see, I'm no threat. You don't need a guard to protect your fragile anxieties."

"The guards are for your protection, not mine." His arrogant grin flattens. "My last interrogation didn't go so well. Was quite messy actually. I've since been banned from consorting with prisoners. If I remember correctly, I believe they said I was . . . unstable."

He sits motionless, refusing to show a sign of fear until I step toward him. A small twitch in his right eye probes my every step. I grab his shackles and notice his bottom lip quivering.

"I don't think we need these anymore, do you? It's not like you're going anywhere."

"You sure that's a good idea?" his voice cracks.

"If we want to trust each other, we need to start somewhere."

"Says the girl carrying a gun," he retorts.

I rustle through the guard's keys until I find one that unlocks the bindings on his hands. He expels a comforting sigh and rubs his chafing wrists. I remove my gun and place it on the table as a good gesture.

"Better?"

"And my ankles?" He points to the shackles.

"Truth feeds trust. Let's chew our food first before we swallow it."

"I don't know what you want from me. I've told the others everything I know."

"Have you?"

"Yes," he smirks.

"Did they ask you about this?" I hold up the metal cylinder the same object Father Joseph spotted on Colonel Dahan's desk. He doesn't flinch at the sight of it.

"I don't know what that is."

"You sure? Look really close." Despite my efforts to expose his lies, he turns his cheek instead, refusing to look. I quickly pull out my dagger from behind my back and rest the edge on his cheek.

"Don't lie to me or I'll shave more than that grizzly stubble."

He answers with a rebellious silence and grits his teeth shut. I press the blade into his oily skin until a bead of blood trickles down his cheek.

"It was given to me," he cracks.

"By who?"

"I don't know."

I move behind the chair, rest my knife on his shoulder, and lean down to his ear. "You might have fooled the others, but I know your game. You and I both know how this is going to play out," I whisper.

"I swear I don't know."

"It doesn't matter. It only proves you're no more than an expendable pawn. No enemy is foolish enough to wander alone in southern Syria unless he wasn't there to purposely get caught. Well, you succeeded, but at what cost?"

Insulted from my remarks, he bitterly objects, "I'm no fucking pawn."

"You said it was given to you, so that makes you a lowly messenger. You really think they care about what happens to you? They offered you a deal, and you were stupid enough to take it. I have no interest in your duty as a messenger or what this object is. I just want to know who you were instructed to deliver this to. Who is your contact?"

"Threaten me all you want, you filthy cunt, but you will get nothing. I'm more than just a messenger."

In order to put a superior man in an inferior position, two things must occur: insult his pride, and inflate his ego. Both have worked, but my patience has worn thin. It's time to end this charade. I hold my knife against his neck, then trail it down his side, his abdomen, and stop at his crotch.

"What the hell are you doing?" he says in a panic.

I slide the knife up and down his thigh. " Did you know that during the Middle Ages a man was punished by castration if he raped another man's wife? A man's lies are no different. Now I can be a patient woman, but I don't have time for an impatient answer, so I'm going to ask you the question one more time, and I pray for your sake that I'm satisfied with the answer. Who is your contact?"

"You don't have to do this. I swear I don't know what you're talking about!"

"That's a shame." I slam my dagger down between his thighs, penetrating the soft flesh of his flaccid penis all the way through to the seat of the chair. His hands tremble violently over the handle, screaming into a bloody fit of rage.

"You fucking bitch!" he curses.

"Shhh, it doesn't have to be this way. I can pull the knife out now, but if you lie to me again, I'll be forced to twist the blade deeper into your crotch, ending any thoughts about sex again."

"Please!"

"Say it!" I grab the handle of the knife and slowly push.

"Yanaton . . . Yanaton Dahan!" he shouts.

"Colonel Dahan?"

"Yes! I swear it, now take it out!"

"You're lucky this isn't a serrated blade, but it's still going to hurt like shit." I grab the knife handle and rip the blade from the chair. The man collapses on the floor, wailing in a small pool of blood.

"You got what you wanted, now help me, please!"

"I did help. I didn't kill you."

I watch him roll on the floor screaming and cursing. A small part of me reaches for mercy, but it's overwhelmed by the other side that keeps me in darkness. In that moment, the pain on Juliana's face surfaces in my mind. Images of those I've lost tear a hole in my conscience. Luke's limp body, Matthew's last dying breath, and Finnegan's stony grave come crashing in on me.

I stand still as a statue while the prisoner writhes the floor in agony. I grow pale from his harsh noises, but I do nothing. Something in me changes, a rising hatred I'm afraid I can't control. A boiling rage erupts inside, nudging me to leave this pathetic man to bleed to death, but just then, a small piece of sympathy surfaces.

"I'll bring back the doctor to patch you up, but that's all I can offer. Your fate is out of my hands now."

I grab my gun and the recording device and exit the cell. Locking the door at this point is trivial. If he escapes from this, then I commend him.

Father Joseph and Ananiah are anxiously waiting for me by the gate.

"Go fetch Roland and Attimus. The prisoner is gonna need stitches."

"So, what's the verdict?" Father Joseph asks.

"We got us a fox in the hen house," I fume, rushing past him.

"Wait, where you going?"

"To kill the fox."

My anger feeds like a brewing volcano, pushing me to the point of no return. While Father Joseph and Ananiah deserve a better explanation, I leave them standing next to the drugged guards instead.

Temper flaring and blood boiling, I head directly to the council chamber. I storm through the doors without warning and plant my fist on Colonel Dahan's face. "You son of a bitch!" He flounders from his seat and falls to the floor. Chaos erupts, men shouting, cursing, and two officers hold me back.

"Arena! What is the meaning of this?" Eizenkot shouts.

I wiggle loose from the officers' hands and lunge at the colonel again. I hold his clean-shaven neck hostage with my knife.

"Do you want to tell them or shall I?" I threaten.

"You're mad!" the colonel screams as blood drips from his nose.

"What the hell has gotten in to you?" Jacob asks with a puzzled look.

"This man—your decorated and trustworthy colonel—is a traitor."

"This is absurd!" the colonel barks.

"That's a serious accusation," Eizenkot adds.

"Arena, put the knife down," Jacob orders.

I pull the back of the colonel's collar and guide him to his seat. "Tell your officers to withdraw their guns and I'll think about lowering my knife."

Eizenkot signals the men to withdraw, but I'm hesitant to remove my blade. Instead, I toss the metal cylinder on the table and observe the colonel's reaction.

"Look familiar?" I ask. He remains silent. I place the recorder device on the table and play back the conclusive evidence from my interrogation with the prisoner. The men are stunned, the room silent and angry.

Eizenkot shoots daggers from his eyes. "Officers, take the colonel to his cell and wait for me," he hotly orders. "Gentlemen, no spy among us will derail our mission. From this day forth, those caught for treason shall rot in solitary confinement for the rest of their days. Whatever deal you struck, I hope it was worth it, Yonatan." Eizenkot rages his fury at the deflated colonel, whose head falls with shame.

Eizenkot is a good and loyal general, but I take umbrage with his soft decision. The wrath I've kept dormant for the last year and a half unravels. I pull the colonel's head back and press my blade against his throat. "If this was an attempt to tear us apart, it has only made us stronger. You can bathe in guilt and slither like the serpent you are, but you will receive no mercy from me. You may have fooled us, but you will never break us."

"Arena, no," Jacob begs.

"Leave him to me. I will deal with his penance," Eizenkot pleads.

My hand trembles as I struggle to pull the knife away from his skin. How can I forgive a man willing to betray the lives of thousands to save his own? No, I refuse to sympathize with a man who prepared to send us all to our death, including my son. I ignore the chatter imploring for the colonel's life and instead heed the angry voices inside my head urging me to slit his throat.

"I'm not your enemy, now let me go," Colonel Dahan begs.

"I find it slightly remarkable that you believe that. No, colonel, you're much worse. You're the slithering worm beneath my enemy's boot," I huff.

"If my arrogance frightens you—"

"The only thing that frightens me is my better judgment to keep you alive."

"Arena, no!" Eizenkot says. Everyone is staring at me, afraid to move.

"Broken or not, we still fight!" I shout. Silence falls over the meeting room. "Remember this day, gentlemen, because the time has come to weed the unjust from the righteous."

I press my blade, ready to slice.

"The war has begun."

Part II

In the Midst of Strangers

CHAPTER 12

The difficulties in saying goodbye are not in the departure, but in the uncertainty of returning. I've left many farewells hanging in doubt, but this one scares me more than ever. It is with the best intensions I must leave my loved ones, even my own flesh and blood. Despite my exit, the smile on my son's face remains burned into my memory. Come hell or high water, I will see him again.

The skies have yet to lift from the dark veil, and rain still refuses to fall. It has been one hundred and twenty-three days since the last rainfall. The sands, still cool, silently drift through the night from stormy winds. Not one star rests above the earth except for one. It peers periodically through the clouds every seven days for reasons unknown, but it reminds us that the vast expanse above still exists. Our world is a revolving shadow trapped in a box. The rising sun is all but a myth now to those born with fresh eyes. Will I ever see the light again?

Morning pushes through, leaving me with another sleepless night, but time has become our enemy. We must make haste to the western region of Damascus to cut off enemy troops.

I'm forced to rest, curled up next to Nadia in the back of a Hatehof Wolf, a light-armored assault vehicle. Nadia has become more than just a confidant, she is my anchor and an inspiration. Her loyalty to fight with me is far greater than the strength of a hundred men. Though I wished she had stayed behind with my son, I'm glad to have her beside me. It's up to Niki now to protect Joshua.

Sadiq, Gabe, Father Joseph, and Jacob follow directly behind us in our large caravan. While most of our troops pack tightly inside cargo trucks, few of us were chosen to ride in these assault vehicles. Beyond the driver, the Wolf's interior can carry up to twelve soldiers if you're okay rubbing knees with one another. Only five remain drivable, and none of them are comfortable. Most of Israel's heavy-armored vehicles were destroyed during the first attacks a year ago. Others have been decommissioned or are waiting in gated military yards on the western and eastern bases.

Nuclear weapons, once the stronghold of defiance and the ultimate threat to civilized nations, are now dormant. When nations fall, so do defenses, no matter who you are. Without deadly weapons of mass destruction and the heavy firepower used to fight from a distance, nations have been relegated to infantry combat. Thousands of years of traditional warfare stands before us, and Russia and China are no exception. When ammo runs dry, we'll be forced to rely on the ancient construction of forged steel. Despite the sheer numbers we'll face, the age of war has returned to the modern era.

Though I've been appointed to Rav Seren, an equivalent to a major, I'm no more than just a grunt willing to fight. A title doesn't protect me from getting killed, but I appreciate the sentiment from general Eizenkot all the same. With Colonel Dahan rotting in a cell, Sadiq now leads the campaign in his place, a daunting task for sure.

I lead one of twenty-five units, traveling the rough roads to southern Damascus in an attempt to lure an enemy advance from Turkey into Jerusalem's government complex filled with explosives. Each unit consists of nearly one thousand troops, but it pales in comparison to the rest of our major forces. While more than one hundred thousand soldiers line Israel's eastern defense along the banks of Jordan and the outskirts of Amman, fifty-five thousand remain stationed in the West Bank protecting the border from northern attacks.

Leading an army into Jerusalem without them knowing will not be easy, but if we want to defeat our enemy, we have to control their decisions. We must stay the course, remain alert, and expect the unexpected. Unfortunately, I'm tired, but I can't rest in this jar-rattling vehicle.

The unleveled streets between the old city and the western border slow our pace, but it pales in comparison to the rocky journey that lies ahead. Major thoroughfares, destroyed by earthquakes, vanish into the desert sands, leaving us with treacherous obstacles. The Natuf pass is kind to no one—a rugged landscape filled with jagged cliffs, unstable ground, and concealed trenches from past wars. It's bad enough being trapped in the back of this assault vehicle with eight sweaty soldiers, much less riding in it across this wasteland. Having Nadia by my side makes the journey less irritable.

I peer through the tiny slits of the armored walls and scan the terrain. The horizon bobs up and down as the truck crawls over the stony ground. The engine idles slowly scuttles before the vehicle comes to a complete stop.

I slide the small steel window that divides the cockpit from us. "Everything okay?" I ask.

The driver exits the car with his crackling radio pressed to his ear. The soldiers look on with motionless expressions, unfazed by our sudden halt. I bang on the side wall for the driver's attention. Something is most definitely wrong. Minutes pass before the back door opens from the assault vehicle. Jacob, Gabe, and our driver stand just outside. Their faces draw an unwanted curiosity.

"What is it?" I ask.

"Change of plans, I'm afraid," the driver responds.

"We've just been alerted of troop movement along the coastal line near Nahariya," Jacob explains.

"What? You've got to be kidding me. That's what, two hundred kilometers away?"

"One hundred and forty to be exact," the driver says.

"That's the least of our worries," Jacob deflects.

"What do you mean?" I ask.

"Our northern adversaries have divided their troops around Tiberias," Sadiq interrupts as he walks over with disgust painted on his face.

"What the hell for?"

"Because they are doing exactly what Colonel Dahan would have done: a simple diversion tactic. That bastard had been working on this days before you exposed him. The southern territory of Turkey harboring this army deployed a day ago from Lebanon. The troop split into two units, one moving along the coast, and the other we believe to be the larger of the two, was discovered just east of the Sea of Galilee near Haspin."

"Where did to get this information?"

"We received an authenticated transcript from our Syrian operatives just moments ago. Our Syrian neighbors held them off as much as they could, but I'm afraid there's nothing left to defend in the lower parallel. The few rebels left fighting have been flushed into the mountains, leaving our alliance severed now. Damascus has been overrun."

"Okay, so we move our troops to Amman and force them into the West Bank. With the size of our defense, they'll have no choice but to detour to Jerusalem. You said it yourself, their end game lies in Jerusalem. Why circumvent it at all?"

"That's precisely what they want us to believe."

"To lead us across the east as far as Jordan? How does that benefit them?"

"It's merely a mirage, a diversion to keep our troops spread thin and focused on the larger brigade instead of the one sneaking through Tel Aviv to take out Camp Ariel Sharon. It's quite smart actually."

The southern IDF base known as Ariel Sharon houses the largest training center in Israel. Located in Yeruham in the middle of the Negev desert, the facility boasts the most sophisticated weaponry in all of the world. Though it lies untouched and inoperable in an underground warehouse, it still remains the stronghold of Israel's military defense. More than one hundred thousand soldiers have trained there. If you want to weaken the IDF quickly, the Ariel Sharon is the base to conquer.

"We can't just allow them to march through Tel Aviv. There's maybe a few hundred soldiers stationed there. We have to help them," I plead.

"Agree, but we don't have the numbers to give up. We can only afford to send one unit to help," Sadiq says.

"Are you bloody mad?"

"Arena, we're severely outnumbered in Amman and the West Bank."

"What are you talking about? Exactly how large is this army?"

"More than we anticipated."

"How many, Sadiq?"

"Two hundred thousand or more."

I gasp. "Please tell me you're lying."

"I really wish I was. Our military is spread thin. We have sixty thousand at most in Amman, and less than forty near Jordan. There are maybe fifty-five thousand soldiers holding the line in the West Bank. They are going to need all the help they can get."

"We cannot abandoned our soldiers in Tel Aviv," I say.

"I have no intension to do that, but I can only send one unit," Sadiq says, frustrated.

"And how many enemy soldiers are expected in Tel Aviv?"

Sadiq looks around nervously. "According to our allies . . . about ten thousand."

Jacob's face falls, but he's not deflated. Unfavorable odds or not, allowing these soldiers to advance and slip through is not an option. It will be the death of us all if they occupy Yeruham. Gabe's sharp eyes gaze fixed on mine like a lion tracking its prey. Not a word needs to be said to know what he's thinking. The subtle nod is more than enough.

"Okay then." I grab the radio from the driver, press the button, and speak into the device, "Sergeant Halprin?"

There's a brief silence before a voice answers, "Go ahead, Major."

"Slight change of plans. We're taking a detour to Tel Aviv. You and Maikef have your men ready to move out. Meet me at point in five."

"Yes, Major."

"Over my dead body," Jacob objects.

"It may come to that if you don't go with her," Sadiq says in jest. "What makes you think you'll change her mind now?"

"I wouldn't quarrel with a crazy woman and her knife," Gabe cracks.

"I'm glad you all think this is funny, because I don't find it amusing one bit," I say.

Jacob gives me a stern look. "Lighten up, I never expected to go without you, sweetie."

"I'm not worried about the task as much as I'm concerned how much farther we'll be away from our son. Something I thought you would understand."

That stings. "That's not fair, Jacob. You and I both know I would do anything to keep Joshua safe."

"I'm not questioning that."

"Then why would you imply it?"

"I don't want to lose my family. Can you blame me for that?"

Once again, I'm on the defensive, and it's a shitty feeling. "I'm doing this to *save* our family," I say in a snippy tone. "If we let those soldiers breach Tel Aviv, we'll be forced to surrender our troops southward, leaving our front line of defense vulnerable. Those soldiers on the front line are protecting our son and everyone else inside that dreary mountain."

"That's what I'm afraid of."

I soften my tone. I know Jacob is worried, and he has every right to be. "They're in good hands, Jacob. We have plenty of soldiers to push back the northern troops into Jerusalem. Our enemy has no intention of moving to the east without any aid. It's just a decoy at best."

"And if they decide otherwise?"

"It won't take much resistance from our troops to force their campaign into Jerusalem, but if they do, my units will be ready for them," Sadiq chimes in.

Jacob huffs in frustration. "And we'll go up against ten thousand? Where's our help?"

"You've got the sea," Father Joseph interrupts. He and Darius, an Egyptian loyalist and leader of the Gaza resistance, walk into our conversation.

"What do you mean?" Nadia asks.

"It would be quite an arduous task to cross a thousand-foot crack in the earth."

"The land outside Rosh Haayin has shifted drastically over the past few months. No man or beast can travel east of Kefar Sava without weeks of rerouting around Shomron's pass. The terrain has been reduced to jagged scars in the earth, leaving no other alternative but traveling the coastline. There's only one road in and one road out, and that's a small window to lead a caravan of ten thousand," Darius says.

"That many troops accessing such a bottleneck of a passage will be to our advantage. We have the sea as an extra line of defense," Father Joseph adds.

I look at him with my brows crinkled. "We?"

"I didn't come this far just to abandon you now. You didn't really think I was going to leave your side?"

"Not for a moment." I smile.

"If we're going to do this, we better do it now," Gabe suggests.

"Well then, going to seem like old times," I say.

"Aye, let's hope this time is better," Gabe replies with a hint of animosity.

His disdain for our enemies has grown beyond rage after they killed Juliana. Our group will never be the same without her. For a quick moment, I catch Gabe looking at Nadia with a secret affection. I know he's in the process of moving on from Juliana, but I'm still struggling to let her go.

"You ready for this, brother?"

Gabe grits his teeth and chambers his gun. "Let's go hunting."

CHAPTER 13

In the dusty, dry desert, there's a long caravan of primed soldiers ready to defend and fight for Tel Aviv. The broken city, once a modern hub of entertainment, sits untouched and inhabited. Brutal battles along the strip ravished the city long before we left America.

Rebuilding the urban landscape fell flat after the long effects of the war. People left in droves to safer locations in the south, leaving an empty city in ruin. Some took the risk and stayed, but it hasn't been the same since. Ananiah told us stories of the earlier earthquakes changing the entire landscape east of Tel Aviv, but I guess the constant shift of the earth has made it impossible now to travel.

Our twenty-truck convoy slowly approaches a dark valley known to the locals as *Os Infernum,* the Mouth of Hell. Not an inviting passage, but it's the only unscathed road to Tel Aviv. Lifeless trees stand bare, covering the scorched hills. This wasteland faces a shadowy existence of oblivion from years of war-ravaged conflicts.

According to our driver, this daunting passage has been known to cast some treacherous resistance from rebellious renegades. The inhabitants of this dead abode hide behind stony crevices, waiting to ambush anyone for food or supplies. Nadia peeks through the small ventilated window and scans for potential attacks. Fortunately, our military presence keeps anyone from trying.

The assault vehicle gradually picks up speed and leads us through the mysterious vale unharmed. I lean back against the metal hull and wait anxiously on the thin padded seat.

Nadia quietly sits next to me and fidgets impatiently with her gun.

The road softens as the minutes pass and the stale air gently blows a horrible stench. I imagine it's the smell of death waiting outside, or one of these soldiers haven't bathed in quite some time.

The uncomfortable silence makes the unwanted voices inside my head unbearable to listen to, and I've had enough. "So, how long have you . . . and my brother—"

"A while," Nadia says quickly. It's almost as if she's been waiting for me to ask. She smiles shyly and avoids looking at me.

"I didn't mean to pry like that," I say.

"No, I'm glad you asked. I was beginning to wonder if you ever were. Secrets rarely last longer than a day around here."

"I guess I've been too busy living in my own world to notice."

She turns to me. "So you're not angry about it?"

"Of course not."

"I just mean, you know . . . your brother dealing with losing someone who's irreplaceable."

"It's fine, I understand," I snap.

"I'm in no way trying to replace . . . Juliana. It just happened."

I take her hand in mine. "I know you're not. If Gabe is happy, that's all that matters to me, and it really isn't any of my business anyway, so forget I asked."

"So, we're good then?"

"You and I are always good. I couldn't think of a better person to be a part of Gabe's life."

"That's kind of you to say, because I really love him."

I have no ill feelings about her affection for Gabe. Juliana has passed and that's that. Whatever issue I thought I had with their relationship has dissipated. We all just want to be happy, safe, and loved.

The engine slowly decelerates and the truck breaks to a sudden halt. The soldiers rustle with their gear while I wait anxiously by the door. Nadia peeks out the window and gasps.

"What is it?" I ask.

"The city . . . it's a complete wreck. Looks like we're displaced in the middle of a warzone."

I grab my gear and draw my gun just as the back door inches open. The pungent air drifts in with a persuasive odor of death. Buildings stand empty like that in Alexandria, a sight I thought I had forgotten.

"Why are we stopping here?" I ask.

"The overpass up ahead has collapsed and our trucks can't plow through all these abandoned vehicles. We'll have to walk from here, but we're not far from the outpost," the driver replies.

Jacob and Gabe exit the truck next to us carrying a wooden crate. They muscle the box across the median and open it. Inside reveals an older B-300 anti-tank rocket system—six thermobaric tandem-propelled rockets with attached warheads and a shoulder rocket launcher.

"We'll need to use these wisely. Unless the outpost has anything similar, this is all we have left," Darius says as he examines one of the rockets. Hopefully the dust falling from it isn't an indication of its expiration.

"Will it work, looks pretty old," Nadia asks. These launchers were produced over seventy years ago. I know the history in and out of these ancient munitions. If there's a book out there about military weapons, I've read it.

"Believe me, it still works. They were developed to last long past their prime," he reassures.

"All right, let's move out," Sergeant Halprin shouts.

Soldiers pour out from the other utility transport vehicles and band together, trekking in ten-by-ten groups. Our three-kilometer hike is on the opposite end of the city near the banks of the Yarkon River. This is the best tactical position to thwart enemy advancement from crossing the only accessible bridge into Tel Aviv.

The highway, blocked by the collapsed overpass, meanders through the heart of the city. Stranded cars and trucks flood the roads, a mere sight of desperation to flee the town. We trudge around parked cars in and out until we reach HaMasger Street, the main thoroughfare that runs to our Israeli outpost. An unnerving quiet rests among the empty buildings. Some are untouched, while others, barely erect, wade in piles of rubble.

I scan the side streets unsure of what to expect. Tel Aviv, once home to more than four hundred thousand people, remains in a state of derelict. A predominately Jewish city and the financial center of Israel, it slowly decomposes by the day. Sadness reflects throughout the vacant storefronts where crowds of onlookers were once alive.

The ground rattles and dust scatters as a flock of birds disperse from a stony corner of a building that's toppling to the ground. No resemblance of humanity remains except for the residual graffiti tagged across scorched walls. Aside from enemy troops, the crumbling structures persuade us to stay alert. Soulless and lost, the empty streets vanish into the darkness, all but one.

A small light flickers between two office buildings. A child's voice echoes from the alley.

"Wait!" I stop in my tracks and urge for silence.Sergeant Halprin raises his fist and the company of soldiers halts.

"Stay here," I tell my squad, "I want to check this out."

Gabe motions me over to the front of the office buildings. I drift quietly on my toes and grasp my sidearm. A woman's voice mutters around the corner, while the crackling light casts dancing shadows on the side of the building.

I peek around and find two women and a young boy standing next to a small fire. One woman holds a jar filled with muddy water while the frail boy dangles a charred rat over the fire. When I move into the alley, the child looks at me and drops the rat. He scurries from the flames and clings to one of the women.

"*'Iinah bkhyr,*" the woman says as she holds the boy firmly to her side. He looks to be eight or nine years old. Both women wear tattered hijabs and grime-covered jeans.

"I'm not here to harm you, see?" I raise my hands in a non-threatening gesture. They cautiously back away. I reach into my bag for a ration of packaged food and offer it to her. Her eyes search my every move as she reluctantly accepts it.

"*Shukraan,*" she nods graciously.

Nadia steps into the alley and hands them a canteen filled with water. The fear of our presence vanishes as the two women take turns drinking.

"Everything okay?" Sergeant Halprin asks, sneaking up beside me.

"Yeah, but not sure they speak English."

The sergeant places his gun on the ground and speaks in an Arabic tongue to the women, "*Hal 'ant huna lawahaduk?*"

"*Nem fielaan,*" one woman answers. The sergeant initiates a conversation before one of the women breaks down and cries. I rush to console her as she falls to her knees in grief.

"They've been here a few days after retreating from the southern Syrian border," the sergeant clarifies. "Both are Palestinian refugees seeking asylum to the north, but after Damascus fell, they were forced into slave camps. With the help of a few rebels, they managed to escape, but she lost her husband and daughter to a band of Iranian militants pouring in from the east."

"Sweet Jesus," Nadia whispers.

"The Russian government recruits radicals to disrupt revolutions from escalating. It's apparent this was one of those groups."

I help the grieving woman to her feet and take her, the boy, and his mother to my squad leader, Eliana, one of sixty-two women soldiers in our unit. The anguished woman embraces Eliana and sobs.

"Please take good care of them, they've been through hell," I say.

"Yes, Major," Eliana affirms.

"And ensure them we're here to protect them."

"*Nahn huna lihamayatk,*" Eliana addresses the two women and boy before she leads them away.

This is what the world has come to, eating rats and drinking puddled water. My heart hardens. I'm done walking on eggshells through this crumbling city. My unit, my rules. I take lead with Gabe, Nadia, and Jacob, urging the others to pick up the pace.

Twenty minutes pass and still no sign of an outpost. The sky rumbles and lightning flashes to the north, but the rare storm is the least of my worries. Just when I give up, the sergeant stops near a large structure where half the building has been decimated. He leads us to the large dome attached to it and calls out a code name, but there's no answer except the grumbling thunder moving closer.

I have a bad feeling this outpost has been eliminated, and Sergeant Halprin can offer no good explanation. "This is where the Fifty-First brigade should be stationed. It's a small unit, but a highly experienced one." His eyes wander about the structure while the rest of us silently wait for an officer to surface from the building.

"Maybe they're on patrol," Jacob suggests.

"Highly unlikely they would abandon their post. You sure this is the place?" I ask.

"Positive, I was stationed here eight months ago," Halprin says in a worried tone.

"Maybe we should take a closer look inside."

The sergeant scans the outer dome before sending two scout officers down the street. They explore the empty road and the dome lobby, but return with no evidence of soldiers.

"Not to be cold, but we don't have the time to waste here."

"I'm going in, there's got to be an explanation," I say, frustrated. I just have a bad feeling about all of this.

"Arena, he's right, our fight isn't here," Jacob advises.

"Just like that, you're not even just bit curious what happened?"

"Admittedly, yes, but we have an agenda, and it's not here."

"Arena, I realize you are in charge, but I strongly recommend we leave. Nobody's here. We must move on," the sergeant proposes.

Something isn't right about this. No soldier would abandon their post and allow as much as a child to pass by. "Move if you must," I say.

Sergeant Halprin motions his men to advance, but I linger back. Though Jacob and Gabe push forward, Nadia stays with me in a last desperate attempt to find some closure. I closely inspect the area with one last scan and discover something peculiar.

"Wait!" I shout. A flickering red dot near the adjacent building catches my eye. I search the source and survey the surroundings. A dust-covered cube hides under a piece of tattered burlap.

"What is it?" The sergeant hastily approaches

"Answer me this: wouldn't we have triggered one of these sensors, alerting our comrades, once we broke the perimeter?"

The sergeant kneels down and examines the cube. His eyes widen.

"What is it?" Nadia asks.

"This isn't ours." He swivels his head like a frightened

owl, eyes alert. Suddenly, my heart races when I look over the sergeant's left shoulder and see a bloody arm from an Israeli soldier who's lying just out of sight.

"Sergeant?"

"What?"

"Behind you."

Halprin turns around, then shouts, "Shit! It's an ambush. Move the troops back . . . now!"

Not a second later, a bullet strikes the sergeant's head and he collapses to the ground. I grab Nadia and sprint across the street to a row of storefronts. Jacob and Gabe split to the far corner as guns fire from the adjacent building above. Bullets freely spray and blast the windows beside me.

"Jacob!" I scream, dashing away from the gunfire. Soldiers disperse and gunshots scatter in a blaze of chaos. Nadia and I dip behind a bullet-ravaged car and wait, but Jacob and Gabe are not in sight.

The fight springs into bloody bedlam, making it far too risky to cross the street to Jacob. Smoke lifts from the top of the neighboring building and fire explodes from its windows. A flood of debris topples to the street followed by few enemy soldiers.

"Arena!" a voice yells from behind. Father Joseph perches on a set of stairs with a metal door cracked open. "Come on," he urges.

I can't get to Jacob, so this is the only way. I cover Nadia as she bolts for the stairs. Another explosion rips the side of the building across the street. I brace the ground as mortar pelts the parked car.

"Run!" Nadia shouts.

A cloud of dust rains down, covering my line of sight from the enemy. I make a quick break, sprinting behind Nadia and Father Joseph and safely inside a dilapidated building. The darkened corridor leads out into a bank lobby. Bullet casings cover the floor. The clank of chains grind together in the back corner.

"Get down," Father Joseph whispers.

An image of a person moves across the lobby, but we might as well be blind. Smoke from across the street smothers any light from entering through the windows. Father Joseph sneaks toward the front, while I inch my way closer to the rattling chain dragging across the floor. Suddenly, the person stops.

The smoke partially lifts and a sliver of light exposes a tall, slender man with raggedy hair standing as still as a statue. I clutch my knife and move closer. Nadia tails behind me and flanks to the right. The man quickly lowers to the floor and out of sight. Like a hunting lioness, I prowl warily on my toes, waiting for the right moment to pounce.

Without warning, the door across the room swings open and the man bolts for it, desperate to escape. He slips through Father Joseph's grasp and races to the entrance. The chain, sliding against the broken tiles, wedges between the swollen cracks in the floor and holds him back.

I strike forward, but Nadia rushes in front of me and tackles the man to the floor. She wrestles him over and shines the torch on his face. His voice cracks in pain. Mouth agape, Nadia stands motionless, almost paralyzed. I look down at the man and cannot believe my eyes.

"Kale?" Nadia whispers.

CHAPTER 14

It's been nearly a year and a half since Nadia's brother, Kale, had left us in Egypt for a world he thought was better. He let his pride lead him to a cunning man, who lured Kale and thousands of others under a false haven. They lined up like cattle, forced-fed with a fabricated ideology of hope. One by one, they held their wrists up, willing to be barcoded in exchange for food and safety, but it was just another deceitful and deliberate scheme for mass tracking. I pleaded with Kale to stay with us, but he refused and alienated himself from the rest of the group, including his own sister. And for what? We've all changed, we've all made mistakes, but we don't have to let that define who we are now. It's a new day, and he will always be my friend.

"Kale?" Nadia says again. Tears flood her eyes.

I grab his hand and help him to his feet. Time wears heavily on his face, but the frail frame standing before me suggests it has been much worse. Nadia, still motionless, stares wearily into her brother's bloodshot eyes. A tear escapes down her cheek before she breaks down into his arms. The emotional reunion, while deserving, must wait. A battle still rages just outside.

Kale turns to me, his eyes sorrowful. "Arena . . . I—"

The front windows shatter and smoke fills the room.

"Save it for later. We got to go now," I assert.

Nadia unhinges the end of the chain from the floor, but the other end is still bound to Kale's ankle. She carries the bulk of its weight and swiftly maneuvers him to the back of the lobby. We exit into the alley and retreat two blocks away to a deserted bus station. The decrepit structure has boarded windows and crumbling mortar, but it's the closest place to hide.

I keep close to Nadia and Kale while Father Joseph struggles to unhinge the chained door. He tugs and tugs, but it refuses to budge. Suddenly, smoke rises into the sky and a flood of gunfire echoes closely behind us. Boots trample the cobbled street around the corner. I slink next to the edge, gun drawn, waiting to unload.

"Hurry it up, we got company," I urge Father Joseph.

Soldiers surge down the street. Nadia leaves Kale against the wall and positions beside me. The rusted door pops and the chain loosens, but it only frees a one-foot gap.

"Let's go!" Father Joseph hurries. He braces himself between the frame and the door edge and pushes, stretching the rusty chain a few more inches.

"Go with your brother, I'll cover you," I say. Nadia follows Kale through the small gap and disappears.

"I can't hold it much longer," Father Joseph says.

Enemy soldiers storm to our position just a half a block away.

"Get in!" I grab the door and pull with all my might to give Father Joseph some leverage.

"What are you doing? You go first." He's straining to keep the door open.

"Stop arguing and get in, old man, or I'll shove your ass in there myself. I'm smaller than you, I'll fit."

"Always so stubborn," he says.

On the count of three, I hold the door while Father Joseph narrowly squeezes through the small gap, scraping his gut on the way. He never once takes his hands off, so now he's standing on the other side to keep it propped open.

I quickly slip through the gap, but my sword catches on something. "Shit, I'm stuck."

Father Joseph pushes the door, but it's useless. I slide back out, remove my sword, and tuck it against my chest. A rush of Arabic voices spew around the corner as I squirm on my side. Heart pounding and soldiers impending, I slip through and close the door with a second to spare. We silently wait in darkness until enemy boots stomp past.

I slide my hands on the dusty floor and reach for one of the others through the dark. "Everyone okay?" I whisper. Nadia shines her torch, illuminating three weary faces huddled together.

"Are you ever going to listen to me?" Father Joseph chastises.

"We're safe, aren't we?" I retort.

"I don't know, can't see a damn thing in here."

"First things first." I grab the band on Kale's ankle and inspect the locking mechanism. "Can you shine the light down here," I ask Nadia. The warped steel bind loosens around Kale's ankle, but it buries against his heel. He grimaces. The long weighted chain attached to it isn't helping either.

"Can you pick the lock?" Nadia suggests.

"I don't have any tools on me. Besides, it appears to be stripped. Going to have to bore a hole through the pins."

"Just shoot the damn thing off," Kale snaps.

"What Hollywood world do you live in? No bullet is penetrating those links. I'm afraid you're gonna have to wear that just a bit longer."

Defeated, he says, "I'm just going to slow you guys down."

"Kale, look at me. We won't leave you, okay? You just hang in there and I promise I'll get you out of here safely, all of us," I say.

"I'm . . . sorry I left everyone. I wasn't—"

"I'm sorry I didn't fight hard enough to keep you, but it doesn't matter anymore, none of it does. What's important is that you are here with us now."

Nadia rests her head on Kale's shoulder and wraps her arms around him. There's a quiet peace, but only for a moment. Somewhere inside the building, shouting erupts. Kale and Nadia quickly hunker to the floor. I pull my gun and dim my torch to my palm.

"Nadia, you stay here with Kale. Father, you come with me."

Father Joseph and I sift through the pitch black and track across the vacant room. With each step, a musty odor creeps in. We cross the rigid floor and reach a broken escalator. A sudden stale draft of pungent air oozes from above and seeps harshly into my nostrils. Small chatter grows in the distance.

"We can't leave them behind," Father Joseph whispers.

"We're not going to. Just stay right here." I shine my torch on the escalator and ascend the debris-covered steps.

"Arena, no." He grabs my arm.

"I'm not abandoning anyone. I just need to take a look and make sure it's clear." He's reluctant to let go, as his keen nature lies on the side of caution, but I must find a safe passage for us. His pursed lips relax and he releases my arm.

"Make it quick."

I climb the cluttered stairs to the next floor. The cacophonous clatter of Arabic accents amble closer, but I cannot tell which direction they're coming from. I quickly turn off my torch and stand in the dark. For a brief moment, the voices vanish, but the abhorrent smell does not. The stench of death dominates the air. I breathe through my mouth, which helps somewhat.

The second floor is veiled in darkness except for a mysterious light flashing from across the room. I follow it like a beacon, brushing my boots gingerly over any debris. With every step, the more I wish not to know what hides in the dark, but it's too late. It reveals itself in a nightmare flashing between the pulsing light.

My boots brush against something soft, but I ignore it. I push quickly across the room toward the light instead. Despite the fleeting effort, I trip over something and stumble hard to the floor. The torch rolls from my hand and flickers on the face of a living nightmare. A roach crawls from a man's decaying mouth. The mysterious blinking light pings in distress still gripped in his cold, dead hands.

I rise to my feet and unwillingly shine my torch across the dark room. Dozens of corpses lie tangled on the floor of the bus station's ticket lobby. What the hell did this? I stifle the urge to vomit.

A six-foot hole in the side of the far wall leads into a dark place I'm not willing to discover. The ticket station stretches a few hundred feet to a set of wrecked doors at the end of the east wing, our only exit. The west wing is showered with broken vending machines barring a sliding glass door. Shattered lights hang from the rafters, blasted by gunfire. Blood splatters, darkened from age, color the bus schedule kiosk in the middle of the lobby. I stand in a war-riddled tomb.

"Arena," Father Joseph's voice echoes. I leave the lobby, stepping over the bodies, and return below. Kale gingerly leans his battered body against the bottom of the escalator and winces.

Nadia's restless eyes stare into mine. "We've got to get him out of here and back to the truck," she says in a defeated tone.

Gunfire erupts just outside.

"We can't stay in here forever," Father Joseph urges.

"We don't have a lot of options," I explain.

"Is there a way out up there?"

"There's an exit, but I don't know where it leads."

Gunshots fire at the back door.

"I don't care if it leads to hell, let's go," Kale implores. He limps up the escalator with Nadia's support.

"Just watch your step up there. We're not alone in here," I caution.

Glass breaks just behind the wall below us followed by shouting. The backdoor slams open and a clatter of voices roar down the hall.

"Go!" I shout.

Guns drawn, I lag behind until Nadia and Kale reach the top. Soldiers spill into the first floor, bumbling in the dark as torches sporadically move about. I climb to the top behind Father Joseph and take one last look below. A light shines past my face.

"*Hnak*!" a soldier barks.

A shot blazes past my ear. I fire back in the dark, chasing the torches, but only a few fall still. The others restlessly file toward the escalator. I grab a smoke grenade from my side, pull the pin, and toss it on the floor. A cloud of smoke cascades down the steps.

"Come on!" Father Joseph yells.

A surge of angry voices vanish behind me as I sprint down the dim lobby. I slip through the doors and follow behind Father Joseph down the hall. The dark corridor leads to a brighter escape where a set of glass doors exit to a skywalk to the adjoining building.

We press forward, but the automatic doors jam shut from a default lockdown. Father Joseph and I maneuver our fingers in the door's crevice and pull, but the tightly sealed doors refuse to budge. Boots clog closely as enemy soldiers advance down the hall. Gunfire echoes around the corridor, zinging through the dark.

"Dammit, I can't get a grip on it," I fume.

Nadia grabs my knife and wedges it between the sealed crevice. She works it a quarter of the way in and pries open a small space. I reach my fingers between the gap and slide the doors apart. Bullets ricochet off the walls. Blood splashes the glass and Kale falls to the ground.

"No!" Nadia screams. She drops next to him and hovers over his body. Soldiers storm down the hall firing at will. Father Joseph braces the entrance as I grab Kale underneath his arms. Nadia grabs his heavy chain while I drag him through the exit just as the automatic doors slam shut.

"Come on!" I shout at Father Joseph.

We exit the building, leaving behind an angry mob, and cross the skywalk. Kale presses against his shoulder and grimaces. His tattered shirt turns red.

"He's bleeding badly. We got to get him out of here," Nadia panics.

Father Joseph lifts Kale to his wobbly feet and helps Nadia aid him across the bridge. We reach midway when a deep thunderous rumble shakes the earth. The glass walls rattle and the bridge floor in front of us cracks.

"Shit, don't move." I stop and warn the others to do the same. A ball of fire explodes in the air across the way, lighting up the street below. Israeli comrades scatter beneath, chasing the enemy into the city.

The blast leaves the integrity of the walkway creaking and shuttering. Two large fissures form on the weakened floor behind us. They crawl slowly in our direction, spreading like a spider's web.

"Okay, let's spread apart and walk slowly along the walls," I caution. "Kale and Nadia go first."

They step along the edge and nearly reach the end, but the bridge weakens and dips slightly to one side. Kale slips from Nadia's arm and loses his balance. He tumbles on the shifting cracks and falls halfway through the crumbling floor.

"Help me!" Kale screams. His legs dangle above the street with the heavy chain weighting him down. Slipping further through, he struggles to find a grip. Nadia stretches her hand to him, but she cannot reach. The hole around him grows, and pieces of the floor fall to the street.

Father Joseph maneuvers over the cracks and stretches the butt of his gun to Kale. The middle of the floor begins to sag. Kale swipes at the gun several times before grasping the stock handle and inching his way up.

Glass shatters from the automatic doors and shots fire across the bridge.

"Go!" I yell, as I fire my gun into enemy mayhem. Father Joseph pulls Kale over the edge and drags him to his feet. The ravaging soldiers breach the doorway and storm across the bridge.

"Arena, come on!" Father Joseph shouts.

I turn and sprint for my life, straddling the cracked floor, bullets whizzing past. The middle of the skywalk sinks in and breaks apart. Soldiers plunge to the street. Glass shatters from the walls, and the bridge collapses beneath my boots. I leap for the exit but fall short, dangling thirty feet from the ground. My stomach drops. "Help!" I shout. Nadia reaches over, but I scrape and claw and slip through her grasp. My legs feel heavy, gravity weighing me down. *This can't be how I die,* I think, as my hands are slipping, my forearms burning. Father Joseph's face peers over the edge, my eyes cling to him, hoping this isn't how we part. He grabs my hand with his brawny grip and pulls me to safety.

Bullets shower across the gap as we escape through a metal door on the other side and into a garage stairwell. I shine my torch through the dusty shaft and lead us down the concrete steps. When we reach the bottom, we find ourselves trapped behind an obstructed exit.

"Oh bloody hell!" I tug on the door, but it won't budge.

"That's fucking great," Kale scoffs.

"Shh, listen."

"*Dhahabuu hunak*!" enemy voices bark behind the door.

"What the hell are we gonna do?" Nadia frets.

I draw my gun and aim it toward the door. "It's our only way out. We fight."

The door swings open and three soldiers push through, each greeted by a bullet to the head. They collapse to the ground. I grab the door handle before it shuts and wedge one of the bodies across the jamb.

"Wasn't much of a fight," Kale quips.

"No, but that might be." I point across the street.

As soon as we exit the building, about two dozen soldiers chase after us. We retreat around the next block and escape inside a destroyed café. Broken windows, toppled patio tables, glass everywhere

"Go to the back of the kitchen and hide," I say.

"What are you doing?" Nadia looks worried.

"Just go, I'm right behind you." I guard the front door, guns raised, and wait until Nadia and Kale leave the dining area. The only way to escape this is to eliminate the threat. I will not have Nadia risk parting from her brother again.

I secure my position by the leaning door and scan the street. No sign of the soldiers. Either we lost them in the chaos or they broke off down another street. Father Joseph stands behind me under a silent tongue, but I know he's waiting to convince me to leave.

"If you're here to thwart my intentions you can forget about it," I say bluntly.

"On the contrary, I'm not carrying around this gun for looks." He flanks to my right and parks the assault rifle through the open window. I spy through the doorjamb and prepare for a fight, but not a soul passes by. The street remains empty and quiet, just like our conversation. I pull away from the door and leave Father Joseph to scout. He squints his eyes through the broken glass and sighs.

"What is it?" I ask.

"They're back." He lowers his gun and cautiously exits the café.

"Are you crazy?" I shout as I race after him. He's not one to do things without discussing, especially in a situation like this. *Has he lost his mind?* Both of my guns are drawn as I follow him.

A dozen Israeli soldiers trudge past, kicking dust into the air. I want to scream to Father Joseph to run back inside, to hide behind something, and then it becomes clear. Jacob and Gabe walk among them, panting from exhaustion. I breathe a sigh of relief. Despite the misery painted on Jacob's face, it brightens when our eyes meet, which is far less than the worry drawn on Gabe's.

"What the hell happened to you?" Jacob embraces me, and his arms feel so comforting..

"We're fine. We got caught up in a bit of an entanglement," I vaguely reply. "Where's everyone else?"

"They're sweeping the rest of area just across the way."

"Where's Nadia? " Gabe anxiously asks. His brows crinkle, unearthing more than just concern drawn on his face.

"She's safe," I assure him. His face relaxes into a small smile.

"Surly this wasn't the entire northern troop we were expected," Father Joseph says.

"I'm afraid not," Command Sergeant Temerls interrupts. He's a large man, six-five, and has a nasty red scar across his cheek. "We suspect they'd been here a while, scouting ahead for troop movement. Maybe a hundred or two, but we've flooded them out. Most are dead. A few retreated north to join the larger brigade that's still advancing."

"How soon will they be here?" I ask.

"Too soon to be hanging around here any longer."

"We must secure that bridge before it's breached. The Yarkon River is our last defense. If we allow them to reach this far into the city, we're fucked," I say.

"Understood. What are your orders?"

"Regroup the company back to Gabirol Street and widen our flanks. I don't want any unwanted surprises," I stress.

Despite the poise radiating from the command sergeant, I'm feeling less confident, not because of the lack of bravery, but from the lack of numbers we'll need to defeat these odds.

Suddenly, Gabe eyes grow big. "What the . . . ?" he gasps. "You got to be bloody killing me."

I turn and see Kale braced against Nadia outside the café.

"My God, is that Kale?" Jacob asks. "How did he . . . ?"

"We don't know. I haven't had the time to delve deeper into his story, and it may have to wait a bit longer. We need to move now," I advise.

Gabe rushes over and braces Kale's minor limp. Nadia closely follows, holding the chain still bound to the iron band around his ankle. A small bit of guilt bubbles inside of me at the sight of Kale gingerly resting his weight on Gabe's shoulder. The last conversation we had before he left our group wasn't exactly kind. I ridiculed him for abandoning us with a man I didn't trust. I was pissed, we both were, but the terms we left on put a small stain on my heart. Not because we were both stubborn, but because I felt responsible for separating him from Nadia. My words pierced sharp and deep that day. I'll never allow that to happen ever again.

"What are we going to do with him?" Jacob asks.

"Well, we can't risk taking him with us. If we can spare a few men, have them take Kale back to the trucks and drive him back to Jerusalem."

We regroup back to the Israeli outpost where the remnants of war stain the streets red. Bloody bodies wait for the beasts to feed on them. Soldiers rummage through their persons and purge useful munitions. A heartless necessity, but war is brutal and it shouldn't be taken lightly.

"The men are ready," Command Sergeant Temerls affirms. He removes a grenade from his pack and gives it to me. "Here, it might come in handy."

I gladly take it and fasten it to my holster.

"Sir," a field officer interrupts. He's holding a tattered olive blanket rolled up like a rug. The sergeant grabs it and hands it to me as if it were a gift.

"Your brother wanted me to make sure you received this. I would have given it to you earlier, but we were too busy trying to not get killed," he jokes.

I unravel the unexpected exchange and find my unstrung bow and a quiver of razor-tipped arrows.

"I thought you might want that," Gabe surprises behind me. "Didn't have much time to fashion the arrows to your liking, but I'm sure you'll make them work."

I smile. "You are full of surprises, dear brother."

Nadia returns with three soldiers prepared for a journey back to Jerusalem. Kale ambles close behind, waiting for their escort. A ragged bandage wrapped around his left ankle replaces the iron-chaffing cuff. Hydrated and reunited, a less strained expression covers Kale's scruffy face. Nadia, however, scrunches her eyes, forging knitted stress lines across her forehead.

"Are you okay?" I ask in a gentle tone.

She glances at Kale. "I'm not going back to Jerusalem."

"But you just found your brother and now you—"

"I'm not going. I came here to fight beside you, and that's exactly what I intend to do."

I let her words hang in the air as they stir inside me. Nothing I can say will change her mind, but I respect her choice.

Kale shuffles over and hugs Nadia, but she refuses to let go. Not a tear escapes from her eyes. I can only assume they've sunken back in and flooded her heart. Farewells are getting harder with each day.

Kale reaches into his pocket and places an object I cannot see into Nadia's palm. Her lip quivers. "Don't be afraid to run," he says.

Though I still don't know how he got here, he leaves us once again, but this time on better terms. Next, he turns to me.

"Arena," he speaks softly. "I was wrong."

Though our last exchange in Suez, Egypt, ended in a heated argument, I see a different man, someone capable of redemption. Before I can offer an amiable response, he stops me with a gesture of his hand.

"Thank you," he graciously adds before departing with the three soldiers. I'm happy Nadia has her brother back. Family is important in these times.

"Let's move out," Gabe says. Troops trudge past, forging a sweeping line about two city blocks. I string my bow, tuck my arrows, and trail closely behind my brother and Nadia. Father Joseph treks along my left, while Jacob scans the perimeter to my right.

The comfort of these two significant men by my side feeds me with hope, but I don't know for how long. I embrace what I have now and leave my future to dwell somewhere else. While a different light casts upon the new fellowship, it shadows the loss of the old. Juliana and Finnegan remain stamped in the folds of my mind. As much as I try to move forward, I still struggle to part with their deaths. But maybe that's how it's supposed to be. Maybe this is how we mourn and celebrate those we've loved and lost. Maybe this is how they never leave us.

CHAPTER 15

The change of scenery morphs into a darker realm as we approach the Rokakh Bridge. Apartment buildings, on the brink of collapsing, line both sides of the littered road. The empty dwellings fade through a gray smoke hung in a haze. Wrecked vehicles, many burned down to the metal frames, pepper the street, barring an otherwise short path to our destination.

A torturous display of human remains are scattered about. Some charred to the bone and others rotting, left by carrion ravaging creatures. A horrendous event laid waste on this end of the city, stalked by famine, disease, and war, but it doesn't discourage our plan to stop another from happening. Soldiers commence, boots shuffling across the battered pavement and meandering around piles of refuse and debris. The treacherous trek makes us more alert.

We reach the south side of the bridge across the Yarkon River, but signs of advancing enemy troops vanish. The clouds part in a circular formation, opening up a black abyss like a dilated pupil. An eerie quiet blankets the edge of the city and the cool air suddenly disappears. A blistering wind swoops down in its place like a shower of heat blown from the breath of hell.

The sand beneath our feet scatters and the skies erupt into a thunderous rumble. A red glow perches on the horizon followed by a faint crowing, drifting in the air. Drawing closer by the second, the clouds fill with frenzied cackling, hailing right over us. The clattering squawks emerge into a full chorus of chaos as thousands of crows fly past. Their coal waxy feathers flap in unison, draping us into darkness.

Sergeant Temerl gawks up at the massive flock. "What mad hell did we just step into?"

"Jacob, hand me your gun." I grab his sniper rifle, scope attached, and climb atop the bridge railing. The last of the crows screech past, except for one that swoops down next to me. His eyes roll back revealing white pupils as the grating caws vanish behind us. Another warning from Michael, I wonder.

My eyes lay pinned to the crow's cold stare. The empty sky stays quiet, but only for a moment. My stomach tosses. Out of nowhere, a raging roar hails down, filling the air with a devilish cry of a horn. The sinister trumpet tempers to an unpleasant key that could trigger nightmares. For two minutes, the dark, terrifying noise blasts, breeching beyond the clouds.

As the acoustic phenomenon dithers, a few soldiers fold to the ground, vomiting. The effect of something evil blows in. Fear envelopes and dispiriting chatter accumulates among the troops.

Michael raps his beak against the sniper scope and flies away. I peer through it and scan the road to our north. Enemy troops pour in through droves around the bend less than a mile across the river. Within minutes, the street fills with thousands of hate-mongering guerrillas trudging forward.

"Sweet holy Lord," I pray under my breath. I expected to fight against all odds, but this scares even me.

Suspicious of my silence, Father Joseph anxiously prods, "What do you see?"

My mind escapes me, numbing my tongue to respond.

"Arena, what is it?" Jacob impatiently echoes.

I regain my composure and admit with honesty, "We may need a change of plans."

"What are you talking about?" Sergeant Temerls interjects.

"We're going to get our arses handed to us."

"Your words are not comforting nor helpful," the sergeant says.

"They weren't meant to be."

"How many of them?"

"More than expected."

Temerls huffs in frustration. "If we retreat now, we risk losing everything."

"I have no plans of retreating, Sergeant. We came here to fight, and it's a fight they're going to get. We just need to slow them down."

"What do you have in mind?"

I'm at a loss, so I scan the road behind me and quickly devise a plan. "We create a blockade on the bridge, bunching as many troops as possible before they cross, and use whatever heavy munitions we have to take them out. It won't stop them all, but it should discourage them from advancing across the bridge."

"And what for the rest?"

"The river won't keep them from moving forward, butit will damn well put them at a dire disadvantage. We'll force them to trek through the water while we have the higher ground, and that's when we strike."

"And if they overrun us? We don't have the numbers to outlast them."

"We won't need to," Father Joseph chimes in. "Indeed we're outmanned, there's no looking past that, but it's our best chance to take advantage of their vulnerable position. I don't see any other way out of this. It's a solid plan."

"And we're wasting time talking about it," I impatiently bark.

"What do you need from us?" the sergeant asks.

"Gather every able man and have them push as many abandoned cars as they can onto the bridge behind us. Pierce any oil pans you can get to. If you can sever fuel lines, do it. Any residual petroleum will certainly help. If those tandem rockets work like you say they will, we should be able to light up that bridge with a wall of fire. It might hold 'em for a while."

"I'm on it!" The sergeant dashes away and barks orders. Soldiers maneuver vehicles near the middle of the bridge, wedging several rows of abandoned cars tightly across the road, many of which leak puddles of oil.

I remain on atop the bridge railing and focus through the riflescope. A sea of enemy troops closes in about a half mile away. Michael sweeps back from the clouds and perches on the edge of the railing beside me.

"What do you think, too many to stop?" I whisper to my feathered friend. His beak stretches agape, and his marbled eyes morph red as blood. Moaning clatter brews from his throat as he bows his chest and flutters his wings. Louder and louder the buzzing grows until a swarm of winged insects exits his beak.

The creatures fill the sky in a tizzy, humming in eerie unison. Emerging fear plagues below as my platoon gawks at the unnatural sight. I peer through the scope and follow the flying pests. They hover above the enemy caravan then pour down like rain. Soldiers scatter in disarray, delaying their advance, screaming. Hundreds of crows descend from the clouds and accompany the insects' assault, pecking out eyes, plucking pieces of hair and scalp, and digging holes in skin. Again, Michael vanishes without a trace.

"Arena, let's go!" Jacob urges.

I climb down on the barricade of cars and scan for a sniper's post. Several troops with empty cans of petroleum dash at Sergeant Temerl's orders. Jacob nudges me to move, but I can't take my eyes off the demolished overpass just across the bridge—a perfect spot to engage by surprise.

"Wait, I've got a better plan," I say excitedly.

"We don't have time to alter strategy. Let's peel back with the others and wait."

"Just give me a hundred men to post on that overpass. There's enough protection up there to keep us safe."

"You don't know that."

"You're right, I don't, but I do know it'll give us an edge, and right now that's exactly what this brigade needs."

"It's too risky."

"I'm running out of ideas here. Risk is all we have left."

"This is a war, the odds are against us, and I'm pretty damn sure risk is not on our side."

"We cannot have our enemy knowing we're outnumbered—they're going to figure it out sooner than later. But if we can engage them from behind their line, then they'll think they're surrounded and lose confidence."

"I can't believe we are arguing over this."

"It's worth a shot, Jacob!"

"It's not worth it to me if you're dead!" His eyes are wild with emotion.

I feel defeated. I understand his stance, but I don't have to agree with it. Gabe and Nadia say nothing. Their silence tells me enough. I'm outnumbered, so I reluctantly give in and join Jacob with my platoon.

Soldiers gather above the grassy hill and set a line of strategic defense behind a small concrete wall. Nadia and Gabe park next to a broken statue while Jacob retrieves additional ammo. I wait, restless and discouraged. I can't get the overpass out of my mind. It just seems like the obvious choice of where to station soldiers.

"Arena, you okay?" Nadia asks.

"Something feels wrong here."

A brisk draft swoops down, brushing across my face. I raise my eyes and follow Michael sweeping down from the clouds and onto my shoulder.

"I really think that bird has an obsession with you," Gabe jokes, leering uncomfortably at my feathered friend. Michael leans forward, mouth opened, and a small silver key falls from his beak. I snatch it before it hits the ground.

"Now what the bloody hell is that for? " Gabe so eloquently asks. "He brings you a peach pit in Cairo and now an old key. Either he likes bringing you junk or that bird is cursed."

Michael leans into my neck and rolls his eyes, revealing the white. Nadia gasps.

A breath of whispers drift from his beak and into my ear: "If you want to save your friends, take the key and follow me across the bridge now."

Without Jacob in sight, a moment of doubt seeps in, but I don't believe Michael would lie to me. I close my eyes and meditate on his words before I carefully heed his suggestion.

"I know it sounds crazy, but I have to get across that bridge now," I say quickly. Nadia and Gabe's face falls deadpan.

"You're right, it's lunacy, enemy soldiers are going to pour in any minute now, and you want to run to them?" Gabe says, incredulous.

"Jacob's not going to like this," Nadia warns.

"He doesn't have to, but I need to do this."

"Why, it makes no sense?"

"I don't expect you to understand, but—"

"Give us a break, Arena," Gabe snaps. Look, I've been through some crazy stuff on this journey with you and I've always trusted you, but this is nuts."

"Have you ever had a gut feeling and you don't know where it manifested from, but you know deep down it feels right? That's exactly how I feel when this crow is around. He's been a call for warning ever since we first met."

"So a crow perches on your shoulder and you think, 'What the hell, I think I'll run off and do some stupid shit'? Have you gone mad?" I hate it when he gets like this; there's no reasoning with him.

"I don't have time to argue with you. You're just gonna have to trust me on this," I snap.

Michael lifts from my shoulder and flaps angrily above us. Nadia grabs my arm and pleads for me to stay. Michael releases a rasping caw before flying toward the bridge.

"I'm sorry, but I don't have time to wait, I need to go now." Maybe I am insane, but it's too late. I dash after Michael across the bridge and reach the barrage of vehicles. While my decision seems dangerously stupid, it's equally embraced. When I turn around, Nadia is directly behind me and Gabe is sprinting toward us. "I don't understand your reasoning, but I vowed to fight beside you, and that's what I'm going to do," Nadia says. Her loyalty will never cease to amaze me.

Gabe slips next to Nadia, panting, "And I didn't think there was enough crazy left. You've had some really stupid ideas, sis, but this is surely at the top."

"So you're coming then?" I smirk.

"Well, of course. You need me."

I welcome his sarcastic presence any day. "Seems like old times, dear brother."

We trod over the barricade of cars and stretch our legs across the other side of the bridge. With troops moving closer, we find ourselves plodding deeper into the mouth of hell. Michael plunges from the dark sky and flies beneath the overpass where the main road will soon fill with thousands of enemy troops marching past.

I grasp the silver key tightly in my palm and quickly follow after. I wonder if I made the right choice to split from our unit. With Jacob across the river, worrying where I am, there better be a good reason why I put my faith in Michael's dangerous advice.

We follow the crow's shadow beneath the overpass closer to enemy territory. The voices of evil men approach from down the street. My stomach knots. What have I gotten myself into? Michael perches on a dusty tarp, nestled in the corner of the remains of an old bank's concrete façade. The interior, charred and hollow, is married to the sands beneath it.

An urgent caw bellows from his beak. I hustle toward his squawking warning and examine the large sandy cover. Gabriel lifts the tattered burlap and gasps. Hiding underneath is a monstrous steel contraption: a fifty-five gallon barrel with fins tapered to the bottom.

"Holy shit, do you know what this is?" Gabe marvels.

I wipe the dust away from a metal panel. "Not in the slightest, but it doesn't look friendly."

"It's a barrel bomb. They were used in War World II and throughout invasions during the 1960s. But this one is slightly different. See this here?" Gabe points to some sort of panel embedded on the side.

"Barrel bombs were detonators, some crudely assembled with fuses. Half the time they exploded before they even hit their target, but this one is a bit more sophisticated. That panel tells me there's electronics crafted in this beast."

"Why didn't it go off?"

"I don't know, maybe it was a dud, maybe someone forgot to set the timing sequence."

I peer at Michael. He thumps his beak above the panel, knocking loose the caked-on dirt where a slot for a key appears. Without hesitation, I fit the small silver key easily into its rightful slot and turn it. The panel glows green and a numeric LED interface lights up. A deep hum vibrates around the girth of the barrel.

What the hell is that noise?" Nadia asks.

"I think I know exactly what your little feathered friend had in mind now." Gabe says. "This is where the timer can be set manually to detonate, but I honestly don't have clue what kind of damage this thing will do."

"Does it really matter?" I sweep my arms at the ruined city.

"It does if you're around," he says with a smirk. "But seriously, this isn't your typical barrel bomb, and judging by the size of the body with the explosives used in the modern era, I'd guess there's enough here to wipe out five city blocks."

"Shit," Nadia mutters.

"Exactly."

"No, not that." Nadia points down the street.

Angry voices perilously loom as enemy troops trample the pavement just two blocks away.

"Look, I don't care, just set the damn thing long enough to lure in the bulk of the troops. Less soldiers, less to kill. It's what's gonna save our arses."

"Okay, okay, ten minutes should do it. Gives us enough time to get back to the other side."

Spotted just to the right, a small enemy platoon advances from a backstreet and storms toward us. Bullets shower the air, pelting against the concrete façade.

"Hurry!"

Sweat drips from Gabe's brow as he presses a few buttons. "Okay, it's done, let's go!"

I pick up a stone and bash the key to the side. It breaks off, leaving the slot in a locked position. We cover the activated bomb with a dusty burlap and sprint back. Gunfire rains down as soldiers follow us to the bridge. Finally, the river is in sight, but out of nowhere, another ban of enemy soldiers strike from the eastern causeway near the overpass. The raging brigade blocks our chance to cross the bridge, forcing us to retreat further away from safety.

Locked in step, we maneuver through the western village with bullets tagging behind us. The battered streets crumble beneath our pounding feet. Chasing on our heels, soldiers drift closer, guns ablaze. I stop behind a car and fire back. Soldiers topple, but more take their place, racing toward us.

"There's too many!" Nadia panics.

Fifty or so soldiers charge from the north, spilling into the streets. We're trapped. Suddenly, a plume of fire surges into the sky behind us, lighting the dark clouds with shimmering amber. For a split second under the bright cascade, I spot an opening in front of a towering hotel across the street.

"This way!" I shout.

We break across the littered road, desperate and outnumbered. Shots blindly shower through the dark, zipping past. Soldiers scatter like cockroaches between the buildings and storm after us.

We escape through the broken door and slip inside. Glass shatters behind us. A deep rumble shakes the building and parts of the ceiling crumble to the floor.

"Down here!" I scramble with my torch and shine it down a long hallway.

"I hope you have a better plan than this," Gabe says as he pulls out his pocket watch.

"Just give me time to think." I cover my ears, hoping it will help me concentrate before hundreds of soldiers ambush the hotel.

"You've got about five minutes to decide before we find ourselves permanently buried. Those angry assholes after us are the least of our worries. I don't know what that bomb is capable of doing."

"How bad is it really?" Nadia urges.

"If we stay here, I'd say anywhere in between *we're fucked* and *we're gonna die.*"

Clamoring voices blast through the front door, quickly filling the lobby. We retreat into the next hall and sprint down until the carpeted floor meets the wall. All the rooms are locked except one behind a set of double doors. A small beam of light breaches through a large window in the nearly blackened room. I shine my torch as we weave around toppled chairs and tables scattered across the spacious venue floor. The doors suddenly swing open.

I shove my torch into my palm before turning it off. We wait in silence, lying on our bellies in the dark.

"We got maybe three minutes before this place buries us," Gabe whispers.

Five soldiers slowly wander into the room. Anxiety boiling, I search the room for an exit. There's a metal door about twenty feet ahead. Locked or not, it becomes a risky mystery if we decide to make a quick break, but we don't have time to wait out these assholes. It's do or die.

"That door is our only hope," I whisper. "You get out and find a way below ground." I slide quietly on my belly to the middle of the room.

"Arena, what the hell are you doing?" Gabe says.

"Saving your arse, now go."

I slither across the floor with a Ballistic Spetsnaz blade in my hand—a terrifying nightmare for anyone hiding in the dark. Gabe and Nadia scoot closer to the door.

While shadows flicker pass the beaming light in the window, a lone soldier stands near me. I quietly crouch to my feet, and like a bullet blazing through the air, I propel the tip of the knife into his throat. He collapses to the floor nary a murmur.

Shadowy figures drift past without even noticing. Creeping on my toes, I push silently through the dark and cut the remaining soldiers to the floor except one: a brawny man who is standing in front of the lit window. He remains steadfast, inching closer to the back of the room.

I slink upon his heels, gripping my knife. He's but a few steps in front of me, but the back door suddenly creaks open. Gabe, stooped in the opening, looks back. The soldier stops and shoots. Nadia fires back and kills him dead, but the damage is done. The gunfire sends dozens of soldiers storming down the hall and into the room..

A parade of torches sporadically beam and shine across my face as I sprint toward the exit. Bullets chase, firing at will. I slip through the door and follow Nadia and Gabe down the long stretch of concrete floor that fades into darkness. Heart pounding and adrenaline surging, I fear I've lost them until the flip of Nadia's hair whips around the corner. My body almost involuntarily follows behind.

A deep rumble echoes and the walls vibrate. "Come on, down here!" Gabe shouts from down the hall. He opens a door and waves Nadia through.

A sweep of warm air pushes behind me and nearly knocks me to the ground. I reach the door and race down the passage to a set of stairs. The building violently shakes, and pieces of the ceiling crumble. I skip every other step, charging below. The railing comes undone and the walls crack and start to collapse. The floor above explodes into chards of debris and sends me tumbling down the stairs.

I brace my fall and slam into the concrete wall below. My lungs fill with dust and my eyes wander into colors of blue before they meet blackness.

CHAPTER 16

I can't move. I'm standing in the middle of darkness, desert sand sifting between my toes. A small shuddering light falls from the sky and stops short before plummeting to the ground. It hovers over the golden sands, unveiling thousands of divots hiding in the dark.

The ground shakes, pulsating pockets of air from the pitted desert like a bubbling cauldron. My feet begin to warm and my lungs burn. The ground splits open to blood-curdling screams as thousands of hands pierce through the sand. The gapping cavern fills with blood, pushing piles of tussling bodies to the top.

My feet stay bound to the desert heat, and my eyes fix unwillingly to the horrific scorched chaos. Fire erupts from the devil's chasm, setting a chorus of screams ablaze.

A dark figure emerges from the sand and passes through the flames. It approaches me, hand extended, and lowers a hooded veil. An androgynous face, pale as winter, flashes a devilish smirk. Brows vanish behind milky skin, accentuating its sallow and sunken eyes. Only a face like this lives in darkness in a world as scourged as this one.

The ground shakes once more as thousands of roaches scurry from underneath the creature's cloak. Its mouth opens wide, jaw stretching to its chest. Restless chatter rises from its throat before blinding light pierces after.

"Arena, Arena!" a deep voice echoes.

I'm caught between a world of chaos and a world my eyes cannot see. Just the hollow sound of my name called over and over. The entirety of my being remains numb. I can't tell if I'm reaching out with my hands. I feel nothing but the bright light weighing on my eyes, until my hand, grasped by another, warms. Pain suddenly throbs throughout the rest of my body while the bright light slowly fades.

My eyes blur for a moment as the faint sound of a woman hovers over me. Shades of black begin to mingle as two figures flash above. My eyes slowly adjust to the dark and meet the faces belonging to the voices.

"She's awake." Nadia places her hand behind my head as I try to sit up. "Take it easy, you took a pretty good blow to the head."

"Where are we?" I ask, dazed and confused.

Gabe shines his torch around the room. "As far as I can tell, in a maintenance tunnel."

"What the hell happened? How did I get here?"

"Well, the barrel bomb did what it was supposed to do, maybe a little too well. The ceiling collapsed and trapped you at the bottom of the stairwell, but you're alive, which is far less I can say for anyone on the surface."

"Shit, Jacob?" I try to sit up further, but I flinch in pain. My body hurts and my ears are ringing.

"I'm sure the explosion didn't reach that far," Gabe responds.

"How can you even know that?"

"Look, even if it did, they would have received minimal impact." The lack of confidence in his answer makes my heart sink.

"Is that your expert assessment, or are you trying to put my emotions at ease?"

"Honestly, I really don't know what to expect out there."

My fingers gingerly graze over the cut on the side of my forehead. The wound has scabbed over and the blood on my elbow has dried. "How long have we been down here?"

"Maybe a couple of hours."

"What?"

"It took us a while to unbury you from the debris. You've been unconscious the entire time."

"If Jacob is out there, he's probably searching for us right now."

"We haven't heard a peep since we've been down here."

"We need to leave now." I rise to my feet and wobble against the wall.

"Whoa," Nadia braces my shoulder, "you're in no condition to go anywhere."

I brush away Nadia's assistance and stand firm. "I'm fine, I just got up too quickly."

"You're as stubborn as a drunk sow."

"Am I?" My head is pounding.

"Yeah, and it's going to put us all in danger."

My lungs burn as I bow over into a coughing fit. I swipe Nadia's canteen on the floor and soak my dust-coated throat. Without warning, I heave a cloud of mud from my gut.

I wipe my mouth and grit my teeth. "The only danger we're in is filling our lungs with more of this ash and dust. I suggest we find a way out of here and fast."

"If there is one, we'll have to go through here." Gabe points to the only exit not blocked by fallen girders and debris. The maintenance channel to the left stretches too far for my torch to reach the end. I balance my way across the room, grab my weapons, and cautiously follow through the unstable tunnel.

The dark passage, unused for some time, is dormant except for the few roaches scurrying across the floor, searching for water. Large rusted pipes run along the edge of the upper walls, hollow and parched while crinkled ducts dangle from the ceiling. There's a solid steel door to the left, but it's locked.

Near fifty paces now and not a sign of light. Though an occasional drift of air swoops past, it leaves us searching for an exit that doesn't exist. The farther we leave the stairwell, the darker it becomes. A soft chill brushes against my skin, now raised with bumps. Something other than the quiet hides in here with us.

A small blip of light flickers in the distance, but just faint enough that it might be my imagination. I stop and glance behind me with my torch.

"What?" Gabe lowers the light from his face.

"Just making sure you guys are still back there."

"We're here, and whatever brushed past my leg."

Nadia digs her eyes toward Gabe with an unflattering twitch. "Please tell me you're kidding."

"Probably just an old cat wandering around."

"A cat, seriously?" I jeer.

"I can't see a damn thing in here, okay? We're wandering in an abandoned underground dwelling, buried among God knows what on ancient soil . . . so yes, a cat. I'm going with a cat. It makes me feel a little better that maybe, just maybe, a cuddly cat wandered in here and decided to brush his fluffy fur against my leg, and who cares that it's creeping me the hell out!"

"Okay, okay, no reason to lose your shit over it."

The faint light flashes up ahead again. "Am I losing it in here, or is there something blinking in the distance?" I ask.

"I see it," Nadia answers.

We pass nearly twenty paces when the tunnel bends to the right, the walls narrowing into a lonely and haunting dead end. A small opening between the broken ducts thrusts warm, stale air into the chamber. I struggle to breathe, still coughing bits of dust from my lungs. And I'm starting to get claustrophobic.

Gnashing metal resonates and pieces of debris crumble to the floor. I shine my torch at the ceiling, which is buckling, shifting, and bulging from excess weight.

"That's not good," I begin to panic.

Surely there's another way out of here, but it's too damn dark to really know. I graze my hand against the wall, probing for a light switch, but instead find something more useful—a ring of keys hanging on the end of a screw.

"Maybe our luck has changed," I say.

The metal duct loosens, creaking and swaying just above my head. The bulging ceiling cracks, sending a warning of inevitable tragedy.

I grab the keys and push Nadia into Gabe, retreating from the unstable chamber. "Run!" I shout.

We sprint around the corner into the wider corridor where the walls violently shake. The ceiling collapses, filling the space with debris. I cover my mouth as a clatter of metal and wood crashes to the floor behind us.

Nadia and Gabe fade in front of me as my eyes blur. I reach out to grab Nadia's shirt, but she disappears in a cloud of dust. Struggling to find my way, I burst forward through the haze and stumble to the ground next to Gabe. The three of us are hacking up earthy soot and powdered fibers.

"Always touching stuff you shouldn't," Gabe says, panting.

"Oh, I'm sorry to put such a damper on things, I didn't realize finding a way out of here was our goal." I sling the keys at him.

"Just remember whose genius idea it was to ignite a bomb," Gabe scoffs.

"Enough!" Nadia shouts. "Quibble among yourselves another time. Let's just find a way out."

The only accessible door is hidden behind a curtain of dust. The collapsed tunnel leaves us trapped underground with nary a drop of water. We share a sip from Nadia's reserve canteen that will soon run dry.

Gabe shuffles through the assortment of keys. He looks at Nadia with a disgraceful grin. "I have no shame in telling you that if none of these keys open that door, I may possibly cry."

Despite my brother's dishonorable admission, he's right. This may be our only chance, and I will also be discouraged if these keys don't work.

"Give me your torch, mine's dead," I say to Gabe.

I cover my mouth with a piece of torn cloth and carefully guide back through the maintenance channel. A peculiar tapping echoes from the walls. In unison, three times it taps, pauses and taps again.

"Please tell me that was you?" Gabe shudders.

I shine my torch through the cascading particles, but see nothing but a trail of fallen debris. Again, three taps, but from where is unknown. Gabe, nearly on my heels, follows along the wall to the locked door. It's dented, as if someone was desperately trying to get out. I hover the light over the lock and anxiously wait.

Gabe sifts through the keys. One by one they struggle to fit. He turns from the lock and sighs.

Tap-tap-tap, the sinister rhythm continues to mock. "Dammit, I can't concentrate!" he lashes out. He pounds his fist against the door. There are a handful of keys left. He clenches his jaw in frustration.

Gabe battles with the unnerving tapping as he tries each key. With a deep breath and a firm twist, the last key refuses to turn. Defeated, he hammers his forehead against the door. The contemptuous tapping continues on schedule, adding to our aggravation.

"Seriously! What the hell is that noise?" Gabe boils.

Three taps every four seconds. I may be stuck in here, but I'll be damned to be stuck in here with that hellish knocking. I close my eyes and lend my ears to the dark, following that disdainful rapping. The sound grows more precise closer to the wall on the opposite side. I open my eyes and lean against the wall, tracing the sound down the hall.

Louder and louder, the tapping echoes behind the pipes until I reach a metal cabinet resonating with its hypnotic knock. The tapping causes my hand to vibrate against the cold metal side.

"Help me move this," I impatiently usher.

Gabe places his hands against the side of the cabinet. "You sure this is a good idea?"

"Is there ever a good idea in pitch black?"

"Not unless I'm seeing the backs of my eyelids."

Nadia raises the torch near the wall—the light is fading. On the count of three, Gabe and I push the cabinet away from the wall, the hellish squeal of metal scraping against the floor slides up my spine.

Hiding behind the cabinet, an old door is recessed into the wall and painted to match. A large padlock dangles from the worn latch. The tapping raps behind the door. Who knows what might be waiting on the other side, but there's no other way out.

"Hand me those keys."

"You really want to open that?"

"It's just a door, Gabe."

"Yeah, but why was it hidden? I'm sure it was locked for a very good reason."

"Well, let's find out."

I shuffle through the ring and stop at a key that's much shorter than the others. The tarnished brass edges, rubbed worn from constant use, slips perfectly in the keyhole. I turn the key and the lock pops open without resistance. The perpetual tapping suddenly ceases.

I draw my gun and slowly pull the handle. The door creaks opens to complete darkness. A screeching breeze blasts through with a rustling sweep of flapping wings.

"Bat!" Gabe shouts.

Nadia chases the bat with her torch as it dips and dives around Gabe, slipping onto the floor. Then I realize it's a crow. Michael, my mysterious guardian, hovers briefly before perching on my shoulder.

"Dammit, Arena, your friend scared the shit out of me," Gabe scolds, pulling himself to his feet. "I swear that crow is going to be the death of us one day."

"Yeah, well until then, I believe a thanks is in order. We just found a way out of here."

I shine my weary torch through the opening, but the light fades before it reaches the end. Twice, Michael caws and lifts from my shoulder, then hovers a few feet ahead. I step through the door and follow after before he vanishes into the dark hall.

The earthy floor crackles beneath my boots. I stop a few steps in and guide my torch to the ground. The floor moves across the light.

"Ah, shit."

"Wh-what is it?" Nadia asks nervously.

"Whatever you do, don't look down. Just concentrate on the back of me."

"*Makak*?" Gabe precisely guesses.

"What does that mean?" Nadia asks.

"You don't want to know."

I quickly raise my torch and try to forget the granola crunching ground. One of the world's largest cockroaches lives in Israel, and our feathered guide has led us to walk among a hoard of them.

"Come on." I move forward.

The tunnel, almost cylindrical, stretches as far as my torch will allow, but I trust there's a way out. The walls, constructed of cobbled stones and ancient mortar, keep anything above from caving in. The work of labored hands crafted by slaves, perhaps. Surrounded by modern structures, this piece of ancient architecture lies beneath the earth with a history untold. What stories might have traveled this ground have now been replaced with what scurries across it.

A sudden warmth of air drifts past and something screeches behind us. My eyes focused, I forge ahead, but the claw-scraping clamor continues, louder and louder. Gabe leans into me, nearly tripping me.

"What fresh hell is that behind us?" he quavers.

"Just keep moving," I advise. No doubt, something sinister is here.

Suddenly, whispers seep across the dark, calling my name. I stop.

"What is it?"

I slowly turn and see red glowing eyes peering back at me. A dark figure lifts from the ground and reaches out with long crooked limbs. Fear floods over me.

"Go!" I yell.

We scamper across uneven floor and chase the light at the end of my torch. It grows wider and wider until it stops in front of a bronzed door, slightly askew. Michael flaps through a small vent just above it.

I quickly pull on the handle, but my hands slip. The latch mounted on the stone frame keeps the door tightly shut. Ominous sounds of an animal feeding draw closer.

"Hurry, help me with this."

Gabe tosses his torch and pushes against the wooden clasp. Even with both of us, it's useless. The door stands firm from years of neglect.

"Stand back!"

I kick the iron latch that's burrowed into the wooden bar, and it rattles askew and loosens. We push once more with all of our strength and free the bar from the splintered frame. It clears the hasp, but the door remains wedged.

Gabe leverages his boot against the wall and tug on the handle, but it doesn't budge. Suddenly, a hellish growl echoes and the ground begins to vibrate. Nadia's light flickers, and like the breath from the devil, a warm, stale breeze pushes up against my neck.

"Help me!"

With a desperate surge of strength, the three of us heave the door from the jamb. The heavy six-inch steel slowly cracks open to a burst of fresh air. When I turn around, I'm stunned in fear as the glowing eyes race quickly toward us.

"Go!"

Nadia and Gabe push through the other side as I slip through after. I peer back through the opening with Nadia's torch and almost faint. A human-like creature gallops on all fours. A hellish shriek bellows from its throat as blood gushes from its eyes. The skin on its chest stretches outward and the face of a child forms, screaming.

I drop the torch. "Close it!"

With the same desperate urgency, we push the door shut, but it doesn't close all the way. "Close the door!" I scream, my voice cracking in pure panic. The creature charges closer. Its human face stretches into the light. We push with all our might, inching the door closed. Teeth gnashing and limbs thrashing, the demonic beast leaps at the door before it slams on its ghastly face.

We lie at the bottom of concrete steps, gasping for air, our hearts pounding and muscles fatigued. The welcoming quiet binds our tongues.

"What . . . the fuck . . . was that?" Nadia breaks the silence.

"I don't know, but I'm never going through another damn tunnel," Gabe says.

"Why was the door locked from the inside?"

"Someone was sure hell-bent on keeping anyone from getting in," I surmise.

We find ourselves safely inside the interior of another stairwell, less threatening than the room we just left. A dimly lit skylight hovers nearly thirty feet above, illuminating traces of blood stained on the concrete stairs. Each step, bloodier than the next, ascend to another door hiding in the shadow. Our feathered friend taps its beak behind it.

"If that damn bird leads us into another shithole, I'm gonna lose it," Gabe grumbles.

We climb to the top without haste, cautiously expecting danger. Thankfully, the door opens without effort. We step into a deserted loading dock untouched from the destruction. Tracks of blood trail across the floor and into an open trailer truck that's resting against the dock bumpers. I don't need to follow the tracks to know how it ends. Instead, we explore farther away and up a small incline to several cargo doors. One door, damaged beyond repair and slightly raised off the ground, draws light from the outside. My doubts abate and find confidence. The only place I want to be right now is outside in the fresh air.

We slip underneath the two-foot gap and stand beneath the darkened skies. I suck in a breath, stunned. I'm in disbelief to a horrific site of unimaginable devastation.

"My God, what have we done?" Nadia whispers.

Tumbled stone, ash, and piles of debris scatter the new landscape. We amble through the rubble where streets vanish into toppled structures. Bodies, more than I can count, lie in waste, some twisted like ragdolls, others without limbs. Clouds of dust lowly float, drifting southward toward the other side of the river. How far the devastation goes, I don't know. I draw a deep breath and hope Jacob and the others were not affected.

Most of the destruction lies scattered on the main street from where we arrived. It's uncertain if anyone made it out of here alive. Gabe stops and hovers over one of the soldiers.

"What is it?" I ask. He stands there in a trance without a response.

The soldier's leg twitches, and his arm raises above his chest. His hollow eyes stare at me. Blood covers his torso. A metal shard protrudes from his ribs.

Gabe pulls his gun from the holster, hand shaking. I quickly grab it and lower it. "No, waste none."

Nadia stands next to Gabe, her eyes teary, and she looks away. The dying man mumbles incoherently before I jab my knife into the side of his head. What's done is done, and it won't be the last. Gabe struggles to look away. I can sense a share of sympathy hiding behind those glazed eyes. We're still human.

"Come on, let's grab what essentials we can."

"How far away do you think they got?" Nadia wonders of Jacob and the others.

"It's been hours. If they haven't searched for us by now, we've got a long journey ahead of us. I suggest packing light."

The arid, parched earth leaves the desert sands awhirl. My dry throat can barely swallow any spit. Gabe takes point while Nadia and I rummage through the carnage. The dead leaves us with no choice but to scavenge a few water canteens. Surviving can be cruel but necessary all the same. Not sure how these men lasted such a long journey. We find only a few carrying small rations of food, mostly jerky made from questionable meat, but I'm not picky.

This side of the river, deserted from political turmoil and hostile advances, lies in ruin. The main street, no longer recognizable, fades into an obstacle course of chaos. Crossing it proves to be a challenge.

We exit the mangled road and stop in front of the overpass, which is partially collapsed. While I can only imagine the bodies buried beneath it, what lies across the bridge keeps my thoughts a scurry. Though it remains intact, there's no sign of our battalion on the other side.

Boot prints stamp the dust-coated cars that block the bridge. We reach the riverbank with no one in sight, but the street that follows tells a much different story. Thirty to forty Israeli soldiers stain it red, many as young as myself.

One by one, we search through the bodies, hoping to find a sign of the others, but find despair instead. I stand next to the last of the soldiers and roll them over. A young woman covered in blood gasps for air.

"Over here!" I shout.

Nadia rushes over. "My God, she's still alive." She gently presses on the bullet burrowed in the woman's side and keeps the flow of blood from exiting into an already large pool.

"What happened to the others?" I ask desperately.

Exhausted breaths exhale as the woman mumbles incoherently in Hebrew. Not a word escapes her lips I can understand. With the little strength she has left, she points her finger down the street.

Blood seeps through Nadia's fingers. "I can't stop it."

The woman's eyes are like a doll's, glassy and cold. Before the last warm breath escapes her purple lips, she lifts her hand and I gasp. Jacob's necklace hangs from the clutch of her balled fist.

"No," I say, a small whisper disappearing into the air. Tears burn my eyes, and fear knots in my gut, growing ripe. I've left little doubt hanging on my decision to come here, but every minute passing without my husband shadows that now. I don't know how Jacob's necklace got in this young soldier's possession. All I can assume is that he's still alive, and I will not let my mind race with anything but.

"Boot tracks!" Gabe shouts down the street.

Nadia slides her hand over mine. "He's still out there. We'll find them."

I peel the necklace away from the woman's fist and tuck it into my pocket. The dead do not deserve to rot out in the open, but there's no time for a proper burial. We must leave before another troop passes. I glance at the woman's dog tags as a reminder that she will not be forgotten. *Ayala,* it reads. I say a quick prayer before leaving her and the others to mingle with the earth. As long as humans exist, the price of war will never be enough.

Just as Gabe observed, soldiers' tracks scuff the sidewalks down the street. We trace their steps as far as they lead us until they vanish across the main road. One of our assault vehicles hides behind an old billboard, but the slashed tires and crushed front end leaves it immobile.

Nadia stops and gazes beyond the eastern horizon. "Would they have stuck to the plan?"

"Father Joseph would never deter," I say, "and I know Jacob well enough that he'd have no choice but to follow. He's a loyal leader, but arguing isn't his strong suit."

"So Beit Shemesh it is."

"Aye."

"Are you kidding me, now?" Gabe exclaims. "That's like thirty bloody miles away. You expect us to walk all that way?" Beit Shemesh, our initial rendezvous, has an underground bunker built in the 1950s, suitable to house up to twenty thousand troops. It sits buried just southeast of here, but it would be quite a journey on foot.

"If you have a better plan, speak now, otherwise I suggest you conserve your water."

"Hello there!" a voice wanders from behind a building.

I draw my gun and aim. A man approaches carefree, unaware of his vulnerable position. He looks quite the fool.

"Stop right there!" Nadia orders with her gun aimed and poised to fire. He halts mid-step, eyes wide as an owl.

"It's okay, it's okay . . . I'm unarmed," he stutters as he raises his hands in the air.

Gabe flanks the careless bloke and tracks his steps behind the building to examine. I cautiously approach the man. "You alone?" I ask.

"Y–yes . . . yes . . . just me."

I press the barrel of my gun to his forehead. "Don't lie to me."

His body trembles like he's preparing for a seizure. "I swear it, it's just me."

Gabe emerges from behind the building and shakes his head. I lower my gun but keep my finger on the trigger. Never trust the predictable that often becomes the unpredictable, even if it sways on the better side of judgment. Wise words I've carried with me from Uncle Finnegan.

"Come on, let's go," Nadia orders the man to move.

We station behind the broken-down vehicle and wait. Precaution can't be understated, even if this bloke is telling the truth. Why he's wandering around these parts alone, while not completely out of the ordinary, remains cause for concern. His cracked lips matches the rest of his worn face and leathered skin. His tussled blond hair is sweaty and dirty. With proper hydration, I suspect this drifter closely borders in his late forties. He's near famished from a long journey.

"What are you doing out here by yourself in the middle of a deserted city like this?" I probe.

"I'd ask you the same, but I don't have a gun to threaten you," he counters with a thick Australian accent.

"Fair enough." I put my gun away and ask Gabe and Nadia to do the same. "Better?"

"I take solace in the fact you've at least made an effort." Sarcasm aside, he's an intriguing fellow and has my full attention.

"Spill it, Aussie, we don't have all day."

"I believe order is in first. What do they call you?"

I'm tempted to leave this man and this conversation behind, but I'll indulge. "I'm Arena."

"Oh, like a venue where gallant men fight to the death?"

I'm not amused by his derisive attempt at humor. I slip my knife halfway from its sheath. "I'm losing my patience with you."

"The name's Donavan, but they call me the Duke of Dealing, the King of Cons. I have that wonderful ability to entice people into decisions I want them to make."

I draw the tip of my blade beneath his chin. "Is it working?"

"Perhaps I'm a bit rusty, but in time, my stories carry weight to my advantage."

I roll my eyes over his arrogance. "So you're like the Shakespeare of bullshit."

"Better, I'm a seal-the-deal savant."

I look into his beady eyes under the notion he may be a threat, but then I realize what this man really is. "Sweet Jesus, you're a car salesman?"

"You say that like it's a bad thing."

"Is there another kind?" Nadia and Gabe sigh as they pick up their bags and get ready to walk.

"Mock if you want, the point is, I'm a nibble-witted negotiator. I believe I would be a great asset to your group," he says.

"Great, when we're held against our will at gunpoint by Iranian militants, you can offer them twenty percent off the sticker price for a new sedan."

He laughs maniacally. "Don't be daft, no one can offer that much. Fifteen percent, perhaps." He's completely mad, but he has quite the gregarious personality.

"Look, I'm gonna be honest with you. We got at least a half-day's travel and barely enough water for the three of us to survive. I'm not the kind of person to leave someone behind, but if you cross me, then you and I are going to have more than words. You understand?"

"Deal."

"Nothing personal, but we know nothing about you and I don't trust anyone."

"Don't worry, I won't hold you responsible for my well-being."

"Good, don't make me rethink my decision. You promise me you won't be a thorn in my side, and I'll find you a safe place."

His face, dry and chapped, wrinkles behind a grin. He slides his tongue over his blistered lips and reaches out his hand. "An honest man leaves no room for mistakes."

"Unless he's following a fool," I retort with a smile. I shake his hand with a firm pact and give him one of the water canteens we picked from the dead. "Use it wisely."

"You hurt, mate?" Gabe asks.

"No, not that I'm aware of, why?"

"You've got blood on your neck."

"Yeah, about that . . ." His eyes look shifty. "Well, if we're going to be honest with each other, you should probably know . . ."

"Know what?" I snap.

He studies my faces for a brief moment before reaching into his pocket. Nadia quickly draws her gun.

"Easy," he says nervously.

She lowers her gun while he pulls out a small microchip. I glower suspiciously at the tracking device.

"Don't worry, it's fried. I had someone dig it out," he explains, pointing to a small scabbed incision near the base of his neck.

"I thought you said you were alone," Gabe prods.

"I am, but I was with a larger group a few days ago, just across the Syrian border. We were being transported on a bus to Cairo."

"Who did you piss off?" I scoff.

"Helped a few guys steal a truck full of guns to aid Syrian rebels."

"So you're a thieving criminal?"

"It appears so."

"Well then, you'll fit right in."

"I'm honored," he grins.

"How the hell did you manage to get all the way out here?" Gabe asks.

"By chance, I guess. I've been wandering this godforsaken terrain to find a safe place with food and water, but instead I found you. Appears I was destined to be here at this exact place and time."

"Lucky for you."

"Yeah, not so lucky for the others."

"How does a man like yourself escape a prison bus?"

"After the bus was refueling in the neutral zone, all hell broke out. A skirmish erupted just outside followed by gunfire. Two of the guards left the bus unattended during all the chaos while the other had an unfortunate meeting with one of the prisoner's fist. We stole the keys, unlocked the chains, and ran like hell."

"Russian soldiers?"

"Russians, Turks, Kurds, shit, everybody who sold their soul to the Ten. The fight continued on as we fled south of Damascus. Found a truck we probably could've pushed faster than it drove and ended up in some wasteland of a town I can't pronounce. We held up there a couple of days with others in hiding, mostly families."

"What happened to them?"

"We stayed as long as we could until a massive army from the northern territory flushed us out. I witnessed more bloodshed than I wanted to. Innocent faces passing by me, women and children rushing for any door that opened. I fled inside a market store where a woman and her two little boys huddled next me, clinging to my legs like a cat. Me? A complete stranger, but it didn't matter. We shared the same fear, desperate to stay alive, even it was for a moment."

Donavan's eyes get teary, but he keeps himself from crying. "I peeled the two boys off my leg to peek out a window, and then gunshots fired and a body slammed against the glass door, nearly shaking it off its hinges. The exit near the back was our only hope to escape. I wasn't going to let that family suffer, but when I returned to the poor woman, I found her sobbing over one of her limp sons. The other boy was shaken and terrified to let go of his mother. A rouge bullet had pierced the glass and shot the boy in the head. That bullet should have been for me. I tried to get her to follow me to the back, but she wouldn't budge, and neither would her son. He clung to her as if he were part of her clothing. I even offered to carry her boys, but she refused and stayed there, languishing over an innocent life. Nothing was going to move her. So the truth is, I don't know what happened to the others. I went out that back door and ran as fast as I could."

With eyes weighted in guilt, he leaves his story hanging in silence for a moment. "I'm no coward, you know," he says sadly.

"No one is judging your actions here. Your will to be free is of your own accord," I say.

"I turned around, but it was too late. I couldn't help them," he says with deep regret.

"There were plenty of people I couldn't help either, but it's not our fault. Just make the best of your life because I can think of a few hundred million other people who would trade places with you right now."

"It's hard having to live with that."

"Yeah, but it's much worse dying with regret. All we have is now, the present, and what we do with it. If you want to make things right, then come and fight with us so maybe no one else has to suffer." I bite back tears as I think of Juliana and all the others.

"And if we fail?"

"I'd rather die for something I believe in than stay here and live for nothing at all."

Donavan looks at Nadia and Gabe then at me. Content with my offer, he nods his head in agreement and flashes a genuine smile.

I pull a piece of jerky from my bag and hand it to him. He rests it between his gums like chewing tobacco and takes a swig of water. "It'll last longer like this."

No man travels across these terrains without some survival experience. No doubt he's resilient, and I have no idea how he got this far on foot. Maybe he's right. Maybe it was destiny. I just hope that same spirit can remain alive because we got a hell of a journey ahead, and I have no plans for stopping.

CHAPTER 17

Miles of roads stretch from community to community, keeping our travel away from the more perilous terrains of Israel. Fields of farmland cover the unexpected mystery of this part of the region—a mere delusion of the long stretches of desert sands people believe it to be.

Each small town remains deserted with the exception of a few, and drifters like us who are searching for a vestige of survival. Domiciles, old and new, scatter across the open ridge of olive trees and rocky soil. This is where many people have fled from the turmoil in Jerusalem. I blame no one for escaping, but these small communities won't hold up forever. If we can't stop the line on the front, they will eventually erode with the innocent people withering with it.

Time fades and the roads change, but Beit Shemesh is still far for hope to emerge. I refuse to stop, but the three-hour jaunt quickly taxes on Donavan's legs. He stumbles across the cracked road before mastering his step on the other side. I may be stubborn, but I haven't lost the courage to admit it.

"Let's take a quick break," I offer.

"No, no, I'm fine. We can keep going," Donavan stubbornly refuses as he stoops over. Adamant or not, I refuse to cater to it. He's genuinely worn and I know he needs rest.

"I don't doubt that you can, but we're about to leave this town behind and I honestly don't know when we'll see the next, so I suggest you take advantage of my kindness . . . cause it could be the last."

"A woman's words are as sharp as the knife she carries with them," he says with a smirk. He roams his eyes across the ragged field before taking comfort beneath a sprawling olive tree.

His assurance, while courteous, still leaves me nervous about his good intentions. I'd offer him a gun, but we haven't quite reached that pinnacle in our relationship. Trust no one until there's no one left to trust. Sounds cynical, but it's gotten me this far.

Nadia's fatigued face hangs as she and Gabe, hands entwined, wander into the edge of town. I've lost the ability to read my brother these days, though I feel a sense of secrecy dwelling deep inside him.

A cool breeze passes by and the skies part across the horizon. A speck of sun peeks with splashing amber behind the drifting clouds for the first time in a month. A shade of gray mingles with the auburn sky, and for a brief moment, there's a display of beauty.

I sit down next to Donavan and gaze at the sky. His chiseled face is highlighted by the sun's rays in a perfectly drawn silhouette. He pulls out a shiny cigarette lighter from his pocket and fiddles with it like a compulsive child.

"You smoke?" I interrupt his annoying tic.

He stares down at the lighter. "Nah, my lips haven't touched the end of a cigarette in fifteen years."

"So why do carry it around?"

He pauses uncomfortably before handing the lighter to me. "To remind myself of the mistakes we've made so we don't make them again."

I'm hesitant to prod. The weighted lighter is plated in gold; the infamous hammer and sickle is engraved on one side and a three-star rank insignia is engraved on the other. No doubt it has passed through hands engaged in some nefarious activity.

"Where did you get this?"

"I lifted it off a Russian colonel."

"How'd you manage that?"

"You always interrogate your guests like this?"

"I suppose I'm not as charming as your mates, but it does make the time pass."

"You certainly got the charming part down."

"We all have our flaws."

"Well, I wish we had the ability to foresee them." Donavan pulls a small flask from his back pocket and sneaks a quick swig. By the grimace puckered on his face, I'd say something stronger than tea hides in there.

"Hey, that's just going to dehydrate you."

"You deal with your demons, let me deal with mine."

His face softens and his eyes glaze with a terrible secret. Heartbreak hides behind them. I've seen this look many times. I have no right to judge another man's tragedies. I've witnessed my own. I hand the lighter back and struggle to leave the conversation without resolve.

"You miss home?" I ask delicately.

"They say, 'Home is where the heart is.' Well, I'd like to punch the bloke in the throat who came up with that phrase. I thought moving my wife and daughter to Riyadh, Saudi Arabia, from Sydney would make life better for us. The economic climate in Sydney worsened like everything else in this world and completely crumbled under Chinese authorities. It became a growing prison for labor punishment, eventually leading to organized slavery. My daughter, Olivia, was only a year old at the time, and I didn't want her growing up wondering where and if we were going to get food.

"I got a chance to relocate under a sweet contract with an upscale car dealer in Riyadh. I was one of the lucky ones I guess. I took it without looking back, but not a single day goes by where I don't regret it. Hustling wealthy clients with more money than sense was just a means to an end. The Saudi government eventually folded by default and submitted to the Ten's concessions, leaving most of us unemployed, as our jobs were deemed unnecessary.

"The New Order has done nothing but threaten our livelihood and crush our hopes. Only a fool's heart would believe anything else. The Saudi central region is just another shithole littered with government facilities and military installations.

"After a resurgence under the Ten's harsh protocols, we were forced to abandoned the city and avoid deportation back to Sydney. A friend of ours in a similar situation aided us into the neutral territory in Syria for honest work and a safer place to live."

My sympathy for his hardship has grown beyond simple curiosity. "And your wife and daughter?"

"Olivia's mom died two years ago."

"I'm so sorry, I didn't mean to—"

"It's okay." He pauses. "She battled with cancer after Olivia turned five. After going into remission for a year, the cancer came back, but it was just too strong for her to handle a second time and spread beyond our control. Treatments were just a means of false hope at that point, but she was willing to do anything to see Oliva for as long as she could. I laid her to rest six months later. The loss forced Oliva to grow up pretty quickly. She was tougher than me, that's for sure. You know, living without Kate made me wonder how human beings are capable of handling the fragilities of life."

"I believe there's a seed planted in us from the beginning. And how we grow that seed determines how we handle misfortunes," I offer a dose of Father Joseph's wisdom.

"Six months ago, Damascus was ambushed by Russian troops. They sifted through for slave labor, while fending off Syrian rebels. Many of my friends became common casualties from an endless fight. All I wanted was a safe place for me and my daughter, but sadly there's no place in this world where that exists." He looks at me. "I'm sure you're no stranger to a dead man."

"I've seen my share."

"Innocence has no place in this war. Well, six months ago, that was stolen from me. The truth is, I'm done trying to handle misfortunes, because now not only do I have to live the rest of my short life without my wife, I have to somehow pick up the broken pieces of my dignity and keep living it without my daughter too."

Donavan's eyes flash a hint of anger. "The only reason I'm still alive is because of this damn lighter I plucked from that miserable piece-of-shit colonel. He took my baby's life, so I took his, but I'm not done. I owe it to her and everyone else who was slain that day. I have nothing left. Call it hate, revenge, whatever. The fact is, there aren't enough dead Russian soldiers that will get my daughter back, but I'm gonna make bloody sure I get my fair share."

He takes another sip from the flask, emptying the last drop before tossing it to the ground. My heart sinks, and for the first time in my life, I witness a grown man cry, desperate for healing.

I have nothing to offer that can tame his grief. He is rightfully entitled to be angry and has my sympathy all the same. I wrap my arm around his shoulder. He grabs my hand softly and hides his sobbing face between his knees. I patiently comfort him until his eyes run dry and the fiery horizon seeps into shadow. The night quickly sneaks up on us.

Nadia and Gabe return from town with a small knapsack and a jug of water.

"Aye, things are looking up." Gabe says with a subtle grin as he tosses the sack to me. The sack is filled with unleavened bread pieces and a dozen dried dates.

"Where did you get this?"

"Some old codger wandering the streets invited us in his store. Said he and a few other drifters had been staying here for quite some time without any hostility. But the worry on his face said otherwise. He offered us a few goods and that was it. He didn't go into any specifics about what's happened or where all the people went. Kept to himself mostly, but he did mention we should be careful when traveling at night. Said scavengers are sometimes seen waiting along the thoroughfares."

"Maybe we should hold up until the morning," Nadia suggests.

"We're already half a day behind. If we wait any longer, we may miss them in Beit Shemesh."

"Why would they leave?"

"The plan is to wait there for a day before heading back to Jerusalem."

"Jacob would not leave without you."

"Maybe, but he may think we were dead." The words feel heavy.

Gabe stuffs a date in his mouth and hands one to Donavan. "Well, eat up then, might be the last good meal for a while."

Donavan ignores Gabe's offer and silently walks away from the tree.

"Is he okay?" Gabe asks.

"Just let him be alone for a bit. He's traveled the darkest recesses of hell. Lost his wife and daughter. If he wants to talk, let him talk on his terms. Everyone deserves to be extended a little grace."

Donavan's mental state adds an uncertainty to the group, but something in me trusts him anyway. I know where his pain is taking him; I've been where his thoughts have roamed. He's a broken man lost in a world of hatred andit's stringing him along on a dangerous path. The only monsters we should be afraid of are the ones hiding inside us. Let's hope his don't reveal themselves.

I grab the jug of water and a piece of bread, and walk over to Donavan. Without a word, I graciously offer it to Donavan. He swallows a big gulp of water and chews on the piece of bread. There's a twinkle in his eye.

"Well, what are we waiting for? Beit Shemesh it is," he says.

CHAPTER 18

It can't be overstated of the dangers that lurk in the dark. We leave the road to travel the grassy farmlands. Fertile grasses camouflage the sandy earth and stony gullets for much of the terrain, but it's important to stay vigilant of the untamed landscape.

My ears stay alert as the chasing wind blows the tall, thin blades of grass. Apart from our shoes beating the ground, silence surrounds us. Not even the creatures of the night stir. We leave our torches off so we don't draw unwanted attention, but the large scattered stones make it difficult to traverse without them. The rocky soil stretches for miles meeting random hills covered in foliage.

We hike nearly two hours before we engage in the first presence of wildlife. The moon glows through the parted clouds and shimmers onto a lone gazelle standing gracefully on the sandy path in front of us. It bends its long narrow face to the ground and grazes on the grass. The clouds fully part and the full moon shines down on the land. The large hill ahead is covered in rows of large well-manicured shrubs. The clouds pass in front of the moon, casting dancing shadows, fleeting between them.

"Get down," I quickly order.

Donavan lowers his big frame to the ground beside me while Gabe and Nadia cover beneath the wiry brush. The hungry gazelle raises its head and stands alert.

Gabe nudges my arm. "What is it?"

"Someone is out there on the hill."

"You sure it isn't just more gazelles?"

"Shh."

Brush rustles and rocks gnash as heavy feet trample across the ground. The statuesque gazelle lurches forward and sprints past in a full gait. Two dark figures swiftly follow after the animal and vanish into the fields. I draw my gun and part the bristled weeds upon a pile of jagged stones. Clouds pass over the hill, casting shadows.

I scan the line at the base of the hill, but no signs of lurkers in the dark except for a few night creatures spying from the sky. We cannot stay here any longer. This open grassland is a prey's nightmare. I dig into my bag and grab one of the guns we swiped from the dead soldiers.

"Here, take it," I whisper to Donavan.

"You sure," he asks.

Doubt washes over me for a split second. "Well, I didn't bring you with us for the conversation."

"Of course not, I thought it was my good looks." A lighter side of Donavan surfaces as an honest smile brightens his disheveled face.

Nadia and Gabe huddle next to me, guns drawn. "So what's the plan, sis?"

"When I say go, you make a B-line to that center row on the hill. I don't care what animal crosses your path, you don't drift away. We need that high ground, and we need to stay close."

My eyes roam for movement like an owl waiting for a mouse to scurry. The field stays calm, but only for a moment. Whatever waits out there, its feet indiscreetly shuffles through the dry brush behind us. I turn and spot two men outlined in the dark nearly sixty paces back. One portly, the other tall and muscular.

Friendly or not, I'm not taking that risk. These could be some of the scavengers the old man in the village warned us about. Donavan aims his gun, but I quickly lower it to the ground and shake my head. No need to call any more unwanted scavengers in our direction.

I holster my gun and quietly retrieve my bow from my back. With the string tightly secured, I position an arrow and balance the bow parallel to the ground. The men suddenly stop.

"*Laqad faqadnahum?*" one of the men babbles.

"What's he saying?" Nadia whispers.

"I don't know, it's Arabic. I only know curse words," I answer.

"They're looking for us," Donavan chimes in. He doesn't take his piercing eyes off the two men.

"How do ya know?" Gabe asks.

"English may be the universal language, kid, but you don't move to the Middle East if you're going to rely on it. You can't negotiate without Arabic—it makes or breaks a deal."

The two men converse back and forth, one in a deep voice, while the other makes crude gestures with his crotch. A slight shimmer emerges as one of them pulls a large machete from his back.

"Are they a threat?" I ask.

"Not unless you think being raped is enjoyable," Donavan loosely translates their banter.

Blood boiling, I stretch the arrow back and release it without pause. It flings above the grass and sticks into the tall man's throat. His machete drops to the ground before he falls over into portly man.

"*Musaeadat!*" the man shouts as he flees across the field. Another voice yells in the distance. I grab another arrow and strike the man in the back. A shot fires.

"Go!" I shout.

We spring up the hill through the soft soil. Small lights flicker to our left. Grape-bearing vines flash past as we sprint between the rows of a large vineyard. Pattering voices emerge and beating footsteps chase closer. Gunshots fling past and a scream echoes. Gabe and Nadia drift into the next row.

I follow after, but someone is closing in on me. I feel a heaviness in the air, hear the pounding footsteps . . . *Run, faster, Arena!,* and then he slams me to the ground. We roll over and tussle about, kicking and swinging. It's frantic in the dark. He reaches for my gun, but I quickly retrieve my knife and cleave his chest. His body retreats back in pain. With a large grunt, I pull out the knife and slit his throat before he can scream.

"Arena!" Gabe yells.

Panting, I dash through the next two rows and follow my name up the hill. Trampling feet swiftly chase. Voices clutter with the wind, menacing and deep. I skip the next row and hide behind a large trellis of vines, trying to catch my breath. I pull my katana and wait. The leafy vines shutter as the pacing boots quicken, growing louder. *Patience, just wait . . .* Then I grip the handle hard and swing at the man surging past. His body falls to the ground, headless, while two others flank me, their machetes swinging. The rustle of leaves mixes with the clanging of metal, and my arms are burning. But I can't stop, I'll never stop. I let out a guttural cry as I dodge their blows, and finally I cut them down.

I stand there, my every muscle pulsing. I loosen my grip on my katana and feel the blood rush back into my fingers.

"Arena," Donavan calls.

I race to the top of the vineyard and find Donavan waiting. My brother is wrestling with a man wielding a knife. Nadia struggles to pull the two apart as the heated exchange escalates. The raving scavenger kicks Gabe off before Nadia marries her knife across his wrinkled neck.

"Thank you," Gabe pants, "is that all of them?" Donavan quickly draws his gun and aims it at me.

My eyes widen, and my mind doesn't immediately comprehend what I'm seeing. Then I realize I've been betrayed. "Donavan, wait!" I shout.

He pulls the trigger, and the bullet zips past my ear and sinks into the man's skull behind me. I gasp. Confused, I rush over the man's dead body, my mind spinning over the idea that Donavan would ever deceive us. I catch my breath under a small moment of clarity and pardon any wild thoughts I have of him.

"I guess I was destined to be here after all," Donavan jests as he walks over to me. Nadia seems confused and holds up her gun.

"So it appears," I say. Donovan hands me his gun as a good gesture of trust. "No, keep it."

"You sure?" he asks.

"You may need to save my life again." We both grin. Nadia's itchy trigger finger retreats and she sighs with relief.

"There's someone definitely looking after you, lass."

"If there is, they're probably having an anxiety attack right now. Let's get the hell out of here before more scavengers show up."

We breach the top of the vineyard and quicken our pace down the other side. With miles still to go through this dangerous landscape, we must stay alert. No man nor woman can be trusted. It's a fool's paradise out here.

We trek past the vineyard housing and escape further away from the main road. It's our best chance to avoid another scouting party, if that's what that was. The landscape marginally changes from tilled fields and rocky soil to a flatter terrain. The land is open, which means less places to hide.

After an hour from the vineyard under a quicker pace, we find ourselves far from the road. With the night still at risk and the moonlight abating, we'll have to wait until morning. Our feet beg to rest under the unforgiving hard rocky soil, and it comes at no better time with a new landscape before us.

A small forest of short, chubby trees sprawling with a large leafy canvas awaits us. The trees, clumped together in tangled rooted foliage, spread across a vast area. Their scented sap smells like the cedar in Texas. Oh, to think of home seems so foreign now. Taller trees sprinkle the center, towering over with twisted and contorted limbs—a sinister sight in the shadows from the moonlight. Their bent trunks hunch over like an old man, their lower branches reaching down, ready to scoop up passing travelers. Open paths weave in and out across the grassy undergrowth. We travel for some time until we reach a coppice of fig trees deep in the woods. I'm comfortably at home here, safe and prepared to camp until night lifts.

The others rest under the canopy of a large fig tree where the trunk is hidden beneath a cocoon of its own broad leaves. I climb midway up a Kermes oak tree, nestle between the thick forked branches, and post watch for the night. I don't know what lurks in the dark, but I'm at peace. Up here, I'm a bird of prey, observing every leaf fluttering, inspecting every shadow dancing, and tracking every creature stirring. I refuse to let my eyes drift, not even for a second. These scavengers, clumsy and predictable, still bear a concern for alarm.

The moon tucks away behind the curtain of clouds and remains reclusive for the remainder of the night. Just as the breeze blows the crackling branches, the native birds return to the air and twitter their calls, reciting in perfect harmony. The peaceful moment turns into hours, and I feel comfortable to ease up a bit. I lean my head against the gnarled bark. Weary and waning, my lids fall heavy and I seep into a slumberous darkness. Deeper and deeper, my mind falls into a realm of terror, a nightmare filled with wickedness . . .

Fire and chaos surround me. Hellish screams echo as a thunderous chorus of winged creatures swoop down from the sky and swipe at the brave soldiers who are desperately trying to fend them off. Women and children flee across the desert sand, escaping the bedlam with black swirling clouds on their heels.

A tall thin man cloaked in black stands in the center of the madness. He carries a large bucket in one hand and a slaughtered lamb in the other. Detached from the death surrounding him, the faceless man tosses the lamb on the ground and pours gold coins from the bucket on top. Each coin, engraved with an X, begins to melt and coat the lamb.

The man removes his cloak and drapes it over the gold lamb. From the shadows, people begin to gather, drawn by its mystery while fire blazes in the sky behind them. Impassive to their surroundings, they wander inertly toward the lamb like cattle. The man smiles as each person who reaches for the cloak and turns to billows of ash.

When all have vanished, the man urges me to come forward. I refuse to move and fall for his deceit. He glowers a sinister grin and lifts the cloak from the lamb. My stomach sinks into a pit of despair. Instead of the slain golden lamb, my son sits beneath the cloak reaching and calling to me.

My feet are cemented to the ground as I struggle to grab him. Seconds seem like hours with a mother torn from her child. Tears run down Joshua's cheeks, crying for me, but I can't reach him. I scream in desperation, but the man just smiles.

He picks up my son by his feet and dangles him in front of me. My blood boils over and unimaginable fury erupts. The man draws a knife from behind his back and holds it to Joshua's neck. I beg for my son's life, tears raining down my face, "No, please no, God, no!"

The man's smile flattens, and for a second he lifts the blade from my son's neck. He stares at me menacingly before his eyes flood red. He returns the knife, grins, and slides it across just as everything turns black.

I bolt awake, sweating, still nestled against the gnarled limbs, but I'm not alone. An unsettling purr hungers to my left. A desert lynx gracefully balances on a stretched branch, guarding its breakfast beneath its paws.

A beautiful creature—short face, tan fur, and long athletic legs that could easily propel its body fifteen feet away. There are two remarkably pronounced black stripes on its forehead, but it's his long tufted ears that distinguishes him from other wild cats. Extremely territorial creatures and this one is no different.

Its hungry purr converts to a snarl before it leans forward on the branch. I slowly back away while the cat's narrow eyes track my every movement. His mouth stretches back, displaying long canine teeth. I stop and carefully reach for my knife. His ears perk, bristled hairs plumed and leans ready to pounce.

"There now, kitty, kitty," I coo.

He lowers his sandy-coated face and clasps the small dead rodent with his jaws. I remain still, inching closer to my knife. He plants his eyes on mine and slinks toward the trunk, breakfast dangling from his teeth. A subtle growl escapes his stuffed mouth before he descends his agile body down the tree. I hover over the limb and watch the hungry cat disappear into the woods.

A small beam of light breaches through the gapping branches. The dangerous encounter with nature quickens my heart, but it's nothing compared than the nightmare my mind still wrestles with. My stomach churns and the fear of my son's safety begins to brew. I've risked enough being alone up here. We must leave.

Aside from the wild creatures roaming, the woods remain still—a lone, peaceful spot surrounded by a wilderness of savagery. I climb down, scraping my knee and check on the others. Protected beneath the fig tree's canopy, Nadia and Gabe nestle together near the sprawling roots. My bow, swords, and pack are lying undisturbed next to them. Though everything appears to be in order, something is wrong. Donavan is missing.

"Hey, wake up." I lightly shake Nadia and my brother.

Gabe steadily opens his eyes. "What's going on?"

"Donavan is gone."

Nadia yawns and stretches. "Why would he leave on his own?"

"I don't know, maybe he's just getting some fresh air."

"His bag is gone," Gabe says.

Nadia reaches for her side. "So is my gun."

"Shit," I whisper. "Pack your stuff, we're leaving."

"What about Donavan?"

"What about him?"

"Should we wait to see if he returns?"

"He left on his own affair. He's no longer my responsibility."

"You don't really believe that, do you?" Gabe says.

"I believe a man makes his own decisions." I grab my weapons and find the gold-plated lighter lying underneath them. I pick it up and rub my thumb across the engraving. The stride of my heart breaks as if neither it nor my soul welcomes another beat. The sympathetic walls I've built for Donavan are now hollow. I can hear Donavan's daughter crying in my mind. Her frail arms reach for him, but they fall limp. My eyes brim with tears. Is it something I said that cast away a good man? My will to leave him behind passes on, and sorrow sits inside of me instead, fermenting. I stand there in silence, waiting for someone to move me.

"So what are we going to do, Arena?" Gabe asks. He has his gear ready to go.

I wipe my eyes and solemnly answer, "We're gonna go find Donavan, he couldn't have gotten too far."

"I got as far as my legs would take me?" a voice says.

I turn around. "Donavan?" A smile lifts from my face and then I glower at him. "Where the hell have you been?"

"Good morning to you too, sunshine."

"You should have told us. You can't just leave like that. It doesn't work that way."

"I couldn't sleep and I didn't want to disturb anyone, so I thought I'd take a walk and clear my mind. I guess the short walk turned into a bit of journey. Didn't mean to upset anyone."

"Did you take my gun?" Nadia glares.

"Oh yeah, here ya go." He carefully hands it to her. "Wasn't sure what to expect out there with just three bullets left in my mag. Forgive me for not asking, but you were sound asleep and I didn't want to wake you."

Nadia bites her lip. "No worries, I hope you found some clarity."

"Does a man good to search his mind for something good to cling to."

"And did you find anything good?" I prod in jest.

"I found something better." He grins like a schoolgirl struggling to keep a secret. "There's a tree line just a mile east of here. Beyond that and over the hill is a ranch."

"So?" I say.

He chuckles. "An equestrian ranch . . . and it's not empty."

"If you're joking with me, you and I can't be friends anymore."

"Scouts honor," he salutes. "From what I could see, there's maybe fifteen or so horses paddocked at the base of the hillside."

My eyes widen. "Did you see anyone out there with them?"

"No, but it was too dark to tell."

The thought of giving our feet a rest and bareback riding the rest of the way to Beit Shemesh stokes a little fire of excitement. Gabe's eyes read with doubt as I grapple with the idea in my head. There are uncertainties with the ranch, but the only thing I can think about is being away from my husband and son. If we want to quicken our pace, this is our best chance to cross the open land.

"Let's go," I decide.

Nadia smiles with relief. "Kind of seems like old times, doesn't it?"

The last time I engaged with a horse, I was slouched on its back, unconscious and nearly dehydrated before Nadia rescued me. Many moons have passed since the day we met.

Gabe looks a little deflated. I grab his arm before he leaves. "Hey, you got a bad vibe about this or something?"

"I don't know. With the hell we escaped from, I'm not overly fond of the idea. And are we not scavengers, stealing these horses as well?"

"If there's no ranch handler overseeing these creatures, then they are fair game, but I won't take a man's horse without his permission, okay?"

"I know you wouldn't, but I want to be sure there's no threat."

"Hey, if you have reservations about this, I need to know."

His eyes wander from me and he stares at the ground. "It seems a bit of a risk, that's all, even for you." Sometimes my brother can be hard to read, but no doubt there's a troubling darkness in his expression. His clairvoyant gift has long faded. I'm afraid he struggles to trust his instincts now.

"When is the last time you felt it?" I ask.

He pauses, his eyes focusing on the dirt. "Too long to remember."

"Try."

He bends down toward the ground, swipes a handful of dirt, and closes his eyes. Suddenly, black clouds swallow the morning light. The fig tree engulfs in darkness and a howling wind echoes in the air.

"What is it, what do you see?" I ask in a desperate tone.

A cold sweat breaks out on his forehead as he strains for an answer. He tosses the dirt aside, opens his eyes, and calmly breathes. "Nothing, everything seems so cloudy. I can't see a damn thing anymore." He slams his fist on the ground. "I'm sorry, I just—"

"It's okay, this isn't on you. Some things aren't that simple and I shouldn't have forced it." He searches my eyes and grabs my hand. Whatever hides behind that hollow stare is something dark and unwelcoming.

"She never goes away no matter how much I try to forget—in my nightmares, my memories. I struggle to see the good things without knowing the bad. Over and over it plays in my head, holding her limp body. I'll never be able to wash her from my thoughts, will I?"

"I don't think we ever can, but it doesn't mean you can't move on and make new memories. That's the only thing you can change."

He gazes at Nadia, who is at the other end of the fig tree. "How do you know if you truly love someone?"

"I think you already know the answer to that."

A small smile tips the corners of his mouth. "Well, I guess I better not screw this up then."

"Pain fades, my dear brother, but love endures.
Remember that and you'll be fine."

Gabe nods and sighs deeply. He seems a little more at peace. Some of the clouds lift, but everything remains in a realm of perpetual twilight. Even if the skies cleared now, not even the twinkle from the stars could help us as only one remains, silent, alone, and waiting to vanish like all the others. We live in a world of fear and mystery now. Our light dwells in darkness.

We gather our things and move out. The trees fade behind us as we travel along a fertile valley dotted with groves of silver-green olive trees. The horizon to the north, when lit, gives way to an area of bare, craggy peaks, strewn across a barren wasteland.

My eyes are alert as I scan my surroundings. We hike through the rocky soil, nearly a mile from our departure without a threat, and ascend near the top of the rising landscape where short and tall trees punctuate the crest of the hill. My face tingles and a sudden rush of blood races to my fingertips. As I gaze down upon the other side, an anxious joy marks itself in the goosebumps on my arms.

Just as Donavan described, a small ranch sits nestled between two enriched valleys surrounded by a sea of wild, rusty-colored brush. Beyond that is unknown. I'm hesitant to leave. While horses roam through a narrow corral, the ranch's inhabitants concern me.

As the three of us look down in silence, cautious and undecided, Donovan stands tall with his chin up and anxiously draws his gun, leaving no doubt about his decision.

"What are we waiting on? Let's tame these bastards," he brashly stokes, bearing a twinkle in his eye.

I grab the back of his arm. "Let's not be too hasty now. We don't know who else is down there."

"How else are you expecting us to find out?"

"Think like a lion, stalk like one. Never storm into the unknown unless you want to get yourself killed."

"Okay, what do you suggest?"

"Stay low, keep your eyes peeled, and move in your grandmother's footsteps."

"Lead the way," he gestures.

We slowly inch through the brush, stopping every few minutes. With fifty meters between us and the paddock, I spot a small building north of the ranch. Behind the building is a thick cluster of trees and a billow of smoke. If there are inhabitants here, they certainty aren't discreet.

Like a snake in the grass, I slink upon a wooden fence and hold my position. Horses creep along the paddock just outside the long narrow stables. The keeper's grounds are quiet and still, not even the stir of whispers except for a horse who nickers faintly in the dark. Nadia and Gabe slither up beside me while Donavan surveys along the fence line.

"No way these horses have been left abandoned," Gabe whispers. "Look at their physiques. Those are not the frames of the neglected."

"Aye, only a fool would believe we're alone, come on." Nadia and Gabe follow close behind me as I hug the fence, edging slowly to Donavan.

"What do you make of it?" I ask him.

"We're not going to get far with these horses out here unless you can ride one of these creatures free rein."

"We may have to."

"Bareback is one thing, but you better be bloody good at controlling them, that's if they are trained on cue. I've tamed my share of horses growing up, but these sure look wild."

"Do we have a choice?"

"Maybe," he says, pointing. "See the end of the stable there? I saw several reins dangling. Those horses didn't bridal themselves. Someone's here, but friend or foe, I don't know."

"Remember, we trust no one."

"So what's your plan?"

"We open the paddock and sneak those horses out of the stable."

"We're no thieves, Arena," Gabe chimes in.

Suddenly, an old man emerges from behind the eastern part of the stable, staggering as if he were drunk.

"Maybe we'll ask him then," I scoff.

A small light shines behind him, casting shadows. Arabic voices shout and the man stops. Two men clothed in tattered uniforms argue with the old man, forcing him to move toward the stable doors. With a rifle pressed to his back, he unlocks the doors and vanishes inside. A moment of silence lingers before a gunshot fires inside the stable. My heart sinks into my gut. *Shit.*

"I think maybe we should move back," Donavan advises.

"Wait, get down," I say.

The man with the rifle exits the stable carrying a wooden box. A shouting match erupts where several men approach dressed in the same garb as the scavengers we tangled with earlier. Back and forth they argue until the man with the box dishes the last words.

"We need to move now," Donavan urges.

"What are they saying?" Gabe asks.

"He's ordered a few men to sweep the fields, now go!"

We quickly track along the fence, masked beside trotting horses. Three men wielding ragged scythes exit the outer paddock and begin sweeping across the wild brush. I stop just short at the end of the fence line where a mangled body, long since decayed, marries with the dirt.

Two other men drift closer, one with an AK47 dangling at his hip while the other leans against the fence and smokes a cigarette. We are quiet and still, hiding in the shadow of the fence post. The man takes a few puffs from the cigarette before joining the others in the field while the other wanders along the fence.

Gabe's face is pallid and filled with fear. I keep hunkered in the shadow, my hand clutched tightly to my knife. The man approaches closer nearly hovering over me without notice. Donavan quietly reaches for his gun, but I signal him to stop. The man peers down and his eyes widen. I thrust my knife into his chest and he lunges over and flops on the ground with a thud. A sharp crack short of a scream leaves his mouth before Gabe quickly covers it. He squirms on the ground, kicking dirt into the air, and tries to reach for his gun. Nadia swipes his gun from his hands while Donavan holds down his twitching body. Only a few more moments and he stops moving..

Not a sound stirs but the chafing of brush as three men continue to scan the fields. I peek through the thin blades and watch the skinny bloke with a cigarette explore the area, completely unaware of his lifeless mate a few feet in front of him.

"Let's go," I hurry, nudging them through the fence.

The backside of the stables remains clear, but drifting in and out, a lone scavenger, with a machete, roams the side.

"Stay here, I got this one," Donavan implores with confidence.

"Be careful."

I scout closely to the men outside the paddock while Donavan lurks toward the stable. Within seconds he grabs the man from behind and wrestles him to the ground. They tussle a bit before the scavenger rolls over limp. Donavan leaves the body and vanishes near the front of the stable.

"Dammit, what is he doing?" I mutter crossly.

Suddenly, a voice from the field shouts. The man puffing a cigarette yells something, but no one answers. He surveys the length of the fence and hollers once more. We quickly slip flat to the ground. There's nothing but silence. I peek between the wooden slates just as Donavan returns from the stable.

"Come on, it's clear," Donavan urges.

I turn to the fields, but Mr. Cigarette is gone. Nadia and Gabe rush over to Donavan, but I remain isolated next to the fence as panic flares throughout my body. I frantically scan the grassy valley for the man and his cigarette.

"Arena, come on," Gabe whispers.

The field suddenly erupts with voices. The three men are back with an anxious alarm in their steps. They must have found the man we'd killed.

"We're not going to get far with those guys. Go get the horses and meet me out by the fence," I order as I string my bow.

"But—"

"Go!"

Gabe, Nadia, and Donovan disappear into the stable. I dismiss the chance to escape and nock an arrow instead. I stand up. The three men spot me, their shouts getting lost in the wind as they sprint at full speed toward me. I peek my bow just above the fence and strike with deadly intent. My arrows pierce both men, one right after the other, in the chest, and they vanish, lifeless, lifeless into the wiry brush. The third dodges my flinging arrow as it grazes his cheek.

I pull another arrow, but it falls from my hand, and he's on me—his arms wrapping around my body, and he slams me to the ground. *No, no,* I think, as we tussle across the dirt, his hands grabbing me so hard. Finally, I squirm from his clutch and reach for the arrow. He lunges, slamming my back to the ground and the world turns black for a minute as I try to catch my breath. He weights my legs with his heavy frame.

I swing with a left hook and drive his chin back. Blood drips from his mouth. He scowls with the furious grit of his teeth and squeezes his brawny hands around my neck. My throat closes without a breath.

"*Ya Sharmouta*!" he shouts with angry venom.

My vision begins to fade, completely breathless, and I stretch my fingers to the arrow beside me. The man's eyes darken a hollow stare and pierces through me possessed. I maneuver my hand around his beefy arm and claw the skin from his cheek. He shrugs back with a horrific moan and releases his strong grip from my neck. A small breath escapes me. Without a wasted second, I clutch the arrow and jab the razor tip into his eye. He rolls over to the ground, squirming in agony before I silence his ghastly shrieking with my knife.

A deep breath exhales and my vision returns, just in time to spot another man running past. With shaky hands, I grab my bow from the ground and quickly notch an arrow into the back of his neck. He stumbles to the dirt, falling dead in front of the stable.

I scan the area, but there are no signs of Nadia, Gabe, or Donavan. One of the horses, saddled and reined, trots outof the stable gate. Voices creep in the distance behind the trees and a burst of light flashes in the sky.

I approach the stable doors and peek inside. "Donavan," I whisper into the dark.

It's silent, and then the back of the pin rings with a clatter. Horses lean over in their box stalls. I slink down the main pin and call out once more, "Donavan."

Still no response except for the neighing and shuffling of horses. My gut begins to shrivel. Then something moves in the shadow in the far back. I draw my gun, sweat beading and blood surging.

A light suddenly burns bright, obstructing my eyes, but only for a moment. My heart sinks as my eyes adjust. Nadia, Gabe, and Donovan are being held hostage by three men, each pointing a gun to the back of their heads.

My hand steadies my gun on the men as adrenaline fuels my veins. Nadia and Donavan look down, anticipating their execution. Gabe looks at me and shakes his head, a sign for me to surrender.

I refuse to withdraw, but he's right. One of them will surely die if I squeeze this trigger. I'm fast, but not that fast. Tears fills my eyes as I stare at my brother and see the fear etched all over his face. I want to run to him, to scream, to do something.

I calmly breathe, waiting for Michael to swoop in and save us, but he doesn't. Instead, the three men push my friends to their knees. One ejects a beastly grunt while another barks to me in his native tongue.

"What is he saying?" I ask Donavan.

"Lay your gun down," he responds.

"I could really use your negotiating prowess right about now."

"Arena, there's no way out of this. I'm sorry," Donovan says.

"There's always a way."

"Not this time, I'm afraid."

I leave my gun planted on the scoundrel in the middle and analyze the scenarios in my head. No matter how this ends, someone I love is going to die. I lower my gun ingood faith and hope this standoff ends in our favor. As soon as I toss the gun, I'm clubbed on the back of my head and fall to the ground, my world throbbing in pain. Gabe leans forward and he seems to be saying something, but my blurry eyes are failing me. "Gabe, I'm so sorry," I say or think, and everything turns to black.

CHAPTER 19

My head, still pounding, rests uncomfortably against a jagged wall. Arabic voices chatter next to me, but I cannot see the faces they belong to. Warm hands graze my neck and a burlap sack is lifted over my head. A thin bearded man hovers over me. He's bald, expressionless, and smells like rotting potatoes. Donavan and Gabe sit across from me, their heads still covered.

A burly man with an eyepatch shoves Nadia inside the stony room and forces her to the ground beside me. He pulls the sack from her head and her eyes turn to me frightened. The two men stare down at us with a sinister grin and mumble to each other with words I can only assume is anything but cordial. They remove the coverings from Donavan and Gabe before leaving us locked inside.

The cell is made of solid rock, impenetrable even with tools. The ceiling hovers close, reaching a confining seven feet at best, making the already claustrophobic prison painfully dreadful for tall people like Donavan. Our wrists are cuffed and our ankles are bound to iron bands with a trailing chain attached.

Breathing is difficult in this horrid dungeon. The only thing to combat the musty air and the stale urine scent is a small two-by-two vented window in the ceiling, emitting the only light from the outside.

A small barred door made of steel rests at the front of this rectangular prison. Without someone guarding it, our chances to flee remain hopeful in an otherwise formidable escape. The wall across from me where Donavan sits can't be more than ten feet, but the length of the chamber remains unknown as it vanishes into darkness.

I grab the chain attached to my ankles and follow it beneath the window where the smell of smoke lingers. The chain hooks to a latch buried deep into the floor, but the rusty clasp refuses to budge no matter how hard I pull.

"You're wasting your time and energy on that," a deep voice seeps from the dark back corner.

I quickly jump back, reaching for a knife I don't have. An amber dot glows and fades before the face of old man emerges from the shadow with half a cigarette pinched between his lips.

"Who are you?" I timidly ask.

"No one special," he responds in a thick Russian accent.

"I doubt that."

He coughs up a small chuckle and struggles to stretch a smile on his crumpled face. Maybe he's right. Perhaps he is just a drifter, caught in the web of a spider's lair. He grabs his chain and slides it across the floor closer to the front and sits down. "I see they brought in new blood."

"New blood?" Gabe curiously asks.

"Entertainment, labor, whatever they see fit. Well, you'll know soon enough I suppose."

"We don't plan on being here long enough to know," I say.

"They all say that, but it always ends the same. I don't suppose you saw a frail gray-haired old man with you."

"Why, is he a friend?"

"In a sense, I guess. He's the ranch keeper who owns this land, or did. I've known him as long as I've been here."

"And just how long is that?"

"I don't know, I've lost track of time."

I kneel next to him and say without wavering, "I'm sorry to tell you, but your friend's dead."

The man stares quietly for a moment before taking another puff of his cigarette. "I guess Yair really messed up. It's very unlikely they killed him for no reason."

"You're not sad?"

"What can I say, it's a travesty, but as long as you play by their rules, no one gets hurt. He broke them and nothing can bring him back."

The old man's sits motionless, arms resting on his knees. I don't have to know a man that well to see pain in his eyes. His clothes, tattered beyond repair, resemble the longevity of his rotting stay in here. His worn body creeks beneath his wrinkled skin, an aging brown. His sagging face, weathered from long, hard years, is punctuated by gray wooly brows knitted together. The motionless, old bird holds his burning cigarette between thin shriveled fingers. His lips are dry and grown together. He leaves the conversation with silence and leans his aging bones against the wall as a waft of smoke drifts from his mouth.

"You know, the air is bad enough down here, you smoking isn't helping," I chide before I return to the other side of the cell.

"It's all I have left, rotting in here."

"And what would they need with an old dying man?"

"Knowledge."

"And they pawn cigarettes off to you for that?"

"It's better than ending up like Yari."

"For now."

"I suppose, but I'm not going down so easily."

"So what is this knowledge you give them?"

"You sure ask a lot of questions."

"Well, if I'm gonna rot in here with you, I'd like to at least know my company."

"Oh, I have strong feeling you won't last long in here, but I'll oblige your curious nature nonetheless. The name is Vaslav. I used to be an arms maker and somewhat of an arms dealer in my younger days, but nothing quite as corrupt as one might have you believe."

"That's debatable, but I'm listening."

"I've worked for many countries under many rulers with shifting ideologies, and despite the language barriers and cultural politics, there's one universal piece of bullshit that never changes."

"What's that?"

"Deceit. The elite will always be power hungry. It's not enough to just control; it's knowing that you and everyone else sees that you are in control. I resigned my work not because I was associated with these monsters . . . I detest them. I resigned because it left a tragic stain on my hands."

"And now?"

"And now I use it to survive."

"By making guns for these barbaric scavengers?"

"Guns, no. I have no tools for that here. There are plenty of arms out there, but they are only as useful as the bullets they use. I fabricate their ammo in return for my life."

"And yet your work continues with more blood spilled. You can live with that?"

"I'm not sure what will kill me first, my conscience or these sorry excuse for cigarettes. Either way, man has lived with a lot worse, but I'm not going down without a fight."

"What do ya mean by that?"

"You ask me if I can live with my actions. Yes, just long enough to destroy everything I gave these assholes and maybe get a little redemption."

"How are you going to do that?"

He sigh heavily and wheezes. He lowers his voice. "Buried in the back corner of this cell is a can with nearly one pound of chemical compounds I've managed to collect over the past six months. That's enough to take their lab down."

Do I trust him? My first instinct is that people lie, but there's something about him that suggests he's telling the truth. Maybe because he gains nothing from telling four new cellmates who he truly believes won't last long in this godforsaken place.

"I guess you and I have something in common after all, but I got to ask, how the hell did you get here?"

"How I got here isn't important. I was baited just like you, trying to survive. What is important is how long we can survive to right our wrongs and hope that there's a shed of grace on the other side."

"Well put."

A door opens and a light spreads outside our cell. There's a horrific grating sound as two men tug on ropes, grunting and moaning as they trundled a large church bell across the floor behind them. The wall next to us echoes a beastly thud bellowing a thunderous crash. The men exit, panting from the laborious task.

"What bloody hell was that all about?" Donavan asks.

"An act of paranoia," Vaslav replies. "Come, let me show you."

He shuffles to the far side of the cell and swings open a square wooden board on the wall. Behind it is another cell, but it's unoccupied with prisoners. Instead, bells of all sizes are piled up on one another in mystery.

"They're not only assholes, they're terrified, superstitious assholes," Vaslav scoffs.

"What?" Donavan's eyes blink rapidly. "You telling me they're afraid of . . . bells?"

"Precisely."

"Do I dare ask why?"

"No bells have ever been used to summon worship in any religion except that of Christianity. Not even the Jews, and these *scavengers* as you call them, are neither Christian nor Jew. Hell, their cultist behavior doesn't even line with Islamic teachings."

"So what's your point?"

"The point is the ringing of bells have different meanings for different people—some good , some bad. The Hebrews had quite a different use for bells, none of which were used to frighten someone."

Donovan's forehead crinkles in puzzlement. "The bells were for the high priest in the Temple," I loosely explain to Donavan.

"I believe in God, but I'm not an overtly religious person, so forgive me if I don't know the story," Donavan admits.

Vaslav continues in an earnest tone, "Moses specifically instructed how the high priest was to dress when he entered the Holy of Holies—the most sacred space inside the Temple. With the purest heart, Moses was to make offerings for the sins of God's people, but if he didn't follow the rules in a place that was restricted from sinners, God would strike him dead for defiling the holy place.

"If that happened, there would be a dead high priest lying behind a curtain in a place with no one qualified to recover him. So before Moses entered the space, the high priest would tie a rope around his waist so his corpse could be dragged out. But because he wasn't supposed to be disturbed during his offering, they would have no way of knowing if he were dead. That's why he was to tie little bells to his robe so the sound of their ringing would indicate that he was still alive and that he was being accepted by God. But if they stopped, it was evident that God had rejected him and he was dead."

"So how is the ringing of bells a bad thing then?"

"The antithesis of righteous is evil, so if you are pagan, the bells call you for other reasons. Folklorists believe the ringing of bells was used to ward off evil spirits, even the devil himself. Which is why many of these cultist reprobates believe the tolling of bells are a call from the underworld for unbelievers. They ring not as an invitation, but as a sentence from the gates of hell, and sending demons out to hunt their souls," Vaslav says.

"All because of a damn bell?"

"I never said they were sane, just assholes, but I getyour point."

Vaslav returns to the front of the cell and peers through the bars of the door. He leans against it, waiting nervously. For the many days he has served inside this stony box, I can only assume he's anticipating a scheduled task.

"You okay?" I ask.

"My internal clock must be off, they usually come by around this time," he mumbles.

"For what?"

He avoids my question and quietly sits back against the wall. Something worries behind that distressed glaze in his eyes, but I decline to dig deeper for an answer. Maybe he didn't hear me. He pulls out another cigarette, then looks at me and says, "May I, please?"

"Sure," I reply, knowing it doesn't matter. If it subdues his troubles, so be it. Besides, it may mask some of the more unforgivable smells in here.

He reaches for a match inside a small box, but it's empty. Donavan flips open the gold lighter he stole from the Russian colonel and hands it to him. Vaslav's face is stunned as he stares at the lighter, like a surfaced memory.

"Where did you get this?" he asks, rubbing his thumb over the engraving.

"Why, have you seen one like it before? " Donavan quizzes.

"Many years ago in a past I wish I could forget. Never thought I'd see one again"—he flips the light over—"from a colonel no less."

"Yeah, well he's a dead colonel."

"That's the best kind, isn't it?" He rolls the flint with his thumb and lights his cigarette. "It's a shame such gifted craftsmanship is floundered in the grips of evil hands."

"How would you know?"

"I've seen a many passed along to such hands."

"You worked for the Russian government, didn't you?"

"Not by choice, no. I and a few other gifted engineers were plucked from our Ukrainian homes to serve under a generous military contract that was anything but. I know what you may be thinking, but I assure you, my loyalty lies with my family, not some ravenous regime. I was told that if I supplied them with my talent, my family would be pardoned from war crimes. I, nor any of my colleagues, were involved with any of these war crimes they accused. The people of my country were pawns in a war we never wanted. It was no more than diplomatic speak for sparing my family. I had no choice but to comply."

"You've met him, haven't you?" I curiously push. His eyes meet mine and he frowns. He knows exactly whom I speak of.

"A year into my contract, myself and a colleague, Petro Yevtukh, were transferred. We became best friends over the years, our families, children. Until one day, Petro was called in by the director of operations to discuss a flaw in our engineering, a mistake that I had made. But like he always did, Petro took the heat for the error. His loyalty and friendship to me cost him dearly. He was severely beaten, ordered by a man spawned by the devil's own seed—Gennadi Olezka Gorshkov, the man who started it all. All because he took the blame for my mistake. I never saw him again after that day."

Vaslav looks away for a moment. His lip is quivering. "I've met many bad men in my days, but none as malevolent as Gorshkov. I'm sure you've heard all the rumors about his menacing acts of anger. They grow evermore, embellished the next time you hear them, but let me tell you, I've witnessed firsthand to prove those stories true."

He takes a deep drag from the cigarette and stares off in the distance, no doubt reliving the dark horrors of his past.

"It was the beginning talks years before the Ten compromise merger. I, like many others were escorted down a long, bleak corridor—the Devil's Hall—to Gorshkov's private conference room. Many diplomats representing various nations were in attendance, along with others who filled the seats by top economic strategists. Myself and some Russian council members stood near the back of the preliminary summit. Gorshkov's wife, Oleysa, who was a former foreign affairs strategist for the Syrian government, sat gracefully next to her husband. You could see the tension drawn on her face the entire meeting.

"Arguments erupted during the talks, but nothing out of the ordinary that provoked Gorshkov to engage irrationally. As the meeting came to an end, Oleysa finally spoke out, but her words, though profound, sliced like a razor with defiance against her husband's ideals. The room remained silent for what seemed like an eternity.

"Gorshkov immediately dismissed the meeting and angrily pulled his wife to the side. They argued while the conference doors remained open for everyone to witness. As she stormed out, Gorshkov grabbed the back of her arm, and with great malice, struck her across the face. At that moment, I knew he wanted everyone to see what he did so that they, too, would fear him.

"Everyone was ushered out of the lobby as Olesya lay on the floor. The only people left in the room was myself, a few ranking officers, the president from China, and two council members. He scolded her in front of everyone to see and strongly warned her to never question nor undermine his authority ever again in front of his peers.

"She was in tears, but what happened next was unimaginable. She stood up, faced him with blood dripping from her lip, and did the unthinkable: She called him a fucking coward. If silence could ever be defining, that was the moment. Seconds later, his eleven-year-old son, Abram, walks in and runs to his mother's side, no doubt, a display he's witnessed before. She continues to ridicule Gorshkov in front of everyone and threatened to leave him with their son and to never return. And then the moment I will never forget . . . it haunts me . . . He drew a gun from one of the officers and pointed it at his wife. He ordered his son to step aside, and Olesya stood there shaking. She looked at him sternly and said, 'Go ahead, pull the trigger and show them what you are really made of.'

"He retorted with an ultimatum, 'Oh no, my dear, I'm going to take from you what hurts the most,' and he shifted the gun toward his own flesh and blood. 'Bitch, if you don't kneel before me, apologize, and remember your place, there will truly be nothing left for you,' and with just five words, sliding from her lips, my definition of evil had changed forever: *You don't have the balls.* Not soon after a shot was fired, Abram fell dead.

"You know no fear of evil until you've stood before that vicious beast. That day I looked upon the face of the devil himself. I believe some people deserve a second chance at life, to be renewed and reborn, but I also believe there are some so inherently evil, they shouldn't have been born at all."

Vaslav takes one last puff from his cigarette before twisting it into the dirt floor. He leans back against the wall, eyes skewered to the cell door. He's silent and detached. We subtly withdraw and leave him with a moment of peace, if there is any.

A few minutes pass before the door creaks open down the dark corridor. Vaslav jumps to his feet, anxiously waiting. There's a loud clank, and footsteps and Arabic voices grow louder. We back away from the cell entrance as a shining light casts the shadows of men. The door unlocks and swings open. A young girl, face covered in dirt, shyly walks in holding a chain. A large man forces her forward while four thugs shove us back to the walls with their guns. Vaslav kneels with his arms extended.

"Please," he begs.

The man locks the girl's chain in place and exits the cell followed by his minions. As soon as their voices disappear, the little girl scurries over to Vaslav and nestles beside him, trembling. He pets her hair until she falls calm. Something purely evil resides outside these walls.

"Is she with you?" Nadia asks.

Vaslav's eyes crinkle shut and his chest throbs up and down. A man stripped bare of his pride painfully sobs inside. Tears trickle down his face.

The young girl, no more than nine years old, reaches up and wipes the tears from Vaslav's cheek with her tiny hand. "*Vse v poryadke dedushka,*" she peacefully consoles.

My heart sinks. Vaslav is her grandad. What happened to her mother is uncertain, and the temptation to unearth such curiosity shall remain that way. The girl's emotional display leaves me wondering if the little good left in the world will ever overcome its enemy. She reminds me of Allison—a girl who will grow into a young woman forced to mature with courage and strength through tragedy.

"This is Anya," Vaslav whispers.

Then something unique happens. Nadia gently approaches Anya. She sits down beside her and offers her hand. And for the second time I've witnessed Nadia speak in her native Latvian-born tongue. Whether it's motherly detachment or purely an instinctive bond, Anya clasps her fingers in between Nadia's and lays her sleepy head in her lap.

Vaslav sinks his head between his knees and sobs. I move to his side, wrap my arm around his back, and morn with him until his eyes dry. The cell grows quiet. While a broken man bleeds for redemption, the bravery of a young girl curls up to a stranger's voice. These are the things that man possess that push him to live, to fight, and to conquer the burdens we share. Our lives may rest in limbo, but our destiny looms in the hands of the Divine.

I lean my head against Vaslav's shoulder and pray.

CHAPTER 20

I lift my eyelids from a weary rest and find everyone else asleep. A jug of water and a wooden tray stacked with stale bread sit next to the cell door. I grab the water and peer through the iron slates. Not a soul creeps about.

"Hey," I nudge my brother, "have a drink."

He opens his groggy eyes, takes a few sips, then looks across the room. "*Vot... davay, pey,*" he offers, holding the jug of water out to Anya. She grabs the jug and takes a big gulp. Water dribbles down her chin and wipes away the dirt. Tiny lips emerge followed by a smile.

Behind her, Vaslav graciously hands out the pieces of bread. His eyes strain red and weary, but he does his best to hide it for Anya's sake. He offers my share of the bread, but I refuse and instead give it to Anya. She happily takes it and returns by Nadia's side.

I take advantage of the moment and lure Vaslav out of earshot from Anya. "She's going to need all the strength she can get. We're getting out of here one way or another, I promise you," I say.

"If you really want to get out of here, you're going to have to find a way to remove these chains. That's your only hope," he suggests. I follow the end of my chain and examine the clasp. Nothing but bolt cutters will cut through this.

The light flickers through the ceiling window where Arabic voices clatter. Everyone draws against the wall while I stand curiously beneath it and listen. Donavan uses his tall frame and rests his ear against the window. The chatter escalates, but their voices drift too far away for Donavan to understand.

"They're talking about a fight of some kind, I can barely hear them," Donavan says. Back and forth the muttering conversation continues until a gunshot echoes in the distance. Soon the voices trail off and disappear.

"Well?" I anxiously ask.

"I don't know what the bloody hell they're up to, but they're coming down now."

Anya's eyes grow wide before she tucks her head into Nadia's chest. Whatever dark depravity awaits outside, her eyes have seen it.

"Everybody stay against the wall and don't look any of them in the eye, no matter what."

"I'm not letting them take her again," Vaslav says.

"No one is taking anyone. Just go sit quietly by, my brother," I calm him. "Nadia, take Anya to the back and stay there."

Donavan addresses me with anger in his eyes, "We've got to do something."

"I know, but we can't take them with these chains on. I need more time to figure this out."

"We may not have the time."

My heart beats with fury as the outside door scrapes open. I hold tight to my brother and wait while boots trod down the hall. Two men approach the cell door, one eagerly smiling while the other unlocks it.

A Middle Eastern man with glasses, clean shave, and tailored hair struts in with a pompous flare. Nothing strikes me curious about him except for the Russian officer's coat he dons. Though it's worn, he wears it with pride. The other men step aside as he walks by. His stoic presence begs for respect and they give it to him without difficulty. Whoever these scavengers are, this man rightfully stands as their leader, no doubt. He straightens the tattered jacket and carefully scans our faces. After a moment of searching, he points to Gabe and barks, "*Hadha.*"

Two men pull Gabe to his feet and force him toward the door. He looks back at me with a fear I have not seen before.

"No!" I shout. I lunge forward at one of the men and slam my fist into his chin. He flops to the ground while the other struggles to hold Gabe. I shove the man back and pull my brother away from him.

Donavan stands between us and tames the scuffle. "Arena, don't! It's not going to make this any better."

The man on the ground grimaces and massages his lower jaw. The pain in my hand pales to the pride boiling from his glare. He stumbles to his feet and begins to charge me.

"*Tawqaf*!" orders the leader. The bruised man stops his advance and glowers beneath his battered ego and broken jaw. Donavan converses with the leader in Arabic, which I can only assume in an attempt to reason with the man. They babble back and forth before Donavan steps aside, leaving me standing eye to eye with the leader.

"I see you like to fight," the leader says in English.

"If I hit a man, it's because he deserves it," I retort.

"Good, I'll keep that in mind when you decide to strike one of mine again."

"What do you want?"

"For starters, respect, but I can see we've got a long way to go before we can earn that."

"You call bowing down to your every whim, trembling in your presence, respect?"

"I call it obedience, and with it respect is born."

"You're nothing without the men standing next to you with guns."

"Perhaps you are the same without your weapons. I guess we will soon find out. Take her, *khudhha*!"

Two men with guns push me forward while one drags the long chain behind me. I look back at Gabe, his eyes stretching wearily to me. "Don't worry about me, my dear brother. Stay strong and protect the others," I say in Gaelic. Then the cell door slams shut.

The men escort me down a cobbled-stoned corridor and up a gradual slope of steps. The squeaky door at the top opens to the outside. I quickly scan the grounds before my head is covered with a burlap sack. We're some fifty yards behind the stable and a small forest is in front of me.

A stick presses into my back, nudging me forward. I'm forcing to rely on my other senses. I count my paces and carefully judge the distance from the cells. Every few steps, a burly hand wraps around my arm and steers me in a different direction. Wood-burning smoke filters in my nostrils; my rattling chains shuffle through the grass. Birds tweet overhead following the cool breeze, flowing against my face.

We stop and another door screeches open. My boots scuff across a wooden threshold into a room where the drafty air dies. Voices mutter while I'm left standing there for a few minutes, wondering what awaits my fate. The chattering grows like a chorus of penguins gathered behind a wall.

A hand grabs the top of the sack and removes it from my head. My eyes squint as I take in my surroundings. A large wooden double door stands before me while the faces of my enemy glow dim in a dark corridor lit only by a few oil lanterns. One of the men smiles as if I said something amusing, though I doubt any of these scavengers could process a simple insult.

Two men maneuverer in front of the large doors and wait. Whatever lies behind them, their menacing grins give me no additional comfort. Am I being escorted through the gates of hell? The two men release a metal clasp and spring open the heavy doors. We exit the room. My ears ring to a lively chorus, prattling in the dark. Tall trees, faintly visible from the night sky, tower in the background.

I'm escorted out about thirty paces to a pile of stones, some stained with old blood. A husky man with the face of a child clasps the end of my chain to a metal anchor that's sunken deep into the sandy ground. I'm left alone in the dark surrounded by burbling voices. Over and over they clatter until they evolve in unison to a collaborating chant.

A plume of fire blazes across the way. The sudden burst diminishes and glows an amber cast where faces appear. Then another and another. One by one, curls of fire spurt around me, blooming with light and revealing more.

When the last torch flames, I gasp. I'm standing in the middle of a small makeshift stadium where hundreds of faces look down on me and shout, *"Qutila, qutila, qutila!"* What bloody hell is this?

The crowd near the top right of the stadium parts, and the man in the Russian jacket enters. The chanting begins to fade as the crowd gives him their undivided attention. The leader looks on with arrogance, soaking in their allegiance. He steps forward into a boxed seat and addresses his peers. When he finishes, the crowd erupts into gratuitous roars.

They bellow into another chant as two guards enter the opposite end of the stadium and park next to another set of double doors.

From the crowd's praising chants, I can only assume my favored opponent awaits behind them. The doors open and a monster of a man walks out to a thunderous frenzy of cheers. The chants continue with fists raised in the air while my fate rests in this gladiator-style modern-day Roman colosseum.

My opponent stands near six-five, with moderately muscular shoulders and a protruding gut peeking beneath his undersized shirt. His beefy arms hang like giant salamis. The colossal fighter resembles more of a donut shop patron than a gladiator, but his large frame will make it that much harder to bring down. My beastly foe proudly stands among a sea of fawning loyalists while I'm ridiculed near a pile of rocks. He blows the mucus from his clogged nose and glowers at to me.

Another guard enters the arena and hands the portly animal two machetes. My anxiety skyrockets as I wait my turn for my weapon. My mind races, my eyes scanning the arena for anyway out. A few moments later, a man from the crowd tosses a small wooden staff, crafted for a hobbit, at my feet. *You have got to be fucking kidding me?*

The double doors close and the crowd cheers. I grab a sharp stone and bang it against the end of my chain, but it's useless. The mammoth man moves forward, snarling and grunting. I stretch my chain as far as I can and wait with a toothpick in my hand and limited mobility. "Okay, assnuts, let's see what ya got."

The man strikes first and slashes the air with one of the machetes. He wields them like a child, clumsily swinging them without purpose. I dodge his swishing attacks, curtailing swiftly on my toes.

He charges me back as far my chain allows and pins me in a corner. I slip through his grasp and strike across his knee with my stick. He stumbles to the ground, but only briefly. The scorn shading his face makes him angrier as he stalks me back to the pile of stones. Our eyes meet, ten feet apart—a brief standoff quickly fading. He sneers like an old bull and slowly steps to his right. We circle each other and stare each other down, anticipating the other's moves.

Our distance closes as my chain wraps around the stony pile. I stop, raise my stick, and wait. He lunges forward and strikes across with his blade. I maneuver behind his swing, but catch a counter blow from his fist to my cheek.

I spill to the ground, my lips bleeding. The crowd cheers and my face stings. *Damn that hurts.* I shake it off and race on top of the rocks. He swipes again, chasing the air and clips the back of my heel.

I tumble to the other side and crash into the dirt. He climbs over and follows like a madman. I crawl away, but my chain tangles. I'm pulling with all my might as he lumbers down the rocks. The chain releases and catches his feet, tripping his massive frame nearly on top of to me.

I roll to the side and clutch on a stone, but he grips my boot and slides me over. My eyes widen. His machete hovers above ready to slice. I stretch my chain between my hands and block its swinging edge. Metal gnashes, pressing down inches from my head.

I swing my boot across his face and escape his wielding blade. The callous crowd erupts in a chorus of boos. The man staggers to his feet, partially defeated, and shouts in anger. The distance between us widens. He picks up my stick and tosses out of my reach.

My only hope falls on my agility against this trotting rhino. That and my chain lying in his path. He grits his teeth and charges at me, but I stand my ground. Closer and closer he springs forward, blades flailing. My eyes peer steady and my rigid boots plant firm in the sand. Within striking distance, he bows back his arm and swings his machete across his chest. I kneel down, grab my chain, and yank it against his fumbling feet.

His ankles tangle and his knees buckle to the ground. I quickly wedge the chain between his crotch and wrap it around his throat. He drops the blades and gasps for air, thrashing his arms about. I squeeze the chain around his thick neck until his mouth gapes breathless.

His arms go limp and his body falls like a timbered tree. The roaring crowd is silent. I scan the stands and find the leader. He stands proud among his peers, but says nothing and instead lifts a menacing smile. He looks down upon me as an expendable piece of entertainment, nothing more.

If my disdain for him isn't clear enough, I grab one of the machetes, sever my opponent's head, and fling it into the stands. Taunts and jeers erupt while I stand, covered in my enemy's blood, amongst a cult of malice swine who couldn't give two shits about their headless champion.

A group of armed men enter the arena and encircle me. One approaches with cuffs and shouts with fervor. I don't need a translator to know where this is headed. I drop the machete on the ground and hold out my wrists. I'm cuffed and escorted out of the arena amid a thunderous reprise of boos. The double doors slam behind me and a sack slips over my head.

We exit and the arena and amble through a grassy terrain. I'm needled in the back with what feels like a gun barrel, pushing me forward. Well over a hundred paces later, a door creaks open. They remove the sack from my head and guide me down the steps and through the rugged corridor. A guard shoves me in the cell and clasps my chain in place before slamming the door shut and disappearing down the hall.

They're all looking at me in anticipation. I smile.

"Shit, Arena, you're bleeding," Gabe exclaims.

"Don't worry, it's not my blood, I'm fine."

"Where the hell did they take you?" Donavan asks.

The sting from my cheek lingers. "To participate in their fecking games."

"What games?"

"Ah . . . so you fought in the colosseum? " Vaslav interrupts.

"You've seen it?" I ask.

"No, but a many of my cell mates have participated."

"Yeah, well where are they?"

"Exactly. You're the first to come back. Should I assume they stopped the fight?"

"When my opponent fell dead? Yes."

"Hahahaha, that's good . . . that's very good. Humility just pisses them off, but at least you have their respectnow."

"I don't want their damn respect."

"What are we going to do?" Nadia shudders next to Anya. "They're eventually going to come for each of us, and I really don't want to know what they have in mind for me."

"After what I just went through, I don't know what to expect from these assholes, but we better find a way to get out of here . . . and now."

Vaslav leans against the cell door and muses through the bars, "There might be away, but it's risky."

"I'm listening," I acknowledge.

"These visits are not random."

"What do you mean?"

"They come down here like clockwork, twice a day: one to take one of us away for God knows what, and the other to bring us food and water. They never break schedule . . . unless you give them reason to.'

"What's your point?"

"Well, they've already come for you, which means the next time they show up will be when they bring food and water . . . an opportunity to be prepared when they come."

"They have guns, we do not, so how does that help?"

"Ah, that's the beauty of it. They won't."

"How do you know this?"

"I've been here long enough to observe. They normally deliver the food when we are asleep, which doesn't garner a fully armed group of men to bring it. I mean, it's just water and bread, for God's sake."

"How many?"

"In the last two months, just one."

"Yeah, but we're still behind a cell door."

"There's one thing about these scoundrels you'll learn; they aren't incredibly intelligent creatures. Instead of crafting a small door to slide the food through, they're forced to unlock the cell and slip it by. When that door swings open, that's your one and only chance."

"So why haven't you tried to escape?"

"I'm too old and weak. I wouldn't have gotten too far before my life was taken, and I certainly didn't want to risk

Anya's. But now, everything has changed. Not until you showed up did I believe it was possible."

"Okay, so all we have to do is pretend to be asleep, wait for the asshole to open the door, and pounce on him. I think we can handle that," Donavan says.

Vaslav sighs. "There's just one problem."

"What's that?" Gabe chimes in.

"We are assuming this man will have a key to unlock our chains. If he doesn't, the rest of his tribe will come looking for him, and I can assure you they won't be forgiving."

"And there's no other way to get these chains off? " Donovan says.

"What about some of that chemical compound you have stored back there?" I ask.

"It would have to be stabilized and completely directional, otherwise it would slowly burn or make a hellish noise and blow your arms off. I'm pretty sure you don't want that."

"So what do you suggest, we take a chance or what?" Donavan dismissively flares.

"That's the risk, isn't it? Sometimes it outweighs the reward, depending how desperate one becomes. So unless you have a key on you, I'm afraid you're stuck here a little longer before you can think of a safer way to escape. Whatever you do, be one hundred percent sure."

Gabe angrily kicks the empty jug of water. "We stay here any longer and we're all going to die."

I grab the end of my chain and mull over the plan. Vaslav is right; we need to be absolutely sure before we even think about doing this. I examine the cuffs attached to my wrists and rub my fingers over the keyhole. As I focus on the rusty slot, it suddenly hits me. I quickly stretch my fingers deep inside my left pocket. Yes, I feel it! The bronzed key the mysterious old man gave me in the mountain. With my wrist bound, it's difficult, but I finally inch the key out and stare at it as if it were the Holy Grail. I place the key in the slot, close my eyes, and hope. Without resistance, the key turns and the cuffs release. My eyes glaze over in a moment of clarity. What doubts I left in the past remain buried, but in this moment, seeing is believing. My spine shivers with delight.

I unbound to the others and toss the rusted cuffs at Gabe's feet. "Let's get the hell out of here."

"How did you—"

"With this." I hold the up the key and smile.

Donavan's eyes glow with excitement. "Where did you get that?"

"My pocket. How I got it is a bit more complicated, but it doesn't matter. We're getting the hell out of here . . . all of us." I look over at Vaslav, but his eyes shrivel and he turns away.

I unlock the clasp on my ankle and pass the key to Donavan. While everyone frees themselves, Vaslav quietly disconnects from the group. My stomach unsettles. I'm no good at burying someone else's pain.

I stand next to him and whisper, "Not the kind of reaction I expected from you."

"You're not out of the woods yet," he softly answers.

"You mean *we*."

He turns to me, eyes grave and cheeks sunken. "You and I both know I'm not leaving here."

"I'm not gonna leave—"

"Yes, you are. I'm on my last leg. I'm too old to be running, and I'm not going to slow you down because you feel sorry."

"Why do you choose to wade in the dark if I can save you from it?"

"My child, you have already saved me, but if it's light you are searching for, then all you have to do is look upon the fires that blaze against the skies."

"What about Anya?"

"Anya doesn't need an old man to raise her. She needs a mother, a protector, and someone to look up to."

"She needs her family."

"By the grace of God, she is still here, but not because of me." His eyes moderately cast down with a secret hiding behind them. "After the third day they stuck us in this prison, Anya's mother was taken away. When several days went by and she didn't return, that's when I knew whatever strength she had left was passed on to Anya. We never saw her again. I don't know how much of that strength is left in her, but I know it won't last much longer. She's a strong girl on the surface, but I'm afraid there's a seed of hate brewing somewhere down deep, and I can't blame her for that. No matter what you do, you get her as far away from here and take her somewhere safe. You owe me nothing, but at least promise me that much."

"Yeah, I promise, but she's going to expect you to come."

"Then you keep her from that, you hear?"

"I'll do what I can."

He places his wrinkled hand on mine. "Thank you . . . now go, get your rest. I have my own planning to do."

I return next to Donavan and lean against the wall. I'm overwhelmed with sadness and look away from Vaslav otherwise I'll cry. To survive this long and not continue is heartbreaking. He's a true hero, sacrificing himself for his granddaughter, for us. My mind races over the grim chance we don't make it, even without Vaslav. Surely this can't be how it ends, not like this. Though I sit with good company, my heart remains dark and alone without my son. I'm tired of living in fear, but I must keep fighting. As long as I'm alive, I will not let his fellowship sever.

Donavan fumbles with his cuffs relieving a nervous but understandable tic. We only have one chance at this. "So, what lies beyond those doors that we should be afraid of? Because I'm hoping you got a better plan than just running," Donavan says.

"The only thing we need to worry about is who's going to be standing outside that door. If we want to escape safely, then those horses are our best chance. We're about fifty yards behind the stable, but I can't guarantee if anyone is or isn't guarding that area. And we have no weapons, so that leaves us in a bit of a fix. Complete silence is our shield."

"Aye, that and swift feet," Gabe clarifies. "Those fields were pretty empty when we got here. We get to those horses and we'll make it out of here. They don't seem too hell bent on taking anymore prisoners unless they have to. They've got us."

"He's right," Vaslav concurs. "This cell has been empty save for me and Anya for weeks before you came. Yair used to talk about their hunting habits. For the most part they scavenge to the north and west, along one of the main roads."

"All right then, saddled or not, we ride these horses south until they collapse. Nadia, you ride point. I want Anya with you. Gabe, you flank Nadia, and the rest of us will protect your lead. No matter what happens, no one stops . . . not for anything. You keep riding like your life depends on it, because it will. We have a few hours before our food comes, so you better get your rest," I say.

I nuzzle up against the wall a few feet from the cell door and keep my ears on guard. Donavan pads next to me and exhales an uneasy breath. "We're going to get out of here, I promise you that."

Whatever small doubt I may have had about this man's valor, it no longer exists. From the troubles he's journeyed, I truly believe him. We may wrestle with our own demons, insecurities, or convictions, but one thing remains strongly steadfast with this fellowship. It will not break easily. What saves us from this hell, rests with our courage. We stand together, true. Now all we can do is wait.

CHAPTER 21

Three hours slip past and yet no sign from any guests. My eyes lazily drift aside as I watch my friends fall asleep. The light fades from the ceiling and the walls grow unusually cold. My arms begin to tingle. I lift my head from my knees and rub down the tiny hairs, trying to stay warm.

Gabe stretches his groggy eyes open. Without warning, a clash of thunder rumbles and the corridor creeps with light. I quietly nudge Donavan awake. A door slams in the corridor.

I press my back against the wall, tucked into the shadow. Donavan nests against the wall, head turned, pretending to sleep. Heavy steps indiscreetly shuffle behind the dim light, crawling closer to the cell.

Peeking through my lids, I patiently wait for the door to swing open. The lock clicks and the entire room vibrates under another dose of echoing thunder. A shadowy image of a man pauses behind the cell door. Is he on to us?

A few seconds later, the door creeps open no more than a foot, and an arm breaches through holding a jug of water. He places it just inches from my boot. My restless muscles twitch, waiting for the perfect opportunity. The guard stretches his arm farther in and bobbles the bread next to the water. Like a prowling cat, I lunge and swing the cell door wide open.

He stumbles back to the wall and staggers frantically down the hall. I pounce on his back and pull him down. His head strikes the floor with a crippling thud, knocking him out. I plant my eyes on the door, anticipating it to open, but nothing moves.

Donavan and Gabe race over and carry the guard's body inside the cell. They hide him in the back, out of the light, and chain him for good measure. Anya's eyebrows raise, drawing together, as she shudders against Nadia.

"You must hurry now before they get suspicious," Vaslav beseeches to me.

"Come with us, we can carry you," I offer him one last chance.

"No, it was meant to be like this. You have your reasons, I have mine." He tucks the can of gunpowder in his arms. "Not everyone is allowed second chances, and I'm not going to squander this one. Don't worry about me, dear, you just run and don't look back."

Suddenly, the sky bellows in raging song, low and rumbling. It approaches closer, soon above us with a continuous burst of furious chaos. The ceiling quakes and the walls shiver beneath an eerie chorus of what resembles thousands of shofars blasting at once. Three times the piercing roar engulfs the air and rattles my eardrums.

"What bloody hell was that?" Donavan quavers.

Vaslav looks up at the ceiling window and his face flattens with fear. "Must be the devil's hour. Go, get out of here now!"

I nod my head as Vaslav . . . there isn't much time for anything else. And just like that, we sprint out of the cell—Nadia holding Anya, Gabe and Donovan ahead of them, me in the back.

"Papa, Papa!" Anya cries as we race down the corridor and up the steps.

"You get to those horses and ride south, no matter what, you hear me?" I order Nadia. She nods, holding tightly to Anya while Vaslav cries a last goodbye down the hall.

Donavan cracks open the door and peeks outside. "Okay, let's go."

We exit into the dark, wind gusting with hellish might. An amber glow flickers from behind the trees near the stadium while shadows of men dart past. Clouds roll by with a thunderous clap and shake the earth. Fat raindrops are starting to fall. Horses flee across the fields while a few men scurry after them. Shots fire from the trees. Voices bark behind us and chase on our heels.

"Go!" I shout.

We barrel through the grass behind the stable and hop the fence. A scavenger rounds the corner and collides with Donavan, and they tumble to the ground. The man rolls over and draws his gun.

"Donavan!" I scream, and jump on the man. His gun fires into the air before Donavan wrestles it from his hand and cracks his neck.

"Arena, they're coming." Gabe points to a dozen men springing out from the trees.

We race inside the stable and through the cobbled galley. Donavan and Gabe unlatch the box stalls where only one horse has been saddled. The others, still bridled, remain bareback.

"Come on, let's go," I urge.

Nadia and Anya mount on the dark brown Friesian outfitted with the full saddle. Anya looks terrified. While Donavan and Gabe wrangle their horses, my eyes settle on a small glimmer sitting against the back corner. I move closer and find my swords, bow, and bloodstained dagger hiding in the shadows, but my guns are missing.

"Arena, come on," Nadia urges.

"I'm right behind you, now go!" I slap the back of her horse. The majestic Friesian flutters its nostrils and squeals before galloping away.

Donavan and Gabe straddle bareback on their rides and whisk shortly behind. I grab my weapons and tug on the reins attached to a gray-speckled thoroughbred. He refuses to move, frightened from the thunder. The stubborn beast lifts his head and utters a soft whinny.

"Dammit, come on!"

He staggers out of the stall and nudges against my side down the galley. My heart races as the barn door blows open. A scavenger storms through with his gun drawn. I pull my katana and strike a fatal blow across his chest. His gun fires and spooks the horse into a frenzy. The horse kicks his front legs in the air and squeals. I reach for the reins and try to calm him, but he resists and backs into the corner. Loud voices creep outside the barn. I grab the man's gun and seep into the shaded corner with my sword raised and wait. My hands tremble. A dozen men gather near the doors and erupt into a gnashing of words before they recognize their dead comrade.

They cautiously roam inside and slink into the galley entrance. One of them shouts. Unplumbed from the shadow I emerge and unleash unforgiving malice, carving my way through a sea of flesh. One by one, their lifeless bodies drop. I'm unhinged with ruthless hatred, and when it's all over, I'm standing in a pool of red and soaked with their blood.

The last voice fades, but a few more usher outside. I sidle through the galley door and shoot three more men running past. More will come. I sheath my katana, hop on the horse, and kick his muscular thighs. He puffs an angry breath from his nostrils and bolts outside into the paddock. The wind howls across my face as he charges into a hoof-stomping gait. Nadia and the others have vanished far into the long stretches of grassland. I race after them, feeling the strength and stamina of the horse's legs.

Menacing clouds swoon beneath a clash of thunder. The horse's steps tremor with an erratic fit and shift me unbalanced. I slip to one side as shots fire from the trees and zip past. The horse stymies near the open gate. His ears snap forward and his head rises up. With a swift thrust of his front legs, he bows and I'm thrashed from his back. I land on my backside on the soft fertile soil while his reins tangle with the fence. I gasp for air and wince.

A lone scavenger sprints across the brush, firing into the dark. Bullets pelt the fence. I quickly grab the reins and hop back on the horse. The raving man closes in when suddenly a shadow from the clouds swoops down and lifts him from his feet. He spews a blood-curdling scream before vanishing into the sky.

I press into the horse's girth and hold on tight. He canters across the open field with little effort as shouting men fade behind us. With the cluck of my voice, I urge the powerful beast forward until he stretches his legs into a full gallop and lengthens our distance. The ranch disappears into the dark.

I look back at the stable and question Vaslav's decision to stay behind without his granddaughter. Suddenly, the ground rumbles under a thunderous roar, and the sky erupts into a blazing plume of orange. Bursts of fire bloom across the trees, exploding like the Fourth of July.

Vaslav did not abandoned his granddaughter because he did not love her. He left her with a love few men are willing to give: his sacrifice. I watch the billows of smoke rise to meet the clouds and know that for all the days Vaslav searched and toiled, he finally found his redemption.

Goodbye, my friend, rest well.

CHAPTER 22

The sky opens and rain pours down, pelting my skin, soaking my clothes, hammering the dirt. Thankfully, the horse doesn't seem too bothered. I keep my head low and squint my eyes as we forge ahead. Nadia and the others are far from my reach as I struggle to catch up. My horse, kept captive for God knows how long, sprints freely with excitement. I lean forward and hug his bristly silver mane, feeling the power surge through his muscular frame. The smooth coat unwashed of dapple gray shimmers through the chasing wind. I've warned myself before about becoming attached to an animal I may never see again, but this beautiful creature deserves a name all the same. Since we left the ranch with fury behind a cloud of fiery dust, I shall call him Ash.

The land quickly changes, making it difficult to pass swiftly across. The rain eases up significantly. The grassland fades and a small desert terrain emerges in the middle of nowhere. Tufts of golden sand scatter beneath Ash's hooves. We canter across the desert floor, stretching nearly a hundred meters before we meet a range of rolling hills that are carpeted with a sea of olive brush and stony soil. Ash powers his way over the rocky knoll and trots gracefully down the other side where Nadia and the others wait. Their horses lap up puddles of water left behind from the quick storm.

I slide down from Ash's back. Donavan approaches and gasps. "Sweet Jesus, you're covered in blood. You okay?"

"A bit of misfortune, but I'm fine. Blood looks much worse when it's not yours."

"You found your weapons I see," Gabe says, and I nod. He stands really close to me. "Don't ever fecking do that again."

"What?"

"I'm tired of worrying about you. You made it out, but you may not next time. I've had enough death haunting me, no need to add to it."

"I'm so—"

"Save your apology, Arena!" he shouts. "I'm your brother, remember? I understand, but I need you . . . we need you, okay?" His eyes, though hardened, are heavy with affection. I haven't the words to respond because he's right. Instead, I hug him. He whispers into my ear, "I'm glad you're alive."

Anya tugs on my arm, and in a small, trembling voice, she cries, "*Gde dedushka?*"

I meet her weary eyes and melt. I haven't the heart to tell her about her granddad, so I lie. "He wishes he could be here, but he can't."

"He's dead," she retorts plainly.

"Honey, your granddad—"

"He's dead! I'm nine, not two."

I kneel down and search beyond her swollen eyes. A girl, struck with unimaginable tragedy, looks at me with brutal honesty. She deserves the truth.

"He loved you very much, more than most could understand, but I suspect you know that already. Whatever it is you may fear he went through, you clear that from your mind. Because I promise you he did not die a hopeless man. If anything, hope is what saved him. Hope is what gave him courage. It's hope that he put in you. No, he did not die for himself. He died fighting for you, for all of us, and that can never be taken away, ever. He was a good man, and he will never be forgotten. I'm so sorry, love."

Her head dips low, and she quietly sobs. She buries her face into my chest. "I want to go home, I want to go home," she sobs. After a moment, she lifts her head and looks at me. Her cheeks are red and tear-stained. In a drained tone, she voices a peculiar but honest question: "What happens now?"

Nadia steps beside Anya and lends her hand. "Come with me and I'll promise you a place you'll never have to fear, where you'll never starve, and always be loved. I will never let anyone hurt you again. I don't have much, but it's all have to give."

Anya reciprocates the offer and clasps her fingers between Nadia's. Sometimes words can ring hollow, but Nadia's compassion give them strength. She musters a small smile and lifts Anya onto their horse. Gabe and Donavan follow in silence. I grab Ash's reins and stroke the side of his jaw. Our eyes meet for the first time and without any distractions, a small connection surfaces. He nudges me with the bridge of his nose and whinnies.

I mount up and press my heels in. "Let's get the bloody hell out of here."

We press forward across the grassy hillside and drift southward through toiled farmlands. The storm fades behind us, but it won't be the last. Our last push into the city of Beit Shemesh must go through the Tzora Forest, a forage of rough hills and valleys steeped in an old age of border tension.

A broken trail of sculptures line a passage through the east, but we steer clear and jaunt southward, deeper into the forest. The sweet scent of pine and terebinth calm the horses. Birds freely chatter and fill the trees—an oasis in a mysterious land.

But they begin to sparse as we amble farther away, deep into the unknown. We exit into an open pocket of land where the timber disappears and the forest's velvet green floor prospers. We cross the grassy basin and bask in the forest silence and a heady smell of hyssop.

An olive tree stands alone in the middle of a nearperfect circle of grass, surrounded by the wild thicket we just wandered through. While their budding limbs around us freely dance in the wind, the air inside the circle is strangely still. Not even a small breeze blows against my cheeks. The olive tree stands at attention, its limbs almost petrified, but no one acknowledges its presence.

We wander past it as whispers begin to appear, but only to me. No one else seems to hear them. They grow louder, emerging from the ground and flutter inside my ears in a language I can't understand. Without warning, the sky moans and the green grass turns red as blood. No one notices but me. Am I hallucinating? Have I gone mad?

The forest returns as we leave the peculiar circle, but my curious eyes wander back. A strange shadow follows behind and covers the olive tree. Its branches uncurl, and its trunk twists before the entire thing vanishes. Either I ate some bad mushrooms, or something is purposefully haunting me. Whatever it may be, I'm the only one to witness the bizarre event. The others press forward through the trees while I timidly follow close behind.

We follow along an abandoned trail, worn into the grass. The forest rises where multiple hills merge. Some bathed in weeds and rocky soil; others cut from the waters many ages ago or split by ancient quakes deep in the earth. Straight ahead and nestled on the heights on one of those hills are two massive trees bowing away from each other. Their gnarled twisted limbs proudly stretch east and west, parting the forest greenery.

We pass through the gaping hole left behind and wander up a gritty hill. The rocky ascent leads to a ruin of an ancient monastery carved into the soil and left in decay. At the top, we perch on one of the stony cliffs and garner a commanding view of a city in the short distance.

"So that's it," Donavan sighs.

"It better be, my ass is numb," I answer.

We descend the rugged slope and exit the storied forest. Two roads cross our path: one stretching to the north, and the other leading around the small city. We bypass them both and instead stroll across a sandy field sitting behind a wall of modern domiciles. Rows of apartment flats scatter along the perimeter, some constructed along the hillside.

We proceed through a neighborhood to the clacking of hooves beating the street. Large concrete buildings, with terra cotta ceramic rooftops, are carbon copies of each other. One rarely looks different from the other. Though they stand in exceptional condition, the streets passing remain empty. We leave the vacated living district and head east to the center square. A web of streets intersect below towering commercial structures that extend in all directions. Though the city is much smaller than Tel Aviv, it certainly rivals its entertainment district. A claustrophobic cluster of retail shops, eateries, and bars pepper the central market, but not a soul scurries from them.

The center of town displays an aging array of architecture compared to its more youthful surroundings. Synagogues built from ancient stones sit on neighboring streets while others rest under dilapidated conditions. Years of history hides here, some good, some devastating.

Though not all has been abandoned; a few faces emerge from the street and stare as if we are carrying the plague. More people surface from emptied buildings to alleyways. I'm afraid our presence may have disturbed their daily rituals. We reach Nieman Square shopping center where hundreds of people gather outside a farmer's market.

Without Father Joseph or Jacob, we're lost, wandering for clues. Faces glow unfavorably toward us as we pass through, some painted with fear. A young woman, holding a crinkled handkerchief, steps close to Ash and offers it to me. I stop and search her face, waiting for her to speak, but she doesn't. I grab the cloth and wipe my face as a kind exchange for her odd and unexpected gift. But then I look down on the blood-stained handkerchief and realize it isn't so strange after all. I must look like a nightmare to these poor people.

"*Toda raba,*" I kindly express.

She nods and sifts quietly back into the crowd where many still run their eyes over our surprising presence. One man stands out. A Tavor assault rifle dangles from a leather strap across his tattered shirt. His charcoal beard hangs low, scraggly and peppered with gray curls. His face is dusky and withered. Without the fear the others possess, he comes forward and bravely engages.

"What do you want here?" he asks while swinging his rifle to my face.

"Lower your weapon, soldier, and ask me again . . . nicely."

He runs his eyes up and down before withdrawing his gun to his side. "Pardon my reaction, but I'm sure you understand why. The name is Asaf. Now . . . how may I help you?"

"We're looking for an IDF battalion, possibly a thousand strong."

"Military you say?"

"Aye, they would have passed through here maybe two days ago."

"You here with the American, aren't you?"

"American?"

"Tall fellow, blond hair. Came here with some troops, but not a thousand as you say. Looked pretty rough, the whole bunch of them. Said to be on the lookout for a crazy Irish girl with attitude."

"Is that so?" I say in amusement. A few chuckles pass from Nadia and Gabe. I'd feel less aplomb with that depiction if it weren't coming from Jacob, but knowing he's alive, I'll gladly accept it with pride.

"Well, I'm no detective by any means, but if that's not your blood, I'd say you fit the description."

"Is that tall lad still here, I'd like to have a word with him?"

"That all depends."

"On what?"

"What are you willing to give me?"

I draw the dead scavenger's gun that's tucked into my pants and aim it at him. "Your life," I say casually. He's an amateur at negotiating.

"That seems like a fair deal to me," he quavers, eyes wide.

"I'm glad you see it that way, enough blood has been spilled."

"I'll take you to him. He and many others have been waiting."

"Your rifle?"

He carefully removes the strap over his head and hands me his gun.

"You'll get it back when I see Jacob," I promise.

Asaf hops on a modified bird scooter, broken down from years of use, and creeps out in the middle of the street. "Come," he waves his hand forward.

We follow on horseback behind him past the square and through several winding streets where few people wander. He stops and parks his puttering scooter next to a withered synagogue with barred windows and a crumbling façade. An aged steel sign with Hebrew text and the Star of David cut into it hangs above the door.

Asaf stands outside the steps and presses a button on the wall. A mumbling conversation in Hebrew chat back and forth into the intercom speaker. Moments later the door cracks open.

"Come, let's go," he ushers us inside.

We tie our horses to the back of an abandoned car's bumper and enter the synagogue. An old Jewish man dressed in ragged priestly vestments greets us. It smells like an open grave inside.

The stained concrete floor glows dingy under dozens of candles that light a path near the front of the Temple. Electricity remains long forgotten in this place as the wax drips down wooden pedestals, gathering in clumps at the base.

Broken pews, stacked on one another, line the crumbling walls. Cracks and divots litter the floor. The arched ceiling slightly sags under old age, but the top wall edges surrounding the Temple thrive, festooned with decretive arcs of blue and golden ropes. A massive lectern crafted with the finest woods and covered in ornate carvings stands near the center front.

"Take them down," the old priest instructs Asaf.

"Down?" Donavan curiously mumbles.

This musty tomb remains abandoned, left riddled with a decaying and lost history. What lies beneath it can only be worse.

I follow Asaf with my hand comfortably nestled around my gun. His brief encounter with Jacob notwithstanding, I'm disinclined to trust him any further, but he's all we got.

He leads us through a door behind the front of the Temple and down a small corridor. Many prayer rooms, left empty, line the back hall. In between each room stands large ornamental bookcases filled with old books. If they were any older in appearance, they'd fall to ash if grabbed.

Asaf stops at the end of the corridor and pulls down on a dust-covered scepter perched on the stoned wall. The bookcase near me rotates inward and opens into a dark and dank crevice. Lights slowly glow bright in the shadow as concrete steps begin to emerge, spiraling downward into the unknown.

"Follow me," Asaf says as he descends the stairs.

No doubt he's trampled up and down this spiraling tread before. We reach the bottom maybe twenty feet below the Temple and wait outside another door where a small camera mounted above slowly rotates.

The lock clicks from the inside and the door swings open. Through the stale air I'm greeted by a delightful sigh as my eyes meet a familiar face.

"Arena!" Father Joseph exclaims as we embrace each other. "Are you hurt, lass, you're covered in blood?"

"You should see the other fellow."

"She's always covered in someone else's blood," Gabe jests.

Father Joseph pulls Gabe over and wraps his arms around him, nearly exhausting the breath from his lungs. "So good to see ya, son."

Nadia joins in the festive greeting while Donavan and Anya awkwardly stand at a distance.

"Who do we have here?" Father Joseph searches keenly over Donavan.

"My name is Donavan, sir. These kind folks gave me food, water, and a chance to survive a bit longer."

"He's just being modest. Truth is, without him we wouldn't have made it here," I proudly explain.

"Well then, I'm forever indebted to you, good sir." Father Joseph extends his hand as the two shake firmly.

"Likewise," Donavan retorts.

Anya's weary eyes struggle to stay open as she shyly nestles next to Nadia. Father Joseph digs into his pocket, squats down beside her, and offers her a piece of gum. Her timid little fingers reach out and grab it.

"And who's this brave, young girl?" Father Joseph asks.

"This is Anya . . . and brave is an understatement," Nadia says. "I'm quite sure she's lived up to it and beyond what any of us have endured, but all that's in the past. She's with us now, in our care, and in a better place."

"And so she shall be then." Father Joseph gazes curiously over Anya, but he leaves her story a secret and declines to further probe.

"Where is he, Father?" I'm eager to see Jacob.

Before he can respond, a torch light beams near the back where a voice calls my name. Jacob darts across the rigid floor with a smile stretched across his face. Without delay, he holds me in his arms and laments, "You scared the hell out of me, love."

My cold cheek nuzzles against his neck and my insides flutter. His skin quickly warms over mine. Though my heart dances in his arms, I feel foolish for leaving him in the first place.

"I'm so sorry, Jacob, we didn't—"

"It doesn't matter," he holds my lips. "You're alive and safe. That's all I want. There's plenty of time for a story, but now let's get you out of these bloody rags. You all must be starved. Come, we have plenty of food and water."

Asaf willfully clears his throat in a rather stroppy attempt for my attention. "You forgetting something?"

"Oh yeah, almost forgot." I hand Asaf his gun back as promised.

"What's this?" Father Joseph nosily interrupts.

"Nothing," Asaf mutters.

"You let her disarm you?"

"She had the draw on me."

"With what, her eyes?"

"With this." I hand Father Joseph my gun. He removes the magazine and chambers it clear.

"This gun is empty."

Asaf shakes his head with embarrassing discomfort. "You tricky, little—"

"Choose your words wisely," I warn.

"Friend?" he humbly responds. I offer him a departing wink and a grin before he shuffles away.

The underground layer beneath the Temple serves more than just a hiding place from enemies. The well-crafted structure, built many decades ago, houses the IDF with an abundance of survival supplies and military operational equipment. This facility—one of three small ones surrounding Beit Shemesh—serves primarily for refuge during a potential cataclysmic fallout.

Sixty to one hundred people maximum could possible live down here for months without returning to the surface, but with it comes flaws. The aging walls are crumbling and the only tunnel reaching to the main IDF underground bunker has collapsed. If the Temple were ever to be compromised, we would be stuck down here.

While the others eat, I clean the sweaty stench off my bloody clothes with soapy water and lay them out to dry. Nothing feels more inviting than hot water cascading down your back, but that doesn't exist here. Instead, I shiver unpleasantly under a cold tap, the water trickling over my bruised skin, but I'll take it.

Over the next few days, our journey will be put on hold as we wait for soldiers to heal from a bloody battle that chased them here. Though they held their own in defeating an onslaught from our raging enemy, nearly forty percent of our battalion died doing so. Those still standing surround us and are responsible for protecting the outer edges of the city. Only half of our vehicles made it to Beit Shemesh and most are abandoned, empty of petroleum. According to the locals, the trucks that normally roll in once a month to refuel the city's holding tanks haven't surfaced for days. We presume the roads north have been compromised, which makes this unexpected impasse more troubling for us to leave. Without aid from the northern troops, I'm afraid our journey pauses here for now.

Before we can return to the Mount of Olive, Jacob waits for orders from Sadiq, who leads a frontline defense of nearly one hundred thousand men defending the Jordanian border. While Lieutenant Yaris protects the West Bank with seventy-five thousand troops, the rest of the division holds strong in the western city. Our numbers may appear meager to our enemy, but we will not cower and hide. We will stand and fight.

This war may be the death of us all before it all ends, but our depleted troops here remain steadfast, not because they made it out alive in Tel Aviv, but because they truly believe there's still hope. Whether or not we triumph, our fate holds on for another day.

I don't know what lies beyond these few days of peace I have with Jacob, but they could very well be my last. These are the times we embrace the small joys in life instead of waiting for great expectations to arrive. Why do we struggle with this so much? I have my brother, my husband, and my friends, but one agonizing question haunts my thoughts: How long will it before I see my son again, or if I ever do?

I hold quiet away from the others in a small bleak room with two cots and a moth-eaten blanket. While my clothes dry, I wrap my naked body in a thin, damp towel and lie on the cot. I stare at the pitted plaster walls, waiting to hear my husband's voice as my eyes slowly close.

Part III

At the Devil's Door

CHAPTER 23

What cures me with sleep disappears when I wake. I wish the tinder moments and warm welcomes would last beyond my expectations, but the truth is, they don't, not in this world anymore.

The room dimly glows from the two melted candles sitting on the table. Their yellow flames sway back and forth, casting eerie shadows dancing on the ceiling. The bed is cold without Jacob, though he's left behind some warmth in the blanket crumpled at my feet.

I stare at the candles, my eyes swaying into a hypnotic daze until something unusual happens. The flames stop completely still, burn the color of sapphire, and bend toward each other without breaking. The silence fades to sinister whispers, seeping through the walls. The room grows dark and my blanket slides ominously across my legs.

I jump to my feet and grab my knife, shaking, when suddenly a man's screams echoes behind the door. I dart out of the room in only a shirt and underwear and follow the blood-curdling scream to the main room. Three soldiers carry a man, arms flinging in agony, and place him on a table. Blood runs over the man's ribs.

Father Joseph dashes from a side room with a metal cart filled with medical supplies. Two soldiers brace the hysterical man to the table while the other grabs a syringe from the cart, draws liquid from a vial, and jabs it near the man's neck. Within moments, the man's frenzied wailing softens to a wheezing murmur.

Gabe, Nadia, and Donavan creep from down the hall and watch the horrific scene beside me. The door from the stairs opens and Jacob rushes in, his hands stained with blood. A uniformed medic with a satchel scurries behind him.

"What's going on here, and why are you holding a knife, Arena?" Gabe asks with worry tucked behind his eyes.

I answer, still shaken from the haunting whispers, "We need to get hell out of this place."

I drop the knife and curiously walk over to the wounded man. Donavan follows beside me anxiously rubbing his fingers.

"Christ almighty," Donavan gasps.

A ten-inch piece of metal shard has pierced the man's abdomen. Blood runs freely. His eyes glaze over and he begins to mutter incoherently.

The medic gingerly examines the wound. He presses around the damaged skin with careful attention and sighs.

"We got to get this thing out of him," Jacob urges.

The medic steps back and rubs his hands over his scruffy stubble. "We take that metal out and this man is going to die. I'm afraid that's the only thing keeping him alive, for the moment."

"Jacob, what the hell happened?" I ask.

"A few of our men spotted him stumbling in from the northern side of the city, wailing and going on about attacks."

"Attacks, from where?"

"I don't know, he's been rambling the entire time."

"He's lost a lot of blood, hallucinations and confusion isn't uncommon," the medic says.

"He's not hallucinating," I snap.

The man mutters again, his mouth barely moving. It opens wider and his voice grows louder before it suddenly ceases. His blue irises fade, and his pupils grow larger until the whites of his eyes are as black as coal. The muscles in his arm relax and his fingers uncurl from the table.

"Is he gone?" Donavan asks.

The medic thoroughly checks his pulse before determining the man's death. I reach over to cover his eyes, but suddenly he grabs my wrist with his gnarled fingers and warns with his last breath, "He's coming."

His hand releases and his arm falls limp. The whites in in eyes return while his pale face rests still and cold.

"This poor man did not stumble in here by accident," I exclaim.

"I've seen some pretty creepy shit from dead people,but that . . . that is not natural," Donavan gulps. "I nearly soiled my pants."

"Those eyes . . . did you see his eyes? Cold and black." Father Joseph shivers. "Deep behind that void is a man who has endured great pain, not by choice. I believe this is an omen."

The soldiers slowly step back from the body while Gabe hovers over the man's ashen face and fixates his eyes with deep study. Gabe's hand begins to tremble.

"Gabe, you okay?" I ask. He doesn't answer and stands unmoved, dazed under possession. "Gabe," I snap once more to get his attention.

He places his fingertips on the man's forehead and slowly slides them across his sallow skin. "There's something more here," he frets.

"What do you mean?"

"I can see this man's past, where he's been. It's not like anything I've experienced before."

"Are you sure, lad?" Father Joseph asks.

"Aye, I'm sure of it."

"What do you see?"

Gabe searches deep, straining for an answer when suddenly his eyebrows narrow and the corners of his mouth dip downward. His face hardens as a great sadness falls from it. "My God," he exclaims.

"What is it?" I ask.

"This man came from the mountain."

"What?"

"Yes, I can see it. Dead bodies lie scattered . . . outside, in the streets, in the halls. Red painted everywhere."

I gasp for a breath. "Joshua! Do you see Joshua?"

Gabe's tongue rests in silence. Distraught and near motionless, his eyes stare through me. A complete void washes upon his face except for a small tear trickling down his cheek. My body flushes into a cold sweat.

Gabe stammers, "I–I can't see him, but I don't know for sure. Not everything is clear."

My stomach churns while tragic thoughts surface. "I should have never left him! I should have never left him!"

"If you didn't, we would all be dead," Gabe offers. "You did what was right, okay? I may not be able to see everything, but sometimes I don't have to. Joshua is in good hands, I can feel it . . . and I know you can too."

"No, no, no, no!" I say in a frenzy. "Pack your shit, we're leaving, now!"

"Arena, just wait and think for a minute," Jacob tries to calm.

"What's to think about? He's our son, Jacob, and he's still out there somewhere."

"I'm not suggesting he's not—"

"Then stop thinking for once and trust me."

"We have no way of transporting our troops, and we're going to need that backup."

"Backup? Jacob, people are dead and our son is missing."

"I understand, but we need soldiers."

"Then they stay behind! I'm going to find Joshua with or without them even if I have to drag my bloody feet across this wasteland."

Jacob grabs my shoulders. "Look, if your brother is right, then we know that the area has been overrun. We left two thousand troops stationed near the mountainside. Even if you do get inside the city, it would take twice that number to reoccupy the position, and we have no idea how many enemy troops subverted our own. So unless your brother can tell us what we are up against, storming in there hell bent without a plan will not get our son back. It will get you killed."

"He's our son!" I angrily snap, and storm away into the hall.

Whatever darkness haunts me in our bedroom, its presence disappears to where it came. Only the shadows from the flickering candles remain untouched. I throw my weapons on the bed and cry. My body trembles and my mind unhinges. I can hardly breathe under this brewing anger, and the knock on my door doesn't calm it anymore.

"If you came here to talk me out of leaving, you're wasting your time," I growl.

"On the contrary," an unexpected voice replies.

I'm surprised Father Joseph walks in instead of Jacob. He looks tired.

"You don't think I'm making a mistake?" I sniffle.

"I believe you choose what you choose because you know what's best."

"Well, that's a diplomatic way of putting it."

Father Joseph sits beside me on the bed. He pulls a small thin metal casing from his pocket and opens to reveal a picture of me and Gabe.

"I believe you and your brother were about five years old here. Your mother gave it to me many years ago."

I smile. "We look so happy."

"Aye, aside from the difficult times, you found a way to smile more then."

"And now?"

"I've known you your whole life, Arena. Watched you grow, change, and make extraordinarily tough decisions, but not once did you give in. Despite the circumstances, even at your worst, you survived. I regret not being around your younger years, but I never stopped . . ."

Father Joseph is almost hesitant to finish his thought. I've never witnessed such a strain hiding behind him before. Whatever it is, he leaves it suspending for another time before continuing. "I believe in you, I always have, but sometimes we lose ourselves in the moment, even if what we know is right."

"What are you getting at?"

"Sometimes it betokens us to step back, take a deep breath, and listen."

"I trust my gut."

"I know you do, and I don't question that one bit, but so does your husband. He loves Joshua just the same and is willing to do whatever to find him."

"So what am I supposed to do?"

"Extend Jacob a little grace, Arena. He's a part of you now. He's not here to work against you, but rather with you, if you let him. I've been around him long enough to know that every step you take and every second you're away, he's afraid he's going to lose you too."

"I'm not angry at him . . . I'm just angry, it's a mother's instinct. I'm allowed to be angry, no?"

"I wouldn't have it any other way with you."

I reach my arm around him and nuzzle my head against his shoulder. I let his words sink in and cling to him in this fatherly moment. I'm almost afraid to let go.

"I'll let you get some rest," he says, and leaves my side.

"Hey," I call before he exits the room, "I believe you would have made a great dad." He smiles, but it's overshadowed by his glassy eyes.

I sit on the bed, contemplating what I'm going to say to Jacob, but I haven't the words. Like Father Joseph suggested, I take a deep breath before leaving and hope my ears will lead instead of my mouth.

The old man's body is covered under a ragged blanket. I watch as two soldiers carry the body out the door and up the stairs. As mysterious or deranged as he may have been, his haunting last words linger disconcertingly in my head. I stare down at the blood stained floor left behind and wonder if they were spoken just for me.

Jacob, Gabe, and two officers, Malka and Peretz, hover over an unfurled map on a wooden table. Gabe voices a strenuous concern during a strategic debate. "We cannot trust the main roads, even if they—"

"He's right," I blurt without knowing where the conversation has taken them. Jacob's eyes search me as I walk over, but he remains quiet under my interruption. The two field officers stand stricken with the same silence as they cast their eyes down at the map.

"I've been thinking about what you said earlier," I acknowledge Jacob, "and you're right. We have no idea how far their troops have occupied. It's better to take the road less traveled than expose ourselves before we even have a chance to think about the mountain. But there's a smart way to go about this even if we don't have backup. I'm not suggesting we storm into a lion's den, but we can at least maneuver close enough to manage our options, and hopefully by that time receive some troop support from Sadiq."

Jacob pulls me into a hug and kisses my forehead. "Welcome back."

"I'm sorry to even suggest—"

"No, don't . . . you were right."

"I just want him back."

"And we're going to find him, I promise you, but if we're going to do this, we need to map the safest passage. I'm thinking we take the south bend to Nes Harim and follow in on Highway 386, then take a slight detour through the south eastern neighborhoods. If those old barriers are still open, we should be able to cross through the university district and maintain our distance below center city. It will get us close enough to establish a midpoint and survey from Liberty Bell Park."

"Possibly, but still too risky. If they've taken the mountain, it's a good chance they moved forces inward to subjugate any livable spaces north of Kiryat Shmuel, but that's probably a stretch and I'm quite sure they don't want to spread their forces thin. I've been through this part of town and there's nothing worth occupying, mostly stragglers and thieves, but it's still an area I'd avoid."

"You could always follow the green line around the city," Officer Malka suggests. "It's not but a few kilometers more, but you'll need to be extra alert. That border may be a barren wasteland, but there's always an uncertainty that lies on the other side."

"Hostile?"

"Resistance is rare, mostly poor independent rebels, but don't let your guard down for anyone. Regardless, I'd take my chances there before I moved deeper into central city."

The green line, also known as the 1949 Armistice Agreements, was a signed compromise between Israel's neighboring countries to end hostilities from the 1948 Arab–Israeli War. This led to these armistice border lines between Israeli forces and Jordanian-Iraqi forces.

"Agree, it would behoove us to circumvent any main thoroughfares running through that part of town. I suggest we take the 386 and drift southward to the green line. We can follow it around until we reach the settlement near Ma'ale ha-Zeitim and hold there. It's unlikely that any enemy troops would breach that far in an area that's crumbling and unstable. That should give us a good viewpoint from the west entrance."

"That sounds like a solid plan," Father Joseph approves from across the room. He enters the conversation with a slightly alarming expression. "I'm afraid we're still cut off from the bunkers in Jerusalem. No radio signal has been detected yet, or at least no codes transcribed. We'll keep trying. In the meantime, I suggest we take a weapons inventory and evaluate our transportation situation."

Three days have past since we stepped into this bunker and not a single radio transmission has been received from Sadiq, which makes our lost signal from the mountain even more worrisome.

"We have four strong, fit horses ready to ride. They've been well-trained and can handle a full gallop at twenty solid minutes. I expect we can make the jaunt in two and half hours with proper rest stops."

"That's a fine start, but four isn't going to be enough."

"Unless you can muster enough petroleum to fill a couple of vehicles, I'm afraid that's all we have."

"We'll talk to some locals in town. We might be able to rustle up a few more horses, but I can't guarantee they'll be thoroughbreds," Officer Malka offers.

"That'll do. I suggest we pack smart and not overburden these horses any more than needed."

Officer Malka dismisses himself up the stairs while Officer Peretz escorts us down a crumbling corridor to the weapons bunker. The secure room contains a mess of tactical gear, guns, and open crates filled with ammunitions. Not a wide array of weapons to choose from, but they get the job done.

I nab two Jericho 941 semi-automatic pistols. They will never replace my reliable Berettas, which are now buried somewhere beneath rubble back at the horse ranch. A gun is just a gun in the eyes of someone who has never handled one, but for me, the feel and weight means everything from its pull, reach, and the slightest recoil. I can already feel a new relationship building as my thin fingers hug around the smooth, comfortable handle, but it quickly vanishes. My cheating eyes drift from the 941 and stake claim to a rare piece of weaponry hiding in the corner.

"What do we have here?" I gleam mesmerized.

"That is Matilda, or as we call it, the Path Clearer," Officer Peretz explains. "The AA-12 is a fully automatic twelve-gauge shotgun, three hundred rounds per minute, stainless steel, and most importantly, very little recoil. Comes with a twenty-round drum magazine, full slugs or pellet."

"I think I just made a new friend."

Before anyone else notices me toting this unnecessary gun, I grab my new toys and exit the bunker. The joyful moment disappears as I leave the hall into the main room. Nadia, knees pushed to her chest, sits alone near the wall and stares at the floor looking distressed. Her head lifts when I pass, but her smile is forced.

Somewhat unexpected, but Nadia keeps her cards close to her vest. If there's anyone she trusts, aside from my brother, it's me. "Everything okay?" I kindly intrude.

Her face softens, but her eyes linger forlornly, "To be honest . . . no. Feeling a bit overwhelmed."

"We've been through a lot on this journey."

"To say the least."

"How's Anya?"

"She's resting. Still out of sorts, but adjusting as much as anyone could."

"Look, I've been meaning to talk to you about—"

"I know what you're going to say, and you can save the speech. I made a pact with myself long ago that no matter the circumstance, I would be by your side, fighting and protecting."

"I appreciate your devotion, but sometimes things change that aren't under our control."

"My loyalty has never changed."

"No, but it can change for a better cause."

"I love that little girl, but in no way could I ever replace her mother."

"And no one is asking you to. Right now Anya isn't looking for a supermom; she needs love and care."

"I promised her a place that's safe, without fear—"

"And you have given her that. I'm afraid until this war is over, this is the best place she has right now."

Nadia's eyes are glassy and her lips press together. The tough decision for her to stay sinks deep.

"Hey, you owe me nothing. This isn't the last of our days together, but that little girl needs you," I say.

"And what about Gabe?" she presses.

I wish I could tell her that my brother would understand, but he'll probably fight me on every level about my decision. Nadia knows me too well to see through my bullshit.

"I'll talk with him."

"Good luck with that." A small snicker escapes her pursed lips and rightfully so.

"I may need some backup," I smile.

"We've relied on each other through some difficult times, haven't we?"

"That we have."

Her smile slips back and her eyes grow weighted. "So why does it seem like every step we move forward something pulls us back?"

My face hardens with no answer. I place my hand on hers and leave the conversation in silence instead.

CHAPTER 24

As dusk settles into its peak, the horizon blooms with swirling smoky gray clouds. A slight breeze blows past the dry desert sands with the smell of burning wood from the far reaches of this city. The musty, bitter scent favors a childhood memory I long to return to.

Ash and the other horses roam the wind-swept gardens behind the synagogue where I wait alone. The gardens, once green and flourished, wither along with the rest of the world, but our feathered critters don't seem to mind. Lively goldfinch flutter in and out and perch atop the cedar trellis while starlings sift through the toiled remains for food.

My patience runs low of wanting to leave this place, but I must concede to our plans. Jacob's trust in me cannotfalter any more than I led Nadia to believe she must stay behind. Leaving her to wrestle with that decision to look after Anya begins to tear at me. I'm not sure if Gabe will ever forgive me for encouraging it, but I know it's the right thing.

Ash brushes his muzzle against my shoulder, seeking attention like a child. I pet his soft speckled coat and cuddle my cold cheek against his. His affection warms me over and lessens the angst steeping inside me, but like all things, it fades. Footsteps glide alongside the Temple, ending this private moment.

"Thought I might find you out here," Donavan says.

"And I was hoping that was impossible," I quip back.

"I didn't intend to invade your solitude, but I can see I'm not wanted, so—"

"Don't be daft, I'm just having a go at ya. Come over and keep me company."

Donavan shyly edges near me and strokes Ash's silvery mane. "Beautiful creatures, aren't they?"

"Who would have thought we'd end up depending on them, rolling back history to an age of simplicity?"

"And yet we've still managed to undermine civility." He calmly gazes at the brimming horizon. For the few days I've spent with Donavan, I know his behavior like my own, and this small exchange isn't what brought him here.

"So what really brings you out here?"

"Do I need a reason?"

"Well, I know it's not for the existential conversation." A quiet pause follows. His eyes disengage from mine, and for a moment I feel our connection separating.

"Everything between you and Jacob okay?"

"Jacob and I have always had the same goals. Sometimes we just go in different directions to get there, but we do get there in the end. Is that what you came to ask me?"

He steps away from Ash; his eyes are burned with worry. "Has it not been bugging you what we encountered down there?"

"Exactly what are you referring to?"

"You know exactly what I mean. That old man, what he said before he died."

"I haven't forgotten."

"Good, neither have I. It's best we heed those words."

"Do you really think he meant—"

"Yes! I do, and it scares the living hell out of me. Vaslav wasn't a crazy old man, and I don't believe he would make up such a vile story. I've seen what Gorskov's henchmen are capable of, and I don't need this bloody lighter to remind me either."

"I know the cruelty and malice Gorskov breathes, but—"

"So doesn't it stand to reason that if he's coming, then every follower is coming with him. He isn't stupid enough to come alone. Jerusalem will be breached with more soldiers than it's ever seen in its history. He's going to bring everything he has to stomp out any hope we're clinging to."

"It's hope that begs me to search for Joshua. What happened to your daughter was beyond tragic, it's unthinkable, and I can't even begin to comprehend the pain you feel, so you can understand why I want to find him. I made the grave choice of leaving him there, so why shouldn't I go back?"

"That's not what I'm telling you."

"Then what is it?" I huff.

"I don't believe in much, but I do believe my fate brought me here to fight with you and to protect you at all costs. We're about to travel into the belly of the beast. These people can't afford to lose you. They need your leadership, your confidence, and your faith if they want to even have a chance to survive this war. Admittedly it's tough to grasp, but I don't see a young woman in front of me trying to survive. I see much more behind her worried motherly eyes. Many of the people we are fighting for may not know who you are, but they will know by the end of this war, the courage you brought, the hope you instilled, and the vestige you will leave behind for generations to come."

I feel a weighted heaviness in my body. "I know what I have to do, but I just wish people didn't depend on me so much," I say softly.

"God has granted you with great things. Use them so others can see beyond what's in front of them. Lead them from the freedoms they can't see and extend their days in a world where they can."

"And if I can't?"

"Then you better start believing you can."

Donovan walks away, then turns back to me. "We will

find your son, no matter what it takes, and I won't leave your side until we do. We live together, we fight together, we die together. That will never change." Then he disappears around the corner.

Dusk gives way to the angry, rumbling sky. Another storm brews from the west, delaying our journey on horseback, but I'm restlessly motivated to travel through it anyway. Donavan's words press deep in me as I search for the confidence I once held, but my mind darkens. Instead I find the devil prowling in the midst, seeping into my fears. Though I refuse to give in, tonight I'm truly scared.

Rolling in on hell's breath, a blast of thunder roars. The carved columns crack and pieces of aged stone crumble to the ground. Something truly wicked spawns from the sudden winds. I leave Ash to his siblings and quickly return to the underbelly of the Temple.

Silence covers the bunker lobby, but not alone. Gabe's eyes hover over the map while the halls remain empty. He's quiet in my presence. I grapple with the need to respond to him, but instead I retrieve my new weapons, still stationed on the table, and leave my brother's solitude.

"I'm not mad at you if that's what you're thinking," he remarks under a weighted tone.

"Gabe, I wasn't trying to separ—"

"I know. I'm just—"

"Just what?"

"Feeling selfish."

"That's perfectly normal."

"Is it? Because that young girl sleeping back there, who's been ripped from her mother, may think otherwise. Anya needs Nadia a lot more than me—I understand that deep down—and yet here I am feeling like an ass because I don't want her to stay. What does that say about me?"

"It says you're human. There's no fault in that."

"I've lost someone I've loved, I can't do it again . . . I can't."

My heart is heavy at the thought of Juliana. "And you won't, because you're going to stay here with her."

He looks shocked at the thought. "But you're family, and I never leave family."

"Gabe, I want you to take a good look around here. Because no matter the circumstance, we're all family here now. Nothing changes that. You don't have to prove your loyalty to me by being by my side. We're always connected. You make your own decisions for you, not me. I'm not here to tell you what to do, but I will stand by whatever you choose."

His eyes slink to the floor and his face solemnly drifts away. With the uncertainties of tomorrow, I hug my brother, maybe for the last time, before I leave the room. I hold my tears as I head back to my room to wait for the storm to pass. That was the hardest conversation I'd ever had in my life. I love my brother so much. We've been together since birth. It was hard enough to handle his separation from me while he was inside the prison at Cairo. But he's suffered through enough, and he belongs with Nadia now.

Jacob is lying on the bed with his eyes shut, but his ears open to my muttering voice. "I wish we would have never left," I lament softly by his side.

"Like your brother said, if you hadn't, we might not have ever seen each other again."

"No, not the mountain. America."

Jacob turns to me. "You don't honestly believe that would have been a good idea?"

"I often wonder."

"If you hadn't convinced me to leave, we'd all be dead."

"But we wouldn't be living out this nightmare either."

"If spending another second with my wife is a nightmare, then I don't want it to end."

I dip under the covers and cling to Jacob's chest. For the precious moments we are given, I hold onto the powerful truth from his words and drift away from the chaos swirling around my mind. Thunder booms in the distance, signaling all that is yet to come.

* * *

Voices linger in the halls as Father Joseph sweeps past our door in a hurry. I grab my sword and head into the main bunker where Asaf, Donavan, and several Israeli soldiers chatter near the stairs. I stand in the shadow of the hall and watch from a distance.

The prattling continues, mostly from Asaf, whose animated conversation elevates into a spewing discourse of pure fright. He stands aghast with arresting fear covering his pale face.

"They're everywhere, sitting, just waiting," Donovan gasps.

"I've seen this once before," Father Joseph recalls.

Curiosity itches as I interrupt, "Seen what exactly?"

They stare at me in surprise except for the stoic gaze I often receive from Father Joseph. "Ah, good, you're up," he plainly recognizes.

"It's probably better if you come see for yourself," Asaf suggests.

My interests grow with every step as I follow them up the stairs and through the hall. Asaf becomes nervous as we draw closer. He stands back and hides behind one of the boarded windows while we approach the synagogue doors. As soon as we exit the building, my arm begins to tingle.

Thousands of crows are perched across the grounds like an ocean of black feathers. They surround us and beyond deep into the city, staring and waiting. Three horses, saddled and reined, stand in the sea of black. They wait calmly as if the birds didn't even exist.

"Soon after we approached the Temple, they just swooped out of the sky in droves, not a sound, just perched on the streets, waiting like statues," Asaf explains. "Look at them, just staring at us with those cold, black eyes. They didn't fly here on a whim. They're here for a reason, but I'm not sure I want to know what that is."

The conversation fades from my ears and instead a whisper calls to me from the middle of the flock. I dip into a small moment of silence as Michael emerges from his crow body. He stands not three feet in front of me, but no one else can see him.

His words flow like a gentle breeze, pushing through noisy chatter. "Terrible danger awaits in the shadow of men. The gates of hell have been opened, giving demons of all kinds freedom to roam. No one is immune to their temptation, especially not you, so be aware. Now, draw your sword."

"Why?" I ask with a timid shiver in my bones.

"You'd be kind to do as I ask."

I feel eyes on me as I pull my katana and hold it steady. Michael clutches the cold steel blade in his hand and squeezes. For a moment, the sword begins to shimmer blue and briefly glows like sparkling sapphires. A tingling sensation crawls from my grip and runs throughout my entire body. He releases his hand, leaving the steel shimmer to vanish.

"Your guns have no power over evil you cannot see. When you come across such a malevolent being, and you will, draw your sword. He will know who you are."

"And who am I?"

"You already know who you are, Arena. Don't allow the illusions of man to cast you in doubt."

"Is that why you've come here, to shed light on my weakness?" I wrangle his words with catty sarcasm.

"I came here to ease your weary heart," he speaks softly from his faceless head. "You must leave for Jerusalem now. The West Bank is on the brink of crumbling and flooding with the enemy. If you want any chance of finding your son, you must go immediately. Do not stop until you get there, for your horses will not thirst nor their legs tire. The favor upon these beasts serves you in this moment, so go."

My beating heart returns to the cry of my son. Michael dissolves into the wind and flaps his feathered wings back into the sea of birds. The peaceful moment disappears.

"Arena, Arena?" Father Joseph snaps his fingers in front of my face. I blink my eyes and lend my attention back into the conversation. "Where did ya go? You left us for a minute, and why did you pull out your sword? Something wrong?"

"Pack up your things now, we're leaving," I order without an explanation. The crows part a path as I exit the front steps to retrieve the horses. Their eyes follow mine, waiting at attention.

"These creatures came here for you, didn't they," Asaf assertively alludes.

I answer with silence, then quickly shout to my feathered friends to fly off, "La' oof!"

The ground disperses with a windstorm of flapping wings into the gray sky and leaves Asaf slightly more frightened than before. I guide the horses to him and hand over the reins. "Gather the other horses from the garden and saddle them if you can, by any means possible—padded blanket, folded rags are just as good. Anything to keep my ass from breaking."

Asaf, alert and filled with terror, grabs the two soldiers and dashes off behind the Temple. Donavan heads inside to prepare the others. Father Joseph stands on the front steps quietly reserved. His eyes cast lowly upon me, and his usual stoic air deflates. He looks sad.

"Father . . . are you ready for this?" I ask as he disconnects with my eyes.

"I'm not sure what to think anymore, but I know you've always been ready. This is what you were born for."

"Was I?"

His eyes drift away before he disappears into the synagogue without answering. The peculiar interaction draws me to follow, but I don't. I leave his aloof behavior to harbor in secrecy. Our kinship struggles not in our silence, but in our desire to understand it. If he wants to unravel his feelings to me, the truth will extract itself one way or another. Until then, it's his to carry before he can no more, and I will hold him to that.

The sky to the north buries itself behind a strange amber glow—perhaps an ominous sign from Michael's warning. Whatever lies ahead, it grows with intensity. I leave it for now and return down below to retrieve the rest of my weapons.

A sense of urgency follows Jacob across the bunker lobby as he scurries next to two soldiers into the communications room. Donavan whisks after, dangling his pack in one hand and resting his gun firmly in the other.

While Gabe stirs past short of noticing me, a lamenting voice carries down the hall. Behind a slightly ajar door, Nadia hovers over Anya under a wistful embrace. Without a hint of being discreet, I stare through the open crack and fall dismayed. What have I done?

Nadia has stood by me through thick and thin, and now I may never see her again. I leave my heart spilled at her door and return to my quarters where my weapons are strewn on the bed and blankets tossed on the ground. I gather my things and sit alone in the empty room, wondering if I pushed Nadia too far into a decision she never wanted. Our fellowship teeters on the edge of falling apart, and I can't deny being responsible for it.

I close my eyes and black out the subtle noises around me. For a moment, everything is still. Only by the beat of my heart do I notice the pulsating grim gloom of a funeral march. The serene dance of my soul loses its balance and returns to the chaos of the world. Noises clutter, and for a split second, my son's cry echoing in my thoughts. I open my eyes and release a cantering breath to the voice of reality.

"The horses have been saddled the best they could," Father Joseph interrupts, standing at the doorway.

"Good," I say in a daze. I can still hear my son's cry.

"Are you sure you're ready for this?"

"At the risk of sounding arrogant, always . . . and yet, never," I peddle back.

"Well, it's honesty that'll push you forward."

"Or hold me back." I grab the last of my weapons and leave this underground dwelling for the last time.

The candles lining a path through the middle of the Temple's sanctuary have all but melted into a puddle of wax. Their flames fade as I exit the dark asylum. Jacob waits outside on horseback. The horses are staggered behind one another in the street, and all but two are saddled and ready. A blue-and-gray quilt, folded long ways, sits atop River, Donavan's auburn mare, and a black afghan blanket that's frayed at the edges hangs over Ash's back. I welcome any padding my bony ass doesn't have to suffer through.

"It's the best I could do under the circumstances, my lady," Asaf addresses. Not sure if he's being a sarcastic ass or if I'm being flirted with.

"My lady? No need to project pompous titles. We're all the same here."

"Believe me, she's no lady, I can attest," Gabe cackles. He mounts on a horse, and I'm a bit surprised with his decision to come, which makes it that more difficult for Nadia's decision to stay. But my brother's presence gives me hope and strength.

Without stirrups, Ash's tall frame makes it quite a feat to mount. "Need some help?" Donavan reaches down and kindly offers his assistance.

I step into his clasped hands and whisk myself up on Ash's muscular back. The sheer strength of this flighty animal can never be underestimated. Ash stretches his neck forward and whinnies excitably. His eager restlessness reverberates with my own.

Under more placid restraint, hooves clop next to me where Asaf sits atop a calm yet hardy Arabian horse with a beautiful chestnut coat.

"And what do you think you're doing?" I ask.

"No doubt something evil is lurking in these parts. I find myself much safer fighting next to you than waiting for it to come to me."

"I wouldn't be so sure. Death follows me like a tick on a pig, but I welcome your bravery."

Netanel, one of our best field officers, crosses the street and joins our plucky caravan. His young face, chiseled with sharp lines but worn from battle, hides behind a short bristly beard that matches his short hair. Thick brows hover above his brown eyes, narrowing together with intense regard. Though what he lacks in intuition, he makes up with a fiery disposition to follow orders. And those are the kind of soldiers I need.

The last horse waits for Father Joseph. I stew with anxiety for him to walk through the Temple doors, but Nadia exits with Anya. They stand on the edge of the steps and wait. Moments later, Father Joseph emerges and stands behind Anya, gazing noticeably doleful. Anya clutches to Nadia's side and her eyes squeeze shut. A weighty stir shrouds over me. I search Nadia's sober face, waiting for her to say her goodbyes to us, but instead, she releases Anya's embrace and mounts on the last horse.

My heart tears in confusion. Though Nadia's decision to ride with us lifts my spirits, Father Joseph's choice to stay back is almost too much for me to handle.

He walks over slightly resigned, hand clasped with Anya's. "Here." He hands me a small satchel. "I took the liberty to pack some essentials for you."

I graciously take the sack and bite back tears. This isn't how this was supposed to play out. I never thought for one second I would go about this journey without him. Despite his kindness, my sadness rises to the surface and threatens to destroy me. My lips tighten as I fall silenced from his unexpected choice to stay. I almost feel betrayed by a man I looked to as a fatherly figure. He grabs my hand and lifts a small smile on his face, but there's a regrettable absence of unanimity drawn on mine.

His reasoning, notwithstanding, I refuse to leave him here until I've forced that one word struggling to breach my lips. "Why?"

His eyes gracefully run over my face. "I must stay back and radio Sadiq. You're going to need all the help you can get."

"Anyone can operate comms, why you?"

"My duty lies here now—"

"Bullshit." I turn my head away to hide the lone tear falling down my cheek.

"I don't blame you for being upset, Arena."

"I'm not upset, I'm disappointed."

"Aye, the sting of truth. People can live their whole life lying to themselves, but sometimes it's the disappointments that hurt the most."

"I'm not disappointed in you . . . I'm disappointed in myself for not trusting you more, for not listening to you when I should have, and for not spending the small moments we could have had," I choke out. "Remember when we first met?"

"Yes, I recall you having a knife in the shape of a stick pressed into my back," he grins.

"You embraced me like my father did."

"Your father was a good man."

"But he wasn't there, was he? You were." His face begins to wither, lowly and somber. "You told me you knew my mother well, maybe better than Finnegan perhaps, but it was special. I could see it gleam in your eye when you spoke of her. She trusted in you, and for that I shall do the same, but I don't have to like it. You told me you devoted your life to protect me and my brother. Where does that stand now?"

"I'm afraid you've grown beyond my defense. Whatever follows you now comes not from this earth. I've seen it with my own eyes and I believe its protection will better serve you."

"But I want you with me," I cry.

He gently pats my hand. "Our paths will cross again, Arena. This is not the end of our journey together, but it is the end of our ride."

I quickly wipe the tears from my face and catch my breath. The clack of hooves clop from behind as Nadia rides her horse beside me.

"I know how you may feel, but I told you from the beginning, I'd fight for you, no matter the circumstance," Nadia reassures. "Well, this is one of those times where nothing has to make sense. It just has to make it right, and in no scenario am I supposed to abandon my leader, my team, or my friend. It may not matter in the end, but if Kale did make it back to Jerusalem, it's worth it to me to at least know if he's still alive or if he lies among the dead."

"What about Anya?"

"I'm strong. I may be young, but I can take care of myself," Anya asserts. "Besides, you need her more than she needs me. I have everything I need here to protect me until she returns."

"I guess there's nothing else to persuade you with."

"Nope," Nadia simply says.

"Don't be sad for your losses, be glad for your gains, because you're gonna need them," Father Joseph wisely offers. He grabs my hand once more and gently squeezes. His eyes swell with tears, but they refuse to fall. "May God be with you, Arena. I'll see you on the other side," he says before returning to the Temple steps with Anya.

For the past three and a half years, Father Joseph and I have forged a relationship from salty disagreements and mistakes to humble beginnings and nurturers of compassion. Bit by bit, we've chiseled away our flaws, imperfections, and pride to become who we are today. I no longer see him as just my protector, counselor, or friend. Our relationship has finally tempered like a resilient sword that refuses to chip. He's been like a father to me when my father wasn't here. And now here we are, at a passing to which I may never see him again . . . at least in this life.

I hold his gaze, our eyes saying what hasn't been voiced. He nods his head, releasing me into the wild once more. I press my heels into Ash's muscular girth and canter to the front of the pack.

"Let's ride!"

CHAPTER 25

What evil waits before us leaves me pressed with anger. It lingers with an unforgivable sting gnawing at my gut and trembling deep inside. My thoughts swirl about my head—in and out, they vanish, all but the crying echo from my son trapped in the folds of my brain. No peace shall find me until I see his face, for tomorrow remains futile. But today we ride.

The chafing wind scores at our backs as we forge through rigid valleys and across a barren scape riddled with spiny bushes and stony trails. The sky begins to darken as we follow the storm left long ago that now creeps in the east.

With the strength of Ash's gait, I press him forward at the front of the pack. Jacob rides slightly behind and to my right while the rest of the fellowship drafts closely behind.

Dusky clouds move past in shadow among the stirring flight of crows surging next to them—all but one. Michael's wings flap rigorously above me, streaming alongside Ash's galloping pace.

We maintain a constant push through the fertile grasslands until we reach the rugged hills, curbing our strides. The land rises up to the dusty ridges, sprawling with jagged cliffs. I slow Ash's step and guide our caravan carefully around the stony path.

The horses, galloping for miles, have yet to collapse from fatigue, just as Michael had promised. What flows in the blood of these beasts manifests beyond my understanding. Still, these animals must thirst after a long and tumultuous journey. Below the hills just a quarter of a mile lies the moorland where we can take a breather.

We trudge across the gritty sands around bended turns, winding gently down a graveled slope. An old military-style jeep, far from the reaches of any road, is upended at the bottom of the hill collecting sandy drifts of dirt and wild vegetation growing around its underbelly. Whoever drove it left the tragic wreck abandoned, but it's not empty. A makeshift covering, made of old quilts and tattered burlap, drapes over the side where an old man sits underneath against his sleeping camel.

History hides behind his leathered face, aged beyond his years. His thinning hair, tousled from the wind, mirrors the ragged clothing hanging from his bony, malnourished frame. Dirty gauze covers his hands from wrist to the end of his fingertips crafted in the form of gloves.

Undaunted by our presence, the old man remains seated without disturbing a muscle. I dismount from Ash's back and offer him a ration of food and the flask of water from my satchel. He gladly accepts and unearths a gracious smile buried behind those aging creases.

"Might be in our best interest to ask him what we can expect up ahead," Donavan suggests. "Maybe he knows something we don't."

Asaf leaves his saddle and crouches next to the old man with his hands turned upward—a common display of an amicable greeting. "Are we wandering along hostile territory?" Asaf converses in Hebrew.

The old man keeps his lips pressed shut and stares blankly into my eyes. Maybe our stranger is deaf, so Asaf begins to ask again, but the man interrupts him and speaks to me in Hebrew instead. "You have come from far away to this land, but you bring death with you."

Asaf quickly stands to his feet and runs his eyes harshly over the old man. "Listen, we don't—"

"It's okay, Asaf," I calm his tone, "let him speak." I appreciate Asaf's attempted refute, but the fact that I can clearly understand this old man's native tongue has my attention, despite the coarse accusation.

"Death comes from all around," I respond to the peculiar man.

"From the ground you walk on, it follows you . . . you cannot escape it, but you can change the path to which you lead others on so they may overcome it."

"How?"

"Now that is a question only you have the answer for, but whatever happens, you do not give up. You and I are no different, child. We both seek to live in a world that is justly reigned without chains, but man cannot do this . . . not alone. The fight against evil is no more imperative than the fight within yourself. When you lose that, then you are truly dead."

"Why are you telling me this?"

"Because I see there's a small crack deep down where evil has the opportunity to slip through and manifest the slightest doubt in your convictions." My heart stirs uneasily at the shameful memory of my attempted suicide. "Our past is what shapes our future."

"I may have stumbled," I say, "but I have not led myself to be taken."

"We all must fall before we can rise. No one is immune to that. Every action you take, small or great, every word that spews from your lips, whispered or shouted, will affect everything and everyone else . . . but for you, your fate has been sewn."

"And you've seen my fate?"

"No, I'm afraid only you can see that."

"I see nothing."

"We see what we want to see . . . until we let go of everything."

Gabe and Jacob leave their horses and approach cautiously, disbelief dripping from their faces.

"How are you able to understand this man? " Jacob curiously asks.

"I don't know, but I do."

"And since when did you learn to speak Hebrew," Gabe adds.

"Apparently just now."

Gabe draws closer to the old man. He stares at him for a moment, as if a silent connection between them permeates. I snap my fingers in front of my brother's face and break his gaze. "Hey, you okay?"

"Yeah . . . yeah, I'm fine."

The mysterious old man turns to me and speaks in English. "Our paths did not cross on a whim. For many moons ago, I've waited for you, standing here before me."

"Why?"

"I was like you once, determined, foolish at times, but always wanting to do what's right. I could never do more than what I was capable, and that's where we differ,because you can."

He turns his decrepit body around and removes a crumpled blanket from a wicker basket. "This is a gift that was meant for you." He reaches in and pulls out a piece of iridescent material. "Take it," he offers. I unfold the strange fabric; it's an oversized cloak. "Go ahead, put it on, and clasp the two metal ends near the neck line."

A strange gift indeed, but I indulge his kindness and put on the shimmering garment. It fits me perfectly, the hood draping loosely over my face. I snap the metal ends together as instructed, and my entourage gasps.

"Bloody hell!" Donavan shrieks, nearly falling from his horse.

"Arena, you there? " Jacob asks awestruck. Everyone looks spooked and startlingly confused.

"I'm right here. What's wrong with you?"

I wave my arm across my face and see nothing but air blur past. Cloaking devices aren't commonly unusual in military science, but no government has successfully engineered metamaterial cloaking like this before. The Chinese came close, using optical-camouflage technology, but it proved to be very limited to wavelength of light and vulnerable to the human eye, which can only perceive visible spectrum. But this is truly a work of art that no man has ever seen before, making anything it covers appear completely invisible. I unclasp the metal connectors and the iridescent material reappears.

"Wh-where did you get this?" I stammer.

"Where it came from isn't important. What's important is that you have it in your possession now. I assure you there's nothing else like it, but it's not indestructible, so use it wisely."

"Why you, why here to give me this?"

"You ask far too many questions that don't need answering. You've delayed enough here already. Your son is waiting."

His words crawl up my spine, raising the hairs on my arms. "How the hell did you—"

"Stay close to the armistice lines just past that ridge up ahead," he informs Asaf, leaving my words to hang. "Keep south, but don't drift too far. Our enemies come in all forms, so take nothing you see lightly. The unexpected should be expected around here, but I perceive you know this by now."

"Thank you, kindly," Asaf answers.

While everyone returns to their horses, I rest my eyes on the strange man, wondering what truly hides behind his ragged appearance. Michael swiftly swoops down out of nowhere and perches on the camel's back, but no one recognizes him but me.

"I see him too. I always have," the old man surprisingly admits as he glares at Michael.

"What's he talking about?" Asaf asks.

"Nothing, he's just old and confused," Gabe interrupts. His eyes drift toward Michael before turning to me with a jovial wink. I grow a disbelieving smirk. That sly, little bastard could see Michael the entire time.

I fold the cloak and place it in my satchel with more questions than I had before. But like the man said, not every question needs answering . . . not yet anyway.

"Now that I'm leaving, I assume you can move on to wherever you're going?" I probe one last time.

"I'm afraid my journey ends here, but yours has just begun. Now, come please help an old man rest peacefully before you leave."

"Of course."

He unravels the gauze from his calloused hand and stretches it out to me. "Many people will perish, but it's not the end," he whispers before I grab his hand.

His cold grip envelops mine, and his skin quickly turns to ash like a dying fire. The wrinkles in his face fossilize like gnarled tree bark, and when a sudden breeze whips past, his entire body ages a thousand years. His hand crumbles in mine, turning to dust, while the rest of him shrivels into his tattered clothes and vanishes.

I stumble back, falling on my ass, petrified.

"Sweet Jesus!" Donavan explodes. "That's not natural."

"No shit."

"What the hell just happened?" Nadia shudders.

"I don't know, but we should heed his advice. We've wasted enough time here."

Gabe boosts me up on Ash's back. "You know we're in this together, right?"

"Why didn't you tell me?" I inquire about him also being able to see Michael.

"We're twins, you should have known better." A small grin rises from the corner of his mouth. Nothing can define the love I have for my dear brother. He means everything to me.

"We live together," I start.

"We die together," he finishes.

Asaf's knowledge of the region puts him at the front of the pack. He safely leads us into the moor and tracks closely to the border edges of the armistice lines. I ride behind him with Jacob budding next to me.

The storms to the east weaken, but the malicious clouds directly to our south roll closer. The stale breeze carries the scent of fresh blood and spoils the air. A sinister crawl hovers at my back. Whatever evil hides among us, it lies close to the edge of the border. The tiny hairs raise on the back of my neck. My eyes hunt and zero-in on two unsettling shadows racing across the fertile moor.

The grassy pasture and all the fauna grazing in it vanish as we canter across and into a craggy vale. Several bodies, freshly deceased, litter the outer ridge. One, seemingly still alive, quakes in the brush. I push ahead of Asaf to examine the survivor, but instead I find tragedy where a black wolf-like creature thrashes its jaws on the remains. The animal removes his ravaging jowls from the body. My eyes grow wide and a tingling jolt erupts through my spine. The face of a grisly man turns to us. His human head sewn to a animal's body snarls with contempt. His eyes shimmer as red as the blood dripping from his gnashing teeth. His gaze follows me as I thrust at Ash's side and retreat back.

"That old man said not to drift too far south. I believe we've stretched our limits," I say.

Suddenly, a bell tolls eerily in the distance, ringing three times before a hellish scream follows. It echoes just beyond the border, then the screeching gets closer followed by a deep, disturbing growl.

"I second Arena's proposal," Nadia urges.

"I've never seen a creature like that in all my life," Asaf trembles.

"It's a safe bet there's more like them. Let's move."

I free Ash into a full gallop and recede the group further away from the southern lines. We ascend into the upper valleys where lotus and thorny broom scatter the hills. The furrowed peaks scatter for miles. We finally reach the closest village near the basin. Multiple sectors, mostly housing, spread across the southern outskirts of Jerusalem. Limestone buildings, great and small, dominate most of the craggy landscape. Mounds of neglected olive groves spread their branchy tendrils every which way.

Aside from the wild beasts roaming the borderlands, our path along the edges of the city becomes increasingly dangerous. One careless move could end this journey. We agree to risk breaching the armistice border and cut across an open strip of land. The ground, scarred with jagged gulches from an old quake, expand nearly a kilometer along our track. Some believe the earth's fracture manifested from the underworld, a recompense for man's iniquities. One chasm burrows deep into the earth where some people often hid during past wars. A few of them stand on the crest of the cavern and watch fearfully as we ride past. Not sure what's more dangerous: being exposed to a potential bloody battle on the surface, or the evil that hides below it.

The rugged gap fades into the earth as we pass over a rocky mound. Rows of limestone flats, stacked on one another, scatter across the base of the hill and into the next. Many still stand, but a few mark the beginning of a war zone crippled outside of the main city.

A few faces emerge from across a battered road, though non-threatening, still a cause for concern. We tighten our caravan, armed and ready while approaching. Three men, two women, and a small child surface in front of us and converse incoherently. Iraqi survivors, according to Asaf.

Nations under the Ten accord forced many immigrants to flee their homelands, leaving them in exile. Most died under cruel banishment, but the few refugees who survived the harsh journey somehow made their way here, while others ventured as far north to the Ukraine. They left everything behind to find a safer place to start a new life. I know exactly how that feels. Unfortunately, those beliefs stretch far from the truth . . . and it may cost us all.

Their filthy hands stretch forward in a beggar's plea. No one is immune to the toils of poverty, and certainty no one deserves to be treated as if they are. Behind their dirty faces love and humility hide, the only things keeping us from being bound to this world and tucked beneath the evil that man perpetuates.

Everyone gives up a day's ration of food and a quenching thirst of water to these straggling survivors. They ravage the food like starving rats without a morsel escaping their mouths. They barely lift their heads to make eye contact. One of the men with a scar across his face offers me a bird feather lined with gray and black stripes.

"What's this for?" I ask Asaf.

"It's like a good luck charm. Some say it represents the virtues of faith, hope, and charity. Apparently he wishes good will to you."

"*Shukran,*" I thank the man with one of the few words I know in Arabic. He pins his knees to the ground and graciously give thanks before leaving with the others. I tuck the feather into my hair and continue leading Ash across the outer rim.

The landscape drastically changes along the armistice boundaries. A city within a city sprawls across, covering most of the southern tip with rows of six-story apartments, matching the congested commercial structures all made from the same tawny stones. The concrete jungle replaces the padded ground beneath the clopping of our horse's hooves.

A network of streets connect blocks of derelict buildings. The crumbling facades leave a once prominent district completely deserted except for the few thieving drifters exercising their nefarious activity.

We ride nearly thirty minutes around the rubble and push northward through the impoverished edge of town. Rebellious wanderers scavenge the central city, but there's no pillaging here. The empty streets and gutted buildings rest in creepy silence, almost ghostly.

Fatigue begins to set in with the group, but not an ounce weighs on the horses as they advance up the sloped streets. Ancient stones mingle with modern mortar, piecing together a wall of disintegrating buildings ascending to the crest of the hill. Hundreds of rooftops pepper the bird's-eye view where a small billow of smoke rises behind the Mount of Olives. Asaf uses the scope on his rifle and surveys the cemetery near the basin a few blocks away.

"Anything?" I impatiently ask.

"Not much, a few men, none in uniform, wander the west side, but the base of the tombs appears unguarded."

"Let's get a closer look." I press Ash forward and follow the bendy street down into the center of the city. There's an enclave of demolished high-rising apartment buildings, many of which are on the verge of collapsing. The cobbled street running between these decaying towers ends in front of a barrier of large rocks piled six feet high. I relieve my sore ass from Ash's back and examine the man-made barricade with Jacob.

"What do you think?" he asks, rubbing his fingers across the jagged obstruction.

"I think someone had the right idea, defending from here," I respond.

I peek over the top and scan the lower cemetery across the street. A lone soldier in shabby Russian fatigues lazily basks on a tomb behind a stoned wall that surrounds the mountain of graves. Iron fencing divides the upper tombs that are scattered across the slops of the hillside.

"How many?"

"Just one from what I can see."

A warm breeze blows in, and a blanket of smoky clouds drape overhead like a grieved widow. A voice whispers behind us, creeping out from a crumbling façade. I turn and face the emerging shadow of a thin man covered in dust and dried blood.

Nadia, mouth agape, eagerly approaches him as he stumbles into her grasp. "Kale, oh my God, Kale," she gasps.

I jump back and draw my gun as several men surface from the dark behind Kale. Their faces allude me, all but two: Attimus and Roland.

"Roland!" I excitedly embrace him. His weary face smiles back, but the crestfallen Attimus steers far from it. His somber eyes avoid mine. I'm almost too afraid to explore them in the attempt to unravel something grim. I anxiously pry apart Roland instead.

"What happened, where's everybody else? Niki, Allison, my son?"

"Arena, let him breathe," Jacob calms. Roland's smile quickly disappears and he casts his eyes lowly at the ground.

"There was so much chaos during the raid. Our troops held the line for a while, keeping most of us away from the battle, but there was just too many of them to fend off. Many of the people fled into the streets and ran for their lives. I could hear their blood-curdling screams from the lobby, but it was a bloody ambush. Maybe some made it out alive, I don't know, but the carnage left behind shows otherwise. While many did escape the mountain, some remained tucked in the lower chambers to wait it out as long as they were able. I'm afraid Niki and Joshua were among them."

My stomach sinks into a hollow shell and I feel sick. My heart completely shrivels. What feeds this pain only comes from the knowledge of not knowing. "And my son, where's my son now, Roland?"

"He and Niki were in my care, safely locked behind my chamber door, well before the gates were breached. I went to retrieve some medical supplies before the mayhem began, but then I heard the doors crash from above. Before I could reach the lobby, the enemy had already stormed the west gates and flooded inside. That's when I found Attimus trashing down the steps and tussling with a soldier. We were forced to retreat back into the galley as both enemy soldiers and our own clashed throughout the tunnels.

"We escaped into the back hall and down the steps in back of the kitchen to the lower level. We searched for your sister and Joshua, and anyone else left hiding. It was complete chaos—people running for their lives, clashing through a torrential rush of soldiers surging down the medical ward. We hoped to escape through the side entrance, but by then it was too late. The halls had filled with enemy forces. Bodies were everywhere. Those poor people . . ."

I struggle to release the words, "Were they among them?"

"No, but it was too difficult to assess everything in the chaos, not until things settled. No doubt it grew grim, but somehow our troops pushed back against the rush, and what seemed like hours took only minutes when the chaos receded. We sustained heavy losses, but those who kept fighting were able to fuel the enemy's retreat . . . temporarily that is. I wasted no time and hurried to my quarters. I told Niki to stay with Joshua in there as long as they could until they were forced to descend below to Elhiym's Hollow as you requested, but—"

"But what?"

"I . . ."

"Tell me!"

"But when I returned, I found only Niki. She was lying face down in the doorway . . . lifeless. I'm so sorry, Arena."

My heart shrivels to nothing, leaving only a hard stone without a pulse. Whatever monster lives within me, it claws on my insides, raging and thrashing to get out. I'm left with only anger now, surging through me with nothing else to see.

Jacob tenderly reaches out to me, "Arena—"

"No!" I swipe away his gesture. "Joshua is still in there." I'm trembling and can't control my body.

"A second wave of enemy troops swept through and flushed us out before we could thoroughly search, but even with the little time we had, we could not find Joshua," Roland explains.

"If he's there, I will find him," I say firmly.

"It was madness, Arena. Even if you find him—"

"If he's dead, then I want to know! I'm not leaving my son behind to rot."

"With most of our own troops gone, you will not survive in there. Even with the ones we did have, it was a miracle we made it out of there at all."

My soul screams and cries in desperation, but my tears struggle to fall as they are now consumed with hate slipping through my grasp. If this is madness, it has found me in complete disarray.

"He's my son! My own flesh and blood! Would you not do the same for yours?"

"A fool's heart . . . yes, but we must wait on Sadiq's men."

"And how long since you've contacted Sadiq?" Jacob asks.

"Two days," Kale interrupts. "The few of us who made it out alive have been hiding and waiting here since then."

"Two days? Two fucking days! Sadiq's men aren't but forty kilometers away. You and I both know they would have been here by now." I storm over to Ash's side and grab the cloak from my satchel.

"What are doing?" Donavan asks.

"I'm going to find my son."

"No," he grabs my arm. "That's not what I mean."

I push him away without an ounce of caring. " This isn't your problem."

He stands unmoved and tireless while the gravity of his eyes rest down on me. "You're right, it isn't mine. It's become all of ours. Emotions aside, that hatred is going to burn you up until there's nothing left. You storm off in there, stirring up a bee's nest and leaving us all out here to deal with the swarm? No, you're not getting off that easy."

"I'm not forcing you to do anything."

"Nor would I let you. You took a chance on me, remember? I admire that. You didn't have to do that. I don't know why bad shit happens, but it just does. We accept it and help each other get through it. That's why I'm going to help you find your son—not because I feel guilty, but because I want to. That's who I am. That's why we're here? We came here together. We leave here together . . . alive."

While Donavan may be right, I refuse to look him in the eye. I'm too angry to reason with him or anyone else. It's all I can do to keep from breaking down in front of everyone. I leave my glassy eyes rested on Ash and exhale a trembling breath.

Jacob moves beside me, pensive in silence, but only for a moment before he calmly takes my hand. I run my teary eyes over his and regret that I've dismissed the same pain hiding behind them. Though hate still fuels my boiling blood over Niki's death and my missing son, his touch leaves it to simmer . . . for now.

"We may look at things differently, but never have I once overlooked your motives. I've learned from them and realized that your opinions only really matter to you, until you listen to your wife."

I grin beneath my tears. "And does he hear her?"

"Loud and clear. Now, wipe those tears off your face for another day and let's go get our son."

CHAPTER 26

The mound of tombs scattered across the southern mountainside is undisturbed, except one. A Russian soldier sits idle on a grave, toking a cigarette. With darkness covering the city, it's uncertain how many soldiers guard the west gates. Our only option to get inside is hidden through a small crevice near the top of the mound. Unknown to most, I frequently used it to escape the doldrums inside the bunker, but more importantly to circumvent officers ordered tokeep me from leaving it.

Donavan, Jacob, and I sneak across the torn street and huddle below the stone wall that surrounds the cemetery. We crouch just below the iron fence and sidle to a section that's been breached.

The lone soldier rests comfortably, but his eyes hold firm in our direction. I signal with my hand for the rest of the group to wait on the other side. While his head turns away, I quickly gesture them across the street. Asaf, Netanel, Gabriel, and Nadia settle quietly next to us behind the wall. While Roland and Kale stay safely behind with the injured troops, a few healthy soldiers are positioned several meters up the road ready to fight and waiting my signal. I put on the shimmery cloak, fasten the magnetic clasps, and instantly transform into a nightmare for anyone wandering the graves.

I climb over the wall and creep through the maze of tombs with kitten feet. The poorly trained Russian bloke leaves his rifle resting against his boots, but Twiddle Dee isn't alone. His idiot comrade, Twiddle Dumb, is holding bottles of libations, one in each hand, while his gun dangles to the side. He walks sluggishly, nearly stumbling over his feet, and offers a drink to his mate. Wine spills from the bottle, but the man's drunken behavior leaves him unaware. A fool's smirk plants across his rugged face. I move closer and eagerly wait next to the tomb with my knife hanging ready.

The men are slurring their words. Vulgar banter spews between them, and my blood runs cold when they boast over a woman's rape. The drunken asshole shouts, "We are the kings here!" He tilts the bottle of wine to his lips. I free my knife under the cloak and slit their throats.

Twiddle Dee, Twiddle Dumb, Twiddle Dead.

I scan the graves on the hill before unclasping the magnets from the cloak and giving a clear signal to advance upward. Section by section, we slink between the tombs, which are layered in tiers until we reach the top. A cobblestone wall with razor wire fencing wraps the crown of the mountain where many buildings are nothing but ash and debris. I spot a small portion of the wall damaged in the collapsed Seven Arches Hotel. A small crevice between the buckled stones leads into the hollow mountain and down through the tunnel gates where I frequently escaped.

I squeeze through the slender opening and descend into the rocky underbelly one nimble foot at a time. Jacob and the others carefully follow on my heels, mirroring every step. The jagged path narrows into a meandering obstacle, and then we approach an even smaller opening where the tunnels begin.

"I don't know about the rest of ya, but my fat ass isn't getting through that," Donavan fairly points out.

I maneuver halfway through and realize the crevice is much too small for the others to pass. "Shite, maybe there's another way."

I creep down a rugged trail where older tombs are buried in the upper crust of the mountain. Just below us, a sliver of light shines through a balcony of limestone. The gates that separate the open atrium are heavily guarded.

"If you want in, that's your ticket," I suggest.

Donavan scoffs, "We'd have better luck squeezing my ass through that envelope slot. There's near fifty men down there if not more. We won't make it halfway down those steps without being shot first. Look, I know your full of good ideas and all, but—"

"Glad you see it my way then. Stay here while I'll clear a path for you."

"You're kidding me right?"

"Trust me."

"Trust you? Are you listening to your wife?" He eyes Jacob.

"Every word, and I'm alive because of it."

"Just bring the others down here and wait . . . and don't do anything stupid until it's clear," I instruct before ascending back to the top.

I slip through the small cleft in the wall and scan the backside of the tunnel below. A few lights glow from the generator, but they'll soon fade. I hop down into the hall and seep into the shadow. An old smell lingers among the everlasting cascade of dust. I activate the cloak and slink through the maze of tunnels. When I reach the end, I tiptoe up the steps to the foyer entrance that stands slightly ajar. A glow of light brushes through the small gap where fifty men wait on the other side in the bunker's hollow atrium. I slowly push the door open and slip through, but no one notices. Besieged by their own drunkenness, the soldiers roam with disorder and vaunt in victory.

The western gates remain closed, but only a handful of soldiers stray outside in the dark. I sneak across the floor under a silent ballet of butchery and slit throats one by one. Hands clutch and knees bend to the floor as men choke on their blood, holding their inevitable last breath. The few remaining, aghast and disoriented by the writhing carnage, rush for the gates. I finish them off with my sword, leaving their tangles bodies barricading the front entrance. I unclasp the cloak and stand among the slain soldiers under a tireless breath.

"Hurry," I call to Jacob, who's waiting behind the stony balcony with the others.

One by one, they trickle down the jagged steps armed and ready.

"How many more are out there?" Donavan asks.

"Just a few from what I can see, but they don't seem to be interested in the mountain."

"We should probably comb the area below," Asaf suggests.

"No, I want you and the rest of these soldiers up here protecting the entrance. This is your battalion now, and I'm leaving you in charge of it."

"We really need this many men against the few wandering outside?"

"I'd rather have enough up here should any more Russians decide to show up. They see this and they're calling for backup, and I assure you it'll be more than fifty sozzled men."

"You sure I'm the best man for the job?"

"I have no doubt. I trust your leadership."

He affirms with an apprehensive nod. "Good luck."

I hand him my AA-12 fully automatic shotgun. "This should get you out of a pinch should you need it."

I leave Asaf a tempered man, desperately seeking the approval of confidence he deserves. No doubt I made the right choice, even if we never meet again. I race out of the atrium with my son solely on my mind.

Donavan, Jacob, and I take point down into the first-floor chamber while Nadia, Gabe, and Netanel protect our backside. We descend the stairs to the second floor below where the lights dimly burn. A wretched smell of death permeates the halls.

"Take the back corridors and meet us at the end of the dining hall," I instruct Nadia's group. "Don't fire shots unless you're forced to. We don't need to stir the den if there're any wandering soldiers down here. And keep a keen eye, there might still be survivors."

We split our paths, covering the largest area of the living quarters. Most of the doors are open. Blood is smeared down the walls. I fear what is hiding behind closed doors, but we must scour every room.

Jacob, torch in hand, leads us through a trench of bodies scattered across the floor. A massacre of innocence are jumbled together, many with cold, dead eyes staring back.

Donavan warily opens the first of several sleeping quarters and shines his torch inside—empty but not forgotten, as blood trickles behind the door and onto a toppled mattress. I hesitantly open the next door and cringe at the sight. An old man hangs from the metal rafter with bed sheets tied into a noose. Uncertain if it's self-inflicted, but gruesome nonetheless.

We pick up our pace and search the last three rooms, but all come up empty except the memories left behind them. The end of the corridor breaks into two sections: Jacob and Donavan take the left wing while I linger down the right. I explore each room but find nothing except cluttered quarters from a desperate escape. The last corridor bends to the right and leaves me clinging to the hollow feeling inside. The glowing light at the end of the hall glimmers above two bodies slain outside my sleeping quarters—a man and a woman I fear I know.

I draw my gun and sharpen my eyes, but I don't want to know the truth that lies ahead. Heart racing and breaths increasing, each step closer worsens, but the light does not lie. Terror, fossilized from her last expression, is frozen on

Mia's pale face. I hold back tears as I approach the man lying face down. I want to believe it's someone else. I turn his body over and break into pieces. Harold stares up at me with cold, innocent eyes, and he's clutching Joshua's blanket in his bloody hand. I whimper at the sight. Nothing can change what's happened here. Our days are numbered, and our enemy is winning.

I stare blankly at Joshua's crib, but I'm too afraid of what I might find. My stomach tightens and my feet won't let me move forward. *It's all right, everything is fine,* I tell myself, as I inch forward. I whimper and clutch the side of the crib. It's empty except for a few pieces of candy left behind.

I feel the presence of Jacob standing at the door with Donavan, but my eyes refuse to turn.

"We've checked all the rooms on this side . . . and nothing," Jacob reports.

"And the dead?" I gravely ask.

"Yes . . . and the dead."

"So we keep looking."

I wipe my eyes and leave the room determined my son is still alive. We track back into the main hall where many more corpses lie, none of whom I know personally, but sadly breaks my heart all the same. Lifting heads and sorting through the carnage leaves me hardened. A wrath of hate begins to brew beyond my control now.

When we enter the dining hall, Nadia, Gabe, and Netanel look somber, as they should. Nadia's bloodshot eyes are swollen, and a streak of dried tears wash clean down her dirty cheeks.

"What is it? Did you find him?" I struggle to ask.

"No, but we found this." Gabe grimly holds out his hand, revealing a single die, and my heart sinks. I quickly sift through my pocket and pull out its partner. These dice are mementos of Luke's that Allison and I have kept. My lips tremble. How have I forgotten about her?

"Her body?"

"She wasn't among them. We checked them all."

"Then she and Joshua are still alive."

"We can't be sure of anything, you know that," Donavan reasons.

"Well, until we are, I'm going to see it that way," I sternly retort.

"Arena, we could search hours on end and still not find them. I'm not saying we give up on looking, but what will it take before we do?" Donovan asks.

Voices suddenly flood the halls and gunfire echoes right after. I rush to the main entrance of the dining room and take aim Asaf and two men fire back at enemy soldiers filtering through the corridor.

"Arena, come on!" Jacob shouts. He springs to the backside of the galley with the others.

I stay at the door a few moments longer exchanging shots into the hall. Our bullets chase past one another while Asaf and a few men retreat. Four Russian fall dead, but more emerge from the stairs.

"Take the Keeper's steps in the back kitchen and get below, now!" I urge Jacob.

"There's too many, let's go."

"I'm right behind you, now move!"

Jacob's eyes furiously glower before he follows the group down to the lower chamber. I refuse to leave Asaf and his men behind. I activate the cloak instead and barrel toward the soldiers like a ghost in the wind. We meet, guns blazing, but I have the upper hand. Unseen and merciless, I cut a path with my sword. Within a flame's flash, gunfire ceases, and the hall is nearly still.

While a few Russian soldiers writhe helplessly in puddles of red, a dozen are sprawled out on the floor without a breath to keep. I unclasp the cloak and glare into the eyes of a dying man. "It never had to be this way, but you've created a war that can't be stopped," I scoff. I draw my gun and point it at his head, but I fight to pull the trigger. My hand shaking, the barrel pointed in the middle of his forehead, my finger trembling over the trigger. I linger there for a few seconds, feeling the burning in my arm and relishing in the power I have over this man. Then I calmly return the gun to my holster. "But today, you will suffer greatly for it."

Why didn't I shoot him? What has come over me? The rage is building and building, and every innocent death I see in these halls is a reminder of all we have lost. But the thought of Joshua somewhere alive softens some of the hate. I just want to find him.

More voices hurdle down the steps at the end of the corridor. A bullet grazes the neck of my cloak.

"Go!" I urge.

We escape through the kitchen and down the spiraling iron steps from behind the chef's pantry. The third-floor chamber is glowing with a few scattered lights. I search through the hall for Jacob, but find nothing but a few scampering rats.

"Arena, over here," Nadia's voice emerges from the dark.

"Where's everyone else?"

"Down the hall, near the supply room. What happened up there?"

"We got trouble."

The pantry door crashes open and the clang of metal scuffs. We race down the hall, past the medical bay while a heaving thud of boots chases after us. How many is uncertain, as gunfire clatters behind us in the distance.

Jacob darts out into the hall with a fiery exchange. "What the hell were you thinking back there? You could've gotten yourself killed!"

"Yeah, well, the day isn't over yet and we got company," I retort.

"Come on, this way," he huffs.

We follow Jacob down a narrow corridor. His jacket nearly vanishes in the dark until a glimpse of figures flash past in front of him and dip around into an unfamiliar passage. I sprint after with Asaf and his men followingclose behind. We reach a three-way bend: we could go right, left, or continue straight. The surge of enemy forces fade into another area, and we wait quietly in the dusky hall. Fatigue finds a few of us under a sprinter's pace. Gabe and Donavan bend over almost breathless, but not weary. "We're not going to outrun them forever," Gabe says.

"True, but we know this place better than they do," I agree.

"How many are we dealing with?" Netanel asks Asaf.

"Twenty, maybe. Most of the damage remains upstairs. We got a lot of them, but if we're going to get out of here, we're going to have to fight our way out, I'm afraid," Asaf responds.

"I didn't come all this way to be driven back by twenty bumbling soldiers."

"I'm not worried about the ones in here scurrying through the dark as much as the many more that will be following after," Asaf points out.

I snap the magnates on the cloak, but the shimmery coat flickers, exposing my body underneath. "Shite, it's not working."

"We can take them."

"Shh, dim your torch," I whisper.

The lumbering pattern of heavy boots plod around the corner. I quietly draw my gun and hug closely against the wall. A faint of Russian chatter between two men grows louder until it stops at the end of the hall. I rest my finger firmly against the trigger and hold.

We hide still and wait for them to slither past, but they don't. The bright beam from a torch shines down the shadowy passage.

"Oni zdes'! Oni—"

I quickly shoot and leave their voices silent, but it's too late. The torch falls to the ground and illuminates other soldiers rushing to their defense not far away.

Asaf turns to me. His eyes burn fierce. "Go," his words hang, tangled with a decision, "we'll hold 'em off as long as we can."

"But—"

"It's my decision, not yours. I came here for a reason . . . with my own admission. This isn't a suggestion. Now go!"

He presses his men forward to the end of the corridor under a selfless act of bravery. I chase after the others through the narrow passage while a blaze of gunfire exchanges in the distance. The walls tremble, and the gunshots ring out to the beat of our feet.

The dim lights flicker out and within seconds, everyone vanishes into the dark. I manage to follow behind the sound of Jacob's trotting boots while the breathless pant from the others spread thin across the maze of tunnels. But his beating steps soon disappear and voices fade. I can't see two feet in front of me.

I stop and search for my torch, but it's gone, left in one of the halls. The hope of my escape crumbles, but I'm not alone. Someone wades in the dark with me, creeping across the floor. I draw my knife and reach forward. A subtle scrape against the wall and a small flame ignites in front of me. Donavan's face emerges behind his lighter and only inches from my blade.

"Sweet baby Jesus, Donavan. I could have cut you. What happened to everyone else?"

"Lost them . . . but it looks like someone has found us." A small light glows pale to the right along with the chamber echo of Russian voices.

"Hand me your lighter."

"What are you going to do?"

"Get us out of here."

I hold the burning flame in front of me and sweep through the dark corridor. I feel the babbling breath of enemy soldiers advancing behind us. While their light grows brighter, our path ends at a cross-section.

"This way," I creep to the right.

"I hope you know where you're going."

"Trust me."

The familiar hall stretches past the medical supply room and through the sickbay. Lights flicker inside, but the medical chambers are empty. *Dammit, Jacob, where did you go*? Boots tread narrowly down the hall and voices mutter just outside one of the examining rooms.

Donavan and I quickly slink behind the open door and wait on ended breath. The shadow of a soldier stands at the threshold. I tightly hold my knife, and Donavan clutches his gun. We hold still, waiting for him to pass, but he inches closer and our eyes meet. I slit his throat before he has a chance to make a move.

A few seconds later, another soldier breaches the door, but fatally meets a bullet from Donavan's gun. The shot lures a roar of Russian comrades and they trample down the hall. We exit the room exposed as heavy gunfire chases after. Bullets whip past my ear and scrape against the walls. We dip into the long corridor around the bend. The tunnel illuminates in bursts of light from guns firing. Voices shouting ever closer catch up to us.

"Arena!" Jacob yells from afar.

I try to follow his voice, but it's too late. The tunnel behind us quickly fills with soldiers rushing in a raging fit. I shoot back and pluck a few, giving us a few more steps to escape.

The lengthy corridor ends, giving us two options: one tunnel extends to the left through the officer's quarters, or we can take the steep stairs to the right down into the briefing rooms. Without hesitation, we fly down the stairs, careful to not trip and fall. When we reach the bottom, we're assaulted by a strong stench of urine.

We scamper into the main hall that's still lit from the generators. Blood stains the floor and trails around the corner to a prisoner who's lying facedown and lifeless. An escape destined to fail. The briefing chamber next to him lies abandoned, but those who fled from the quarters left it in disarray. There's a pile of burned papers, most likely with classified information. Furniture is turned over and thrown about.

Suddenly, the doors behind us crash open and a slew of soldiers storm through. I part from Donavan to the backside of the corridor while he exchanges gunfire behind me. A lone door at the end of the hall is our only choice, but if we exit through it, we'll descend into the cell block on the lower chamber in which there is no escape.

"Come on!" I urge Donavan.

He fires at the few soldiers still standing and rushes down the stairs behind me. Bullets spray against the walls, edging past us. I scramble down the last step and turn around, but Donavan isn't there. His footsteps climb back up to the door.

"Donavan," I scream. A metal-scratching sound scuffles against the door, before his footsteps scamper back down to me.

"My rifle wedged against the door won't hold for long, so make the best of it. I was outta bullets anyway."

"Here, take this," I hand him one of my guns. I search the dank chamber for a place to hide, but there's nowhere to go except for one place I have yet to journey. The thuds and pounding against the door leaves us with no other choice.

"You better think of something quick," Donavan panics.

"Come on, this way."

I burn Donavan's lighter along the backside wall and down through a narrow gap where the construction of this resilient bunker ends. Jagged rocks protrude from and open into a hollow chamber.

Suddenly, the clashing metal of Donavan's rifle springs from the door and soldiers crash through. The patter of their boots tramples across the dusty floor and close in on us.

"Go, go, go!" Donavan nudges my shoulder.

He fires back at the charging men while I slip through the cavern and rush down the stony spiral steps that are on the verge of collapsing. I'm surprised the small door that leads into Elhiym's Hollow is open. The door is always locked to keep children from wandering inside the dangerous tunnels.

A beam of natural light pierces through a hole in the ceiling and reflects against two mirrors positioned on the rocky walls. The twenty-foot hollow chamber illuminates enough to see Donavan scuffling with a soldier near the top of the stairs.

I carefully aim and fire. The soldier plummets over the steps and crashes into the cavern floor below. "Come on, down through here!" I shout to Donavan. He descends the coiled steps, firing back at the entrance above.

I slip through the door into Elhiym's Hollow and wait for Donavan before closing it. A cascade of bullets shower the chamber in an echoing fire fight. I cover Donavan as he struggles to move and return shots through the chamber door. Two soldiers stand at the top, firing back at us.

"Donavan, come on!" I scream. He dashes to the bottom of the stairs and exchanges fire one last time before his magazine runs dry. One soldier falls dead and gunshots cease. The last standing soldier holsters his gun and plucks a small pipe from his side. *Oh, shit.*

"Run!" I yell, holding the door and ready to flee.

The soldier tosses the pipe grenade at us. Donavan's eyes widen. "Go, Arena!" he shouts. He springs to the ground as the grenade bounces toward me. I have no other choice but to close the door behind me.

I dash away from the entrance a few steps before a thunderous quake bellows, like a roaring lion. The tunnel ceiling explodes near the door and sends rocks and dust crumbling down. My ears are ringing, and I'm coughing up dust and dirt. After the debris settles, I pull out Donovan's lighter and survey the scene—a pile of stones barricades the entrance and the door is no longer visible.

I lean against the wall, separated from one of the most selfless friends that I could not save. I stand there, hoping to hear Donavan's voice on the other side of the rubble, but there's only silence. His sacrifice will never be forgotten, for I will remember this moment until my last days. I'm completely alone now, away from my friends and loved ones. There's nothing I can do but close my eyes and weep in the dark.

CHAPTER 28

As I journey through the Prophet's Path, the flicker from Donavan's lighter separates me from total darkness in this ancient tunnel. Every step without my torch remains a perpetual pitfall. The hollowed underbelly of this mountain hides a mysterious history beneath piles of tombs. It's no wonder people believe it to be haunted.

Strange ruffling flutters against the walls while a light draft blows against my cheek. Something tells me I'm not alone in here after all. The farther I walk, the less dim the path becomes.

Around the tunnels bend, an old, rusted canister, housing a light bulb, dangles from the ceiling. It burns a dirty amber, illuminating the recesses of the subterranean walls. Several more hang below nearly fifty feet apart, leading me to believe that these tunnels may not be vacant.

I draw my gun and press forward, slithering across the sandy floor. My name floats upon a whisper in the dark, calling me, but I ignore it. What evil hides in here knows my deepest secrets and I will not give in to it.

A shiver rolls throughout my body, and I stop in my tracks. Fear wraps itself around me. At the far end of the tunnel, a ghostly figure with no face hovers like wisps of black smoke. We stare at each other, with neither one of us budging our position.

"Arenaaaaa," it says in a slithering whisper. Then it torments me with unforgivable words. "You killed your mother the day you were born. Without you, she'd be alive, but you gave her no hope, slithering from her womb, and now the ones you love will wither away just the same."

"Go fuck yourself, demon."

"You should have killed yourself when you had the chance. Your incompetence of such simple things makes you a living failure."

The creature's coarse words rings hollow, but they fall hard on my ears. Try as I might, I cannot quell the rage burning inside of me. My skin stings like the cold of ice pressed against it. My gun is useless to this demonic presence, so I pull out my katana instead, as Michael advised. Within seconds, the spineless anomaly dissolves in front of me, vanishing into thin air.

I'm riddled with anger but refuse to let a taunting of words mingle with my psyche. Sword clutched tightly, I creep down the end of the tunnel. A metal door recessed into the wall opens into an echoing chamber, vastly wider, where two beams of light shine from the floor to the twenty-foot ceiling. Water trickles along a carved channel of limestone beneath a humble but sturdy bridge made from Lebanese cedar.

I warily cross the bridge and stumble upon a torch. I have no idea how it got there, but I'm thankful for the light. Large limestone bricks encase the slim passage, reaching near ten feet to an arched ceiling engineered with precision. Though it remains unclear why these ancient tunnels were constructed by Jewish stonecutters, I can only imagine what's left behind is a disheartening history of fear. Perhaps a place of protection for priestly ceremonies, or a secret channel for pilgrims to pass in the night from enemies abroad.

I reach the end of the claustrophobic tunnel and find Hebrew text etched into a stoned archway. The carved letters, preserved but worn, loosely translates to "The King's Passage"—a gateway or an escape route for men of high power in the likes of the last king of Judah, King Zedekiah, or engraved after the infamous King Herod. For whomever they were built for, they have stood the test of time, meandering underneath the most sought after piece of land in human history.

The chamber behind the archway hides deeper into darkness and farther away from my group. Where it leads, I don't know. Desolation begins to crawl inside as I press forward. The stony walls sweat over the unusual tannin stains. When I reach another opening, I find blood, still fresh, smudged against the arched entrance. The spacious chamber is less dark and smells like a sewer; it echoes under the slightest scuffle against the hardened floor.

I shine the torch against the walls and find a shadow of a hand trembling above. A mumbling voice accompanies whispers behind a shallow cove in the wall. I quietly raise my sword and creep closer, prepared to face my demon once more, but I'm met with an unexpected surprise. I drop my blade to the ground and fall to my knees, weeping joyfully instead.

"Godfrey," I tremble from my tongue.

His eyes, swollen and red, drip tears down his cheeks. Joshua is wrapped tightly in a dusty shroud nestled against his chest. The tiny voice from my son I've longed to hear is silent, and his body doesn't move. My heart teeters over a pit of despair before his small cry emerges from the tattered blanket.

I grab him with a mother's caress, my cheek nuzzled against his, and secure him close. "Oh, Godfrey, thank you . . . thank you, my dear sweet man," I cry.

Godfrey rattles off his usual rhyming response with honesty. "Hungry baby, no more soup, stinky baby, making poop."

"Soup?" I wonder. He points down to the ground to several bottles of empty baby formula and several full diapers. Aside from Godfrey's jovial response, he deserves much more than a *thank you.* He's truly a gift in my life, and I'm indebted to his unselfish sacrifice.

Joshua flounders from his last loaded diaper and screams. I replace his soiled diaper with the tattered shroud he's wrapped in. Godfrey's dispirited face scrunches up. Aside from the harrowing escape through these dreadful tunnels, he's been through a lot. He dips his head between his knees and mutters Mia's name beneath his breath. Whether or not he knows her passing, he shouldn't have to relive that ugly memory.

Though Joshua tucks safely in my arms, still my heart grieves for another. Godfrey sits dejected in silence, but he's the only one left alive to have witnessed the atrocities that have unfolded inside the mountain. His knowledge is imperative and I need answers.

"Godfrey, I wouldn't ask you if I didn't have to, but I must know . . . what happened to Allison?"

He lifts his troubled face and stares blankly, looking lost. His brows crinkle and his eyes narrow, blazed with an anger I've never seen before.

"Bad men took her," he says sternly.

"Did they hurt her?"

He rocks back and forth without answering and repeatedly gabbles, "Bad men, bad men, bad men."

"Godfrey," I calm, petting his shoulder. His eyes widen and his mouth slumps before his muttering ceases. His blood-covered hand trembles on mine.

"Oh, Godfrey, are you hurt?" He shakes his head no. "This isn't your blood, is it?" His lips remain silent, but the tears streaming down his cheek tell me that this blood belongs to someone he cared for. I can't imagine what his innocent eyes had witnessed until his stuttering tongue reveals something far worse.

"B-b-bad men do n-n-naughty things."

His simple words, regrettably telling yet honest, sting like the pain from a wasp. My blood boils with fury. I stand determined to find Allison no matter the cost. I pull Godfrey from his lamenting stupor and salvage what strength we have left.

"No matter what anyone says, despite what evil men do, you are mighty, a man above all others who deserves to see a better day. I trust you with my life, Godfrey." I carefully hand Joshua over to him and grab my sword. "You protect him with yours just a little longer, and I promise you that better day."

"I guard little one from bad men."

"I promise you I will find Allison. Whatever they did to her, they will pay. Fuck the bad men. I'll kill them all myself if I have to."

"You say bad word."

"Yes I did. Sometimes grownups say bad words when they are angry."

"Fuck," he says, grinning. "Am I a grownup?"

"Yes, yes you are, dear."

He stares vacant at the ground for a moment. "Hm, I know lots of words that rhyme."

"I bet you do." I shine my torch through the bleak, shadowy tunnel and search for an exit while Godfrey freely mutters those rhyming words behind me.

"Truck . . . duck . . . luck . . . stuck . . ."

CHAPTER 29

If misery loves company, Godfrey and I were paired for destiny. As we wade through these dreadful tunnels, Godfrey has been anything but miserable with his light-hearted simplicity.

We've wandered for nearly thirty minutes now in search for an exit, but all we've discovered remains hidden behind blocks of limestone in this subterranean city. A flight of uneven stairs ascend at the end of the small vacant room. At the top there's a door made of stone, heavy and immovable. No other paths lead us forward except for the one we cannot pass.

No matter how hard I pull, the door will not budge. With no way out, I pound my fists against the stone in frustration. A wooden plaque dangling just above the door comes crashing down. I pick it up and wipe the grime from its ashen rot. Hebrew text is scorched into the wooden grains that reads: *Only the righteous man walks before God.*

It seems rather silly, but I scour the walls anyway for a secret latch with my torch. I discover no more than rigid stone and crumbling mortar except for a small slit conveniently cut into the rock beside the door. It expands no longer than my pinky finger and just slightly wide enough for a blade to slide through. I indulge the crafty lock and my slip my knife effortlessly through the slot, but nothing happens. The door doesn't budge.

"Your sword," Godfrey plainly suggests.

When I slide the katana through, it stops halfway before I firmly nudge it forward. The iron clasp clicks and the heavy door freely ejects open. Another arched tunnel reveals itself, but it's not like the others.

The walls sparkle with specks of golden emblems embedded into the stone. The illuminated corridor parts into two separate tunnels to the left and right, but the deteriorating steps in front of us garners my attention. They ascend steeply a few feet to a broken wall where a soft light shines through the other side. I climb up, peek inside, and find a sewer grate hovering a hand's reach above us.

"I think I found a way out. Come on," I usher Godfrey up the steps.

He timidly climbs up as Joshua settles still in his arms, quietly asleep. Without the strength and leverage, I take my sleepy son from Godfrey's grasp while he bulls his shoulders into the grate. After a few grunting heaves, he lifts the rusted grill from its edge and pushes it aside.

I place Joshua back in Godfrey's arms and crawl through first to inspect our surroundings. "Damn," I whisper. We've escaped not far from the mountain but dangerously closer to enemy territory. We are near the exterior wall that surrounds the Temple Mount on a street that serves as a gateway into the old city.

Voices strike in the distance as several soldiers dart past the end of the street and toward the mountain. I slink on my belly and wait for them to vanish, but Joshua begins to wake. His cranky little voice cries out. Godfrey struggles to quiet him while two more soldiers emerge from the Temple steps.

I slither across the pavement and reach down and gently rub Joshua's hair. "Shhh, don't cry, Mommy is here."

Godfrey panics and flounders through his pockets. "He make too much noise."

The soldiers move from the steps of the Temple wall and out into the street. At that moment, Joshua decides to belt a monstrous yelp.

"Shh, shh, baby," Godfrey begs.

The two men advance curiously toward Joshua's distressing cry, and I draw my gun. Suddenly, Joshua stops. My hand trembles, waiting to pull the trigger, but the soldiers halt. They take pause, searching for a cry that has vanished.

"Come on, turn around," I utter under a nervous breath. They stay rooted to the spot, listening for sound of a cry.

When all is silent, they return up the steps and out of sight.

I exhale the breath I'd been holding. When I look down into the sewer, I smile at the sight of Joshua suckling on Godfrey's pinky. "He likes finger foods," Godfrey unknowingly jokes.

"That's good, but we need to move quickly. Here, hand me Joshua."

Godfrey passes him through the hole and lumbers out after. Once he's emerged, he carefully takes Joshua into his arms and continues to use his finger as a pacifier. "I protect him . . . you protect me," he says, swaddling his thick arms securely around my son.

"Exactly, now stay close to me."

The street remains quiet, but a party of voices bustles atop the ridge of the Temple wall. I scan across the street and survey the south side of the mountain tombs. All is still, but the edge of the Temple grows dangerously louder with Russian chatter.

"Come on, this way." I lead Godfrey down into a valley below. He stumbles to his bottom and slides down the dirt mound, securing Joshua like a football. "Weeee," he happily squeals, which is far from his frightful experience in the tunnels.

We reach the bottom and take cover beneath a sagging cypress tree while gunfire erupts near the southern courtyard. Soldiers scatter across the scape to our north, chased back into the limestone hills. Unfortunately, the skirmish extends inside the congested bundle of buildings where Ash and the other horses wait—our only transportation out of this warzone.

We hunker through the valley to the south and move closer to the passing streets near the cemetery. Shots fire just feet from us as two men, robed in black, fall to their death. The noise upsets Joshua. He unlatches from Godfrey's finger and screams.

Three soldiers dash across the road, one slightly ahead of the other two, and storm toward us. Godfrey hovers over Joshua and covers him like shield as fast as I draw my gun to the men. Blood expels from the soldier's head in front before I can even pull the trigger, and the two men following behind immediately tumble beside him.

My gun remains drawn, steady, and scanning for more until the flap of a jacket flutters around a broken fence. I fix my eyes on it, but like a ghost in the wind, it vanishes. Boots creep behind the shadows and inch toward us. I rest my finger firmly on the trigger and hold my breath, ready to kill.

"Arena, don't shoot. It's me," a hopeful and wonderful voice surfaces from the dark.

"Donavan? My God, it is you? I thought you were—"

"I'm not going down that easily. Looks like the radio calls got through. Your backup has arrived."

"And the others?"

"They're alive . . . looking for you, along with a fella named Henry who's convinced you have more lives than a cat. I suspect he's right," he says with a grin.

Godfrey is shaking with Joshua wrapped quietly in his arms, and looks straight at Donavan with a frightful gaze. "Fuck!" he shouts. "It's okay, I'm a grownup."

Donavan looks confused. "Well, I suppose it's rightfully appropriate."

"You can thank Godfrey here for my son's life. You two have a lot in common, you know," I say.

"What, other than screaming expletives?"

"The bravery of a true man can never be measured."

Gunshots rain down on the western tombs and flashes of fire explode into the battled breeze.

"You can note that on my gravestone if we don't leave now. Let's get out of here while we still have the chance."

We race down a street that is strewn with bodies. In just the little time we parted from the southern district to search for my son in the mountain, an urban war has manifested. A row of storefronts blaze with fire, while other buildings smolder in ash and rubble.

We flee past a small enemy battalion and escape into the streets of a vacant village. Pieces of stone and plaster fall from the tops of apartment flats that are barely standing. I jog next to Godfrey, whose breathless fatigue takes hold of him. Donovan slows his step as well and peeks around the corner of a pharmacy.

"What is it?" I ask.

"We got two stragglers, lost but armed."

"Friend or foe?"

"Most definitely bad men."

"Bad men, bad men, bad men . . ." Godfrey mutters.

"It's okay, Godfrey. I'm here to protect you. And so is Donovan, okay?" I say, calming his startled face. He nods his head and stops trembling.

I advance around the corner and shoot both men in the head. The ground rumbles as war rages behind us, sweeping the sky with fire and smoke. Broken glass drops like shrapnel from shattered windows. Clouds of dust envelop the village, forcing us closer to the cemetery.

"I see them!" Donavan shouts.

Israeli soldiers filter past, storming along the outer wall of the graves. A frenzy of gunfire exchanges. A hellish clash of bullets fill the night sky, blazing over us and shredding the ground. Russian fighters scurry back into the old city, but our attacking battalion stalls at the western gates.

Another enemy line of soldiers surge over the hill and push back.

I plod close to Godfrey and retreat on the heels of Donavan to the backside of the apartment flats. Every alley exit is blocked by debris and leaves us searching farther down a war-riddled street.

"This is it," Donavan affirms, ruffling near a pile of rubble.

He lifts a splintered board from the side of a building wall and ushers us through a narrow but accessible back street. We flee behind the debris and exit into the enclosed encampment where Ash and the other horses wait. Rattled by the clash of combat, drumming in the distance, they hunker beneath a rickety awning.

Several Israeli soldiers dart past while a few limp sluggishly behind. One, carried on a stretcher, leaves a trail of blood running from his leg. I lurk closer inside and find more men sitting on the ground while Roland treats their wounds. Some grimace from minor injuries while others thrash about in puddles of blood.

The tragedies of war prevails, and here I stand in the middle of it, among a crude field triage. The battle beyond the mountain weakens and the fire in the sky fades. Our troops retreat to the encampment while the smoke continues to rise, mingling with the dark clouds.

I follow Donavan and Godfrey away from the trauma and wait for Jacob and the others to return unharmed. What seems like hours passes by minutes before Gabe and Nadia filter through the chaos.

"Arena!" Nadia sifts through the crowd of troops and embraces me. She nearly squeezes me to death under the grips of elation. "My God, I thought we'd lost you."

I wrap my arms around her, but my eyes drift toward my brother's solemn face instead. I'm afraid to read too much into that look because Jacob's absence from the group. His eyes fill with tears, and he holds me like he's never done before.

"We live together," he whispers.

"We die together," I respond.

My brother leaves his warmth on my shoulder and approaches Joshua, still nestled in Godfrey's arms. He pets his curly blond hair with a gentle touch. "I knew you would find him. Seems strange to say, but I could hear his tiny cry echoing inside my head ever since we got here. Don't know how to explain it."

"Some things don't need explaining," Donavan says. "They speak to you and that's what matters."

Suddenly, Henry pushes through the crowd and his voice rings upon my ears with joy. I greet him with a welcoming embrace. "Henry, my old friend, I didn't think I'd ever see you again."

"I wish it were under different circumstances," he laments. My heart descends swiftly into the pit of my stomach. With my husband still missing, I nervously ask, "Where's Jacob?"

"I'm right here, love," Jacob swoops in unexpectedly. He swallows me with a hug and kisses the pain inside my stomach away. I soak up his affection as much as I can before leaving this moment for another time.

"Go hold your son before he forgets his father."

Jacob lifts Joshua from Godfrey's grasp and cuddles his sleepy head against his chest. A crabby moan sneaks from Joshua's lips as he clutches his father's shirt.

"It's a miracle," Jacob says with tears in his eyes.

"If you want to keep that miracle alive, we better get him to a safer place," Henry urges.

"So, I take it you received a radio dispatch from Father Joseph?" I ask.

"We did, but Sadiq could only spare this small battalion. We'll soon be pushed out if we stay here much longer, I'm afraid."

"I don't understand. What happened with the northern line? I saw Russian soldiers flood near the Temple."

"We didn't anticipate the breach into the old city . . . at least not this early. A day after your battalion left for Tel-Aviv, Gorshkov's troops split into two units from the original two hundred thousand we accounted for. One unit left from Damascus heading south while we believe the other deviated into the far east of Jordan where they're waiting for the arrival of the remaining armies to join them. Our Egyptian allies found cause for concern when they stumbled upon large military caravans filtering through Iraq," Henry says.

"And what came of the southern unit?"

"They advanced under no surprise and attacked near the West Bank about three days ago. Yaris and his troops quelled their assault and forced them back into the mountains."

"That didn't seem to stop their agenda."

"Precisely, that's why we sent scouts to monitor their movement. They found traces of Russian and Iranian forces camped just outside the Palestinian village of Nabi Samuil. A little over a day ago, they pressed forward across the northern border and settled in Grinbaum Square, like we expected, but our tactics team was unable to detonate the charges."

"What do you mean unable?" Gabe interrupts.

"Exactly that. Everything was in place, but the detonators failed. We suspect one of their counter-explosive squad may have found and disabled the charges."

"That's impossible!" Gabe exclaims. "The explosives we planted can't be disabled alone. They're tied to the parent warhead. Trying to dismantle each bomb by themselves would trigger it, causing a chain reaction. It was purposefully set up that way in case they did find them. I made decoys—dummy charges for each one. The only way to deactivate this tethered beast is to go through the parent."

"And this *parent warhead,* how easily could it be deactivated?" I ask.

"Assuming they could find it, someone with impeccable intelligence would have to break a twelve-digit code just to unlock its core. So it stands to reason the device is still active, but somehow the remote carriage is either disconnected or faulty."

"Can it be fixed?"

"With a reasonable set of eyes, sure, but it can't be fixed without understanding its electrical construct."

"Then we find someone who can understand it."

"Whoa, wait just a minute, Arena," Henry cautions with a heavy breath. "Let's not allow our confidence to dilute our thoughts here. Before we make a foolish decision, know the consequences that come with it. Besides, I don't have anyone in this battalion who can offer those kind of skills. We'll have to dig elsewhere to find someone who knows what to do."

"I'm the one who built it." Gabe's eyes harden. "I'm afraid I'm the only one who knows what to do—more importantly what *not* to do, but I'm sure I can fix the issue. If I can get it back online, I'll be able to detonate it remotely, but it's imperative we're far enough away before that happens. "

"Where is this warhead?" I ask.

"It's hidden in the Wohl Rose Garden."

"No, no, no, you can't be seriously thinking about going through with this," Jacob argues.

"We have no choice."

"Christ, Arena, we just got our son back! Does that not mean anything to you?"

"There's a hundred thousand enemies hungrily waiting to sweep through here and clear a path straight to Jordan. Where in the hell do you think we're going to hide then? We can't keep running to the edges of earth and expect to be safe."

"There's a lot more than a hundred thousand waiting somewhere else to do the same."

"Probably, but it's a hundred thousand less than we have to worry about. The devastation alone would at least subdue their hunger for a while. It will mount us some time and deliver a clear message to Gorshkov that we will not back down. If there's a weakness he submits to, it's his ego. And the tiniest prick into that could chip at his confidence. I've convinced this army to fight and they have put their trust in me. This was the original plan all along. We cannot just abandon it now. "

"You're never going to stop, are you? You're going to let this fucking war eat you away," Jacob says, frustrated.

I bite my lip. His words sting, leaving our fleeting affection to sour, but deep down I know that's not his intention.

"We cannot allow Sadiq and our army to be surrounded. It will end us, Jacob," I say softly.

"So will risking our lives to ignite a bomb."

"A risk that could save our son?"

"I've followed you, I've fought with you, and I will stand by you until the bitter end, but I'm afraid that's all it will end up being. Can I not indulge in the moment with my family?"

"Jacob, I didn't mean to—"

"Savor these moments, Arena, because they're not going to last," he snaps.

I'm frustrated as well, and also saddened. My actions have always been for the love of my son, my husband, and my friends. But I can't forget about the innocents either. We've gone this far and been through so much. We have to keep going.

"If you do this with me, Jacob, you will give us a little more hope to hang on to. And we need that hope. We need that hope to stay alive so maybe, just maybe, there's a greater chance for that moment to last."

Jacob's words falls silent and just short of slipping from his tongue, but I know my husband's pain often hides behind his eyes. He casts them down upon me and lifts Joshua's sleepy head on his shoulder. He brushes my hair back and says nothing, but he doesn't need to. I wrap my arms around him and enjoy this moment, savoring every second and imprinting its details in my mind and heart.

CHAPTER 30

The storming clash of battle wanes on the hillside, and we're given a rare pause to heal and plan. The field triage fills with soldiers who are mostly packing for a return to Jordan though a few still languish with injuries. The last thirty minutes painfully lingers as we stretch our goodbyes as far as we can.

Gabe leaves Nadia sitting in the back of a military vehicle with her face pressed into her palms. Nothing can undo what has already been promised, but it stings evermore. I secure Joshua in a fabricated car seat next to her before they set off for Beit Shemesh.

"Promise me just one thing," Nadia says. Her eyes are puffy from crying. "Stay close with him. I trust he won't do anything stupid, but I trust him more if he's with you."

"Of course," I agree. Her unselfish request for me to protect my brother forges stronger the bond we already have. Godfrey opens the door and sits quietly next toNadia. For the first time, he has nothing to say or rhyme. I'm afraid to know what may be swimming in his mind. Whatever it is, it has changed him. I will forever hold Godfrey close to my heart because he saved my son's life.

I grab his and Nadia's hands and give them one final squeeze before their small armored caravan drives off. Joshua will remain under her safeguard until I return. Nadia's courage and loyalty may rival the best, but her love and grace for my son can never be replaced.

My stomach knots and my anxiety reaches its pinnacle. Will this be the last time my eyes look upon them? I lean up against Jacob's side and watch with a broken heart as a piece of me departs down the battered road.

"Don't worry, my dear, they'll be much safer there," Asaf wanders near.

My eyes widen under his unexpected presence. "My friend, you made it!" He winces as I swipe a quick hug. "So sorry."

"It's fine." He grabs his shoulder. "The pain is beginning to dull. I'll live."

"It's good to see you."

"I hear you are planning a suicide mission."

"Why, you interested?"

"I wouldn't be asking if I wasn't." He manages to lift a small grin from my face, something much needed.

"Come on, then. I could use someone who isn't afraid to die."

His eyes crinkle as I walk away from his fading voice. "Maybe we can refrain from the word *die* on this mission."

Gabe rummages diligently through a bag of tools sitting on the back of a transport truck while Henry and Donavan debate among a few officers. I join the end of a conversation before a senior field officer finishes his proposed advice.

"That complex will be crawling with soldiers. You're going to need every armored vehicle we have."

"No vehicles," I interrupt.

"Huh?" Sergeant Hazan tips his head. "So what, you're just going to walk in there?"

"That's the plan."

"You really—"

"Look, the last thing we need to do is rattle a snake's den. You storm in there with reconnaissance vehicles and armored trucks like a parade and you're asking to get your ass kicked."

"You realize how many soldiers are in there?"

"I don't care about the numbers, it doesn't matter. What concerns me is drawing unnecessary attention. As far as I'm concerned, we're ghosts, and I plan on keeping it that way."

"That's hardly a plan, especially with—"

"Just hold on, Sergeant," Henry interrupts, "hand me your map."

Sergeant Hazan pauses for a moment, then complies. Henry unfurls the tattered map and stretches it on the ground. The faded blue ink labels most of Jerusalem's districts, and the quarters inside the Old City are smudged in red.

"What exactly are you proposing, Arena?" Henry says in a serious tone.

I look over the map. "If we're going to reach the complex undetected we'll need to circumvent the gates of the Old City completely. There still could be stragglers roaming in there. We get caught near one of those gates, this operation will be over before it ever begins. I suggest we break southward through Trotner Park and flank west to Gazelle Valley. We'll shore up here before sifting north through the Botanical Gardens. That should keep us away from the main thoroughfares for the most part before we cross into the complex."

"You're talking about three hours on foot with no plan to thwart any potential attacks from enemy ground munitions. Going to be a bit difficult to flee without vehicles," Sergeant Hazan points out.

"I hardly believe any enemy would waste heavy munitions on seven strangers scurrying in the dark. Not even the Russians are that stupid."

"Seven?" Henry's eyes lift with curiosity.

"Seven horses, seven riders. No more, no less."

"That's suicide," Hazan responds.

"If this is going to work, that's what I want. I'm not expecting you to come with us."

"I–I . . . I'm just trying—"

"But I will need your help. As much as I disagree with you, Sergeant, you're right about one thing. We'll need an exit strategy if things go awry."

"What is it you want?"

"A transport truck ready to leave south of the Gazelle Valley. You'll have to drive further south so they don't detect any suspicious movement."

"That I can do."

Gabe walks over and tosses his pack on the ground. "Okay, I've got what I need. When do we leave?"

"As soon as we find our other five riders," Henry answers.

"Four," Donavan corrects. "I'm in."

"As am I," Asaf follows.

"I'm not here to enjoy the scenery," Jacob adds.

"Well, it's been awhile since we last rode together, but if you'll have me, I'm ready to saddle up," Henry offers.

From warrior to warrior, I gaze upon his eyes with mutual respect. "Gentlemen, I'm honored to ride with you."

"Guess that leaves just one spot left," Hazan says.

"Good, because we're going to need a sharp shooter."

"Sharp shooter?" he questions.

"I need eyes, impeccable ones, to cover Gabe and me in the Garden. I need someone who can shoot a flea off a dog's ass at a thousand meters."

Henry and Sergeant Hazan look at one another but remain silent.

"What?" I ask more curious now.

Hazan avoids my eyes and stumbles over his words, "There's a . . . well, we have, a—"

"Dimitri," Henry answers plainly.

"Okay, where's this Dimitri?"

"Before you go and recruit this fellow, I have to warn you, he's a bit—"

"Unbalanced," Hazan finishes.

"All I care if he's good with a sniper rifle."

"Damn good, better than you even," Henry assures. "He can clip a hair off your head at two thousand yards."

"So what's the problem? You both act like he's contracted some kind of disease."

"If mentally unstable is a disease, then yeah, he's teeming with crazy," Hazan warns.

"How unstable are we talking about?"

"He's a reclusive being of uncertainties, a hidden gentleness, but an enigmatic madman nonetheless. If you poke the beast, you may wake the devil."

"Oh, that's comforting," Gabe scoffs.

"Let me talk to him," I say.

"Wait, you're seriously thinking about bringing along a crazy man with a gun?" Donavan says.

"He's no more crazy than us walking into a camp with a hundred thousand men itching to kill us."

"You have a point."

"If I may," Hazan says, "I advise enlisting some of our other decorated soldiers who can take decent shots."

"If I wanted decent, I'd shoot myself in the leg and get it over with. I'm not looking for chest candy, Sergeant. I need a remarkable shooter, a man who can take the shot and reload without blinking. If Dimitri is as good as Henry says he is, then I want him. So, skip your sales pitch and take me to him."

"As you wish," Hazan concedes.

Hazan leads Gabe and me to the corner of a building where a man sits alone. He arranges his bullets on the ground in front of him and meticulously spaces them evenly apart from one another.

"Why is he sitting by himself?" Gabe asks.

"He prefers to be alone. The last of his comrades died about six months ago during a field reconnaissance in Damascus. His squad was overtaken by an unexpected surge of rebels from the Turkish border. He was the only survivor.

"It was his only family he had. Most of our Russian soldiers stick together in cliques. Since they don't speak Hebrew, they feel more comfortable around their own language and culture, which I can understand, but they are very loyal to the IDF, don't get me wrong. Most have lived here ten or more years, fighting for what they believe is right, just like you and me."

Hazan approaches Dimitri, but he doesn't seem too interested in our presence. He's in his fifties, with thin blond hair that fades into silver streaks on the sides. His dark brown eyes, wide and cold, stare intently at the ground. Instead of looking up at Hazan, who hovers near him, he curses the spacing between the line of bullets and adjusts them accordingly. One by one, he inches them apart perfectly before applauding his work.

"Aren't they beautiful, shiny bastards? " He joyfully delights in a thick Russian accent. "One skull for each point, a magnificent display of death awaits, wouldn't you say?"

"It's simply stunning," Gabe humors him.

Dimitri looks up at Gabe and bursts into maniacal laughter. "You remind me of a turtle."

Gabe's cheeks burn. "Is that right?"

"Without the shell of course, because that would just be ridiculous."

"That it would," I say flatly. *My God he's crazy.*

"So, what brings this surprise visit, Sergeant?"

Hazan clears his throat. "Well, I wanted to . . . um . . . just see if . . . you—"

"Having a disagreement with your lips again I see."

"Sergeant, may I have a word with him?" I ask, and usher Hazan away. He gladly leaves, taking his stuttering words with him. Dimitri runs his eyes over me. His crooked smile falls and his chiseled jaw relaxes.

"So, what can I do for you?" he simply asks.

"My name is—"

"I know who you are. No need for introductions, unless of course you keep your tongue as loose as the sergeant keeps his tied."

"Look, let me cut to the chase—"

"What is it they call you now . . . Eater of Souls, Destroyer of Men? That sounds dramatically absurd, but wouldn't it be something to be introduced in a conversation, 'Everyone, I want you to meet, Soul Eater.' Ah, but my personal favorite—oh, you're going to love this one—it has to be, Cock Chopper?" Dimitri laughs so hard he starts choking. "Yes, I know, it's crass, but there's just something about it that sends a man and his balls running, don't you think, Turtle?"

"My name is Gabe," Gabe deadpans.

"Ah yes, Gabe, the twin. I still think Turtle has a much better ring to it."

I'm not amused by his banter. "Look, I don't mean to sound curt, but I don't have a lot of time. I need your help," I say in a serious tone.

The smile wipes off Dimitri's face. "Okay, I'm listening."

"I hear you're a bloody good shot."

"The best."

"Willing to put it to use?"

"What's the objective?"

"We have ten highly explosive charges sitting inactive and sprawled across the municipal government complex. Because they failed to detonate, we now have a hundred thousand enemy soldiers encamped there and ready to deploy. I've assembled a small team to help aid me and my brother to remedy that."

"Sounds dangerous, so what do you need me for?"

"I happened to have a position open for a sniper who's willing to put himself on the line. I need someone to cover us while we sneak into the Wohl Rose Garden to fix the warhead's remote detonation. You interested?"

"Depends, are there free tacos with this job?"

His response leaves my words still for a moment. "No, but maybe there's some grilled unicorn if you play your cards right," I counter his absurdity.

"Hmmm, let me discuss this with my comrade first."

"Comrade?" I look around but don't see anyone.

"Yes, Ivan, my therapist. He's generally better at dealing with these types of decisions."

He digs in a black crumpled bag and pulls out a large potato that has arms and legs made of twigs. Strangely enough, he converses with the spud as if it's a real person, mumbling in his Russian tongue.

Gabe's face shrivels. "He's clearly mad," he says under his breath.

"Aye."

"And you're going to trust this nutcase who carries a gun with bullets he treats as if they were his kids?"

"We're all a bit insane."

"He's seeking advice from a fucking potato. Does that not concern you just a wee bit?"

"I really don't care if he pisses his trousers and barks like a dog. If he's really that good with a gun, we're gonna need him."

"I really hope you know what you're doing."

Dimitri finishes his imaginary conversation with Ivan and slips the potato back into the bag. He rummages through a satchel of tangled dog tags and pulls two from their chains. He hands one to each of us. "Wherever Dimitri goes, his friends follow."

The tangled mess of tags wear thin on Dimitri's eyes as they droop sorrowfully. Within that satchel he carries memories but also feeds a pain that will not let go. I don't know this man's origins, but even I can see the loss of friendship weighing heavy on him.

"You sure you want us to keep these?"

"Aye, we are friends now. You, me, and Turtle here."

"The name is Gabe. Seriously, how hard is that to pronounce?" Gabe mumbles.

"So what do you say, Dimitri . . . for your comrades?" I offer one last time.

"I suppose they do deserve better. Yes, Ivan and I are in. We'll help you."

"Thank you."

"So, when do we deploy?"

"As soon as you gather your things. I hope you're comfortable riding a horse."

"Well, if it's anything like riding a boar, then Ivan and I will be just fine."

Great successes come from the camaraderie of a group's admissions. This is one of those groups I'm proud to ride with. We all have our stories and struggles, but despite our personal demons trying to tear us apart, we all share the plight of this mission, even the insane.

CHAPTER 31

The night obscures our journey under an already stormy sky. The seven of us ride into the southern district and filter through the dark barren streets. A few faces emerge from the alleyways, some pressed against the windows, watching us from abandoned storefronts. While most of the locals have fled farther south, these brave citizens ride out the trials of war in a city diminishing by the day.

The cool, stale air is quiet except for the yipping call from a lone jackal wandering behind a dumpster. Few animals hunt this close to urban areas, but the city's vacancy invites them to roam freely now.

After an hour-and-a-half trek, we leave the decaying dwellings and the impoverished district behind. An eerie buzz creeps upon us as we stop just short of the moorland that feeds into Gazelle Valley. Our conversations remain quiet, but what follows us grows louder in the shadows.

"What bloody hell is that noise?" Donavan shudders.

Jacob swivels his head, searching for the ominous hum. "There!" he points to the south.

Like a spreading cloud of smoke, a swarming field of insects fills the sky, clapping their wings with a menacing roar of the wind.

"Arena, we best find cover," Asaf advises.

"What are they?"

"Black beetles . . . go!"

The winged bugs dive from the clouds and swoop past as we flee through the grassy moor. They pelt my back like rain and sweep their jagged legs across my face.

The prickly beetles continue to shower down on us, needling Ash's gallop. Ash thrashes against the coarse brush and knickers in a panic. I slip from his back and nearly drag to the ground. My arm dangles from his reins before Donavan closes beside and pulls me back up.

"Over there!" He points to an old fire station.

Gabe and Henry flee in front of us and escape through the bay door. Ash stomps into the dirt. He lowers his head, whipping it from side to side. I kick my heels against him, but the swarm worsens. Ash rears and strikes and tosses me into the air. I hold tight to his reins, and Ash's sharp movements tug my body back down on him. I grab hold of his silver tresses. He lunges forward with a forceful kick from my boot and follows Jacob and Donavan into the station.

Henry scampers over and calms Ash from fleeing. "You okay?" he asks, wheezing from the trying escape.

"I'll survive." I slide from Ash's back, a bit sore from the bucking, and quickly account for the group. Dimitri sits in the corner with his horse tied securely to the back wall. Everyone else stands clear from the door and watches the invasion of beetles storm past. All but one.

"Where's Asaf?" Gabe asks.

I walk to the edge of the bay door and peek outside. "I don't know. I lost him in all of the chaos." Suddenly, a dark figure emerges from the haze of insects and rambles toward us. "My God, I think that's him."

Asaf bats away at the beetles before his horse tosses him to the ground. I run after to help him while Donavan and Jacob keep the agitated horse from running off. They tightly hold his reins and pull. With each struggling step they inch him closer until he stammers safely inside the garage.

Asaf shakes off dozens of beetles left stuck in his hair while Jacob and Gabe scrap the few stragglers clinging to the horses.

"I guess this is the best time as any to suggest that we probably should hold up here for the night," Asaf says with a grin. "What do you say, any takers?"

"I could bloody well use a drink right now," Donavan sighs.

"Aye, mate, we second that." Dimitri holds Ivan in his hands. "If I wasn't so fond of my friend here, I'd squeeze his little rotting corpse into a glass of vodka." He chuckles. "Oh, I'm just kidding, little buddy." He pets the potato and lays it on in his lap like a cat.

"Sweet Jesus. Well, at least someone is enjoying this," Gabe blithers as he secures Asaf's horse.

I'm anxious to move forward, but the flying pests are forcing us to wait a little longer. I grab my journal from the satchel hanging on Ash's side and unfurl my thoughts on the empty pages. Though my story may vanish through time, it shall remain inked on this dingy parchment for my son to read one day.

I look around and see faces strung with fatigue, but one in particular grabs my attention as his eyes modestly cast down at the floor. I grab my satchel and sit next to Dimitri. He looks confused, and it's clear he's used to being alone. I rifle through my bag and offer him a granola bar. He graciously takes it.

"You and your brother are kind souls. Not many people, if any, take the time to befriend someone like myself."

"I really appreciate you coming along. I know you didn't have to, but you did, and that means more to me than just friendship."

I catch a passing smile from Jacob as he gazes at me from across the garage. Dimitri quickly takes notice. "That's a good man you got there."

"Yes, he is."

"So why you sitting over here?"

"He understands."

"Does he?"

"Why you so concerned?"

"Because our days are fleeting, my dear, and every moment we're not spending with what keeps us alive destroys the very fabric of those moments, thread by thread, until one day you forget what it was like that made those feelings special."

I let out a huge breath. Any snap judgements I'd made about this man has completely vanished. Memories of the first day I met Jacob at school flourishes in my mind, a memory almost long forgotten. My insides shrivel and my heart feels deserted. What have I been doing?

"Well, go on," he urges with a soft push.

"But, I—"

"This isn't a suggestion. Now go be with your husband." His eyes sternly narrow under a purposeful but subtle wink.

I leave his side without further debate and curl up next to Jacob. I keep silent beneath the warmth of my husband's embrace and enjoy the moment before it fades. While the night feeds this pestilence of insects, we rest and wait.

CHAPTER 32

The horde of beetles fade into the wind as fast as they stormed through, but they leave behind a foul stench in their wake. I gather my things and lead Ash out of the garage. A few beetles still flutter in the air, but most have left, extinguishing any real threat.

We ride north through a small valley and exit into an older district where the buildings along the street are riddled with propaganda posters, many of which are plastered with Gorshkov's face. The image alone makes me heated. There's not enough hate in the world that can fill the wrath I want to release on this evil man.

The abandoned buildings vanish behind us as we cross over into the Botanical Gardens. I catch a fleeting light just beyond the trees in front of us, but the sky remains dark, leaving our presence obscure through the shaded foliage. My ears and eyes parade vigilantly as we troll closer into enemy territory.

I stop Ash on a hill in front of a cluster of trees. "Wait," I signal.

Movement of troops filter past the mingling branches across from the Ministry of Finance building, though how many guard the perimeter is uncertain.

"Dimitri, let me borrow your rifle," I say.

I scan the grounds with the scope and find thousands of soldiers roaming beyond the finance building while thousands more are stationed with armored vehicles inside the east complex. Hundreds of tents pepper the gardens at the foot of the Supreme Court building, fringed by tall clumps of trees. The central lawn remains clear, but the encampment draws dangerously close.

"How bad is it?" Jacob moves to my side. "Can wereach the gardens undetected?"

Dimitri grabs his rifle and peers through it. "I'd say you have a better chance of catching syphilis on a deserted island."

"We have to try," I strongly submit. I feel Jacob's eyes on me, but I don't leave myself to look. I know what he's going to say.

"Hey, I know you want this and so do I, but don't let it be worth your life," he reasons. "If things get too dangerous in there, you promise me we bail, okay?"

"We didn't come all this way to—"

"Promise me!"

My heart slinks back at the look of worry and love in his eyes. "I promise."

I dismount from Ash and loosely tie his reins to a branch. His head lowers. I reach for his face, but he withdraws my affection and leans away. I'm afraid both he and Jacob share a similar resentment.

"You sure you can detonate these explosives remotely," Donavan asks Gabe."

"Aye, but like I said, we need to be a good quarter mile away if not more before I do."

"And what if there's someone left behind," Asaf asks. Everyone looks at me, waiting for a response.

"We all knew the risks before we signed up for this objective. No matter what happens, these explosives are going to detonate, but I have no plans for leaving any of you behind," I say.

"We'll make it out," Donavan reassures as he looks at each one of us.

I scan once more down the hill and tie Ash's reins to a tree. "Leave your horses. We travel on foot from here. If you start feeling the heat before we reach the gardens, don't hesitate to leave. You get the hell out of here and race your horse until it can't breathe. Asaf, you follow Dimitri and give him cover. The rest of you fall back about twenty meters behind me and Gabe. We move slow and quiet. Remember, we're ghosts."

We sift through the end of the trees and descend to the bottom of the hill that meets one of the two roads that lead into the complex. The danger of crossing them sinks in as a military vehicle passes by. Its brake lights vanish down the street and out of sight. With the aid of darkness, we scamper across the road and through a strip of barren land under construction.

Voices tangle near the garden entrance and a gunshot fires. I immediately drop to my belly. Dimitri slithers through the brush next to me and searches the voices through his scope.

"Nothing, it's too low here, need to find higher ground," he whispers.

I draw my head from the grass and push to my knees.

"Wait!" Dimitri grabs my arm and forcefully pulls me down.

"What is it?" I ask.

"We got us a solo in the street, hijacking a bottle of booze."

I signal the group behind me to stay down while Dimitri digs inside his bag.

"What are do doing?" I ask.

He pulls a suppressor from his bag and carefully screws it to the end of his rifle. "Going to eliminate this pup so we can cross over and get a better looksee."

"We're trying not to draw attention."

"Don't worry, he won't be missed. I'll wait until he's out of sight."

The lone soldier stumbles one foot in front of the other and drunkenly meanders across the road and into the brush. He stands a bit shy of fifty meters from us.

"Hold still, ya drunken bastard," Dimitri whispers. He focuses through the scope as the soldier dances from side to side. He holds his gun steady, but before he can squeeze the trigger, the drunken bloke collapses to the ground under his own volition.

"Well, that was easy," Gabe says in a sarcastic tone.

Dimitri scans once more before he motions us to move. "Now, go."

We swiftly cross the road and dip behind the security lot next to the garden entrance. Jacob grips his gun and parks beside me. The streets clear until another transport vehicle passes by. Like the other, its lights fade into the dark.

"I'll have a better shot up there." Dimitri points to the balcony of the Parliament office behind us. "How far inside the gardens is this warhead?"

"Maybe two hundred meters from here," Gabe answers.

"Perfect, let me get comfortable and I'll signal you when it's clear."

Dimitri tosses his grappling hook toward the roof and scales up the side of the Parliament building. Within a minute, he vanishes over the side. I anxiously plant my eyes on the edge of the roof and wait.

"You sure this is gonna work?" I ask Gabe with a hint of doubt.

"One way or another, I'm gonna blow up some shit."

Dimitri raises his hand over the ledge and gestures us forward. Gabe and I creep in front and breach the side of the garden entrance. The rest of the group hangs back twenty meters, staggered apart in cover formation.

Ancient olive trees and towering pines flourish the grounds, shading the vast overgrown grassy field with their cascading branches. Countless rose bushes, sans their blooms, line the weaving trails that divide the lush lawn.

"How far is it from here?" I ask.

Gabe scans across the shaded trees. "It's through there about a hundred meters, just behind the pond."

I follow Gabe into the wooded landscape and parade my eyes like an alert owl. We approach enemy territory as heckling men brashly banter in the distance. The smell of smoke filters between the tall pines from the Russians' campfire warming the crisp night. The amber glow lifts above the trees and casts onto a disturbing image in front of us. I gasp. An Israeli soldier dangles from a large branch, strung by his arms stretched from their sockets. His face, severely beaten, drips with blood. Death awaits for this poor man if it hasn't already found him. Suddenly, his left leg twitches.

"He's still alive?" Gabe gasps.

I reach my hand to the man's boot. He mutters from his swollen lips, "Help me."

I search frantically along the branch for the rope that holds him, but mumbling voices suddenly approach behind a cluster of bushes. I pull Gabe by his collar and dip behind the trunk of the tree.

Two soldiers emerge from the shadows and stop, oblivious to even a mere bird shitting on one's shoulder. One of them breaks for a cigarette while the other swings his rifle around his back and walks toward us.

"I need to take a piss," the soldier crassly announces in Russian. He stops at the side of the tree and unzips his pants. I grab my knife and wait, my body hugged against the bark. While his comrade remains enamored with his cigarette, this drunken fool struggles to stand, unaware of the urine splashing his boots. The chance of avoiding conflict ends when he stumbles forward and sees us. I pull his staggering feet behind the tree and slit his throat. He clutches his gushing neck and tumbles into the soft grass.

"Quit fooling around over there," the other soldier barks.

I slip back against the tree and wait for him to approach, but instead he stares contempt at the man hanging from the tree. The Israeli soldier, near breathless, mutters once more, but the Russian looks up at him with a sardonic grin.

"Shouldn't you be dead by now you filthy Jew?"

He inhales a deep puff on his shriveling cigarette before tossing it to the ground, then raises his rifle up to the Israeli soldier. I swing back to toss my blade, but I'm too late. Blood sprays from the Russian's head before he falls dead. *Nice shot, Dimitri.*

With Dimitri looking on through his high-powered scope, I point to the limb holding the dying Israeli. Three shots later, the ropes that are tied to his wrists snap from the branch. I break his fall and gingerly lay him on the ground. His eyes flutter and his face grimaces in pain before he speaks his last dying breath.

"He's in the Temple."

"Who?" I desperately ask. Before he can answer, his body falls limp.

"Come on, sis, we have to move now. He's gone, there's nothing you can do."

I look into the man's cold, dead eyes before leaving and remember similar words exhaling from the dead man who escaped to Beit Shemesh. What's revealing from their warnings is no coincidence. Gorshkov is here in the Temple, and if Godfrey was right, then Allison may be there as well.

We leave the bodies and slip between the trees behind a covering of thick vegetation. The garden remains clear of any wandering soldiers, but the pocket of trees end, leaving us exposed in an open landscape near the pond. We stop and wait before running out into the unknown.

"Okay, where is this warhead?" I ask.

"On the opposite end, just beneath those cypress trees." Gabe grabs a pair of binoculars from his pack and scans across the water.

Jacob shuffles through the brush and crouches beside me. "Are we close?"

"Aye, we're here."

"Good, let's make this happen so we can get the hell out of here. We'll cover you on the perimeter."

I creep beside Gabe with my gun drawn, protecting his every step. He parts the drooping cypress branches like a curtain and removes a pile of brush from a metal cone that's sticking out from the soil. The fabricated device is as wide as a tree trunk with three protruding steel prongs buried deep in the earth. Just the sight of this devastating killing device makes my hands tremble.

"How long is this gonna take?" I ask.

"Depends on how much you're gonna nag me. Now, make yourself useful and shine your light down here."

"If you weren't my brother, I'd punch you in throat right now."

He removes a small metal plate from the bottom of the cone and sifts through wires. I survey the grounds, anxiously waiting to leave, when an exchange of voices echoes across the small rigid hill next to us—unintelligible gibberish from drunken fools, no less.

Jacob and Donavan move closer while Henry steadily positions near the pond. Voices grow louder. Two shadows ruffle through the bushes before surfacing on the ridge. Shots fire and a shrieking whistle rings out behind us.

My patience wears thin. "Brother, tell me you're getting close."

"I'm working on it, I'm working on it."

The two soldiers creep behind the dangling branches. Both tumble to the ground before they reach the tree. Dimitri's shot proves to be deadly from afar.

More voices emerge, but this time among a crowd of shouting from the encampment. A screaming siren, brash and fierce, fills the sky. Soldiers pour over the hill and fire near the pond. Henry, Donavan, and Jacob exchange shots clashing in the dark.

"It's done, let's go!" Gabe quickly covers the warhead.

We part between the wilting branches and meet face to face with a soldier and his rifle. "*Ruki vverkh!*" he barks before Dimitri strikes him down with a headshot.

Jacob and Donavan retreat to the pond next to Henry as gunfire rings back and forth. A few soldiers tumble down the hill, but many more emerge in overwhelming numbers.

"Come on!" I shout.

We dash back into the trees, bullets chasing and the siren blasting. Jacob flanks to the left and heads to the main entrance. I sprint after him as soldiers open fire to our right. A bullet pierces Jacob's shoulder and he shouts in pain. He grabs his arm and grunts as we exit the garden.

Dimitri climbs down from the roof and fires into the horde of soldiers trudging after us. Gabe, Henry, and Donavan sprint past while Asaf races over and aids Jacob across the street.

"Come on, there's too many. Let's go!" I shout at Dimitri. He exchanges shots into a flood of men exiting the gardens, then sprints after me. We climb up the hill and fetch our horses as enemy soldiers gain ground. Shots sling through the trees, gouging branches.

"They're coming fast, blow it now!" Asaf shouts.

"We're not far enough away. Another quarter-mile we'll be clear of damage," Gabe explains.

A soldier breaches the trees and lunges for me. Jacob pushes me to the ground and wrestles with the soldier. "Jacob!" I shout. Donovan rushes up beside me and aims his gun. *Bang!* The soldier's body goes limp. Jacob holds his shoulder and rolls onto his back. Donavan hovers over the dead soldier, his gun smoking. "Let's go!" he shouts.

I help Jacob up and we escape the hill on horseback, galloping away as shots fling past. We manage to create a large enough gap between the soldiers as the residual gunfire fades. We exit onto a narrow street that leads into the Botanical Gardens.

Suddenly, two military vehicles approach from a connected street and force us to detour. Two soldiers man the machine gun perched at the top of the vehicle and rain their bullets down at us. A stray bullet pelts Ash in thehind, and he jerks and knickers in pain, but still gallops. We exit to the next street over, evading more gunfire. Jacob and I trail behind the others. I power Ash forward under the pain, but notice Jacob slowing. His head begins to tilt down and his horse veers away, fading across the street.

"Jacob!" I scream.

With no response, his head drops to the horse's mane and his body straddles limp. I chase after and grab the reins of his horse. The trucks surge a few block behind us. Anexplosion rips the street near Ash; he wobbles to the side, grunts, and tumbles to the pavement. I toss from his back and cling to the reins still gripped in Jacob's hands. My boots drag across the street a few meters before his horse stops at the corner of a building. Ash whinnies with painful breath and lays helpless on the street.

My heart plummets as Jacob turns his head and stares at me with glassy eyes. Blood soaks the side of his shirt. Suddenly, the earth shakes and the building rocks. Gabe's warhead detonates, filling the air with a menacing roar. The surging force vibrates my chest. The sky blooms with fire, spreading across in a wall of blazing orange behind us. The rambling trucks stop down the street and the soldiers pause and stare in awe at the massive explosions. Within seconds, the shockwave plows through the air and strikes the vehicles onto their sides. I quickly pull Jacob's horse behind the bricked building. The end of the wave pushes past like a gale force wind in a storm. The explosives were successful, butat what cost?

Jacob's face pales, and his pupils enlarge. I pull him off the horse and gently lean him against the side of the building. In the wake of his condition, a surprising grin lifts from hisface.

"Well, I guess I can say I went out with a bang," he jokes.

"Just stop, everything is fine," I say, but I find it difficult to smile back. Tears run down my face. I put pressure against the wound in his chest, hoping there's still time left in him. "Come on," I whisper under my breath as I wait for the others to return, but they have long departed.

"Just hang in there, we'll get help."

He grabs my hand and opens his parched lips. "It's too late for that."

"No!"

"Arena . . ."

"Don't worry, you're gonna be okay." I pat his hand. "It's okay, everything is going to be fine."

"Arena, look at me."

Blood seeps between my fingers and my lips tremble. "I'm not going to let you die."

"You can't control that now. It's okay. Just lie here with me."

"Jacob," I cry.

"I'm afraid this is where my journey ends, but I'm glad it's with you."

I bury my head against his soaked chest and hold him until my tears run dry. My heart finally escapes the delusion that he's going to be okay and seeps into complete darkness. His hand, clutched to mine, loosens, and his face blankly stares into mine. I shut his cold eyes and let him go, but not without the sting that comes with it. What have I done?

My insides tremble and my body goes numb. For a brief moment, I feel nothing, absolute emptiness, until I wake the rage hiding deep in my soul. Anger fuels my blood with a flowing hatred I cannot control. I want nothing but blood to spill for this. If not now, when?

I look up in the sky and beg God, "Why . . . what have I done? Have I not done what you have asked? Why then this? Grant me grace, oh Lord, I beg of you. Take my place if you want it, but I beg you now . . . please, at least give me my vengeance."

Jacob is still, and I feel lonely and lost, until I finally lose control. I scream and pound the wall. My body rises in temperature, boiling with a wrath I've not felt before. Every vein strung through my arms glows in a web of blue, and my eyes burn like a raging fire.

"I will be back for you, my love. You don't deserve to die like this . . . I will have my vengeance." I leave my husband's lifeless body and exit the alley.

Ash lies dead in the middle of the street, his dapple coat stained red, pierced with a slew of bullet wounds, and his hide peeled back to exposed ribs. His brown eyes, now coated black, drip with the last of his tears.

I approach the two vehicles, wrecked on their side, and fume. Soldiers, thrown from the trucks, slither painfully on the ground, while some limp down the street. I draw my sword and slash those who still stand. The rest, I leave to crawl in agony.

Boots pound the street around the corner, but I'm not afraid. I stand waiting, guns drawn for those who survived the massive explosions. Dozens of soldiers flee around the corner and scatter like roaches. Most with nothing in hand but a knife and the will to run. I pick off as many as I can until my magazines empty.

I draw my sword and evade the rest, thrashing in a frenzy until I'm nearly out of breath. My knees suddenly buckle. A soldier, crawling out from of one of the trucks, grabs my legs and pulls me to the ground. I swing my sword, but he punches my side and the blade strikes hard against the steel frame instead. It splinters into several pieces leaving the handle in my hand with just a two-inch jagged shard.

I try to get up, but he slams me back to the pavement, knocking the handle from my hand He wrestles his body from the truck and lands on my chest. I swing my arms from his grasp and grab at his head. He presses his heavy body on mine and forces my face into the pavement. I free my hand and clutch his jaw, ripping it from its sockets. He rolls over from my chest and screams in agony.

Instead of walking away from this miserable piece of shit, fury consumes me. I pull the grenade from his belt and stuff it down in his wide open mouth, jaw hanging by a thread. His eyes grow wide as I pull the pin and walk away.

Two soldiers emerge at the end of the street and charge forward, guns firing. Their bullets chase past without a scratch as if I'm a ghost in the wind. I stand firm my ground and draw my other sword. They advance until their guns run dry, stopping just feet before me with fear pouring from their face. I unleash my anger and strike both to the ground.

The last soldier falls to the pavement spilling blood into the street and painting it red. I stand over the slain bodies strewn on the ground and tremble with rage. Nothing I've done here will bring Jacob back, not even a thousand deaths can serve the life of another. My husband is gone, but I stand here anyway, screaming into the dark, and waiting for more soldiers to come running. I've been a bystander of tragedy for far too long. My vengeance has just begun.

I hear my name called under a bright light shining behind me, but I struggle to move. My thoughts leave me fixed on nothing but killing now. My body shakes uncontrollably as the voices grow louder and louder in my head, "Arena, Arena, come on!"

I stand there nearly unconscious until Donavan and Gabe pull me from the street and into a transport truck. Faces grimly stare at me as I lean down over Jacob's body lying at the front.

I can't bear this pain anymore. I scream in a raging fit and pound my fists to the floor until they bleed. "No . . . no . . . nooo!"

The group remains silent under my violent outburst. I feel their eyes on me as the truck turns around, but all I see is a bloody massacre left behind filling my heart with emptiness.

I feel so alone, so utterly alone. Just then, Michael swoops down from the sky and perches on Ash. He looks at me with his beak agape, sending whispers only my ears can receive. "I'm still with you." He hovers over Ash and screams a hellish caw as the truck speeds away.

My body no longer trembles, but my heart flutters with a pain I cannot cure. My anger subdues just long enough to completely fall apart. Tears pour from eyes as I look upon my husband's pale face. I lay my head on his chest and hold him until all is lost around me. My thoughts fade while old memories vanish, all but one: Jacob's first kiss. I hold on to that moment and fall deep into a place of darkness where no one can reach me.

CHAPTER 33

The walls surrounding me grow grimmer every minute that passes—in here, out there, it doesn't matter. I feel lost without my husband beside me. Three days have passed since Jacob's death, and my heart still lies in a pit of perpetual darkness. His body now rests in Beit Shemesh, where my brother and Donavan have traveled to bury him.

They have yet to return, leaving me here in the dusky hills of eastern Jerusalem on my own accord. I've said my goodbyes. What's done cannot be undone. Jacob is gone and I'm alone once again, stricken by grief so painful even the chance to see my son evades me. Not a second goes by that I don't regret looking upon his tender face. Instead, I sit on a moth-eaten mattress isolated twenty feet below the surface in a bunker along the central West Bank valley.

This underground fortress pales in comparison to the mountain, but the three levels vital to this networking facility serves uniquely and sustainably perfect for military usage. The top level facilitates the operations quarters. Level two bunkers house and feed the soldiers, and the lower level holds a storage of weapons.

With the devastating crush at the government complex, General Eizenkot pulled back all troops from the Jordanian border and the West Bank in hopes to capitalize a stronger defense along eastern Jerusalem.

We buried nearly one hundred thousand enemy troops in ash, but all we really did was wake the devil. A multitude of enemy battalions, far more than encamped in the gardens, ascend from the north, and Gorshkov himself is rumored to be among them, though some believe he's been here for days, hunkered in the Temple mount, plotting his advance into the old city. I'm inclined to believe them.

If I stare at these walls any longer, I'm afraid I'll be a part of them. My insides feel completely empty, memories whisked into a void, and heart still numb. I'm not sure what to think anymore. I lean against the wall and unravel my thoughts inside my journal. It seems to be the only place I have left to grieve.

The door knocks.

"Come in," I mutter in a dull tone.

Ananiah stands at the doorway. Like clockwork, he checks in on me every several hours and greets me with the same discomforting stare. Under gray bushy brows. But this time he's smiling.

"I have someone here to see you," he says with a crackling voice.

"I'm really not in the mood."

"Not even for an old friend?" Father Joseph appeals lowly outside the door.

My eyes wander with surprise as he enters the room and sits next to me on the bed. The sadness strained from his face accompanies the pain drawn on mine. Not even his presence can soften my heart in this brief wonderful moment. I want to celebrate with joy, but I bury my tears into his chest and lose myself.

"It hurts so much," I cry.

He swallows me with a warm hug and keeps silent. The door shuts behind Ananiah while I'm left sobbing and trembling in Father Joseph's arms. Whatever happens in this war, I will never forget the true heart of this man's affection and his will to embrace my burdens.

I unbury my swollen eyes from his chest and gaze upon his weary face. "Thank you . . . thank you for coming back."

"I wish I could have come back sooner. I'm so sorry."

"And Joshua?"

"He's safer where he is, I assure you. He's well cared for."

"I miss him . . . and now he has no father. What am I supposed to do?"

"Love him. If I had it my way, I'd suggest you go to him and stay, but you and I both know that's not going to happen, is it?"

"How are we supposed to rise against our enemy if we have not fallen? I just want this to all be over, and I can't see that happening if I leave. Not now . . . not tomorrow. Jacob knew that too. The world is a fragile place, but sometimes we treat it as if it isn't, and it got Jacob killed."

"He saved your life—"

"But I couldn't save his!" I shout.

Father Joseph puts his arm around my shoulder and rocks me back and forth. "We can beat ourselves up all day long for all the things we could've done, but it still won't change anything."

"I'm sick and tired of losing everyone I care for. Does it never end?"

"Life cannot exist if death is not a part of it, but it doesn't have to be the end. The truth is, maybe you couldn't save Jacob's life, but you still have a chance to save your son's."

"So what happens now?"

"Now? Now we wait, but first we're going to get you out of these depressing walls and get you some fresh air. Come on." He grabs my hand and walks me out of the room.

The halls, dingy and bleak, are roaming with soldiers. Their faces grow increasingly distressed as they pass by. An inevitable war brews.

We ascend to the first level where a skirmish of voices clash near the end of the hall. Sadiq, Ari, and two officers detain a man who's been beaten from head to toe. I hurry down the hall before they take him away.

"What's going on here?" I eagerly ask.

"Arena . . ." Sadiq pauses. We haven't spoken to each other since I've arrived here. Only in passing have our eyes met, but from a sorrowful glaze. "It's good to see you," he continues.

"So what's this all about?"

"Apparently, we have a defector seeking asylum. We found him wandering on the outskirts of the valley."

His Russian uniform is tattered and bloodied, marred from battle or from an unavoidable scuffle. Nevertheless, he's now bound in custody and primed for interrogating. He looks to be in his sixties are older with a face aged like tree bark.

"Where are you taking him?"

"The officer's quarters. We need to learn more about his situation before we consider his refuge."

"I'm going with you."

"Is that such a good idea?" Father Joseph interjects.

"It's okay, Father, she can come," Sadiq insists. "In fact, it might be better. She's witnessed what we haven't, and I could use the insight."

Father Joseph grazes his eyes over the Russian man, then he looks at me. "No weapons."

"No weapons," I agree.

I shove off through the door behind Sadiq and wait outside in the hall while Ari preps a room for our so-called asylum seeker. Admittedly, this man's condition warrants questioning, but his story still seems suspect. This isn't the first time a deceiver has roamed among us.

I follow Sadiq inside the room and sit quietly across the table from our Russian refugee. He clasps his bound hands together and dips his withered and scarred face down.

"State your name, please," Sadiq immediately begins.

He lifts his head and lowly answers, "Petro . . . Petro Yevtukh."

"Where did you—"

"Wait," I interrupt as a chill crawls across my arm. "What did you say your name is?"

"Petro."

His name surfaces a memory.

"You worked with Vaslav, didn't you?" I say quickly.

His eyes widen. "How do you know that name?"

"Because he told me about you. Where you worked . . . your friendship. What they did to you. He felt terrible about what happened."

"He's here? Can I see him?"

"I'm afraid not." Tears threaten to escape but I push them back.

"Why?"

"I'm sorry, but . . . he's dead."

His eyes slope and his mouth quivers. I unhook the keys from Sadiq's belt.

"What are you doing?" Sadiq asks. I remove the cuffs from Petro's wrist. "These aren't necessary."

"Are you sure?"

"I vouch for this man's life. He's no threat to anyone. The only threat I see here is the person who did this to him."

Petro grabs my hands and peers deep into my eyes. "He's here . . . in the Temple."

"What is he talking about, who's here?" Sadiq asks with a curious shift in his eyes.

"The man you want and yet the man you can't get to."

"How long has he been here?" I ask.

"Six days."

"I was beginning to think President Gorshkov was a ghost, a story made up to scare men," Sadiq quips.

"He's very real, I assure you, an unkind soul."

"That's a rather charitable description." I say.

"He's a depraved fucking madman, a sick, evil savage. And he's bringing an army that shadows yours."

"We will not back down no matter how many men he sends," Sadiq strongly ensures.

"You cannot win this war, not by his rules anyway."

"I will die trying then." Sadiq assures.

"You will lose."

"Then I'll see you in hell."

"No need for that. The devil is already here."

"If we can get to him, we may have a chance," I interrupt.

"Perhaps, but you still have to deal with the armies that are advancing, that's assuming Gorshkov hasn't changed any plans, and he gets what he wants. They are loyal to him like a dog to a man. They obey like one too."

"If they truly follow his rule, then we must sever the serpent's head. I'm afraid this war will never end as long as Gorshkov is alive. So, tell me more about this Temple."

Petro sighs. "There are two levels beneath it. Operations are facilitated on the first, though he spends most of his time massaging his ego in the lower chamber with his animals."

"Animals?"

"Lions, he has two locked away in cages, a gift from his allies. He brings them with him everywhere and looks upon them like his own children . . . and yet treats them with the same umbrage. This man extends no grace for anyone without projecting some kind of unspeakable cruelty on them, expect for maybe the girl he keeps in his quarters."

I clench my fists. "What girl?"

"*Molodoy tsvetok*, that's what he calls her, his young flower, though rarely has anyone seen her."

"Have you?"

"Once, briefly down in the lion's den. She was chained to the floor when she was first brought in. She was cold and frightened. I could see it in her eyes. She looked at me, desperately begging for me to let her go . . . and I wanted to. I've never wanted to help someone so badly than at that moment, but I couldn't, not with all the armed guards. I would have gotten us both killed. But I knew in that brief moment that I had to escape this prison, even if it killed me. The next day I went to look for her, but she was gone."

"What did this girl look like?"

"Brown hair, covered in filth, eyes as blue as the ocean. Without the dirt covering her young skin, I'd say she was no older than thirteen."

My blood boils. The sadness and grief trapped inside me escapes and plants behind a burning rage instead. The pendulum of my thoughts leads me down into a darker place, and I'm afraid I cannot turn back now. I leave Petro's guilt hanging and exit the room.

"Arena, wait!" Sadiq orders.

I turn my sullen eyes to him, heart pounding. "Allison is in there with that cruel beast and I'm going to get her."

"I understand, but now is not the time."

"No, now is the perfect time." I storm down the hall.

"You can't go!" he barks, following after me.

"Under whose authority?"

"Mine."

"Then I guess we're at an impasse."

"Look, I'll help you get her myself, but right now we have to deal with the reality surrounding us. Gorshkov's armies are not going away; we have to accept that fact. And you, of all people, would not abandon us, not like this after everything you stood for and fought for. Every soldier took an oath to fight for what's right even if it feels wrong. They did it because of you, not in spite of you. In the end, we all may die, but at least these brave men will know what they died for. It is you who gives us hope, and they need to see that, whether you believe it or not."

My insides rankle and my mind fills with chaos, running lost and hopeless. A small part of me breaks, creeping subtly to the surface. "Promise me one thing," I say.

"Of course."

"Whatever advances over the hills, we stop for nothing. After we defeat the first wave and gain momentum—and we will—you and I are going to get Allison and kill that son of a bitch with her."

"Deal." Sadiq shakes my hand. "Now, why don't you go outside and get some fresh air. You look like hell." He smiles with jovial intent as I grin back and heed his advice.

Fighting will not cease until all the devils have vanished from this war. Death may be unavoidable, but we can make peace with it. This is our last stand or our last fall. Whatever happens now is beyond my control.

I leave the long hall, stretched to the back of the bunker, and exit the surface doors that are recessed into the earth at the top of a barren hillside. Jagged stones scatter across the hills down into the valley ridge where an old Palestinian village lies tucked in the middle of desolate land. Only a few farmers remain, but they survive nonetheless.

A cool breeze blows steady the desert sands from afar near the peaks of the rocky hill where scarce vegetation grows. The skies remain dark as always, with not a star present except from a single twinkle that has yet to leave us.

I round the stony ridge and catch a glimpse of light glow behind a large rock. Its intrigue begs me to get a closer look. I peek around the edge of a crevice and see a small fire burning. A pile of tree limbs stripped from a single olive tree sit next to the fire.

Suddenly, Michael swoops above the fire and flaps past me. He unravels his feathers and forms into his darkly figure of a man without a face. For the first time, his black wings unfurl from behind his back, casting a menacing shadow from the flames.

"It's nearly time, war is coming," he states with powerful admission.

The wind blows with force and the clouds begin to sweep across the skies. They part like drifting smoke and leave a blood moon glowing above us.

"How can we possibly overcome what's coming? These people look up to me . . . and for what? That I gave them a little bit of hope so they can perish and feel better about it?"

"Is that what you believe?"

"I believe a lot of people are going to die. Is that not enough?"

"Death is not the end of everything."

Jacob's face flashes in my mind and I bite my lip. "I've lost too many people I care for in my life. It certainly feels like it."

"But you're better than that though. You always have been. That's why He chose you. You've been asked to do unspeakable things—and suffer for them as well—but it never changed your course. Not once. Even when you felt alone, lost, and begged to be taken, you still found a way to reach this very moment. A crucial one that you must carry out and finish. Bad things did not happen because of you. Bad things happen because you live in a world where tragedy thrives. But you can change all that—for your friends, your son, and for Allison."

"And what am I supposed to do?"

"Lead them into battle. Give them confidence and show them who you really are. Let them see the Arena that the world was meant to see."

"I'm just one girl."

"You're much more than that." He turns and shouts into the dark behind the fire, "*Shelkha melekh kara.*"

A large shadow moves across, snorting and huffing. Its heavy breaths grow louder as its feet trudge slowly against the ground. Out of the dirt and dust, a creature emerges next to the fire.

"This can't be . . ."I move closer to prove my eyes do not deceive me. "Ash?"

"He belongs to you now."

"But he died. I saw it."

"And now he's resurrected to serve you."

His ashen coat is stained with blood from the bullet holes still pierced into his thick hide. Flies dance around his meaty ribs, still exposed, and his coal eyes have fallen white. My bow, left behind, dangles from the bloody afghan matted to his back.

"This is not the same Ash."

"He's alive and he's dead all the same, but he still remembers you and trusts you. Go ahead, greet him."

I step up to him and gently touch his face. He nudges me with his muzzle and wraps his head over my shoulder—the same loving affection he's displayed before. He lifts his head and whinnies, and the fire next to him suddenly blows out. His cloudy white eyes begin to swirl in an amber glow, twitching and rolling. Like a strike from a match, they ignite into orange flames and flicker inside his sockets.

I step back, aghast. "What the hell just happened?"

"He's ready for you."

"Ready for what?"

"Ready for you to ride him into battle. Tomorrow, when the moon fades and the skies turn black, armies from the north will advance through the valleys from the east into the Western Bank, and from the Old City across the tombs."

"I–I can't do this without Jacob," I say in a moment of weakness.

"You will not be alone," Michael says in a booming voice.

The sky abruptly bursts into a thunderous roar and the wind screeches. A myriad of crows swoop out of the clouds and descend around us on the rugged hill.

"We will be waiting for you," Michael says as he stands in the middle of his flock. "Whatever you do, do not let your men be deceived. This war cannot be undone. You must stand and fight."

I stand there in awe and frightened as Michael returns into the shadows and vanishes like a waft of smoke.

CHAPTER 34

When I return to my quarters—my mind occupied, frantic, going over everything Michael told me—I stop short when I see Gabe and Nadia standing at my doorway whispering in secret. A pang of sadness stabs me at the thought of these two loving each other, touching each other, while my love is gone in this life. I secure my interest behind their motive and forget I notice. Then it dawns on me that I haven't seen Nadia since we parted last, and here she is now in the cramped tunnel.

Her eyes drop before she reaches out to me. She keeps silent about Jacob and offers me simple affection instead. Her embrace leaves me warm, but I know it won't last long.

"I'm glad you're here," I whisper into her ear.

"Joshua is safe," she assures me before I'm able to ask.

"And Anya?"

"She's a very mature, young girl. She'll make a great mother one day." Nadia turns to Gabe under an awkward pause. "Well, I need to go . . . check on something. I'll let you two talk."

I walk into my room with an uncomfortable silence following me. I sense an unwelcoming conversation. I plant myself on the bed while Gabe tensely sits next to me.

I'm afraid to ask, but his nervous expression begs concerning. "Is something wrong?"

He timidly pauses before answering, "I saw everything."

"Saw what?"

"You . . . and Michael and Ash."

"Eavesdropping were you?"

"Really? We're twins, you didn't think I'd find out."

"I wasn't trying—"

"He talks to me too ya know . . . in my sleep, tangled in my thoughts. Sometimes I don't know if I'm imagining the voices or not. I do know that you and I are connected in this."

"Then you know what has to be done?"

"I'd rather not think about it. It just all seems so—"

"Real?"

"To know tomorrow will change everything. I don't know if I'm ready to accept that."

"You will be when the time comes, dear brother."

"Why are you always the calm one?"

"I'm just better at hiding it."

"Must be a woman thing." He grins under a soft chuckle.

"Do you ever wonder what Dad would say to us right now?"

Gabe's smile flattens. He stands from the bed and his hand slightly trembles. "Maybe you should ask him yourself."

"What are you talking about?"

"I didn't come here to talk to you about Michael." He pulls an envelope from his pocket and hesitates to hand it to me. "I . . . I'm so sorry. I should have given this to you long ago. I took it from your satchel before we left Beit Shemesh. I didn't want you to be distracted, and I know now this isn't any better. But you shouldn't be mad at anyone else but me."

"You're freaking me out, Gabe," I gasp. "What is this?"

"Closure." He exits the room with a mysterious guilt and leaves me with pending ambiguity hiding inside this envelope. I'm almost afraid to open it. With a trembling hand, I remove a letter.

My beloved Arena

For many years on end, I've struggled to reveal the truth, not because I was scared of a reaction, but because I felt it would change everything that has transpired to this very moment. I've loved you since the day you and your brother were born. I've never once let my absence change who I am. I've let guilt drive me enough, but I can no more. You are everything to me. You've kept me on my toes, nervously waiting and watching ever since you were a little girl, but now you are all grown up.

Your mother and I have known each other since we were kids. We grew up together, played together, and fell in love together. But it all changed the day I was called to join the priesthood at the Vatican. Our love never vanished, but our relationship parted that day. Six months later, she met a man, William, your dad, my good friend. They married not six weeks after. It was only then when your mother told me the truth she had kept hidden while I was gone.

When your mom went into labor, I was not there just as her priest, but I was also there to witness the birth of my children. I know I wasn't always there for you. You deserve more than me—I can't change that—but I offer you the truth. I at least owe that to you. I'm your biological father, and I'm proud that you're my daughter. I can never replace your dad, as I had no intentions of doing, but you are my heart, my soul, and my blood. I can't change the past or predict the future. I can only offer you what's now. I love you with every ounce of my being. I beg you to forgive me, daughter, if I've caused you any pain. I hope you can accept this truth and allow me to love you as I always have.

Your loving father,

Joseph Merrick O'Sullivan.

My head spins in a daze. My heart flutters, seeping deeper in the pit of my stomach. The walls close in and my body tingles as the blood flushes from my face. I fall to my pillow, numb and withdrawn, waiting to wake from a dream. My mind tangles, lying in a puddle of emotions swirling about.

I want to find Father Joseph and hold him, but I soak my bed with tears instead, leaving this moment suspended in disbelief.

What seems like days in a world tossed upside down turns into just a few hours as I struggle to comprehend all of this. I can sit here no more. I leave my tears on the pillow and search for Father Joseph, but when I open the door, he's standing there.

Our eyes meet, but our words are silent. This emotional ride of a relationship between us festers no more. My love for him has not changed; it's just begun. I wrap my arms around him and cling like a wounded child.

"I'm so sorry for not being there for you and your brother," he laments. "I regret not telling you sooner."

"I lift my glossy eyes from his chest. "Did my father know?"

"It was his face your eyes first looked upon when you were born, and it remained that way. Yes, he knew, but we all agreed to keep it a secret. It doesn't change your childhood. He was a good man and deserved much better than what I received."

"What's in the past is in the past. What's important is that you're here now."

"Can you forgive me?"

"You've done nothing wrong. The truth is, you've done more for me and my brother than anyone else, but if it's forgiveness you're searching for, then I absolve you for any guilt you hold on to. No more secrets. I am your daughter, and I will always love you until the end of my days."

A stir of voices rankle down the hall with an abrupt slam of a door. Sadiq and Gabe bustle across the floor toward us, animated with fury.

"We got a big problem, Father," Sadiq flurries his words with deep concern.

"What's going on?"

"It's Eizenkot. The Russians reached out about an hour ago to arrange for a private meeting."

"Meeting?"

"To offer Israel an extended position to the accord. He believes there may be a common ground that's worth the sacrifice."

"He's a fool!" I bark. "It's just a ruse and you know it. They have no intentions of negotiating."

"Perhaps, but the general has conceded that we can't win this war."

"Let me talk to him."

"He's beyond listening to reason, Arena. Not even you could convince him at this point. Besides, he's already sent Lieutenant Yaris and Major Beris to negotiate the terms."

I scoff with frustration. This idiot will send us to our grave. While Lieutenant Yaris and I haven't really had any confrontations, his ability to negotiate suffers from thinking outside the box. He's a good man and platoon leader, but this task isn't for him. Major Beris has come a long way as a soldier, but he's still better suited from a far rather than in the trenches. I storm inside my room and grab my sword.

"Give me your gun," I order Sadiq.

He draws for his holster with an uneasy fix, "Don't do anything foolish."

"An empty hand is no lure for a hawk. Prepare you men on the north side of the hill and you wait for me. Where's this bloody meeting taking place?"

"Near the basin by the village. What is it you plan on doing?" Sadiq asks.

"I'm gonna go poke the devil." Father Joseph and Gabe stare at me, but neither one say anything. They realize by now they must accept the decisions I make without debate.

I dash outside in search for Ash. He waits, eyes burning and nostrils flaring, on the rocky ledge. I skip from stone to the other and leap upon his back. Like the roar of a trumpet, he squeals over a brushing breath and rears forward across the hill. As we travel, his legs stretch a pulsing gait, pounding the earth with his bloody hooves. His breath blows like steam from an engine with every galloping step. The flames from his eyes blaze past my cheeks as we ride. I have to stop this. My friends—my Jacob—didn't die so we could surrender to the Russians.

We reach the basin and trot into the small broken town. Only but a dozen buildings still stand, most in derelict condition. Two military vehicles sit positioned near the end of a dusty road that stretches through the center of town. Ash slows his pace and the fiery flames cool from his eyes.

Four men stand in the open—a rather unorthodox engagement for peace negotiations. The village is in darkness except for the red hue from the moon shining down on this unusual arrangement. Lieutenant Yaris and Major Beris stand on one side while two Russian diplomats stand on the other. Their eyes follow me as I interrupt their meeting.

"And what is the meaning of this intrusion, Lieutenant?" the Russian spouts.

Yaris's mouth drops open at the sight of me. "Who authorized your presence here? This is a private affair."

"I did, do we have a problem, Lieutenant?" I sneer.

"I may take issue with it," The Russian answers.

Lieutenant Yaris nervously clears his throat. "She's of no concern, there should be no problems that would otherwise terminate a fair agreement."

"Let's hope for your sake."

"Arena, this is Colonel Volkov and the gentleman next to him is intelligence adviser, Gurkin," Yaris says in a hesitant tone.

Volkov runs his eyes over me like a piece of meat dangling from his fork. "That creature looks like it's been through hell and back."

"I'm sure he's seen better days."

"I wasn't speaking of the horse."

I grit my teeth. Ash lifts his head and huffs a roaring sneeze toward the colonel.

"You better tame that sick beast," Volkov angers.

"You'll have to forgive him, he's allergic to assholes." I say.

"I don't know who the hell you think you are or what you're trying to accomplish here, but that mouth of yours is going to lead you to great pain," Volkov seethes.

"My apologies," Yaris says, trying to calm the situation.

"Might want to put a leash on this animal if you're serious about negotiating," Volkov says.

"She's only here to witness, that's all. Right, Arena?" Yaris leers scornfully at me. I keep quiet for the moment, but I refuse to let my eyes wander from these Russian fools.

"Our terms are quite simple," Volkov addresses. "Give up your entitlements, all principal assets and wealth, and we'll offer your country a fair piece of the global market. Your assets will be retained by the accord and compensated back to you under the policy and guidelines of global contribution. All requested subsidies are subject for review under the head council. Your lands will be absorbed and partitioned accordingly and barred from any border restrictions."

"And what of our people? They have been stretched thin from the city that your regime has left in ruin. What clemency will you offer?"

"Lieutenant, we are not in the business of charity. What your country contributes to the system will reveal the value of your people."

"Don't get ahead of yourself, Colonel. The value of our country overwhelmingly outweighs yours. You wouldn't be here if it didn't," Yaris says.

"I find you overcompensation amusing, but I'm afraid these are our terms and they are non-negotiable," Volkov states.

"Everything is negotiable. You can stand there and belittle, but I will remain superior in this deal."

Volkov chuckles. "I believe the stench in the air has caused you to hallucinate. I see the façade of a superior person in an inferior position."

"Look, we're not here to piss anyone off," Major Beris interrupts. "We're all looking for common ground to seize what's best for both of our countries. I'm sure we can come to a fair arrangement."

Volkov looks at Yaris and smirks. "Looks like we have a misplacement of rankings. The major here is the only one making sense. Maybe he's the superior one."

"We still have an army," Yaris leers back.

"Is that what you call it?"

"Make no mistake, are forces are strong—"

"And ours are bigger!" Volkov shouts.

"Are you done with your pissing match?" I interrupt.

Volkov glares at me. "You'd best tie that tongue, woman, or put it to better use."

I grip my sword. *Calm down, Arena,* I think.

Volkov continues to chide, "Now I know where this beast got its stench. I believe you will find your place wallowing in the mud somewhere."

He smiles, and the sight of his crooked yellow teeth turns my stomach.

"That seems to be the only fitting place for a woman . . . in the dirt."

I churn, bereft of patience. With a dizzying swing, I whip my arms around and behead the Russian colonel with my sword. Gurkin trembles for his gun, but I draw mine first. "Drop it!" I demand.

"My God, what have you done?" Yaris gasps.

Gurkin tosses his gun on the ground and shivers in fear. "This can only end badly for you."

"Pick up your comrade's head," I say.

"Wh–what?" Gurkin whimpers.

"Pick it up!"

Gurkin grabs Volkov's severed head and holds it by the hair. He stands nearly paralyzed, eyes bulging.

"You take that head back to Gorshkov and let him know that we've offered our terms, and that they are non-negotiable. You tell him death is coming . . . and hell is coming with me."

Gurkin stammers to his vehicle and races off in a cloud of dust. A war, now set in motion, awaits us all.

"Do you know what you've just done?" Yaris shakes his head.

"Yes, I did what you couldn't. I didn't come to this meeting to measure cocks. So don't lose your sight, Lieutenant, 'cause it will be the death of you. Now, go help Major Beris find his balls, we have a war to end."

A small plume of smoke rises from the ridge of the bunker on the hill. Ash turns his head with a gruff and pushes his muscular legs up the side of the rocky mound. He stops near the rugged ledge. The same small pile of charred wood smolders where Ash had first emerged. Michael reaches his hand into the dying fire and stokes it. Blue flames ignite and dance like the wind.

"Come," he gestures.

I climb down from Ash and creep close to the fire. My entire body erupts with a sensational force, like nails brushing against my warming skin. I feel charged and alive, tingling beyond any experience as if every cell in my body has awoken.

Michael stretches his wings, and hovers next to the fire. "Hand me your sword," he says with his face cloaked in shadow.

He takes my katana and dips the steel into the flames. The fire ignites into a blaze, rising above him. Ash kicks his restless legs in the air and screeches like the sound of grating metal. Everything around me fades and my eyes descend into darkness. I stand in the middle of pitch black where I can reach for nothing. For a brief moment, I hear my mother's voice calling before my skin cools and the light returns to my eyes. Michael removes the sword and the fire abruptly dies.

"Long ago, you chose this sword, and its edge has kept its promise. Now it chooses you to finish what you've started." He hands the sword to me; it feels light in my grasp. "Wield its wrath behind the power of a thousand men, forged by the power of God. Now, go mark yourself with the ashes from the fire and protection shall be granted unto you."

I break off a piece of charred wood, crumble it between my fingertips, and smear the soot across my face. Dark clouds begin to gather as a thunderous roar erupts. Three crows descend from the dark and perch atop Ash. Their eyes ignite with fire. My breaths grow deeper and my heart pounds. I can feel rage building inside a brooding tempest ready to blow.

I sheath my sword and hop on Ash's back. The crows scatter, flapping and squawking. They follow me to theedge of the ridge and fly in a circle just above us.

Michael stands on a rock next to me, as we both overlook the barren landscape below. The moonlight rests on a battlefield waiting to be trampled on by a bloody war. Tens of thousands Israeli forces scatter across the hill and form multiple brigades near its basin. Many more from the eastern front pour in and establish a line of defense.

"Death among men and demons alike cannot escape this. When the moon hides and the skies blaze with the roar of a horn, ride your beast into the middle of the storm and strike wrath upon all who are against you."

A hellish shriek rings out and the crows above us begin to caw. Countless more flood the clouds and swoop down onto the hill around me, staring and waiting.

"You legion awaits," Michael reveals.

What has fallen from a dark past now shapes the hope for a grim future—all because of me. In this ill-omened moment, I look at Michael and finally realize who I really am and what I've become. And if I don't already know, he stares into my eyes, wings unfurled and reminds me, "What say you, Pale Rider?"

I take a deep breath as my mind shows me everyone who's been taken from me.

"Kill 'em' all."

CHAPTER 35

Time stands still in the midst of death that's consumed by the fear of the unknown, but it doesn't have to be, not for me anymore. I know my place now.

I lead Ash down the hill to search for my brother while my three feathered soldiers fly above me. They squawk loudly as thousands of alarming faces stare up at the sky. Gabe stands calmly among them, waiting behind a brigade of men next to Father Joseph and Nadia.

The grounds flourish with soldiers prepared to fight, but the illusion of victory evades them. They part a path for Ash and watch in terror as we pass through. Nadia's face draws numb as she and others around her stare at his wounds.

Voices mutter my name, but I'm too transfixed to respond. My mind remains absorbed by what lies before us. I stretch my eyes across the rocky dunes to a sea of enemy soldiers far too many to count. They pour in from the north and flood the Western Bank, gathering in droves. Nations stand by nations, mingling as one as they prepare for a battle, unrivaled.

"Arena . . . Arena?" Gabe begs my attention. I unfix my eyes from the endless army and meet his. "Are you okay?"

I look upon my brother's unruffled face, but I know there's an honest fear hiding behind it. "Ask me again when this is all over."

"We're gonna get through this, aren't we?"

"Come, closer." I wipe the residual ashes from my fingertips across his forehead. "We shall not be parted, dear brother. We live as one."

He pauses briefly, jaws clenching, before responding, "We die as one."

"Arena!" Donavan shouts, as he weaves through restless soldiers. He scurries across the crowded hillside with Sadiq following. "Just wanted to see you once more before all hell broke loose," he says. "My God, I wouldn't have believed it if I didn't see it for myself. So . . . this is really Ash?"

"Yes and no, but I don't expect you to understand."

"I've forfeited all logic and understanding long ago."

"Wise man."

Sadiq approaches, eyes tense and face troubled. "Yaris is in position and ready to flank his forces."

"Good." I take a deep breath and scan the horizon, slipping away. The clouds begin to drift over the moon, sending all beneath it to seep into the shadows.

"So, it really has come to this?" Sadiq says.

"I'm afraid so, my friend, but the threat to this nation does not stand before us on the other side of this valley, it cowers inside the Temple. As long as Gorshkov is alive, this war will never end. No matter what happens today on this battlefield, I'm going to kill that son of a bitch and end it for good."

"You know, I look across the way and see how severely outmatched we are, and yet I look at you and somehow none of it matters. The truth is, a lot of men are going to die today, but at least they know now what they're dying for."

"And where's General Eizenkot in all of this?"

"I'm afraid he's resigned his command to me."

"That may have been the best strategic decision of his career."

The sky bellows with a crash of thunder and continues to rumble in the distance. The moon fades from the sky while a small front of enemy troops spreads to the edge of the valley and waits.

"The time is upon us. Get your men ready, and don't advance until I give you a signal."

"What are you going to do?"

"I'm gonna clear a path for you and your men."

"Alone?"

"I'm never alone."

I guide Ash forward as the three crows circling above us swoop down and perch on top of him. My feathered legion swarms the skies and turns the gray clouds black as the night. I reach the basin of the hill and hold my wrath in the grips of God's hands. Silence covers the ancient land, and the desert breeze suddenly stops. A moment of truth reaches its pinnacle before the sinister roar of horns calls out the sky. They blast so loud, men cover their ears and hunch over. Then it stops, the quiet before the storm. Already I smell blood and sweat hanging in the stale air.

Ash huffs a breath of steam and stomps his legs. His eyes ignite into raging flames. The tepid solace of my body vanishes and burns with scorching heat beyond my being. I unsheathe my sword and press my heels in. Ash thrushes forward in a furious gallop and screams like a banshee across the barren earth.

A sea of enemy soldiers quickly take notice as their eyes perch on me. Their uniforms clash into each other as nations stand by nations hell bent on a bloody battle. Some don desert sand fatigues while others wear traditional garments from a mingling of Middle Eastern culture.

The three crows lift from Ash and fly in front of us with fiery eyes. Gunshots rain across the valley. Men from all angles begin to push forward, but Ash thrusts faster, his hooves pounding the ground.

Soldiers rise from the dunes, stacked upon one another, their faces heated and bent. We approach the frontline and a crash of thunder roars. I raise my sword against the first line and swing into a clump of angry men.

Limbs scatter and bodies by the dozens fly near fifty feet, tumbling to the ground. Chaos erupts. Thousands sprint toward us, howling and screaming. Gunfire hails across, but misses, slinging through a ghost in the wind.

Ash kicks forward as we press on in a crowd of furious men. I unleash the wrath behind the power of steel and slice through them like butter. We drive a bloody path through a flood of enemies.

Rows upon rows of desperate soldiers sacrifice their bodies, plunging themselves in all directions. Ash sweeps across them effortlessly as I slash with rage. Men fling by the hundreds with each passing swing, bowing into the earth by the touch of my blade.

Still, thousands more advance. Soldiers from the east attack and fire at will. They scatter under relentless fervor like an army of ants. Ash charges, eyes flaring, and plows in the middle. Men fall by the hundreds and are trampled under their comrades' feet, while thousands greet the edge of my powerfulblade.

We drive through them and circle around, slinging soldiers from their feet. Bodies tangle, bashing across the field until thousands lie broken and dead. Ash stops and whinnies a hellish screech. The fate of my enemies drips from my sword.

Thousands of soldiers spill their blood into the soil, but it's only the beginning. I've cleared an opening where only the first wave of soldiers now marry to the earth. Many more spill over the ridge from brigades so enormous, the horizon moves in shadow.

I hold my ground and wait to wield my merciless blade once more. Soldiers advance closer, but not under the power of gunfire. Instead, they rush into a suicidal run with swords, knives, and metal weapons alike. The day of reckoning approaches at the hands of ageless warfare.

"Do not cease!" I shout over Ash's ears. "We leave none to scurry."

I turn back to the hill and raise my sword high in the air. Without hesitation, Sadiq's men shout and charge toward the basin. I grab a fistful of Ash's silvery mane and fix my eyes on impending bloodshed. The enemy floods toward us under thundering steps.

Sweeping across the clouds, the sky breaks into a squawking song of raging warriors. A legion beyond the power of man dives down into the belly of the gulch.

Ash charges forward into a mass of storming soldiers. Bodies crash and bones snap. He barrels through, stomping and gnashing without ceasing. I unleash my wrath on all around me, carving up men by the thousands, but thousands more take their place.

They charge fiercely without stopping and blanket the battlefield. Ash plows ahead, bashing bodies. Soldiers toss and tumble to the ground, but more storm past. Feathers flap, swooping past and caw the cry of death. My legion of crows spreads out and plunges deep into the enemy. They dive-bomb, clipping limbs with their razor-sharp beaks. Many swarm those fleeing, removing their eyes and exploding clear through their chests. Bedlam sweeps across the valley.

Eyes burning and blood churning, my veins surge with a pulsating fire. I boil into violent madness as Ash kicks up his front legs and storms back into the middle of a sea of charging men. I swing my sword with a fury unseen and strike unceasingly.

Soldiers fling, blood spewing as the never-ending charge of men keep pushing. From the north, east, and west, dead soldiers cover the battlefield in red.

Thunder rolls and lightning strikes as an exchange of heated gunfire erupts to the east. Sadiq and his men rush the moor and storm another army that's flanking the upper vale. Bullets shower on both sides, pelting one another like slaughtered lambs.

Chaos explodes in a raging tempest. Soldiers scatter, dying and fleeing. Many sprint like madmen and clash in a ballet of bloody bedlam. I turn my eyes against the madness and see Donavan, Gabe, and Nadia running from a slew of men. I rush Ash in a blazing gallop, but I lose my way in the sea of bloodshed.

"Arena!" voices shout through a barrage of soldiers.

Ash charges into them, and I'm able to part my way through the crowd with my sword.

A soldier wrestles Nadia to the ground. Donavan pushes him off, and the soldier slashes his cheek with his knife. I storm through and behead the man before he makes another move.

"You okay?" I ask Donavan.

"I'm fine, just a scratch."

Nadia jumps to her feet, searching across the field. "Where's Gabe?"

I scan through the melee and spot him next to Henry. They're fending off a small platoon charging from the west front.

"Stay here!" Ash sprints off, eyes flaming. His bloody hooves pound the earth faster and faster. Finally, we approach the storming platoon, and my sword goes to work. Bodies flail, dismantled within seconds. The crows have had their way with the others I haven't gotten to.

"Arena!" Gabe screams and hunches over Henry.

I ride Ash over like the wind and dismount. I kneel next to Henry. Bullet wounds have pierced his torso. I hold his head in my hand. "No, no," I cry.

"It's okay," his lips tremble, "it was always meant this way . . . I'm free now." He releases his last breath.

I look on the battlefield and find hope slipping away. Sadiq's army, nearly half gone, waits for impending death to flush them out. While the eastern front fades by a myriad of frenzied crows, a large troop is flooding in from the west. They advance in numbers beyond the eyes can see.

I lead Ash into a raging storm of unbridled wrath. He races into a full gallop without ceasing and breaks through the wind under a hellish scream. I lift my sword and swing with all my strength into a wave of charging soldiers.

Fury unleashes from the stroke of my blade as thousands of men are thrown from the earth. Blood spills and bodies clash. Ash sweeps around, stomping on dead men into the soil. A path clears in front of me, but a second wave of soldiers grows larger.

I pull Ash back and retreat to my brother in the middle of the moor. Michael swoops down from the clouds next to me and morphs into himself. Thousands of crows fly past, screeching across the field. They attack the front line and delay the enemy's advance.

"There's too many of them," I concede to Michael. "We've lost half our men already."

"Are you not the Pale Rider, Destroyer of Men?"

"No matter how many I slay, still more come."

"You stand here, blood spilled from your hands, and still you question who you are."

"I know who I am."

"Then leave your beast and face your enemy. Your fate brought you here for a reason. Now go and finish it."

"How?"

"Search deep inside you. Find what it is you have lost—everything that has been taken from you, every moment that man has left the innocent to suffer because he prescribes to his own lies and selfish desires. You were not born to save souls, Arena, you were chosen as a beacon of hope to lead them. And now it's time to rid of that which wants to destroy them."

I jump off Ash and turn to Gabe. Tears spill from his swollen eyes as he hovers over Henry's body."

"You must hurry," Michael urges. "Your legion cannot hold them for long. Go forth and feel the power of which God gave to you. Draw your sword and strike down upon the earth with every ounce of rage that surges through your veins. Your destiny awaits."

I approach hell bent in front of my enemy not fifty meters. Only but blood and the dead separate us. The crows fade into the clouds, leaving me to face near a million soldiers hungry for murder.

Every pain I've ever harbored surges through my body like a razor sliding against my skin. I raise my sword high as their eyes glare at me. For a brief moment, every person I've lost flashes through my mind. Especially Jacob. I can hear his laugh, his smooth voice. I feel him with me now. I let out a piercing war cry, grip tight, clench my jaw, and plunge my sword down into the ground.

The blade sinks into the soil, glowing and shaking my hands numb. The clouds break into a thunderous roar, and the entire land rumbles, rocks rattling and trees swaying. Cracks race across the stony earth, and then the valley splits open into a web of jagged canyons. Soldiers flee, screaming, but their escape is futile. The growing chasms chase on their heels until the quaking ground swallows them.

Tens of thousands fall instantly to their demise while the rest scatter stumbling into the cavernous abyss. The handle of my sword heats and melts away from my grip. I fall back and watch the rest of the steel sink into the ground. The sky bellows once more before the last few fleeing soldiers dip into silence below.

As fast as the earth opened, it closes back just the same like a zipper on a jacket. The dust-filled air settles and the thundering sky wanes. Three crows dive from the clouds and swagger brazenly on a pile of corpses in the middle of the valley. They screech a hellish caw like the battle cry of victory, but something unsettles me. I look upon the land scorched by the breath of God and fear that not every enemy has fallen. The sky blazes with fire near the Mount of Olives where soldiers still hold the Temple captive. The war only ends when we've taken it back from the grips of a tyrant who's not willing to surrender. Finally the day has come that I shall face my true enemy.

Sadiq's depleted army moves across the valley over half a million bodies strewn across the landscape. Donavan and Nadia, soaked in fatigue, hover next to Henry's body. An emptiness suspends inside me.

Father Joseph sifts through the carnage in sorrow. He kneels by Henry and places his hands together. "My dear friend, may you be at peace now." His lips tremble before he recites an Irish blessing.

May your soul rise through the swift wind,
Under closed eyes until the end.
From the splendor of fire to the radiance above,
We comfort in thee and remember your love.
Let us heal your deathly price,
and never forget your sacrifice.
In nomine Patris et Filii et Spiritus Sancti

CHAPTER 36

The desert valley is blanketed in a heap of corpses and waits for a cinder to burn them to ash. But for now, they must stay and rot. Gorshkov and his last line of defense lies in the old city—a war we must finish.

Sadiq advances his men along the stony hills and marches them through the northeastern valley of Zurim. I ride Ash out in front and scout the empty roads that lead into the center of a once active district now in ruins.

Fire swells from two burning buildings and lights the dark sky with raging amber. Enemy soldiers this far in the outskirts keeps everyone on edge. I sweep through the empty streets but find nothing except for the remains of broken homes and haunted memories.

Ash stops at the bend in the road where a ridge overlooks the north side of the Mount of Olives. The rocky valley below is barren, but traces of enemy soldiers still lurk along the western passage. Several roam through and cross into the Temple grounds.

Sadiq presses his scope to his eyes and pans across the small stone wall that lines the road. "We got troop movement surging from the north?"

"And the Temple?" I ask.

"A line of defense lies mostly along the basin, maybe a hundred or so positioned on the mount. But after what we witnessed on the moor, I can't imagine Gorshkov has anything less than fifty thousand troops guarding the old city."

"Perhaps, but now the war remains in our favor. He's not expecting anyone to knock on the front door. I've wiped his army clean and left no one to escape the valley. There's no way of him knowing any of what happened. And if he did, he's not the kind of person who's going to give up. We finish this now."

"If you can make it down to the lower graves, we'll distract the guards outside the Temple grounds. It may give you enough time to get in, but I suggest not going alone."

"She isn't." Gabe lunges himself on top of the stone railing. He smiles when our eyes meet. "Allison is still in there, I know it."

"Good to see you, brother," I say, and he nods. "If you can draw them out to the north, we'll get in."

"Consider it done . . . and for what it's worth, none of us would be here without you. You've been right the entire time, and for that I owe you, "Sadiq says.

"You owe me nothing, just your friendship. That's enough. Now go spill some blood."

Sadiq whisks away and leads what's left of our army through the ravished city to the north of the Lion's Gate. The fatigued brigade clears the road, and Donavan, Nadia, and Father Joseph are standing there.

"What, you thought you were going to leave without us?" Donavan teases.

"Never crossed my mind," I smile.

"So what now?"

"Let's go knock on the devil's door."

Ash jumps the stone barrier and carefully descends onto the rocky slate below. We sift through hillside homes, forsaken for years. They lean tired and vulnerable, yet still stand in defiance. I notice innocent eyes watch us through broken windows as we pass.

The closer we approach the base of the mountain, the colder it becomes, almost deathly. A faint mist develops and hovers eerily across the ground. We reach the north side of the mountain and wait inside a cove beneath the Tomb of the Prophets.

The mist thickens around us and begins to crawl up the mountain slopes. I leave Ash beside the tombs, and grab my bow and quiver hanging from his side. My sword is buried in the earth, so I'm left with only my knife and two arrows.

We slip lightly along the mountain base and stop near the northwest edge where the Temple rises above the hills. Near a thousand troops line the lower wall silenced and disengaged. I don't know what to make of it, but something sinister looms in the air, even my brother can feel it. The hairs on his arms stand erect. He leans next to me and gazes across the graves sprawled along the slopes of the mountain.

"Why is it so quiet and still?"

Not a creature stirs nor a breeze blows. Even the chirping crickets are silent. The entire landscape falls soundless and dead that even a single raindrop falling on the soft soil could be heard.

For the first time in over a year, the clouds break, parting a small opening beneath an empty sky—all except for a lone star twinkling. Our eyes draw to its mysterious wonder until the clap of thunder bellows. The silent moment vanishes, and the sky erupts into a disturbing moan of distorted horns and screaming voices, roaring and grating.

Dead insects fall from the clouds and pelt the earth. The troops scatter as the bugs shower down, but the bugs soon fade and the sky returns to black. The hellish horns cease and everything lies still, but only for a moment. The sound of grinding stones echo on the mountainside. I quickly turn my attention to Donavan; he looks utterly frightened.

"What is it?" I ask.

He trembles as he points to the upper western slope. "What the bloody hell?"

The mist thins over the tombs and the ground begins to vibrate. Gravestones crumble. Deposits of dirt surface through the chafing rocks and gather in small mounds. A rotting hand stretches out over one of the open tombs and a body rises from its stone casing.

"Tell me that just didn't fucking happen." Donavan shuffles for his gun.

"Put your gun away, they're not here for us," Father Joseph says in a calm manner.

"A bloody fucking corpse just walked out of his bloody fucking grave. Does that not disturb you in the slightest?"

Another corpse lifts from the mist and stands paralyzed next to Nadia.

"My God!" She stumbles back. "Then what are they here for?"

Father Joseph peers to the top of the mountain and says, "Your dead will live; Their corpses will rise. Those who sleep in the earth, will awake and shout for joy, for your dew is as the dew of the dawn—"

"And the earth will give birth to the departed spirits," I finish.

"What is that?" Nadia asks, shaking.

"It's from the book of Isaiah," Gabriel replies. He looks at me with fear in his eyes. "Judgment day."

One by one, bodies spring from the ground and stand beside their tombs that are scattered across the mountain. Their eyes draw into the sky and never move. Many are decomposed beyond recognition still clothed in ragged garments, while some stare preserved behind crackled faces and spoiled flesh.

"Leave them, our duty lies elsewhere," Father Joseph says, dismissing the dead and exiting the graves. We follow him across the valley and stay close to the lower barrier that divides the street from the Temple. Many soldiers remain stationed along the towering walls.

Suddenly, fire blazes to the north and gunshots exchange across the city's edge. Enemy soldiers escape into the firestorm, leaving the Temple wall clear.

"Come on, now's our chance," I urge.

We race over rocky groves and climb through the many headstones that are tucked below the walled compound. I quickly hide low to the ground as soldiers sprint past. Dozens dash across the street while battling chaos erupts on the north hill. We keep discreetly on our stomachs until the last soldier vanishes in the dark.

"Let's go." I scrape myself from the rocks and rush up the cobbled steps. A shooter spots us, but Donovan quickly takes care of him. "Let's move before any more show up," he presses.

We traverse around the great wall until we reach the Mughrabi Gate, one of two entrances to the mount. The rocky stairs ascend into a darkened archway where the unknown waits at the top.

"Let me go first," Donavan offers. He slowly climbs while the rest of us follow on his heels. We reach the top to the stone floor and sneak behind one of the shrines. Several soldiers scout over the ledge at the far end, and witness a battle raging not far from their post.

Centered in the stony courtyard, where the Dome on the Rock used to be, stands a reprised vision of an old Jewish temple. A large tower decorated with ornate pillars sits in the middle of the inner court surrounded by stone piled ten feet high.

"I'm not so sure about this, Arena. We don't know how many are inside the Temple courtyard. There's got to be another way in," Donavan suggests.

"We don't have time for any other options. We need to move now," I advise.

Voices bark below the step entrance. Their shadows grow wider, inching closer to the top. I break across toward the inner court just as six soldiers emerge from the stairs. The hesitation to follow keeps the others at bay while the soldiers mingle in the middle of the courtyard. Father Joseph,

Donavan, Gabe, and Nadia hunker against the backside of the shrine and wait. Father Joseph looks at me with that all too familiar stoic gaze and nods. My only chance is slipping away, but I'm afraid to leave him. Time races against us, and I'm conflicted. When I look back at his face, I say a small prayer that I'll see it again.

I dash under the sprint of a gazelle and stop at another wall. Two soldiers roam past the entrance that leads inside the inner courtyard. I slink slowly and dip inside before they return.

A one-hundred-foot towered structure stands inside the main entrance. The double doors, as grand as any architecture in the old city, are recessed on the opposite side where golden ornate carvings decorate the sash and handles. stone buildings connected to each side of an arched entrance. Smaller buildings decked with pillars line the walls. On the east side, the dreaded sound of boots pound the slated steps that descend below the mount.

I quickly slip behind a pillar and unsheathe my knife. Two soldiers surface, one carrying a rifle and the other holding a bucket. They inch closer, laughing. I prowl in the shadow like a hungry lion and lunge for the soldier with the gun. He stumbles, clutching his bloody throat before choking to death. The other drops the bucket and flees, screaming. I tackle him to the ground and jab my blade behind his neck until he falls silent.

The mysterious bucket tips over and a foul odor punches me in the face. Flies dance around the rim where traces of blood drip inside. With Gorshkov reigning over the mount, I can only imagine the horror that hides below it.

I creep down the steps beneath the Temple and find two narrow tunnels. Glowing lanterns line each channel that stretch fifty yards before they bend. I sidle through the right arched corridor and stop just before the bend. I hear voices, but I can't tell where they're coming from.

I peek around the bend and see three soldiers. A voice shouts behind them before their pace quickens. I have nowhere to hide. Their shadows grow closer. I grip my knife in my sweaty hand. Boots pound faster and louder. Their shadows merge as one as the soldiers dash around the bend. I pounce forward like a rabid dog and sink my blade, cutting and gashing. Blood gushes and arms flail until the last floundering soldier falls limp.

I hear a voice, but it fades. A small sliver of light flickers behind fissures in the wall to the left. I follow it through a dusky passage and find a small crevice big enough to slip through. It leads to a jagged edge where a vast chamber lies below.

Two soldiers emerge from stairs that hide behind and enormous wall crafted in wood. The aging timber has the Star of David carved deep into its grains. The seven species—wheat, barley, grapes, figs, pomegranates, olives, and dates—are etched around the tattered border.

The soldiers walk toward the back out of my line of site where the voice of a man pleads. I climb down over the rocks and crouch behind a stone slab to get a closer look. A man in his twenties, scarred and beaten, sits chained to the wall. A Russian uniform, bloodied and ripped, lies in a pile next to him. I can only assume this soldier defiled the colors that could reach to such abuse.

He grovels at their feet before they unbind him from the chains. They drag his fatigued body and dump him in front of the prison bars on the far side of the chamber. A shadowy figure moves inside the cell that extends into the dark recesses of the hollow stone. The sound of a hungry growl reverberates the entire chamber.

The tortured prisoner pleads and begs, but the two soldiers ignore him. They grab his arm and force his hand between the bars. Gnashing teeth emerge and thrashes about under horrific screams. The man springs back with a bloody stub and flounders to the floor.

"Who was it . . . who?" one of the soldiers barks.

The wincing prisoner casts his eyes to the floor and sputters, "I . . . I told you . . . I don't know!"

"Perhaps a starving beast can remind you." He nods to his comrade who walks over to the stairs and pulls a lever attached to the large wooden wall. The cell door pops open.

"No, no, please . . . please don't do this."

"Who? If you don't tell me, I'll be forced to cause you considerable agony." The soldier lifts the man from his grimacing stupor and shoves him to the open door.

"Petro!" the man fearfully concedes.

The stalking lion dips out of the shadow and lunges but the soldier is able to slam the cell shut. They drag the poor man across the floor and dump him by the back wall. I've had enough of this shit. I slink down and tip toe behind them. While they cuff the man back in his chains, I knife them both to the ground. Their legs twitch and blood mingles before a last gasp escapes their lifeless bodies.

I look down on the disgraced Russian soldier, but he doesn't look at me. While his right hand hangs cuffed to a chain, his severed left bleeds out. I grab the key still clutched in the dead soldier's hand and unlock the man from his binds. Though his colors bleed with the enemy, his gratuitous treatment is unjustified.

He peels his eyes from the floor and meets mine, trembling, "Thank you."

"Bravo, bravo," claps a voice behind me. I slowly turn. I'm face to face with the devil. "Your sympathy has become arrogant," Gorshkov continues to chide.

Gorshkov's menacing scowl overshadows the aging wrinkles hiding behind a nasty scar. He stands a little over six feet with salt and pepper hair cut short to his scalp. His thinning lips rests permanently under a sinister smirk. His well tailored uniform is as sharp as his acid tongue. The distance between us divides the ageless conflict between good and evil. No amount of rage can fill the hatred brewing inside me right now. I sheathe my knife as we stand our ground.

"You're not getting out of here alive," I promise. I grab my bow and reach for an arrow.

"Everything has a price, you should know better." He tugs on a chain trailing by the stairs. Allison stumbles down. She's bound around the neck like a dog on a leash. He grabs her by the hair and presses a gun to her head. I stretch the arrow back and call his bluff.

"I'm quite sure my trigger is quicker than your release, but go ahead and test me. It'd be a shame to see this young flower wilt to the floor."

"Let her go!"

"Your heart begs for her, doesn't it? Strange how one little muscle in your chest can become so selfish. It leads you astray, controls you, and gets you in trouble."

"You murderous piece of shit."

"Surely you don't mean that. Please tell me this hypocrisy is just a feeble attempt to destroy my good name. You don't for one second believe you truly can save her?"

If it's the lies that suppress my will to converge, then I shall die by its perpetuating agony. Because I refuse to listen to this man. I steady my bow, heart pounding and teeth gritting. "You and I both know you're going to die here."

"But at what cost, hm?" He pulls Allison closer to his chest and smells her hair in a creepy gesture. "It's a shame she has to go. Such a young and tender bud to pluck. You should be thanking me. I've done you a favor. I've broken this young girl open into an extraordinary woman, and she can now know what it's like before she leaves this earth."

"You sick, twisted fuck."

"So what now . . . should we share a lover's fate?" he asks in a sing-song manner, "or am I at the hands of mercy?"

"No mercy will undo you."

"Perhaps, but taking away what's dearest to you makes it all worth it, don't you think?"

He pulls back Allison's head and presses the gunharder. I leave myself, knowing I cannot save her. This cruel man has no intentions of keeping her alive. There's no way out of this but to plead under my breath, "God, please no . . . I beg of you, save her. Take me instead."

The room deflates into complete silence. A strange stillness surrounds me. My fingers wrapped around the string of my bow refuse to move, nor my feet. I'm completely paralyzed. The callous smile on Gorshkov's face remains undisturbed, almost suspended like in a painting. Allison's frightened face stays unmoved; even the tears have stopped midair. Her hands, reaching out, remain frozen, and her long brown hair springs to the side in suspension.

Michael walks in and peers at me with that faceless mystery. "Her blood will spill before you can aim," he says.

"I have to at least try—"

"You cannot save her, I'm afraid. Her fate ends here."

"Then I'll change it!"

"Let go, Arena. She will feel no pain."

"You know nothing of pain."

"I know more than you can imagine."

"Why would God take her from me like this?"

"I assure you His love for her measures beyond what we understand."

"Taking an innocent life is what you consider love? Is it death that serves Him now?"

"Man caused his own death. From the beginning, he left that up to choice. The choices he makes can be cruel in a world like this."

"I'm pretty sure Allison doesn't choose to die."

"No, but the world she lives in now will choose for her."

"Then change it!"

"I cannot change her fate."

"Then change mine. Let me take her place."

"Your destiny does not end here."

"I don't give a damn. Take my life and spare hers." He does not answer. Instead, he stares in silence.

"Well, go ahead. Tell Him."

"He already hears you . . . and He already knows what you have asked before you even thought it. That's why I am here now. I've anticipated this very moment and this very conversation since you were born. I had hopes it would change, but I was fooling myself."

"Then this has been my fate all along."

"I'm afraid so. This is the path you want? You're sure of this?"

A sudden flash of events since the beginning plays out in my mind's eye: my parents' death, my stepmother, Myra dying in my arms, Finnegan bleeding out in the car, Luke lying limp on the ground, Julianna's grave, and Jacob's last dying breath. All these memories will finally vanish someday. I want to be free from all this pain.

"I want to take her place."

"Don't ask lightly, my dear. Your words are forged with great conviction. They will take you from everything—your son, your friends, your loved ones. Know this sacrifice will not come alone."

"What do you mean?"

"Since birth, you and your brother have been connected in ways none other can understand. You know this to be true. That connection cannot be undone. One cannot live without the other. Your brother's life is in your hands now. What you ask you ask of him too."

I swallow the lump in my throat. "If Gabe were here, he would do the same thing. We live together, we die together. I ask of this . . . save her, please."

"He will hold you to your words. From this moment on, I can no longer protect you, but it's not the end for us."

Michael vanishes into the dark, the last my eyes will see of him. The ground begins to shake, and the floor rattles. The stone wall behind me splits open with a thunderous clap. My hands and feet move freely and everything held in suspension continues in motion.

The violent vibration pushes Gorshkov against the wall and his gun slips from his grip. I stretch back my arrow and fling it, piercing his right hand into the wall. His heartless voice shrieks. I string my last arrow and puncture his left arm the same.

Allison escapes his clutch and braces the floor, crying. The Russian prisoner limps over, barely alive, and removes the keys from Gorshkov's pocket. He unlocks the metal collar from Allison's neck and lifts his weary face to me. "An evil man is a dead man and deserves no mercy," he mutters before exiting up the stairs.

Gorshkov writhes, cursing and spitting, "You bloody whore!"

"I'm pretty sure you're in no position to cast out such vulgar repartee."

Allison stands up, her eyes narrowed and lips pursed. Her face blooms red with unforgiving fury I know all too well. "Make him suffer," she grits.

I press my knife against his prickly neck, but I refuse to gift this vile man a merciful death. The unspeakable cruelty he's perversely created will not go unpunished.

"Go ahead, I'm not afraid to die, you cowardly bitch," Gorshkov scoffs. I refuse to let his abrasive tongue rattle me. I grin for what's forthcoming.

"Death is just a passing into darkness. It's the grisly moments building up to it that should frighten you. Do you know that dreadful sound of bones crunching, macerated flesh thrashed between the grips of gnashing teeth?" His smug face shrivels. "Perhaps you do."

I glare into his cold, devilish eyes and grab the cell door lever on the wall. "You know, man and beast have coexisted since the beginning of time, but there's just one problem. If you starve a man, he'll beg for his life. But if you starve an animal, you'll beg for yours."

I pull the lever and the cell door creeks open under the clank of clenching metal. Paws shuffle across the floor and a deep growl emerges. Saliva drips from the lion's jaws and the famished beast dips out from the cell. His eyes narrow and his watering mouth stretches back.

"Come on, Allison, this isn't for your eyes to see." I grab her hand and leave Gorshkov's fate in the clutches of this beast. We climb the steps under the gnawing sounds of a feasting lion and his meal's bloodcurdling screams—torturous yet justified. We reach the top and quickly exit through the door, leaving behind the horrid suffering.

Suddenly, the ground beneath our feet trembles, and the crumbling floor buckles in the middle. Veiny cracks run beneath our feet. Dust and debris cascades above us. We sprint through the outer doors and flee the building behind a collapsing ceiling. Pillars buckle on our heels and crash to the Temple mount.

We escape to the outer courtyards, but Gabe, Donavan, Nadia, and Father Joseph are nowhere to be seen. Dozens of soldiers lie dead, trailing from the far corner to the bloody steps below the mount. We leave the Temple behind and race across the street. Enemy soldiers flee from the northern banks as gunfire blazes past.

I cling close to Allison, searching for a clearing, when I see Gabe running down the hill. "Arena!" he shouts. He's being chased by three Russian men. They raise their knives.

"Gabe!" I scream back. I plunge down into the valley, my legs churning.

Out of nowhere, Ash barrels through and plows the men

into the ground, cracking their bones He wickers with a haunting shriek and gallops toward me under a warrior's chase. Horns blast the air and thunder booms. Gunfire scatters behind us.

A small surge of Russian soldiers flee from Sadiq's men. They scurry along the Temple walls and exchange shots—a desperate escape of chaos. Allison clings to me, trembling. Ash stomps the ground beside me and whinnies. His eyes, fueled with rage, dance like flames in a fire.

Gabe rushes over, wincing and pressing the side of his ribs. "What's wrong, you okay?" I ask like a worried mother.

"I'm fine, just a bit of nick."

"Where are the others?"

"I don't know. We all scattered when soldiers flooded back toward the Temple."

"Gabe!" a voice shouts. A Russian soldier wrestles Nadia to the ground and pins her down. I grab Ash by the mane, but it's too late. Gabe sprints like a bolt of lightning. The bedlam raging behind us begins to fade, but not before dozens of Russians charge at us.

I quickly lift Allison on top of Ash. "You grab his mane and put your head down. Don't let go no matter what. Just keep your eyes closed."

"What about you?" she cries.

"I'll come after, now put your head down."

I grab the side of Ash's face and look him in the eyes. "You ride like the wind, you hear me? Keep her safe, now go!"

Ash buries his ears back and whips his hooves against the stony earth. Within seconds his pressing speed fades across the vale toward the Mount of Olives.

I race after Gabe with gunfire hailing behind me. Nadia, still pinned, struggles from the man's grasp and screams. Gabe lunges full speed and tackles the soldier to the ground. They tussle, rolling over and over. I pull the soldier off and jab my knife into the back of his neck.

The pounding of enemy boots closes in, chased on the storm of Sadiq's men. We sprint across the valley near the mountain and reach the outer basin. Bullets crackle and pop.

"Go! I shout.

Donavan and Father Joseph emerge from the western tombs and exchange fire. Gabe's legs begin to slow as Nadia churns past. I leave my feet upon the fleeing wind and gasp. A sudden sting strikes my chest and my eyes slowly blur. I find myself running in slow motion until my knees buckle to the ground. Gabe collapses next to me. Blood seeps through his shirt.

I grab my burning chest and feel the warm blood escaping between my tingling fingers. My body is numb and fixed like a weight, pushing me into the earth. Gabe reaches his trembling hand out to me. I secure every ounce of my strength and grab a hold of it, clasping my fingers with his under shallow breaths.

The sounds of war fade around me and leave the faint crying voices of Nadia and Father Joseph. I choke back my last words as blood drips from my mouth, "I'm so sorry, brother."

He looks at me with fluttering eyes, with a smile now fleeting. "It's okay, Arena. It was always meant to be this way. I can finally rest now, knowing it's finished." His cold eyes stare ahead, into some unknown void.

"No, wait . . . Gabe?"

His fingers unclasp from mine.

My brother is now gone from this world, and he waits for me on the other side. Voices cry beside me, but my fainting eyes stay fixed on the parting clouds. They begin to dissipate and uncover the last and only star that shines like a beacon.

It glows beyond my eyes can see and falls from darkness, blazing like a ball of fire. It shines a blinding white and strikes just south of the Jewish quarters. A wave of energy follows, rolling across the land. Trees bend and the ground shakes.

Men fall to their knees. Enemy soldiers spread over the vale and disintegrate to dust. The sky opens up and the shadows below disappear. For the first time in nearly three years, a glimpse of the sun peeks through the endless mist above.

My eyes witness the end of my journey. The burning fire in my chest vanishes and my body grows cold. My heart sputters, slipping deeper away. My arm drops limp and my eyes look one last time at the tears rolling down my father's face. I fall breathless into darkness before I'm pulled from my body and released from the world.

Every feeling I've ever experienced leaves me all at once. Though my loved ones hover over our bodies below, my fate has been fulfilled, and for the first time I see the truth resting with my destiny. I'm no longer bound to suffering, guilt, or shame.

I'm restored. I'm free.

CHAPTER 37

Six months later

The door to humanity can open and close at any time, but for me, it revolves. I briefly leave my place with Michael and gaze through the misty portals between man and his future. The world my son lives in now slowly restores, but not without human hardships. It remains a place of emotions, death, and choices, but it's ruled upon the ideas of freedom. I watch from across a garden gate in Beit Shemesh where Nadia stands below a budding peach tree. She cradles her bulging stomach, shirt stretched tightly around it, and searches the branches.

I move closer to the back of the garden unseen, but my spirit brushes like the subtle breeze against the skin. Nadia plucks a piece of fruit and watches my son waddle joyfully through the rows of tomato plants. Her face briefly brightens as she follows him to the end of the row, but it soon flattens. She gazes on three graves near the back of the garden: Jacob, Gabe, and mine. Strange standing next to my own tomb. Nadia kneels beside Gabe's headstone and places the peach on top—a memory far from home now.

She struggles to lift a smile until Joshua leans his head against her and pets her belly. She rubs her hand against the gravestone. "I'd trade my life just to see your face for one second. I know you probably get tired of me talking to an empty tomb, but I just wanted you to know how much I miss you. And whether or not you can hear me on the other side. You need to know you will never be forgotten. From me, Father Joseph, Joshua . . ."She looks down to her swollen belly. "Our daughter will know what a great man you had become, and I'll never let a day go by that she doesn't know who you were. Allison and I came up with a name that I know you'd be proud of: Abigail Arena Power. I refuse to let your surname be washed away. I love you, Gabe."

She leaves his grave like she does every day with Joshua tagging on her heels.

"It's time to go," Gabe softly says as he sidles up next to me.

"Give me one second."

I whisper my son's name on a gentle breeze and watch his little head turn. He stops in the middle of the garden and toddles over to the fence. I reach out my hand and his round face lights up. For a brief moment, only he can see me cross over into his world. He grabs my hand and my heart melts. His smile grows as he rubs the side of my cheeks and spurts just one word: "Mama."

As much as I want to stay and keep this feeling forever, I must go. While I'm able to watch over and protect him, Nadia must nurture him now. She picks up a basket of peaches and calls for him.

"Joshua! Time for your bath." His head turns around and he lets go of my hand. I back away from the fence and watch his short legs shuffle off through the garden. A great innocence walks away. Even before he can fluently speak, his leadership is being molded. Day by day, a little more is chiseled away from my son as he grows into the man that he was meant to be—to help lead a new people in a new world. I leave this world for now and rejoin my loved ones on the other side.

Though the light casts down on new fellowships, the shadows will return one day, for a war to end all wars has yet to come. My part is finished here, but my son's has just begun. A new age is born for Joshua to live, lead, and love.

Our fate has been sealed, and there's nothing we can do to change it. We must accept it, for the reward is greater than the story told.

While I watch my son grow, I prepare for a new war beyond this earth—a reckoning for all generations that have passed into the wind. Until the last days come, a new beginning awaits. A great void will swallow humanity and deliver us beyond the vast expanse no man can explain.

What's left in the shadows shall never return, but into the light a door will open to a realm of eternity where time and space will cease to exist. Man's pilgrimage never ends . . . it just changes like the second hand on a clock, one tick at a time. While my son learns his way in this world, I wait patiently in another. It is my will, it is my destiny.

With our eyes perched on the heavens, one day humanity will gaze upon the last light falling, covering the world in eternal darkness, and leaving behind what once was in order to become what will forever be.

Our purpose was never to understand questions that can't be answered because in the end, none of it will matter. In the end, life will escape us and death will seize. In the end, our brothers and sisters, mothers, and fathers will disappear. Though no one will remember, in the end our final thoughts will wisp from existence and our stories will all vanish.

But the end is only the beginning.

THE END . . .

Acknowledgments

I would like to pay tribute to the following who gave their talents, support, and kind contributions to the Last Light Falling saga. To my poor family who suffered my absence through endless writing sessions while I submersed myself in a fictional world. Thank you to my pets for tolerating my story building conversations with them when they'd rather be licking themselves. To my Irish whiskey and your timely submission for getting me over those pesky unresolved chapters. Tacos, my first love, you pulled me out of the writer's block gutters many times. You have my respect. To my sarcastic and devilish co-workers, Philip Felux and Aaron Rainbolt, for allowing me to slay away on my manuscript while I should have been helping you. Thank you, Melanie, my supportive, beautiful wife for encouraging me to pursue my dream and finish what I started. Also, thank you for shaping my story with your proofreading and editing skills. Thanks, mom, for your continual support and giving me your honest and constructive feedback. Thanks Mr. espresso for your caffeine surging resilience, flooding my bloodstream during those oddly hours of writing. To my awesome kids, Gabriel and Mikaela, for your expressive and squirrely suggestions on characters and story arcs. To my few, but loyal fans. Without your persistent badgering, I wouldn't have finished my story. Speaking of stories, mine would be buried beneath piles of incoherent drivel if it weren't for my professional editing savant, Alison. Thank you for helping me transform a pretty good story into a great one. To my wonderfully talented graphic designer, Giovanni Auriemma. Your book cover and jacket designs clearly stand out amongst the best. Your inspiration behind every detail on the covers live brilliantly with the words inside them. And lastly, but certainly not least, thank you Mela Hudson for your support, encouragement, and inspiration behind the entire saga. Your drive and passion to build this novel into a film adaptation goes beyond than just the screen. Though you are no longer with us on this earth, you have giving me hope that there's more beyond a story we couldn't finish together; There're are no endings. I hope your next journey is filled with as much kindness as you offered me.